"John Thorndike displays a mat.. this intriguing first novel . . . the reader be... wholeheartedly in his Middle Western setting, in Anna, and in the others who occupy her life. . . . Thorndike has invented a world we can live in, accept as authentic, and relish to the last page."—Doris Grumbach

"In lyrically powerful prose . . . without sentimentality, John Thorndike portrays the intricacies and difficulties involved in the establishment of new relationships. He handles his characters' fears and fallibilities with compassion and understanding, respecting them enough not to provide them with easy consolation."
—*The New York Times Book Review*

"A brilliant first novel, written with power and delicacy . . . lyric prose and sensuous imagery . . . a master's touch."
—Daniel Keyes, Ohio University

"Eminently readable . . . his insights into human nature and his sense of story serve him well in this appealing work."
—*Publishers Weekly*

JOHN THORNDIKE grew up in New England, graduated from Harvard, and taught English at the National University of El Salvador. He farmed for twelve years, two in southern Chile and ten near Athens, Ohio. Thorndike was the recipient of an Individual Artist Fellowship Award from the Ohio Arts Council in 1982. Currently at work on a second novel, he lives in Boulder, Colorado.

John Thorndike

ANNA DELANEY'S CHILD

A PLUME BOOK

NEW AMERICAN LIBRARY

NEW YORK AND SCARBOROUGH, ONTARIO

NAL BOOKS ARE AVAILABLE AT QUANTITY DISCOUNTS WHEN USED TO
PROMOTE PRODUCTS OR SERVICES. FOR INFORMATION PLEASE WRITE
TO PREMIUM MARKETING DIVISION, NEW AMERICAN LIBRARY,
1633 BROADWAY, NEW YORK, NEW YORK 10019.

ACKNOWLEDGMENTS

"Only Love Can Break Your Heart" written by Neil Young.
Copyright 1970 Cotillion Music, Inc. & Broken Arrow Music.
Used by permission. All rights reserved.

 PLUME TRADEMARK REG.U.S. PAT. OFF. AND FOREIGN COUNTRIES
REGISTERED TRADEMARK—MARCA REGISTRADA
HECHO EN FORGE VILLAGE, MASS., U.S.A.

SIGNET, SIGNET CLASSIC, MENTOR, ONYX, PLUME, MERIDIAN and
NAL BOOKS are published *in the United States* by NAL PENGUIN INC.,
1633 Broadway, New York, New York 10019, *in Canada* by The New American
Library of Canada Limited, 81 Mack Avenue, Scarborough, Ontario M1L 1M8

Library of Congress Cataloging-in-Publication Data

Thorndike, John.
    Anna Delaney's child.

    I. Title.
PS3570.H6497A8   1987   813'.54   87-11212
ISBN 0-452-25998-3

Designed by Jack Meserole

First Plume Printing, October, 1987

1 2 3 4 5 6 7 8 9

PRINTED IN THE UNITED STATES OF AMERICA

For Janir, who reads

Thanks to a dozen friends and writers in Athens, Ohio, who helped with this book. Lady Borton, in particular, read closely and gave affectionate, merciless advice.

I am grateful as well to the Ohio Arts Council, whose Individual Artist Fellowship provided both financial help and recognition.

ANNA DELANEY'S CHILD

CHAPTER 1

ANNA DELANEY jammed the claw end of a hammer under the two-by-four nailed across the doorway to her son's room. She pried but couldn't budge it, not even by propping her feet against the door and hanging all her weight from the hammer. Three months before, she had driven a pair of twenty-penny nails through either end of the board into the oak door frame. Now she beat on the two-by-four in frustration, dropped her hammer to the floor and strode outside in the sunlight.

Anna liked seasonable weather, not this heat before its time. April's sudden warming had leapt ahead of everything green in nature. The pearly grey extremities of the maples on the Kentucky side of the Ohio showed a faint salmon color, but the trees on this side of the river were too close to show the change. Anna followed the path to the barn. She walked inside past the tractor and field cultivators, into the deep shade and silence of the tool room, where the farm's steel wrecking bar hung from a nail on the back wall. She nudged it and listened as it pivoted back and forth, clanging sweetly against the wood.

The three-foot bar was heavier than she remembered, and still cold from the night before. Anna's legs felt like rags. She carried the bar home and sat down at the kitchen table until her strength returned. Then she hammered the chisel end of the bar under the poplar two-by-four and pried. The nails didn't give. The board pried off, but the four-inch nails remained imbedded in the oak jambs as if set in concrete, pulling through the poplar board, head and all. Anna let the two-by-four clatter to the floor. Damnable dry oak, it firmed up a building like steel but was merciless on mistakes. Using all her leverage, she

1

attacked the nails directly and pulled them creaking from the jambs, then lay the bar on the floor and curled her fingers around the doorknob.

She rattled the knob in warning and opened the door.

The air in the room was cool and still, like a poised animal. Everything inside looked the same. Anna wished the room had changed—it would mean she herself had changed—but every detail was the same. Kevin's books and albums lay on the naked mattress along with his baseball mitt and a pile of toys. His dump trucks were still parked on the floor next to his boots and sneakers.

Anna knelt and put her face against the musty clothes hanging in Kevin's open closet. She fought down the emotion rising from her chest. She wanted to be in the dark, but not to cry. For an entire year she had cried, weeping on the floor, on her bed, on her father's couch. She no longer wanted to scour herself with tears, nor turn her back on Kevin's room. She stood up.

From the top of the dresser, Kevin's hamster cage gave off a stale, abandoned odor. A few dried hamster droppings lay on top of soiled wood chips and decayed pieces of lettuce. Anna put her nose to the miniature bars.

She had once promised Kevin a dog, if he'd start with a smaller pet and take care of it. He chose a hamster and tended it faithfully for six months. But after Kevin's death, the hamster went on living. Month after month it followed the same schedule, waking at night and running in its spindly metal wheel, destinationless, futile, uncared for. Anna sat in her living room and listened to it spin. In the mornings she fed it and gave it water. It slept all day, surviving month after month without affection, without space, without Kevin. During the long nights of autumn it began to run its wheel earlier in the evening. One night Anna entered Kevin's room and found it arched backward inside its tiny wheel, its ballpoint eyes fastened on her own. She put her face to the cage. Couldn't it recognize danger? Opening the small door, she grasped and lifted the animal. It trusted her, completely ignorant of her resentment that it had gone on living all this time. She came close to crushing it in her hand.

Stepping outside into the chill landscape of December, she released the hamster at the edge of a field. It didn't move. Fifteen minutes later she returned to the same spot and found it curled up and shivering, its fur cold to the touch. She picked it up and returned it to its cage. A week later, realizing she hadn't heard it run for a couple of nights, she entered Kevin's room and prodded the animal under chips of wood and bits of tissue paper. It was cold and stiff.

She didn't want the hamster in her house, so it had obliged her and died. She understood that. What she couldn't understand was how it had gone on living for so long without anyone to hold it or let it out of the cage to play, or even to look at it. After its death she missed the sound of its wheel spinning in the darkness, and a few weeks later she nailed the board across the entrance to Kevin's room. She didn't expect to think of her son any less because the hamster was dead and the room closed off. Like everything else, it didn't help. Anna was sorry the animal had died—but she'd been sorry it was alive.

She picked up the empty cage and set it on the living room floor, not knowing what to do with it—or with anything else in her son's room. After a full year, everything of Kevin's was still in his room. A shirt stuck out of the chest of drawers exactly as he had left it. She plucked it out and threw it into the living room. Then a pile of comic books, one after another, and a poster of a dolphin. They skidded across the waxed pine floor. If she threw them out of the room, she'd have to do something about them.

But take all his clothes out of the chest of drawers and throw them on the floor? She had only opened the drawers once, to get the corduroy pants and red-and-black cowboy shirt Kevin was buried in. The funeral parlor had asked for clothes, and the cowboy shirt was his favorite. They asked for dress shoes, too, but he didn't own any leather shoes. They called her about them twice, but Anna couldn't bear to think of her son lying inside the casket with his track shoes on grey silk. Let him go barefoot, she thought.

Somewhere in Kevin's book there was a snapshot of him wearing a cowboy shirt. Anna rummaged across the mattress and found his album, on whose black matte pages she had glued photographs, letters and schoolwork. Leafing through it quickly, she found the picture and sat down on the dusty mattress to look once more at her child. He was as beautiful as sunlight. Below the snapshot she had written in white ink, "The Ultimate Badman."

MORE THAN anything in the world, Kevin wanted a cowboy suit with two guns and holsters that tied to his legs with strips of rawhide. His father, Paul, wanted to buy a suit for him, but Anna said never in this house. For two years running Kevin asked for a cowboy suit for Christmas, and she gave him a racetrack or a toboggan or some expensive present that didn't have anything to do with guns.

Anna's father hated guns, and her mother hated them as well; it was a family mania. Paul didn't share the feeling. On one of his visits after the divorce he took Kevin out for a drive and showed him a .22 pistol he kept under the front seat of his car. Anna found out about it when she discovered a half-dozen empty shells in the pockets of Kevin's blue jeans. She complained to Paul about it over the phone, but he said, "Hey, Kevin loved it. We shot up a couple of cans, that's all." She was too angry to ask if he had actually let Kevin shoot the gun.

It got worse when Todd down the street was given a cowboy suit for his birthday. Kevin gave her no peace for weeks. He called himself Silverman and Tough Stuff. He wanted a suit and two guns like Todd's. He needed them. One Saturday he left for Todd's at eight in the morning and didn't return until noon. He rode full tilt into the garage, braked with a streak of rubber across the concrete and pushed his bike against the back wall. With a snapshot in his hand he burst into the kitchen shouting, "See, Mom, I'm a cowboy!" He had gotten Todd to loan him the suit and Todd's dad to take a Polaroid picture of him with full scowl and guns up.

She never had a sadder moment with him, realizing how she had denied him a harmless fantasy for years. But he paid her no more attention now than when she gave him sermons on violence. He had finally gotten into a cowboy suit and had the photo to prove it; that was all that counted. He danced around the kitchen and shot into the air with his fingers, saying, "I'm Jesse James! I'm Pretty Boy Floyd!" Anna could hardly keep from crying. Guns were playthings to Kevin, there was nothing in him that was violent or tough. He didn't want to hurt anyone, he just wanted to blast the light bulbs and the clock. He didn't even remember her resistance to guns. Grabbing the picture from her hand, he looked at himself and said, "Isn't it great, Mom?"

He was eight years old.

WHAT could she do with his clothes? And with his tool kit and dartboard and collection of baseball cards? Send them all to families in the South Bronx? Give them to the Salvation Army and have them show up at local yard sales in Fell River? She didn't want to find one of his trucks for sale some Saturday morning on a card table along with some other child's leftover toys.

Anna paced the floor of the living room, unraveled the telephone cord and dialed her father's number. Six rings and she almost hung up.

"Hello, Dad?"

"Hi, Anna. What's up?"

"You sound out of breath."

"I ran back inside to get the phone."

"You were going out, then?" she asked.

"Down to the courts. I've got my first real match of the season today. How've you been?"

Alex Delaney was in his sixties, but still an accomplished tennis player. The previous summer he and a woman half his age had won the town's mixed doubles tournament.

"I spent the morning in the greenhouse," Anna said.

"That's always your favorite, isn't it? Do you want to play some tennis later? My match is only a couple of sets."

"Thanks, Dad, but I'm . . . I'm working on my house."

"You're not going to start working sixty hours a week again, are you?"

"I might, if I need to stay out of trouble." Anna's eyes fell on the hamster cage and the pile of comic books scattered over the floor. "I wanted to ask if you knew what happened to Mom's cashmere sweater, that beige one from London she liked so much."

"I sold it, along with all her other clothes. Or gave them away, actually." Alex's tone implied that he'd told her this before.

"I thought you might have saved some out."

"They would have been too small for you."

"You're probably right," Anna said. "But . . ."

"But what?"

"Didn't you ever worry about seeing someone else wearing those clothes?"

"Minneapolis is a big city. Anyway, I left the next morning."

Anna paced slowly, only two steps, back and forth. "What about those boxes under your bed? You didn't get rid of all that stuff?"

"No, I didn't. Those are all Freya's books and papers." His voice dropped. "I've never meant to hide them, you know. If you ever want to look through them, you're welcome to."

"I was just wondering about the sweater. But now that you mention it, what's in those boxes?"

"All the letters Freya wrote me, and almost everything she

saved in her own files. I've looked through most of it."

Anna's mother had died two years before. Her sudden death from bone cancer followed a stormy divorce from her father, a decade's separation and two years of passionate revival. Anna knew that Alex could not have read Freya's papers with equanimity.

"You were brave to keep it all."

"What else could I do?"

"Burn it, or . . . something." Anna's voice cracked, and she made a joke of the idea: "You know, the way they burned books at the Inquisition."

"It's an idea," Alex said, gently.

"Well, Dad, I only called about the sweater. Don't let me hold you from your match."

"I should go. But I'll see you this week, for sure."

Anna hung up the phone—and imagined burning the books in Kevin's room, and the clothes in his dresser, and the dresser itself. She felt giddy, as if her head floated far above her limbs. She had to do something about Kevin's room.

The small, square room was built into one corner of her house, its pine walls anchored only to a floorplate and a ceiling joist. Gently, Anna picked up the crowbar and wedged it under the baseboard molding. The wood splintered lightly and sprang away from the wall. The tongue-and-groove siding popped off almost as easily and twisted to the floor. Dust dropped from the joist, filling the air.

Anna knocked the pins out of the door hinges and dragged the heavy oak door outside, around to the back of her house. Instead of carrying out the pine boards, she opened the kitchen window and pitched them directly onto the lawn. She finished one wall and attacked the other. Once she had a pile of wood outside, she went back with matches and newspaper, knelt beside the boards and started a fire with some of the splinters. The pine caught quickly. In five minutes she had a small blaze, the resinous wood crackling and sucking at the dry air. She propped the long siding boards into a pyramid.

The flames burned a black oval in the grass. Anna contained it by beating out the edges with a shovel, her face tucked away from the heat. Her hands were shaking—not from exhaustion, but from fear at what she had started. She tore out the last of the boards, flung them out the window onto the fire and started with Kevin's clothes. An armful of books went into the blaze, volume by volume. Acrid smoke swirled back into the house, smarting her eyes. Without resting, she gathered up her hair and pinned it up on top of her head, a few blond strands hanging past her face.

The mattress was a struggle. She lugged it outside, leaned one end of it close to the fire and tipped it in. She dismantled the wooden bed, smashed the dresser apart and threw the drawers out the window. A stream of Kevin's goods passed into the fire: his records, his shoes, his football, the encapsulated globe of snow Anna had shaken for him every night before he went to sleep. The lamp beside the bed, the table it stood on, the pillow, a game of Parcheesi: everything went. Anna breathed hard, her eyes blinking against the smoke. Her neck hurt and she had to carry her head to one side, peering out of the window as she threw the baseball cards into the fire, then a plastic flute, then a slingshot.

It went on and on, she never thought it would take so long. Like an obsessed housekeeper, she persisted until there was nothing left but the marks where the two-by-four plates had rested on the wooden flooring. She swept meticulously and scrubbed the floor with a mop. The room was gone, and everything of Kevin's. She had removed it all from her house.

Except for his book. Anna sat down with it on the living room couch, holding it open on her lap. Large and well thumbed, its black pages smelled of dried glue. It was filled with naked-baby shots and drawings from school, as well as a list of Kevin's first spoken words and the "books without pictures" he had read. Anna skimmed through the album, her temples pounding as the fire rushed and whistled outside. She felt as if she had been driving the freeway and drinking coffee for three days straight.

She read the letter from Kevin's day-care center, formally typed on eggshell stationery, announcing his four-year-old transgressions: he wouldn't take a nap, wouldn't keep out of the bushes and trees in the playground, couldn't paint without making a mess, didn't pay attention in prereading class. Even Paul had been outraged by that letter. He stayed up half the night with Anna's books on child raising and marched off the next morning to defend his son to the center's stout directress. He quoted from Leo Tolstoy and John Holt, and told her, "The reason Kevin is like this is because he's a child. You've had kids in here before, haven't you?" Even though his antics got Kevin bounced for a week, Anna loved Paul for having stood up for his son.

The album, in fact, had originally been Paul's idea. He bought it on the day of Kevin's birth and pasted in the first entry himself: the front page of the *San Francisco Chronicle*. Over the next few months he added a copy of Kevin's birth certificate and a few photographs, but then he abandoned the project to Anna. At Kevin's funeral the album was never mentioned.

The thought that someday Paul might claim the album brought Anna out of its cluttered pages in a rush. She didn't want him to have it. Rising from the sofa, she carried it to the kitchen window and stood tautly, holding it upright between her palms. It was the last object. Its dry pages would catch and burn fast; it would be gone in a moment.

"Anna, no."

Her father, dressed in tennis shorts and a white sweater, stood in the doorway, his eyes going from what had been Kevin's room to the dense column of smoke outside the kitchen window. He took five quick steps toward her. Anna pressed the album flat against her chest with one hand and held off her father's approach with the other, like a cop against traffic.

"I can burn it," she said. "I can, if I want to."

"Yes, you can."

She hugged the album to her chest, ashamed of herself but wanting the demonic feeling of rebellion. She wanted that feeling—or any feeling—because after tearing apart her son's room and throwing everything he owned into the fire, she didn't feel anything at all.

Alex sagged in front of his daughter, his tall frame humbled by the lift of her palm. She lowered her hand. "I'm sorry," she said, "I'm not myself." But she went on clutching the album to her chest.

Her father nodded. His shaggy grey hair protruded over the tips of his ears and over his wide, elevated forehead. A pair of bushy eyebrows hinted at his age, though he looked a good deal younger now than he had in the worst of times after his wife's death.

"You could never replace what's in that book," he said.

"I could never replace Kevin."

Some perverse streak drove her to make such comments. She wanted to see her father at a loss—though the desire passed immediately when his face turned sad.

He disappeared upstairs, returning with a blanket to drape over her shoulders. Anna let him sit her down on the couch like an invalid, glad to be taken care of. He tucked the blanket over her feet and slipped a pillow behind her head. Within seconds, almost as if she had been knocked unconscious, soft images of the ocean swept over her, green and flickering. Her father gently disengaged the album from her arms, but she opened her eyes and drew it back.

"Anna, I'm not going to take it away from you."

She was halfway into the dream and wanted to go on, into the slanting ocean waves. She gave up the album to her father, who stepped into the kitchen and put it on top of the refrigerator. "You take a nap," he said, "and I'll fix something for dinner."

Anna let her head fall back against the pillow. The ocean was close, if she could only let herself drift toward it. She thought of the salt smell and fogless nights in the little town of Seal Rock, on the Oregon coast, but she could not reenter the dream itself. A tight band stretched across her abdomen and would not let up. She tried over and over to go into the dream, but in the end she couldn't do it.

Softly, she stood up from the couch and stared at her father's back as he sliced vegetables at the counter. Alex wanted her to sleep, of course. He wanted to protect her, and sleep was the great protection. But Anna didn't want to sleep off the fact that she had just burned Kevin's history out of her house. She walked unsteadily across the floor.

Alex looked around at the sound of her steps, surprised. Didn't she want to rest?

No, she wanted to stay awake and help him with dinner. She set the table but moved through a haze. Her father started three pots on the kitchen stove. Anna washed her face at the sink and looked at herself in the mirror. The light outside had begun to fade, and she had trouble focusing her eyes. Her hair smelled like old margarine, and her hands were the color of an opossum, even after she washed them. When her father served dinner she was unable to eat more than a few bites. He worried about her, she could see.

After dinner she picked up the album with one hand and led her father outside. The clear evening was chill, the last red light fading from both the sky and the fire. Anna passed her father the shovel so he could rustle the coals and pile on a few unburned pieces of wood. She ignored his wary look. In the burst of flames, his white shorts and striped athletic socks stood out against the dark. He had put a jacket on over his sweater, but his knees and long legs remained exposed.

Holding Kevin's book under one arm, like a student, she asked, "Why should I keep it?"

"What if you had another child sometime who wanted to know about Kevin?"

Anna imagined a dark-haired girl of Kevin's age. Of course she would ask about her dead brother, her half brother. She would want to know what Kevin had looked like, and how much Anna loved him. And how would Anna ever explain about her child without a photograph, without anything he had owned or painted or written? No matter how she told the story, the girl might think she had never loved Kevin at all—and might fear being abandoned in the same way.

Alex saved her from throwing the album into the fire—but Anna resented what he said nevertheless. Like everyone else, he assumed she would have another child.

The fact was, she was ovulating even now. That was the tension that had stopped her from slipping into the dream. The pressure had been there for hours, though she had been slow to recognize it. It angered her still that every month her body should prepare itself for another child, repeatedly and insistently tendering an ovum. She didn't know how to tell that to her father.

Alex rustled the fire again, which blazed up and illuminated her face. He still looked worried. "You're not going to burn that now, are you?"

"No, I'm not. It's a good thing you came out, though, because I probably would have."

"There's nothing else left?"

"Probably the whole idea was pigheaded."

"Maybe in the end it'll help," he said.

"I doubt it, since he had his hands on everything I own." She had to get in the last word.

ALEX DELANEY, who had bent his mind to the question for forty years, came to lunch early so he could sit for an hour and think about love. He took a corner table at the restaurant, unfolded the morning newspaper and pretended to read the front page while letting his eyes wander out of focus. Certainly he had loved his children and his parents and a few close friends, and perhaps some of the people he had worked with. The word was impoverished from overuse. Had he loved his friends? It was more exact to say he had loved his wife, passionately. But on the subject of passion Alex no longer trusted his memory, or his feelings. He only opened himself up to the topic now on the chance of stumbling over some explanation of why he should still be thinking about romance at the age of sixty-three. On occasional awkward days his desires seemed to be those of a twenty-year-old.

Through the window and gauze curtains, Alex stared at the Ohio River and the Kentucky shore, a quarter mile off. Every other Tuesday Anna drove into Fell River for lunch at the Bradford Hotel. On alternate weeks Alex went to her house for dinner. When they met in town he often came early, to sit in the quiet hotel dining room and think about what he would say to his daughter. Sometimes he made notes on a yellow pad. At first Anna had laughed when he put on his glasses and consulted a list of emotional topics. But in recent months she had done the same, bringing scraps of paper or store receipts with questions on them about Alex's childhood in Fell River or about the early years of his marriage.

Alex raised his eyes to catch the waitress for a cup of tea, but she was busy setting tables at the far end of the room. He smiled at himself. He brought a newspaper to avoid looking like a vacant dreamer, yet no one gave him any thought. He and Anna had been eating at the Bradford for over a year, attended by the same aging waitress in a white nylon uniform. They chose the hotel not because of its food, which was American common, but because the dining room was old and formal. Although the Bradford had outlived its pretensions, it had once been a stylish place on Fell River's fanciest street. The Elks and the Redmen now held their luncheons at the Holiday Inn outside town, and the Rambler and Deacon motels got the illicit-affairs trade, but the Bradford still had riverfront rooms to let, a long dining room with chandeliers and floor-length windows, and a staff of septuagenarians.

At ten after twelve Anna strode through the door, wearing blue jeans and work boots. She had rolled up the sleeves of her

shirt and carried a sweater in one hand. From her rough clothes
and outdoor bearing, Alex knew she had come directly from
work. He was surprised, once again, that he had fathered such
an attractive woman. Her expression of high alertness—as if
she had caught herself at the start of a fall—reminded him of
her mother, Freya.

They didn't quite embrace. Sometimes they did, and sometimes not. They had no fixed habits for when they met.

"You've brought me a twig," Alex said, reaching out to loosen
it from his daughter's tangled blond hair.

"I've lost all my city ways," Anna said, smiling as she sat
down. She studied the twig for a moment before dropping it
into her shirt pocket. "Ash, probably. There's one next to the
barn. I know I shouldn't have come like this, but I didn't have
time to change clothes. We were transplanting lettuce and barely
finished before noon."

"It's fine," Alex said. "You look great. You look wonderful,
really."

"I didn't want to be any later."

After their first visit to the hotel, they had agreed to match
the Bradford's formality, which was why Alex now wore a blue
sports jacket and a pair of smooth-tongued black loafers. Anna
usually wore a dress or a skirt.

"It's the season," she explained.

"Tell me about the lettuce. Did you get it all planted?"

"We got this week's rows in. In ten days we do it all over
again—if Deal can fix the planter that's been acting up."

Leaning forward against the table, sunny and relaxed, Anna
detailed the progress of the early spring crops. Alex was glad
to hear her talk about farmwork; she didn't look anything like
the woman who had stood bent beside the fire outside her house
ten days before, the flesh around her eyes a blotched, irides-
cent orange. Her complexion was smooth now, and her back
straight. The ends of her nostrils flared slightly as she breathed.

The waitress took their order, writing it out slowly and precisely. The eraser at the end of her pencil described small cir-

cles in the air, and her head wobbled to the same rhythm. In over a year they had never learned her name, though she called Alex "Mr. Delaney."

After the waitress left he told Anna, "Working has been good for you. I see it every week."

She twisted in her chair and sat back. "I guess it has. I had another dream though, Sunday night."

"A bad one?"

"They're always bad about the accident. In a whole year I haven't had a single peaceful dream of Kevin, where he just shows up and we do something together."

"Dreams are worse than memories," Alex said.

"They're stronger. When I dream about Kevin, it's as if he's alive and has to die all over again."

"I know."

Anna nodded, calming down. "You do know. That's why I can talk to you. There's no one else I could say these things to."

Alex edged his silverware to one side, clearing the table-cloth of imaginary crumbs. "Still," he said, "work is good for you. And in the end, time smooths everything out."

"Do you really believe that?"

"I have to. But yes, I believe it."

"Don't you ever think time might crush you instead?" she asked.

"It could. The older I am, and the faster the years go by, the worse the odds seem against getting what I want. But at least the dreams let up."

They had with him, anyway, sometime in the second year. He still dreamed of his wife, Freya, but not of her death. In the morning he lay in bed thinking about her.

After lunch, Alex walked with his daughter in the narrow park beside the Ohio, beneath the flaking white branches of giant sycamores The river, which had looked fat and intransigent from the hotel, was actually full of movement. Smooth on the surface, it swirled and rolled downstream, muddied by springtime rains. Branches, sticks and human effluent bobbed along close to the muddy banks, while farther out whole trees or saw logs floated by. In Fell River they said that everything came down the Ohio in the end. The man at the hardware store told Alex once, "If you wait long enough your mother will come down the river. 'Course she might go by at night and you'd never know."

On this beautiful day almost no one was in the park. Alex noticed that people from town didn't watch the Ohio anymore. Maybe the implacable flow upset them. The river moved four miles an hour, a hundred miles a day, and almost twice that during floods. Because they had desperately needed to have time pass, Alex and Anna had always come to the Ohio.

"There are still things we don't talk about," she said.

"Like what?"

"Like whether you get lonely. You never complain about it."

"I'm lonely sometimes. After those last two years with your mother, I got used to living with a woman again. I miss that. I've met a couple of women here, but . . ."

"But no one you could love."

"No, I don't know if I can do that anymore. Not the same way."

"You're young, Dad. You don't look any older than you did ten years ago."

"I'm hot on the tennis courts," he said, smiling. "I've even started playing volleyball. But there's no getting around it. Sixty-three is a little old to go courting."

"Times are changing. It depends on the sixty-three-year-old."

"And don't you get lonely?" Alex asked. "You might not be ready to think about it, but you'll find another man someday and start over."

"What do you mean start over?"

"Well, you could get married again. Or whatever you want to call it. Freya and I never went back to a church the second time, or even to a judge. We swam out into the middle of Lake Harriet and whispered our vows."

"But you mean start over with another child."

Alex looked out over the water. "I didn't say that."

"Still, you think it would be a good idea."

"I guess I do."

Anna leaned against the iron railing at the top of a set of stairs that led down to the river. The wind blew back her hair and puffed out her shirt; she tapped on the bar with her nails, making small, metallic clicks.

"Let's say," she began, "that the person you love leaves you. You can't patch it up by finding somebody else, because you want the one who left. Well, that's how I feel about Kevin. People act as if children were interchangeable—as if another child would absorb my attention. Maybe that's true, I don't know. Maybe if I had another child I could forget about Kevin and not have these dreams. But I don't want to forget about him. And I don't want some squalling infant, either. It isn't a child I want, it's Kevin."

The breeze off the river grew stronger. Anna drew in her shoulders and put on her sweater but still looked cold. Alex took her arm and led her along the path beside the river.

"When I wake up from a dream about Kevin," she said, "I'm outraged. The dream is always stronger than I am. It turns out to be the truth and everything I do during the day is just a trick to keep me going."

"The dreams are true," Alex said. "But so is what you do the next day."

"Maybe so. I get up and work like crazy, and think about Kevin. I think of what he looked like as a little kid when I checked up on him at night. He'd have both hands curled up underneath his face, with his eyelids all shiny. If I moved him over on the bed and covered him with blankets, he'd fend me off with his little fists."

Alex didn't say anything. He knew Anna wanted to talk about

her child and speak his name out loud. She had to let someone know she still suffered. Alex understood, for often in this same park he had confided to Anna his own desperate memories.

AFTER twenty-seven years of marriage, Freya had told Alex she wanted to leave. He argued, he made her explain, he couldn't believe she had to go. If she needed more freedom, he said, she could do whatever she liked. If she felt tied down, he'd release her. He told her outright to sleep with other men if she wanted to—but he hated the idea, and she knew it. "I can't breathe," she told him. "I can't relax around you anymore. Everything in this house stifles me."

The battle erupted into late-night arguments, tears and shouting. In the end, Alex helped her go. They baited the case with known lovers and refined Freya's sense of guilt. It took months to wedge themselves into a place from which the only exit was divorce.

After three years Freya moved to Chicago for a job—though she flew back to Minneapolis every summer for Alex's birthday and again at Christmas. Eventually she followed a man to London, and although the affair didn't last, she made friends in England and stayed. Altogether, though they never lost their friendship, she and Alex were separated for ten years.

One spring afternoon, with no warning, she called him from the airport.

"You're in Minneapolis?" he said. "What are you doing here? I'll pick you up."

"I've come back. But don't drive out to get me, I want to take a look at the city first, and I have a few errands to do. Can I come to your house?"

"Of course, I'd love to see you. Why didn't you tell me before?"

"Ah . . ."

After her call he took a shower and tried to read a magazine. He had moved to an older house in a haphazard neighborhood, and thinking Freya might have trouble finding it, he touched up the faded street number with a small brush and a can of black paint. He watered some plants and straightened up the yard. Finally he sat down on the porch glider and waited through the warm afternoon.

Freya waved gaily from the back seat of her taxi, as if returning from a weekend trip. Alex hadn't seen her in six years. She stepped onto the sidewalk in a pair of low heels and a maroon knit dress, looking older but as slender as always. Her hair was still straight, and her eyebrows still threatened to meet on her forehead.

Alex stood up but stayed on the porch. Freya climbed the steps, placed a firm hand around his back and kissed him on the mouth.

"Where's your luggage?" he asked.

"Ah . . . I dropped it off. I wanted to see you like this, with nothing in the way."

He didn't ask her where she was going to live.

The Minnesota afternoon declined peacefully. A neighbor mowed his grass with an electric mower, and the first of the year's mosquitoes hovered over the lawn. Freya sat down on the porch swing, dropped off her shoes and tucked one foot under her thigh. Alex sat next to her, only a foot away. She brushed the floor with a stockinged foot, rocked the swing and yawned.

"To me it's eleven o'clock at night. I'm still on London time."

Alex shifted the bend of his knees, trying to create some leeway for his erection. "You could lie down on the couch and take a nap," he said.

"No, I'll stay up late. At least until sunset! I'd forgotten how beautiful these evenings are. We're close to Lake Harriet, aren't we?"

"Half a mile."

They walked it. First, though, Alex ducked into his house, changed into a loose polo shirt and tied a sweater around his waist to cover his stubborn erection. It didn't subside until they had walked halfway around the lake, and it rose again when they lay down on the grass below the rose gardens. A hummingbird hung over the smooth grass, its wings viridescent. On the asphalt path around the lake, the young adept on roller skates pumped and coasted by.

"Why did you come back?" he asked.

"Ah . . ."

"Are you going to stay?"

"Yes, I've come back to stay." She didn't touch him, except to undo the first button on his shirt. Their arms had brushed on the way over. "I was happy enough in England, but I got to thinking."

"About what?"

"I thought how we've been friends for more than thirty-five years. Can you imagine that? I was much too young when we met—so I guess I had to jump ship and travel around. But after ten years, I figured out you're still my closest friend."

"Tell the press we're just good—"

"Sssh." Freya rolled a finger across his lips. "No sarcasm. I want you to answer one question. Just one, will you?"

"All right."

"I want to know if you always cared about me."

"At first I hated you."

"That's okay, I was a hard case."

"You were," he said.

"And then?"

Alex stretched out his legs. Lying on the cool grass, his knees had begun to shake. "And then I missed you, and I got over it. But I always wanted you back."

"Well, I've come back."

"What if I weren't interested?"

"If you weren't interested," she said, laughing and untying his sweater, "you wouldn't have wrapped this around your waist, and you wouldn't be shaking so hard." Still, she didn't touch him. "And if you weren't interested, I'd stay in Minneapolis anyway. I've already got a job lined up."

He thought about the danger, and about how much he'd been hurt.

"Take your time, Alex. It scares me, too. That's why I left all my bags over at Elizabeth's."

"You don't look scared."

"Ah . . . but I am."

They walked back to his house, and rather than go out to dinner, they cooked hamburgers over a grill in Alex's backyard. As it grew dark they sat close to the coals, on a blanket. Alex's knees were shaking again. He felt hollow. He wondered if a middle-aged man could faint from desire. When Freya put her hand on his chest, he burst out crying. She folded the blanket over him and held his head against her breasts so he could weep. He didn't know if it was love, or fear, or sex, but he cried a long time, lying against the woman he had fought to give up.

She laid him on his bed, took off his clothes and smoothed his muscles with her palms. It was sex, and love, and fear. She pulled her dress over her shoulders, took off her underwear and brushed his entire body with her chest, tracing his skin with her nipples.

A week passed before he could get into bed without shaking—though by then he was laughing, not crying. Freya woke a sexual response in him that had almost died. Her gestures and movements in bed had changed—suggesting unknown scenes with other men—yet he wasn't jealous.

Surprised by the passion of their revival, Alex worked with less ambition, ignored half his friends and even stopped playing tennis. Freya had broken her ankle in London a year before, and neither of them missed the game. They spent more time in each other's company than they had since they first met as teenagers.

Their daughters, ensconced on either coast, had become partial strangers. Anna worked in a greenhouse in Eugene and took care of Kevin; Lisa was in business with her husband in Philadelphia.

Anna came to visit one summer, alone, having sent Kevin

to his father for two weeks. At first it embarrassed Alex to have Anna discover him kissing Freya in the kitchen pantry, or hear them arguing loudly about a movie or laughing late at night after making love. Freya, on the other hand, didn't seem to mind if her daughter heard everything that went on in the house, including the bedroom. Freya hummed and moaned, and came with the same noisy abandon as ever. In the cool early mornings, Alex watched her amble naked to the bathroom, her smooth haunches reproving the sluggish. She weighed herself on the floor scales and sang out, every morning, "Still a hundred and thirteen!" She said it louder when Anna was there.

Anna outweighed her mother by twenty pounds. A half hour after Freya she would call out from the bathroom, "Still a hundred and . . . remember I'm three inches taller than you are!" The two women would laugh from different rooms but were not always relaxed when face to face. Alex, the last to weigh himself on the pink scales, called out, "No competition from the Hulk." His instinct was to shield Anna from her mother, and her mother's ardor.

It lasted for two years: a cascade of friendship and laughter and sex. Alex turned sixty, then sixty-one. He believed no man his age had ever had such luck.

At the start of a cold wet spring, Freya's leg hurt. She thought the weather brought it on, along with her old break at the ankle—even though it was her calf that ached. Her whole leg swelled slightly for a week, then subsided. One morning she got out of bed, took a step toward the hall and fell. Alex drove her to the hospital.

Against the advice of the doctors, he told her the truth as soon as they let him know. She had bone cancer.

She looked away for an instant, out the window. "I want to be near you," she said. "That's all I care about."

Alex took off his shoes and lay down beside her on the bed. Freya touched his arms and legs, even slid her hand briefly into his pants and cupped his testicles. She felt his ears, kissed his wet cheeks, counted out loud the disks of his spine. Then she threw up softly into the pitcher of water.

Alex knew two members of the hospital board and got Freya into a private room after only three days. He brought his own cot and moved in with her, returning home for books, a tape recorder and music, and some of Freya's clothes. He accompanied her through the underground maze of the hospital, to diagnostic tests and special treatments.

"Alex, I don't care about tests and lab reports. I just want you to lie down beside me."

"You might puke on my shoulder," he joked.

She had lost her sense of humor completely. Lying on the white pillow, her dark eyes open, she said, "I love you, and I'm glad I came back. All I want now is for you to be here."

So every day he climbed onto her bed and lay beside her, trying to loosen his heart, until either she fell asleep or pushed him away softly with her fingertips and said, "That's enough." Nurses found them side by side and did not complain. Soon, Alex stopped being embarrassed. He could no longer enjoy sex and laughter with his wife, but he could still lie beside her.

After a month in the hospital she said, "I'm going to die, and I don't want to stay here. I'd rather live out my time at home."

Alex balked, for he had never given up hope. He had read furiously in the literature of bone cancer and talked to every doctor he could corner. "Give it another week," he asked her, "please."

"A few days," she said. She knew he had an appointment with a specialist in Kansas City. On the morning he left she told him, "After this, take me home." She didn't look well: thin and neurasthenic. He promised her.

The specialist offered no particular hope, admitting that if Freya wanted to go home, she might as well. Alex flew back to Minneapolis, picked up his car at the airport and drove straight to the hospital.

He took the stairs rather than the elevator. The ward was quiet. A young nurse, standing near the main station, saw him and walked off quickly. Oh no. Not on the one day he left her. His eyes ached, and the corridor swept past him. He reached the doorway ahead of two of the older nurses, who took his arms. Freya's bed, freshly made, looked as if no one had ever lain there.

The nurses sat him down on his cot like an invalid. He didn't care, he let them. All he wanted was to lie down beside Freya—even if she was dead. They had taken away her body. Alex lost his hearing under the ocean roar of his heart.

She had died alone, had never called out or rung for anyone. One of the nurses gave Alex a piece of paper she had found beside the bed. Written in pencil, without salutation or signature, were three uneven words. *Now go on.*

Alex clutched the scrap of paper. The nurse loosened his tie and called an intern. She took his blood pressure, unbuttoned his shirt and put her stethoscope to his chest. Satisfied, she asked if he'd like to sleep on the bed. He nodded and allowed himself to be moved. He was aware of being surrounded by women, the true attendants of death and birth.

At the funeral, his daughters treated him like an old man in delicate health. Both Anna and Lisa invited him to live with them, in their homes, but he declined. He put up a stronger front, and after a week they went home.

Alex was head of the university's career counseling office but hadn't gone to work in a month. He quit without notice and put his house up for sale. The city turned meaningless after Freya's death. Worse than that, the streets were malevolent without her. Although he had lived in Minneapolis on and off for fifty years—ever since moving from Ohio as a child—the needle memories of his last two years with Freya threatened to pith him like a frog.

For two weeks he wandered through the streets and parks of the city, gripping the canister of Freya's ashes. Although the can had been provided by an ostentatious mortuary, it looked cheap, as if designed to hold coffee or paint. Alex was surprised by its weight, and after his daughters flew home he pried off the cover to look inside. What people called ashes were in fact the remnants of Freya's bones and teeth: dull, clean white chips the size of river gravel, packed into the canister like a mangled collection of seashells. Alex carried the can in a leather bag, trying to decide where he should scatter the ten pounds of miniature shards.

He knew Freya's life from start to finish, but he didn't know where her bones belonged. He knew her history, her family, her laughter. He knew the sweet aging flesh of her body, and her smell. For forty years she had given off the same clovish odor, unchanged by either childbirth or menopause. Alex opened the can a second time, but the dry chips gave off less of a smell than the canister, with its double lip and crimped metal seam.

He threw a handful of Freya's ashes in the Mississippi River, close to the falls below the Washington Avenue Bridge. They popped into the smooth water like raindrops. A second handful he let dribble through his fingers onto the tiny garden where Freya had grown tomatoes and bell peppers. Another he threw into Lake Harriet. The white chips, floating down through the water, attracted the ducks.

Late one night, overtaken downtown by a rainstorm, he slung the last of the ashes directly onto the pavement. They spattered down onto the black asphalt and lay gleaming under the street lights as the raindrops exploded minutely around them. Alex dropped the canister into a garbage can and walked home, soaking wet.

Someone bought his house. Before deciding where to go, he rented a U-Haul truck and packed it with furniture, clothes and utensils, enough for a small apartment. He gathered the rest of his and Freya's things, tacked up signs at the nearby street corners and held a sale. On Saturday morning he sat on a three-foot stepladder in the middle of the living room, quoting prices.

Early in the day, a young woman looked patiently through Freya's clothes. Alex had strung them on a sagging length of clothesline between two wooden columns on the front porch. The girl, whose long blond hair hid her face from Alex's view, inspected one garment after another, down to the buttons and zippers. After fifteen minutes she picked up Freya's laced velvet dress, held it against her shoulders and looked around.

Alex stepped down from the ladder and spoke through the open doorway. "There's a mirror inside," he said.

"Do you . . . are you selling all these?"

"Everything here is for sale."

She held the velvet dress against her with two hands, at shoulder and waist, turning her upper body back and forth in front of the mirror. "I'd like to buy this dress," she said, "if it isn't too much." She wore rope-soled shoes and a blue cloth belt. She was young, but not very pretty. A girl of twenty, with a gap between her teeth, and glasses. Her skin was smooth, though. She might have a boyfriend. Someone might love her.

Alex held the dress at arm's length. He tried to look as if he were calculating a price, but in fact he panicked. He didn't have the faintest idea how much to ask—and this was only the first of many dresses. He'd never be able to price them, nor watch as one woman after another lifted them to their shoulders. He handed the velvet dress back to the girl.

"How much do you weigh?" he asked.

"A hundred and ten." She said it without hesitation, folding the dress over one arm.

"My wife weighed a hundred and thirteen."

The girl took a step backward toward the porch. The soft ellipses of her eyes turned circular, their lids faintly shadowed in blue. Pivoting on the heel of her back foot, and keeping her eye on Alex, she retreated to the clothesline and hung up the dress.

"You don't want to sell them," she said.

"No, I do." He followed her outside. "Maybe to someone who likes them."

"Your wife had beautiful clothes," she said primly.

"I don't think I can sell them. But I'm leaving tomorrow, everything's already in the truck."

"I don't understand."

"They have to go to someone. My wife died a month ago. I have two daughters, but neither one can fit into her clothes."

"I'm sorry she died," the girl said.

"Would you take them? I want you to take them all."

"Oh no." She looked at him as if he had asked her to take off her own clothes and get into bed with him. "I hardly have any money. I just picked out one I liked."

"For free," Alex said, stepping past her and sweeping the dresses together on the clothesline. "If I sell them one by one I'll go crazy. Let me give them to you."

"No, I couldn't. What would I do with so many clothes?"

"Keep the ones you like, and give the ones you don't want to friends. You'd be helping me out."

"It's not right."

"*Please*," Alex said, as the girl took another step back. "If you don't take them, I'm going to throw them into the garbage."

"You wouldn't do that." She looked at him, eye to eye.

"I would." He grabbed a dress off the line and threw it over the hedge onto the unmown lawn, where it fell in a lump. The girl looked at it coldly. "All right," he admitted, "I wouldn't do that." He stepped out on the lawn, picked up the dress and came back to the stairs.

"Please take them," he said. Without sobbing, without even a catch in his breath, his eyes filled with tears.

He helped her carry the clothes to her car, where she folded them carefully into the back seat. After the last load, she stepped toward him. Alex looked away as she kissed him on the cheek. At least he thought she kissed him. He heard the soft sound but didn't feel her lips. After she drove away he touched his fingers to the spot, until someone asked him a question from the house.

Before the day was over, hundreds of people passed through the living room. Alex sat on the stepladder with a tackle box on his lap to hold the money and sold the accumulated paraphernalia of decades: furniture, paintings, records, power tools, automobile tires, the food out of the kitchen, a croquet set, some of his own clothes. He sold the cherry dresser Freya had inherited from her mother; he sold her silver bowls. He even sold Freya's old Mustang, forging her name on the title.

At four o'clock he stood in the middle of the room—he had sold the stepladder—holding the tackle box full of checks and twenties. A half-dozen people still rummaged through the clutter. "Free," he told them. "Take anything you want now for free, I'm closing up." He took in the sign from the lawn, called the Salvation Army and told them they'd find the remnants of the sale on the porch, and closed the door behind the last of the browsers. Stuffing the tackle box under the front seat of his car, he drove across the Mississippi to St. Paul. There he sat in a bar, drinking beer and watching the Twins play a double-header on a five-foot television screen. They lost one and won one. Drunk, he drove home in second gear, stumbled into his house and wrapped himself in blankets on the living room floor. Sunday morning, mildly hung over, he threw up into the toilet of an empty bathroom.

By eleven in the morning the temperature had dropped from fifty to thirty-five. It was still the middle of May. Alex packed a few last items into the U-Haul, attached his car to the truck with a tow bar and headed out of Minneapolis. He still hadn't decided where to go. Maybe to Anna's, he thought. Snow began to fall just as he reached the interstate, and on the radio he heard that a last blizzard was loose in the Dakotas. He headed south. Two days later he drove into Fell River, his childhood home.

AFTER lunch with her father at the Bradford Hotel, Anna drove home in peace. She watched the sunshine on the river and the rough-plowed earth, ready for seeding to field corn. In the greenhouse she went back to transplanting tomato seedlings into grower trays, one at a time. There were days when her flesh crawled at the repetition of such a task, leading her to break off after only an hour to do some brusque work with a shovel or with large machinery. But this afternoon she welcomed the endless, minute precision of nestling two-inch seedlings into a mixture of peat moss and vermiculite. The work set her mind free. The sky, seen through the greenhouse glass, had the deep blue color of high altitudes.

At six o'clock, Deal stopped by to invite her to dinner at the farmhouse. Anna didn't want to go but felt obliged, for Deal and Shelley had already asked her over twice since the fire. This time she accepted.

Deal had worked all afternoon on the planter's trip mechanism, finally getting it right. He smiled a manic grin of success as they walked to the farmhouse. Like Anna, Deal was an improbable farmer—even though he knew plants better than the county agent. He had dropped out of the upper end of a Ph.D. program in botany at Stanford to play pedal steel with an L.A. rock band. After three years on the road he left the band, swearing never to sleep in another motel or eat in a fast-food restaurant. He came to Fell River with a woman. She left, and he stayed on. A few years later he married Shelley, and when her parents moved to Florida the two of them took over the family's eighty-acre farm on the Ohio River.

Their three-year-old, Shane, ran up to her on the front lawn, saying, "Hey, Anna." She lifted him into the air. How light he was, how small and delicate. She held him up by his squiggling chest for a moment, then lowered him to the grass. Shane was young and blond and quiet, hardly a child to remind her of Kevin, yet Anna often stayed away from the farmhouse because of him.

"My eyes are giving out," Shelley said, standing up from the farm's computer. With a degree in agronomics from Ohio State, Shelley kept all the farm records and managed the pest control program. Anna liked her, and the two women often worked side by side in the fields—yet Anna seldom visited at the farmhouse. "You should come to dinner more often," Shelley said. "No need to ask first, there's always plenty of food."

"I hardly go out anymore, except to see my father. We had lunch today at the Bradford."

"I saw his car in front of your house the other weekend."

The day I burned Kevin's room, Anna thought. The bonfire had gone unmentioned on the farm, even though no one could have missed the column of grey smoke rising from behind her house. She stepped to the door to watch Shane ride across the lawn on his father's back. Deal wiggled like a dog on all fours, his boy's palms clapped to his ears.

Washing vegetables at the sink, Shelley said, "I noticed you burned something over at your house that day."

"I burned Kevin's room."

"His room?"

"His clothes, the furniture, even the walls."

The two women stood ten feet apart, leaning against sink and countertop. Anna rubbed the scar on her forehead. "I know I'm not the partner you hoped for."

"Oh Anna." Shelley turned off the water. Her wet hands hung at her sides, dripping water onto the floor.

"I'm not. You'd have a better time with somebody more relaxed, who'd join in with the things you do. I started out that way, but after the accident . . ."

"No one could have known what was going to happen. We'd help, if we knew what to do."

Anna stuck her hands in her pockets. "You do help. Everything is a help here, because I can work."

"You work so much, Anna, we feel guilty. You work all day, and then late at night we hear you nailing."

"Oh, last night. I was building some shelves. But sometimes I have to work day and night. Without work I'd have died, I swear." Anna took a half step toward the other woman. "I know I've been distant, and I never talk to you or Deal about anything except business. But I have to have someplace where I don't break down. I've cried so much, and complained, and been crazy. Farming's my refuge. Just let me work all hours and pound things into the night. It doesn't upset you, does it?"

"No, no. We just think about you. We worry sometimes."

"A couple of months ago I came home drunk in the middle of the night and threw my hammer out the kitchen window. I was afraid you'd worry, after that."

Shelley laughed. "We never heard it. You smashed the window?"

"Yes. Maybe I thought it was open or something. I put the framing hammer out in the first row of onions." Anna smiled briefly. "That was a little crazy. And after the fire I felt bad about tearing down Kevin's room, since you and Deal both helped build it."

"Anna, don't worry about things like that. You've done so much on the farm, we'd be lost without you. To be honest, after the accident I was afraid you might leave."

Anna had joined the farm as a partner, after she and Kevin drove to Fell River to visit with her father. Anna's sadness over her mother's death was less than her concern for Alex, who had rented an apartment and was looking for a part time job. Months after Freya's death, his grief was still obvious. But from the start of that visit he hit it off with Kevin, and the two of them did something together every day.

Why go on living in Oregon? Anna thought. She was at a low ebb in Eugene, where she had just been passed over for a promotion at Valley Florists. She practically ran the greenhouses for the Judson brothers. She chose the varieties, did all the ordering and supervised ten other workers. She knew the wholesale and retail markets better than the owners, but they gave the new job, and higher salary, to a nephew. In addition, Kevin's father, Paul, had grown distant. He rarely called or wrote, and his child-support payments had long been irregular.

What clinched the move was a classified ad she found in the *Fell River Express*: "Experienced grower wanted to invest and share work at established truck farm. Must know horticulture, machinery, sales. P.O. Box 187." Anna didn't know much about large machinery or the field culture of vegetables, but she did know cooperative markets, crop brokers and the vegetable greenhouse industry. Shelley and Deal's farm had run skimpily in the black for three years, but too much produce had rotted in the fields, or on the delivery truck, for lack of sales. Anna found a market for every crop, and the three partners' first season together was a good one.

Deal came buzzing through the door with Shane on one shoulder, the boy's arms spread out like an airplane. Life was often gay at the farmhouse, Anna thought, with music after dinner, picture puzzles on the coffee table and visiting children. She relaxed. After dinner, Deal asked her what she'd burned in back of her house ten days before—but Shelley said quickly, "I asked her about that already." The three of them drank a glass of wine, and Anna stayed for a half hour of television. "No more banging nails late at night," she said as she left. "I promise."

"Bang away," Deal said. "Don't worry about us, we'll be fast asleep."

Anna walked home in the dark, feeling that once again she had cheated her partners. She had told them a little, but not the truth. Something closer to the truth was still written in Magic Marker on the white plastic finish of her refrigerator, the scoured, half-legible remains of a drunken message she had left herself the same night she threw her framing hammer through the window: "There's a hole in the bottom of my life, and when I get drunk I fall into it."

Sometimes she thought she would rather live in an eight-by-ten shack in the woods with no telephone or books or farm clutter. Just for a year or two, until Kevin lost his power over her. But farmwork and the soil had become her life. She immersed herself in the complex machinations required to grow sweet corn and tomatoes by the Fourth of July, five acres of lettuce in strict succession and fifteen other crops. She lived in the middle of her work. But there were memories everywhere. She took a sponge and Comet cleanser to the refrigerator, one more time.

Anna's small wood-frame house, one story set squarely above the other, had been built in a two-month flurry during her first autumn on the farm. The downstairs, now clear of Kevin's bedroom, was both kitchen and living room. It held the wood stove, a couch, a kitchen table and a desk piled with books and wholesale seed packages.

There was no staircase, only an oak ladder to the second floor. Anna climbed through the trap door and shut it behind her. In the upstairs room there was only a mattress and a chest of drawers, a bar for her clothes, a lamp, a clock, a journal and a book of dreams. Anna stood beside the window, looking toward the river.

At dusk she sometimes opened the window and watched the bats drop out of the eaves, exploding into flight eighteen inches in front of her. Bats, mice, snakes, opossums, sow bugs, spiders: they had all moved into or under her house within months of construction.

Three hundred yards away, beyond a field of early cabbage and a row of sycamores, a towboat roiled against the current of the Ohio River. Squat and businesslike, it guided a string of barges decked with red and green running lights. Its diesel engines throbbed over the banks of the river and vibrated the window glass. Anna touched the panes with her fingertips and thought of nothing, until the towboat disappeared around the first bend upstream.

She hadn't written down her dream about Kevin, and after two days its details had faded. She couldn't remember the first part at all, except that something peaceful had happened, and then something confusing. Finally Kevin had climbed into a large oak tree in the middle of a field. The branches were spaced far apart, but he got up into the tree by himself and climbed toward the top. Anna stood underneath and tried not to worry. She watched the sunlight reflect off his legs

He yelled down to her, "I won't fall, Mom. Don't you remember I climbed up here before? I can climb high."

Far up in the tree, she saw his red shirt and the white bottom of his sneakers, If he fell, she'd catch him. He yelled again, "You can really see from up here." Anna lay on the grass and thought, My darling prehensile boy.

Then he fell, slapping from branch to branch with his soft eyes open. He hit the ground with a muffled sound as Anna fought to stand up. The dreams always ended that way. She struggled to help but couldn't.

KEVIN died in the emergency room at the Fell River hospital, surrounded by doctors, nurses and paramedics. They all struggled to help but couldn't.

The accident followed two days of rain and an unexpected freeze at the end of Anna's first winter on the farm. The warm, slow, straight-down rain saturated the ground and swelled the creeks, which rose to the edge of their banks before disgorging into the Ohio. Although spring had already established a foothold—the redbuds were in flower at the edge of every wood—a cold front swept the skies clear, the temperature dropped forty degrees overnight, and the surface of the ground froze.

Kevin jumped out of bed at first call. Every Saturday morning he took a tennis lesson from his grandfather at the indoor courts. Generally, he objected to lessons of any kind, in school or out, but when his grandfather coached him he paid full attention, chased the tennis balls in good humor and said merely, "Okay, I'll try," when told to work on his backswing.

As usual, Kevin fixed his own austere breakfast, a bowl of Wheaties with milk. No fruit, no juice, no toast. At any hour of the day he was apt to repeat the meal with another, identically stark serving. Rarely, he strayed as far as Rice Krispies.

"Would you like an apple?" Anna asked. "Or a banana?"

"No thanks."

He read the sides of the Wheaties box, ignoring the bright

cover picture of a bowl of cereal topped with fresh peaches. Could a nine-year-old boy, sixty-two pounds and growing, survive for a year on only cereal and milk?

"How about half a grapefruit? I'd cut up the sections for you."

"No thanks. Are there any strawberries?"

"There are some in the field, but they're not ready yet."

"Oh Mom, you just buy them at the store."

"I will," she promised. "I didn't know you liked them."

"I had some at Ben's house last week." Kevin looked up from the box of cereal, mildly accusing. "You never told me they were so good."

"Oh yes I did."

"Oh no you didn't." He mocked her tone of voice, then went back to reading the fine print on the side of the box, out loud: "Vitamin A, palmitate; Vitamin B two, riboflavin; Vitamin B one, thiamin hydro—"

"How about a slice of papaya?" Anna said.

"Papaya? Yccch. We don't have any papaya."

"No, we don't. I was just testing to see what else you've been eating over at Ben's."

"Fruit leather. His mom buys it at the health food store. Can we get some?"

Fruit leather! Anna smiled, thinking of Kevin's secret life. After school he went to Ben's house and ate strawberries and fruit leather. He'd probably get through the year without scurvy after all. "Sure," Anna said, "I'll buy you some fruit leather."

"It's great. It comes from Damascus, Syria."

"That's on the label, right?"

Kevin had scrutinized the label of every package in the kitchen. He also read baseball cards, comic books, junk mail, the newspaper classifieds, and *National Geographic World* from cover to cover. He only got onto a book every month or so, but then he read it like a zombie, eating, or riding in the car, or even walking down the street.

After breakfast he changed into white shorts, a hooded sweat shirt and tennis shoes. Anna told him he had to put his sweat pants on over his shorts, it had frosted during the night.

"I don't have to, Mom. It's always warm at the courts. They're indoors."

"But we have to get there."

"In a *car*," Kevin said. "Look, I'm warm enough." He opened the door of the house and stood in the cool air, holding his palms to the sunshine. His legs, pale after a long winter, poked thinly out of his shorts.

Anna told him to put on his sweat pants and pointed an unrelenting finger toward his room. Then, having imposed her will, she wondered why he gave in to her. How long could she go on forcing Kevin to wear a particular piece of clothing or eat this or that food? Maybe he was right. If he could go to town in short pants without getting cold, why not let him? Or let him suffer if he did get cold.

Kevin didn't entirely give in, for he strode out of his room with a scowl, carrying the sweat pants in his hand. "I'll put them on in the car," he said.

"Okay."

"And can I say what I want?"

"I guess so."

"*Damn. God damn.*"

He marched angrily from the house to the car, got in and pulled the grey sweat pants over his sneakers with exaggerated difficulty, twisting around on the front seat of the Volkswagen as if in pain. That done, he stared out the side window with his chin resting against the glass and his tousled hair hiding his face.

Anna skirted the driveway's ice-ringed puddles and turned west onto the river road, toward town. The pastures of the neighboring farms were glazed silver, each bromegrass and rye blade encased in ice. In the direct sunlight some of the frost had already melted. It would all be gone soon, for the temperature was forty and rising.

Kevin fastened his seat belt with a click. "You better put

yours on, Mom. You didn't remember this time." Pleased at having caught and corrected her, his resentment vanished. He tucked his feet up beneath the seat belt and said, "I had a funny dream last night."

"About what?" She held his hand for a moment.

"About going back to Seal Rock. The water was all different colors, like camo, and instead of seals there were dogs. Do you think we'll ever go to Seal Rock again, Mom?"

"Some year. At least I hope we do."

She wasn't sure they would, since Oregon was so far away. The Atlantic would be easier.

Halfway to Fell River, just as Anna slowed for a pair of reversed curves, a bluebird flashed in front of them and almost hit the windshield. Its bright wings pumped wildly, holding its small blue body, for a brief moment, at exactly the same speed as the car. Finally it spun off toward the river.

"Did you see how blue it was?" Anna said as they came out of the first curve.

The second curve wasn't as sharp, but overflow from two days of rain had seeped across the entire road and frozen in a sheet. Anna braked hard, let up at the last instant and sailed onto the ice. The road veered left. The rear end of the car drifted, broke loose and slid broadside toward a tree at thirty miles an hour. Anna shot out her hand against Kevin's chest.

The right side of the car crumped hard against the tree. The Volkswagen jammed through a cattle fence and skidded onto the icy pasture, then turned and rolled, over and over. Anna bumped her forehead, hard. She reached for Kevin but couldn't find him as the car skidded to a stop on its side, its roof crushed. Anna's seat belt pressed against her neck, her eyesight was blurred and her mouth tasted of blood—but where was her son? She pushed against the door and screamed, "*Kevin!*"

Had he crawled out or been thrown? There was no answer from him, no sound at all. The glass in every window was either shattered or covered with mud. All she could see was the icy grass of the pasture in front of her. Oh God, where was Kevin?

She kneeled and beat upward on the driver's door, but it wouldn't move. Painlessly, her forehead trickled blood into the corner of one eye.

"Are you all right?" A woman's timorous voice made Anna jump. "Can you get out?" The woman wore a turquoise blouse, as blue and vivid as the bird. Her pop eyes stared at Anna through the webbed cracks of the windshield.

"My son," Anna said.

"I wrapped him in my coat. Someone's calling the ambulance."

"Is he all right?"

"I don't know. He's breathing, but I don't know what to do."

"Help me get out. Open the door."

The woman looked at her. "There's blood on your face," she said.

"Get up on the side of the car." Anna pointed up wildly. "I'm all right, just open the door."

The woman scrambled up on the fender, pressing her blue shirt to the glass; her small brown city shoes were covered with mud. Twice she slipped, then managed to climb onto the side of the car. But the door had been jammed tight beneath the flattened roof and wouldn't budge.

"*Shit,*" Anna said, pressing hard from inside. "My son. See if he's all right."

The woman scrambled down, and a few minutes later Anna heard the high pulse of a siren. The hospital was only a few miles away. The sound grew and wavered and grew again, winding down in back of the car. Anna heard voices and another siren in the distance. Finally a man in a blue uniform— hardly more than a boy, Anna thought—ran up to the car.

"My son is outside," Anna yelled through the vent window.

"We have him. Was anyone else in the car?"

"No. Get me out, please."

The paramedic disappeared for a minute and returned with an open knife. With four long strokes he slit the rubber molding around the windshield. The glass sagged but fell out in one piece, and Anna started to crawl through the window.

"Wait," he said, "you're bleeding. I'm coming in first."

"In here?"

"Yes, I want to look at your forehead."

"Forget about me." Anna put her hand against the man's neck, grabbed his collar and crawled through the window.

Another paramedic, a woman, hovered over Kevin on the icy grass, adjusting a white foam collar around his neck. Fastened in back with Velcro strips, it looked like an athlete's neck support. Anna crouched beside the two of them, touching Kevin's leg. She allowed the first paramedic to wipe her forehead and tape on a bandage.

The woman wrapped a blood pressure cuff around Kevin's arm, glanced up and asked her partner, "Is she all right?"

"I think so," he said.

"We'd like you to lie down," the woman said.

"I'm all right, just take care of my son, please."

The man had already stretched a second black cuff around her arm. Anna submitted, her eyes going from Kevin's face to the woman's. Kevin looked peaceful and untouched. The only mark on him was a trace of milk at one corner of his mouth. The woman grew distant as she listened to her stethoscope. Kevin lay under a blanket.

"Ninety over sixty," the woman said calmly. Short and stocky, she was no older than Anna, but completely grey-haired. She told her partner to bring a backboard from the ambulance, and the two of them logrolled Kevin onto the board. They strapped his head down with a triangular white bandage and packed orange vinyl sandbags around his neck. Then they lifted the backboard onto a stretcher and rolled it onto the back of the ambulance.

The woman attached an IV bag to a hook in the ceiling and glanced at Anna. "You can ride in back if you like."

"What's wrong with him?"

She bent over Kevin's arm with a needle. "His breathing is

normal and his pulse is good so far. He may have hurt his neck, or he may have internal injuries. We're extra careful with an unconscious patient."

"But why is he unconscious?" Anna's words flew out of her throat, uncontrolled, her voice rising.

The woman went back to her stethoscope and held up a watch on the inside of her wrist. Her eyes went out of focus as she counted. Then she spoke to the driver: "Ninety over fifty. No lights and siren."

Anna sat down on the bench inside the ambulance. She was close enough to the woman to see her blue contact lenses. The name on her badge was Panofski. She wore a wedding ring.

"Do you feel dizzy?"

"No," Anna said.

"Good. It's not that far."

The driver shut the rear doors and walked to the front. Maybe I do feel dizzy, Anna thought. No, it was just her heartbeat. She was afraid. She studied the downturned face of the woman for some sign but discovered nothing.

The ambulance pulled out gently, past a dozen cars on the road and a police car with flashing lights. Through a small door Anna heard the driver of the ambulance radioing to the hospital: "Unit One bringing in a boy, age nine, unconscious, unresponsive to voice, touch, pain. Initial BP ninety over sixty, pulse ninety-eight, respirations sixteen. Current BP ninety over fifty, pulse one-oh-four, respirations twenty. Child's mother accompanies patient. ETA ten minutes."

Anna sat on the bench and studied Kevin's face. He looked pale and distant. She wanted to embrace him, to hold him, to hold his neck. Glancing at the medic, she picked up his hand. The woman nodded.

She yielded to them the care of her son. Kevin's eyelids were blank and opaque, he was much farther away than in sleep. The grey-haired woman pressed her fingers to his elbow, unable to use her stethoscope over the sound of the ambulance. Kevin's eyelids fluttered momentarily, then his mouth turned down. He didn't look like himself at all, his face had grown as long as an adult's. The woman was busy counting.

She looked up directly at Anna, then spoke through the door. "Hank, go code one, we've got a palpated pressure of forty."

The ambulance leapt forward, and the siren howled. Turning up the IV, she told Anna, "He may be going into shock."

Within seconds they hit sixty miles an hour, screaming into the outskirts of Fell River. It was only blocks to the hospital. The ambulance slowed on the first warbling brick streets, and Anna heard the driver on the radio again, though she couldn't make out what he was saying. They wheeled through one curve and then another under the whip of the siren. Anna's face burned with the noise, but Kevin showed no signs of hearing anything. Strapped tightly to his board, he hadn't moved. He looked closer to hibernation than to sleep, Anna thought. Closer to death.

The doors opened, inches above a concrete platform, and two nurses reached for the stretcher. The paramedics held Anna back until Kevin disappeared past two more sets of swinging doors, into a corridor with pale green walls. Anna watched as they wheeled him away.

CHAPTER 2

TWO DAYS after Kevin's death, Anna drove to Columbus in her father's old Buick to meet Paul Dunham's flight from San Francisco. She went alone, convinced that all her old arguments with Paul would vanish in the face of their son's death.

She was early, and the plane late. Under the fluorescent light and forced-air ventilation of the lounge, a skin closed over her feelings. She neither read nor watched the other passengers but sat upright in her chair, her eyes out of focus, waiting for the plane to land.

Paul entered the terminal at the end of a long line of travelers—and walked right past her. He didn't see her, didn't appear to be looking. "Paul," she said.

He turned abruptly. "Oh Anna, you came."

She had forgotten how tall he was. Either forgotten or adjusted her memory. He wore a rumpled khaki suit, a black shirt—his idea of mourning?—and a narrow, striped tie. In one hand he carried a small, dented aluminum suitcase, his only luggage.

"What a flight. Planes drive me crazy with that buzzing." He touched his free hand to the small of Anna's back. "Let's get out of here."

The carpeted hallway muffled their steps as far as the exit. Paul walked close beside her, his right hand pressed against her waist, impelling her along faster than she wanted to go. Outside, they followed the yellow arrows to the parking lot.

They should stop, Anna thought, and look into each other's eyes; they should acknowledge that Kevin was dead. But a stream of families and businessmen passed them face on, all staring. A wind gusted through the parking lot, flipping paper bags and candy wrappers into the air. Anna led the way to her father's Buick and unlocked the driver's side of the car.

"You got hurt," Paul said, touching his own forehead where hers was covered with a bandage.

"Just a cut."

"Did they sew you up?"

"Three stitches, it's nothing."

"Still, maybe I better drive."

She gave him the keys, partly because she'd been in the accident and partly out of habit. Paul threw his suitcase on the back seat and folded himself into the car.

"You didn't have to come get me," he said. "I could have taken a bus from the airport. What is it, a couple of hours?"

Anna pressed herself against the passenger door, fighting tears as Paul drove south from Columbus through flat soybean and corn land. Tractors in first gear stumbled across empty fields, pulling five- and six-bottom plows through the heavy soil. Behind the plows, grackles swooped through the air in tremulous throngs and alighted on the freshly turned earth.

"That ice must have surprised you," Paul said. "I don't see any on the road today. Isn't it late for a freeze? Of course you can't tell what's around a curve. You said you hit a tree—how did Kevin get thrown out?"

"I don't know. When the car stopped rolling he wasn't there."

"He probably grabbed the door and slid out under his seat belt. That could happen with a small child. In the middle of an accident you can't remember anything, it's like being in shock. Even if you're not going that fast you can really bang yourself around if you hit a tree or something."

Anna looked at the speedometer: Paul was doing seventy miles an hour. "Please slow down," she said.

"Oh yeah. But at least the road's in good shape. And this is no Volkswagen. VWs are terrible on ice with all that weight in back. Once the rear end breaks loose, it's all over."

Paul's left wrist hung over the top of the steering wheel, and his knees jerked up and down. He talked like a taxi driver, his eyes on the road. "I wish I'd called him last week. I was going to call him and then my phone went out. Someone asked me about him and the most recent photo I had was two years old."

In the last year Paul had called and written his son infrequently. Now he wanted to talk about the old days.

"Kevin always loved cars and going places. Remember how excited he'd get before a trip? He'd pack his clothes the night before and wake up early, like it was Christmas morning. He got a kick out of leaving when it was dark. I remember one time he came in and jumped on our bed at four-thirty in the morning. Four-thirty! And we were only going an hour and a half to the ocean. He couldn't get his fill of vacations and trips. Airplane rides, too, we went on a couple of those. What an imagination that kid had! If he was on an airplane—or if he just saw an airplane—he'd pretend he was flying to the moon, and talk about everything he'd do when he got there. He could have been a writer, he was so full of stories."

From Paul's tone, Kevin might have died months ago.

Anna waited for him to ask the questions she would have asked. Had Kevin suffered? What did he die of? What did he look like in the ambulance, what was he wearing, what did they do to take care of him? Did he have any dreams the night before, did he ever ask about his father? Did he have friends at school, was he still shy, was he still beautiful? Was he happy in the last conscious moments of his life?

Paul drove on past Washington Court House, past Hillsboro, telling Anna what Kevin had been like as a child. She waited for him to ask the crucial question, "Was it your fault?"

When he finally stopped talking she said, "I never had an accident before. In twenty years I never had an accident."

Paul drove a mile in silence. "It could have happened to anyone."

She couldn't tell if he blamed her. All his talk was distant. "I had the casket sealed," she said.

There was another pause. "Okay. I'd rather remember him the way he looked the last time I saw him. Besides, after the accident . . ."

"He's dead, but there's not a mark on him. His neck was broken, but that didn't kill him. It was a ruptured spleen. He died of internal bleeding."

Paul asked quietly, "What's the spleen?"

"It's some spongy organ below the heart, filled with blood. A sharp blow to the chest can rupture it."

Paul drove the rest of the trip without talking. Anna had finally gotten through to him, but all he did was clam up. He didn't say anything about going to a motel, so she directed him to the farm. She felt incapable of deciding anything. An hour before dark she threw a couple of blankets on the couch for him, climbed the ladder to her room and lay down on her mattress with her pillow over her head.

The next morning Paul dressed for the funeral in the same khaki suit and black shirt he'd worn the day before. If he had other clothes, he didn't remove them from his locked aluminum suitcase. It was a cloudy, cold morning at the start of April, yet Paul wore only his rumpled suit and a pair of dark glasses, as if the temperature were in the seventies. Anna drove them first to her father's apartment, where Paul and Alex shook hands neutrally. They had never been close.

Alex's presence, however, seemed to animate Paul, who fidgeted in the back seat of the Buick and asked Anna a stream of questions as they drove to the cemetery above Fell River. He challenged Anna to recall details about Kevin as a young child, but his questions only induced amnesia. All she could think of was the sickening thump of her car as it exploded against a tree and rolled over the icy field. Paul cleaned his glasses on his black shirt and leaned forward from the back seat, grazing Anna's shoulder with the ends of his fingers.

"Remember that canoe trip down the Green River? I'll bet Kevin wasn't four years old, but he was trying to paddle. Remember he wore those red overalls and jumped into the creek?"

Anna did not remember the red overalls. It annoyed her that Paul should remember something about Kevin that she'd forgotten, and she didn't believe in the nostalgia that had apparently overtaken Paul on the way to the cemetery. If she wanted to tell him anything now, it was that he had never had enough time for his son, and it was too late to do anything about it. Paul went on talking, first leaning forward in the car, then slumping into the back seat, then jerking up again. At the cemetery he jumped out and paced around the casket, inspecting the tidy excavation and the pegged green tarpaulin covering the dirt.

Shelley and Deal had come without Shane. Ben's parents were there, and two other families of Kevin's friends. They all looked formal, like professional mourners. Anna wore her grey overcoat with a hood. She hadn't been to a funeral since she was a child, when her grandparents died. Looking out over the brick buildings and white wooden houses of Fell River, her eyes kept losing their focus. The sun came out briefly, then disappeared as gusts of wind pushed against her.

"No dust to dust here," Paul said loudly. "No sign of the earth at all."

It was true. A line of folding chairs, too many for the number of mourners, was set up on one side of the gleaming wooden casket. The casket itself, suspended by two webbed slings, hung six inches in the air, nowhere touching the dirt. Everything was arranged and orderly. Anyone could see that funerals took place here all the time—as if the death of a child were an acceptable fact. Paul's critical nervous pacing made it all look cheap. And it was cheap, Anna thought. It was cheap and mannerly and ceremonious. But by now she didn't want to share anything with Paul, even if they had the same reaction to the funeral.

The April wind blew at Paul's hair and flapped his unbuttoned suit coat. He looked down at the ground, then straight up in the sky, as inquiet as the wind. When Alex read from the Bible, Paul disappeared for a moment. Anna heard him shuffle up on the dry grass behind her, heard his suit coat flapping, and then his own mumbled passages from Scripture. Her father read on. When the cemetery men lowered the casket into the ground, Anna turned and whispered vehemently, *"What are you doing?"*

Paul moved off and circled the grave, but even from the other side Anna could hear him. With his jittery ways he took over all her grief, and she lost whatever connection she had felt between the ritual of burial and her son's death. When her father stepped forward to drop handfuls of dirt onto the coffin, Paul knelt and threw in clods, rocking back on his heels and keening like a tribesman.

"Why is the coffin so big?" he wailed. "He was just a little boy."

They had put Kevin in an adult coffin. Anna hadn't asked about it at the funeral parlor—what difference did it make? But she hated Paul for calling attention to it now.

He groveled on the dirt in front of everyone, smudging his pants and jacket. Alex put a hand on his arm and drew him to his feet. Paul didn't cry, but contorted his face and let his neck go slack. Then he jerked out of Alex's grasp, tore back a corner of the tarpaulin and scrabbled soft dirt into the grave with his thin city shoes.

"For Christ's sake," Alex said, "stop that noise. Stand up here and be quiet." Disgusted, he walked off to get his car. Anna turned her back to the grave and to Paul as the other mourners passed by in consolation. They touched her arm and said a few words. The skin of her face, taut and dry, stood out from her cheekbones as if she had lived a year at extreme altitude.

Alex had arranged a late lunch at his apartment. A wake, Anna thought, a party, a vigil. But Paul was jumpier than ever as they drove into town. He talked about Kevin's visits to San Francisco and said he'd been planning to take him to a lake in

Montana that summer, a great place for a boy. There were ca-
noes to rent and campsites where no one ever went. Paul had
been there once with his own father, years ago, and the lake
probably hadn't changed at all. They could have gotten up when
it was still dark and driven all day to get there.

Alex told him to shut up.

"But he would've liked it. He was good in a canoe, even
when he was little."

Anna wheeled on him and hissed furiously, "You're doing
speed, aren't you?"

Paul sank back. "Just a little to get through the day."

"Then shut the fuck up."

That's what he'd been up to the last year in San Francisco,
Anna was sure. In the last year of their marriage he'd sometimes taken speed for weeks at a time: a hit in the morning and
another in the afternoon. He'd shaken it at the end. Later he
wrote her that he was off the stuff for good—and she believed
him. When he came to Seal Rock the last time, he was clean.
But she should have known he was speeding when he got off
the plane in Columbus and started talking so much. Instead of
challenging him, she had numbed her own feelings and let him
run on.

Early the next morning she drove him back to the airport
and put him on a return flight. By now he was humbled and
quiet, but Anna was glad to have him go. She wanted to mourn
her child alone. Standing at the gate, his ticket and boarding
pass crumpled in one hand, Paul looked defeated. Spiky hair
jutted over his ears, and one black shirttail drooped below his
jacket. But Anna felt nothing for him. Under the weight of
Kevin's death she had lost all charity for others, including Paul.
It was too long, she thought, since they had loved one another.
They embraced stiffly at the opening to the accordion walkway,
and he disappeared.

Anna climbed to the observation deck and stood in a chill
wind, surrounded by juggernaut airplanes and wide expanses
of concrete runway. In the corridors below, thousands of alien

humans pressed forward on their way to distant, useless cities. Paul's plane taxied, waited and took off, trailing smoke. What if, instead of lifting on its cushion of air, the plane abruptly nosed down and crashed onto the end of the runway, spewing metal and jet fuel, killing everyone on board? Two hundred people could die in an instant, including Paul—and what difference would it make?

For thirty minutes, while one metal envelope after another roared into the sky, Anna sat alone on a cold bench on the flat roof of the terminal. The air, pocked with uneven gusts of wind, swirled by her face. Finally she struggled to her feet, walked unevenly to her father's car and backed out of her parking space. But she couldn't find the exit from the lot. She cried, slumped across the front seat of the car with her head under her coat, until someone honked at her to move. Reparking the car, she walked to the airport Sheraton. There, lying on the bed of an isolated, soundproofed room on the fifth floor, she wept, praying only for time to go by. She fell asleep, woke once in the evening and called her father, then lay down and slept again until eight in the morning. Alex took a bus to the airport and drove her home.

Later, Anna heard from friends that Paul was still in San Francisco. She sent three letters to his old address, but he never wrote back. In the next year she heard from him only once, when he called collect in the middle of the night. She was completely asleep when the phone rang and had to ask the operator twice who was calling. She wasn't sure she wanted to accept the charges.

Paul's voice jumped onto the line: "Forget it, you bitch, you've never helped me with anything anyway. Just screw yourself good."

For an hour after the call she lay in bed, staring through the windows into the darkness and trying to make sense of what Paul meant to her. He had once been her husband, and the father of her child. Was he still a father? And she a mother? If in fact Paul grieved, his manner seemed inhuman and inexplicable to her, having little to do with Kevin. Yet the feeling nagged at her that she had not been entirely fair to him.

ON A BRIGHT SUNDAY MORNING in late May, more than a year after the funeral, Anna knelt on the front steps of her house sharpening her garden hoe with a new file. The hoe had a long, wasp-waisted handle of mountain ash and a curved steel blade. Like a runner with an addiction, Anna tried to hoe every day. She loved the balance of the tool in her hands, the rhythm of the work and the weedless rows after finishing. Because it was Sunday, and Deal and Shelley still thought she worked too hard, she took the long way to the broccoli, walking behind an old fence row of arborvitae. She spent an hour chopping lamb's quarters, chickweed and velvetweed.

The days had grown as warm as summertime. Anna changed into a pair of shorts after lunch, retrieved her bicycle from outside the tool room and rolled it along the gravel drive to the gates of the farm. She pedaled upstream along the river road, the ten-speed wingy and precise beneath her. As she coasted, the bright tick of the gear cluster swelled like the hum of a cicada.

Three miles up she turned north onto Turner's Run, where loose gravel and a slight grade slowed her speed. The road ran past a series of narrow farms—not really farms any longer, but worn-out bottomlands still hayed to support a few head of cattle. Last summer Deal had showed her a pond in the middle of the woods, and twice she had gone there on her own to swim. A path left the road beside a large sweet gum, wound uphill for half a mile through maple and beech trees, and opened onto a pond with an aging earthen dam.

Anna hid her bike behind a stand of sumac bushes and walked the half mile to the pond. She stepped into the clearing—and found an old man on the other side of the pond, sitting on a three-legged stool with his back against the smooth bark of a sycamore. He was stark naked. She stopped instantly, but he saw her and spoke, his voice carrying neatly across the water.

"Don't mind me, miss, I'm just out for the sunshine." The man flicked his fishing line without changing the lay of the bobber and raised his smooth chin at her hesitation. "I'm old enough to go without my clothes, and I own this pond anyway, so make yourself at home. Take a dip if you like."

She was relieved that he was old. But how strange to find an old man completely naked in the woods. He looked eighty at least, his smooth bald scalp fringed with remnants of white hair. Although he wasn't fat, soft rolls of skin lay folded over his stomach. His penis lay between his thighs, looking at a distance like any younger man's.

Unsure of what to do, Anna lingered on her side of the pond. "Do you live out this way?" she asked him across the water.

"No, I moved to town twenty years ago. My missus drives me out when she's had enough of me around the house, and picks me up again at the end of the day. I don't get out very often."

"She doesn't come with you?"

"Her legs are bad, she says she can't make it up the path. The truth is, she gets bored in the woods. She's scared of snakes, too."

"Snakes?"

"I wouldn't worry about them, I've never seen but a couple of black snakes out here. And they drive the copperheads away."

Anna wondered if the man's wife knew he sat beside the pond on a little stool, stone naked.

He cast, and cast again. His head angled back against the sycamore as if he had dropped off to sleep. He didn't say anything for ten minutes.

Finally Anna slipped off her shoes, shorts and underpants, pulled her shirt off and dove into the pond. She didn't look around but swam vigorously back and forth across the pond's shortest distance. She came out at her original spot and stood drying in the sunshine, forcing herself not to turn her back to the old man. Not having a towel, she brushed the water off her arms and legs with her hands. Once dry, she put her clothes back on.

"Now that's as pretty a sight as a man has right to see," he said. "I've been coming to this pond for sixty years and I've never seen anything as pretty as that."

"I thought . . . since you were sitting there . . ."

"Yes indeed, I'm sure it's what the Lord intended. I'll have to give Catherine this story, if I dare. What's your name?"

"Anna."

"Well, Miss Anna, I'm Sam Turner. You use my pond here and don't worry about a thing. I hardly get out anymore, like I said, and most people don't know about the place. My father had it dug with horses and drags when I wasn't much older than a boy, and it's lasted all these years. It'll outlast me, and it might outlast you. Ponds are just like animals, though, they live and die. This one would have filled in years ago if the cattails had caught on, but something must have stopped them. Now I'm talking too much. Old men like to do that with pretty young girls."

"You're not talking too much," Anna said. "And I'm not a young girl. I'm thirty-seven."

"That's a young girl to me. But I don't mean to pry into your life. You just come up here any time you like and go swimming, I'll be glad to think you're here."

Without waiting for her to say anything, he picked up an old baseball hat and tipped the brim down over his eyes. He leaned his head back against the tree and dozed off—or at least he stayed motionless and didn't speak. Anna waited a few minutes, then turned and walked back to the road through the thin underbrush. Her bike still leaned against the sumac where she'd left it.

EARLY the next morning, direct sunlight bored into Anna's bedroom before six-thirty. The sighs of mourning doves eased her from sleep while the light expanded the dimensions of her cell, flushing before it the memory of dreams. No depression could withstand such a flawless, cool morning.

The last frost had already passed. After a week of rain and two days of sunshine, the temperature hadn't dropped below forty, even under clear skies at night. Anna slipped out of bed and splashed her face with water, stopping only to eat a piece of toast before heading for the barn. She wanted to be the first, the earliest, the only one awake on the farm or on the face of the earth.

The one-row seeder, already connected to the back of the Farmall tractor at the entrance to the barn, was still set up for beets. Anna changed the plastic disk to accommodate the larger zucchini seeds, lowered the coulter a notch and poured ten pounds of seed into the hopper.

The moisture of the soil was perfect. The coulter wavered through the ground, and the packing wheels rolled smoothly behind the seed drop. Anna jumped down once from the tractor, dug her hands into the sandy loam and found a seed every six inches: just right. The earth smelled rich, the warm weather having roused the soil's bacteria and fungi, millions to a thimbleful of dirt. The sun climbed straight up in the east, quickly warming the surface of the ground.

Ten rows took no time at all. Anna slowed the tractor, savoring each pass; she didn't want to finish.

Halfway down the last row, Deal jogged onto the far end of the field and waved to her. She finished the job, eased off on the throttle and leaned over to hear what he had to say.

"Kevin's father is at the bus station and wants you to pick him up. He just called the house."

"Paul? He's in Fell River?"

"He says he spent all night on a bus from St. Louis."

What the hell was Paul doing here, without any warning? Anna jumped down from the tractor, wondering if he expected to stay at her house again.

"What did he sound like? Was he hopped up?"

Deal shrugged his shoulders. "I don't know, he sounded fairly normal. Maybe I should have told him you were away or something."

"No, I better go get him."

"We'd be glad to help. If you want him to stay in the farm-house, we could put him up."

"You're a prince, Deal, but I probably have to work this out myself."

Even though they had been divorced for five years, Anna's response to Paul was automatic. She returned the tractor to the barn, got into her car and drove to town.

He was leaning back against the outside of the bus station, wearing a sweater and a pair of baggy grey pants. He looked ten years older. What had he done in the past year, Anna wondered, to have aged so? His lumpy, irregular flesh hung on a stranger's frame, and he had lost an incisor from the once regular white march of his teeth. The dark space drew Anna's gaze, over and over. Save for the gap, his expression was as bland and soft as a spitball.

Paul talked about the long trip and bad food and dull passengers; about nothing in particular. Anna waited for the first mention of Kevin. Halfway out of town he drummed his fingers on the dashboard and pointed to a carryout.

"How about stopping so I can get some beer? I didn't have a drink the whole trip."

Anna pulled up in front of the store. "I want to know if you're taking any drugs."

"I never take anything off the street anymore."

"What do you mean, off the street?"

"Well, sometimes I'm on a medication. But I don't always take that, either. I'm no drug hound."

He spent five minutes in front of the cooler deciding what beer he wanted. Then, in pantomime, he opened his empty wallet toward her. She loaned him enough to buy the six-pack.

"What about money for the return trip?" she asked.

"Don't worry, I've got a check coming, I'll pay you back."

He had already abandoned the diffident pose of his arrival, and his tone had a surly edge. A hundred yards down the road he opened one of the bottles and tossed the twist-off cap out the window.

"*Hey,*" Anna said, "what'd you do that for?"

"What's it to you? It'll rot in the grass."

"The first week I was in Fell River Kevin cut his foot on a broken bottle in the grass. They gave him eight stitches."

"So what, I didn't toss the bottle, did I?"

Anna felt the ancient rift between them. She asked as neutrally as she could, "How come you don't have any money?"

"I get a check every month, but everything costs double these days. You'd hardly know San Francisco, the whole city is going downhill."

"You're on unemployment?"

"Welfare. Everybody's on it, but it's tough at the end of the month. That's why I'm broke. I spent everything on the bus and I'm waiting for a check."

"I want to know if you've been taking speed."

"I swear to God, Anna, I haven't done any speed in months. Even on the street they tell you speed kills. Everybody knows that."

"What did you call me for that time in the middle of the night? I probably would have accepted the charges if you'd given me a little time to wake up."

"That was from Napa State," Paul said. "I might have been a little wired then."

"Napa State?"

An image came to her, in the instant before he spoke, of a younger, more graceful Paul, stepping down to meet her from a moving cable car in Chinatown. He had smiled, his legs resilient to the shock of descent. Walking to her quickly, he had lifted her hair and kissed the side of her neck.

"I was in there for three months before they let me out," he said.

"In jail?"

"Felt like a jail. It's a nuthouse where they don't let you out. Every day they give you a drug, or maybe a couple of drugs. Some guys get three or four. That really stews your brains. I got out of there because I played the right game, but I'll bet a lot of those suckers are still locked up. Like Jasper. They might let him down to the first floor, but they'll never let him out on the street."

"Listen, Paul, things didn't go well for me when you came the last time. You go the whole year without writing once, and now you take a bus all the way to Ohio. Why?"

"Hey, don't get steamed up about it, I'm just passing through. I've got some friends to see in New York. Besides, you and I spent a long time together and we had a child, so don't pretend you don't know me. You might have found some other men, but I've been inside you plenty."

"Shut up, Paul."

He leaned away from her and sipped his beer. Her car was too small to allow a defiant posture; he could only slump a few inches and stare fixedly out the window.

As they approached the farm Anna saw Deal leave the small walk-behind tractor in midrow and step into the drive to intercept them. He was looking after her, in case Paul turned out as weird as he'd been at the funeral. Paul sat up straight in his seat and put the can of beer on the floor.

"That's the guy you work with, isn't it?"

"That's Deal, one of my partners. He's married to Shelley. You met them after the funeral."

"Look, Anna, I was a little crazy then, I can't even remember exactly what I did. I made a fool out of myself, didn't I? Don't . . . tell him I was in Napa State or anything, will you?"

Anna glanced at him, surprised to see his macho pose dissolve. Her heart went out to him. She was sorry about his missing tooth, which made his expression so clumsy.

Deal came up to Anna's side of the car. She rolled down the window and said, "Hi, Deal, you remember Paul Dunham."

"Sure, how're you doing?" Deal stretched his arm over the steering wheel and shook Paul's hand.

"Pretty good. I had a long bus ride, but it's nice to be out in the country."

"It's more like a factory out here right now, we're doing so much planting. We can't slow Anna down."

"I'd be glad to give a hand," Paul said, "if you get in a bind."

"Well, sure, that might work out."

After a few more words, Anna drove Paul to her house, surprised at how relaxed he had come across with Deal. He carried his suitcase inside—it was larger than the one he'd brought the year before—and set it down on the living room floor. Then he took off his shoes and stretched out on the couch with a second beer. Lying with his head on the armrest, he faced where Kevin's room had been yet said nothing about its absence. He dropped off to sleep before finishing his beer and snored lightly as she laid a blanket over him.

In the next few days Anna threw herself into farmwork and stayed out of her house as much as possible. When she did go inside she usually found Paul lying on the couch reading magazines or just staring. He went out for occasional walks, took a nap every day and cooked himself scraps of food at odd hours, eating directly out of the frying pan with his fingers. He never washed a dish or cleaned anything up. He pissed off the front steps until Anna asked him to urinate farther off.

"Where did you pick up these habits, anyway?" she asked. "How about cleaning up the house a little?"

The next morning she saw him shitting in the open field. He scraped dirt over it when he finished, but it didn't look like he cleaned himself. When he came in she asked him to please use the outhouse, or there was a flush toilet at the farmhouse.

"Sure," he said. She had expected an argument.

That evening he made himself a peanut butter sandwich and ate it standing up in the middle of the living room while Anna cooked dinner. He pulled his shoe sideways along a line on the floor where the bottom plate to the wall of Kevin's room had once been nailed.

"What happened to his room?" he asked.

Anna stood at the kitchen stove, frying potatoes. "I tore it down a couple of months ago."

Paul traced the discoloration on the floor with the toe of his leather shoe, brooding. "What about his things?"

"I burned them."

He stepped up beside her at the stove, his lank hair falling into his eyes. "You what?" He took hold of her right elbow.

"I burned everything." Anna picked up the skillet with her left hand and tipped the potatoes into the sink, where the boiling oil crackled against drops of water. Paul released his grip and stepped back.

"What do you mean?" He asked her all about the fire and Kevin's room. "And then what?" he kept asking.

Anna told him what she'd done, but not what she'd felt. "So what's happened with you?" she asked him. She had to know if Paul had suffered too, before letting him know how bad it was for her.

"Life is shitty, what do you think. *You* spend three months in Napa State and tell me about it."

"But what about Kevin?" Anna insisted. "Do you miss him? Have you cried about him?"

"Don't be so goddamned sanctimonious. Of course I miss him, what do you expect? You think I should lie down on lilies every week and think about death? So you burned his room, big deal. What else?"

In fact, what else had she done? Stayed awake nights. Got drunk in town and come home to lie on the floor with the stereo on so she could cry out loud. Never considered suicide. Mainly, she had thought about her son.

If Anna had ever done anything courageous in her life, it was to think about Kevin, to remember him every day and let him back in, over and over. As for Paul, she didn't believe that the first thing to come into his mind in the morning, and the last at night, was his son. She thought he had returned to Fell River to feed off her grief, instead of suffering on his own.

Still, how could she judge what Paul had done? Maybe he'd spent three months at Napa State because he couldn't cry. Maybe it was easier to go crazy than to cry.

"How can you have slept on that couch for three nights in a row," she asked him, "and never said a word about Kevin's room? How come you never ask me anything about his life here? I don't know if you even care."

"Of course I care. Just because Kevin lived with you doesn't mean I forgot him. How could I forget my son?"

"I didn't suggest you had forgotten him," Anna said coldly. "I just can't figure out what you're doing here. What we're doing here."

"I suppose you've got something better to do?" Paul shuffled around the living room. He had stuck his sock feet into his shoes as if they were slippers, the backs crushed flat.

Anna could hardly remember what Paul had been like as a husband. In the past three days she had grown used to his slack, listless body, but his mind was a stranger's. She thought to herself, testing the words: I don't care what happens to him.

But that wasn't true. Even as she watched him standing at the kitchen table in his crushed shoes, eating doughnuts out of a box, she remembered the agreeable young man she had married. Without a word, she climbed the rungs to her loft and flipped through a pair of old manila folders until she found the snapshot that had come to mind. No, she had not been mistaken. In the photo Paul looked tall and attractive, his hair fluffed up by the wind. He stood with one foot on a cable fence in the Presidio, holding a cigarette in his raised hand. A few months later he quit smoking altogether; she asked him to quit and he did, overnight.

Paul had turned out crazy, sure enough. But here was proof of a handsome young man with all his faculties and an easy smile in the wind.

After some hesitation she climbed back down into the living

room and handed Paul the snapshot. She was aware of prodding him, like an animal in a lab, to see how he would respond to such evidence of better times.

"Hey, I remember that!" He examined the black-and-white photo in detail. "I had that old mohair scarf on, and you wore your plaid skirt. That was our celebration day at the Wharf, right? This is great!"

The day before she took the photograph, Paul had waked her early, promising a surprise. He served her breakfast in bed, then took her by bus and BART and another bus to a marina across the bay, in Alameda. There he had reserved a small fiberglass boat with a thirty-five-horsepower motor. The outboard had padded seats, two life preservers and a little six-inch windshield that ornamented the deck.

With amiable stubbornness, he refused to tell her where they were going. They walked down the wooden ramp to the floating dock, their street shoes clacking on the bright grey paint, and climbed gingerly into the boat. All they had brought, aside from their coats, was a bottle of wine in a paper bag. Paul cast off. He was comfortable in the outboard and ran it with some skill.

Planes from the Naval Air Station roared overhead as they nosed out into the bay. Anna put her coat on and leaned against Paul's shoulder. To the west, San Francisco's white buildings stood out against darker streets and parks, forming an uneven, stepped horizon against the blue sky. Paul increased their speed until bits of spray began to catch them in the face. Anna asked him to slow down, and he did. She preferred meandering across the wide bay, sharing the padded driver's seat with Paul and feeling the sun on her hair. They passed under the Bay Bridge below the roar of trucks and buses, and rounded Treasure Island toward Alcatraz. But Paul gave the old prison a wide berth. He sat upright and intent, holding Anna against him with his left hand as he set his course for the Golden Gate.

A mile before the bridge, the ocean swell reached under the little boat and set it pitching. Anna asked again where they were headed, but Paul merely lifted his chin toward the ocean. She sat up straight, watching the grey-green rocks of the Marin headlands and staring out to sea, the same as Paul.

Passing in the other direction, a giant tanker swept by doing five times their speed. The boat was so large it made the ocean look calm—but its wake sent them crashing and plunging.

"We're going to get soaked," Anna said. "Haven't we gone far enough?" They had passed under the bridge and reached the last headlands of the Golden Gate, with nothing but open ocean before them. Most of the swells rolled smoothly under the boat, but an occasional renegade wave sent up narrow flyers of spray. Paul wanted to push farther into open water. By alternately gunning and releasing the throttle, he tried to minimize the spray and still keep moving.

"Paul, I've had enough, I want to go back."

"All right," he conceded. But instead of turning around, he dropped the engine to an idle, just enough to keep the bow into the wind, and reached under the seat for the bottle of wine. The wet paper bag came off the bottle in shreds. It wasn't wine after all, but champagne. Paul stood up, steering with his knees as he uncrimped the wire basket and popped the cork into the wind. Half the champagne foamed out of the bottle and down his hand, but he only laughed. "Anna, stand up."

"I don't want to tip over."

He took her with both hands and pulled her up, holding the bottle behind her back. The rhythmic waves pushed under them, lifting and dropping the little boat.

"I want you to marry me, forever." He gestured behind them toward the bridge and the cliffs of town. "Forget all that stuff, it's nothing. Let's get married and have children."

When she hesitated, he reached down and gunned the engine. The boat jumped forward and they fell together onto the seat. "I won't turn back!" he yelled over the sound of the engine. "You'll have to marry me in Hawaii!"

She laughed and clung to his neck as the outboard scudded over the waves, lifting sheets of spray into the wind. She loved him for saying forever. She told him she'd marry him.

"You will?" He eased off on the throttle and howled into the wind. They shared salt kisses and champagne as the boat followed an untended arc back toward land, rolling side to side between the waves.

Even then Paul had been a little crazy. But that autumn day, sliding down the front of the waves on their way home, Anna had yielded to him and released all her doubts. His persistence had won her over. He had asked her to marry him a month after they met and had never let up. He was hot for her night and day. He made her feel that willpower was properly the domain of the male, and if only she would yield to it, all would go well.

And for a time everything did go well. But then Paul changed. Anna hesitated, staring at the crumpled backs of his shoes, trying to be fair. But it was true, Paul was the one who had grown strange and unpredictable. Someone in San Francisco must have seen the strangeness and chaos in his life and sent him up to Napa State.

Paul didn't scare Anna, but chaos did. A year after Kevin's death she still feared she could go that way herself. "When you get your check . . ." she said.

"First of the month, any day now."

"What are you going to do?"

"You want me to leave Fell River?"

"No," she said—and found, unexpectedly, that she didn't. Even though she wanted to be left alone in her house, she didn't want to run Paul out of town. More than that, she still had things to tell him. "But it's awkward for me to have you living here," she said. "Why don't you rent a place in Fell River?"

"I've been thinking about that. I'd like to get to know Fell River a little, since Kevin lived here."

Anna wasn't sure whether to believe him or not. He might have just figured out what to say. She stared at the opaque expanse of Paul's forehead, below which his unmoving eyelids were raised a fraction of an inch. Maybe he still had business here, with Kevin and his memories. She couldn't fault him for that, if it was so.

Paul's check arrived three days later, forwarded by a friend. Anna loaned him her car so he could look around, and after a couple of trips to Fell River he found a room that would be available in five more days.

Though it was only five days, Anna felt trapped in her own house. She was fed up with Paul's offhanded, vaguely sexual comments about her and her clothes, about her and birth control, even about her and Deal. "Don't you think Deal looks at you funny?" he asked her one night.

"No, I think you look at me funny."

"Hey, we were married, I know every inch of you. I know all about those secrets. As if you had any. You're up in your room alone every night, don't you ever go out with anyone? Have you turned into a nun or something?"

Paul never touched her, but she couldn't relax around him.

One night after dinner she broke away. She grabbed her sleeping bag and burst out of the house, only stopping to tell Paul she'd be back in the morning. Then she drove upstream along the Ohio, going fast. To her right, the setting sun lit up the smooth surface of the water and the upright oak trees. Anna slowed, left the highway for Turner's Run and sped up the gravel road, a plume of dust trailing behind her. She parked near the sumacs and locked her car.

At the pond she stripped off her clothes and dove into the water. It was warm near the surface but still frigid at the bottom. She hovered over the soft mud, then shot to the surface and swam a few laps.

She used her shirt to dry off, standing by the edge of the pond in the grainy dusk. The fading colors of the water surprised her vision with shapes like hallucinations, curious patches of light flashing and disappearing. At this hour the nighthawks liked to hunt above the surface of the pond, pulling out of suicide dives with a booming explosion of wings. A few bats nicked across the sky like erratic machines and disappeared into the trees.

As the last light faded, Anna walked around the pond looking for a smooth place to lay her sleeping bag. Instead, she found a pile of beer cans lying in the tall grass. Goddamned men had left their trash. She stooped to investigate. The grass had grown up around the cans, but she couldn't tell how long they'd been there. A couple of weeks? A couple of days? What if men came to the pond at night? What if two or three of them came and got drunk and found her there?

They wouldn't find her. Instead of sleeping next to the pond, she'd stay under the trees. She tried to convince herself it was stupid to worry about it. After all, Sam Turner had told her hardly anybody came to the pond.

But she gave the beer cans an angry kick. What woman would leave a bunch of cans in a place like this? It had to be men. In the morning she would carry the cans down to her car. Shit, her car. Anyone who drove up the road would know she was at the pond. She cursed herself for leaving the car next to the path and thought of walking back down and moving it. But night had come, enforced by low clouds. Above the clearing of the pond she could still see light in the sky, but the waning moon wouldn't rise for hours, and the woods were black. Three steps under the tree cover, she couldn't see the ground she walked on.

Her hands raised face-high in front of her, she walked twenty yards into the woods, exploring with her feet until she found a level spot. She dropped to her knees, hand-swept the space to clear it of dead branches and stones, and pulled her sleeping bag out of its sack. The woods were as dark as the farm's root cellar at midnight. Anna took off her shoes, socks and pants, laid them out as a pillow and climbed into her down bag.

Wide awake and too hot, she unzipped the bag. A single mosquito buzzed around her head but didn't land. Back at her house, Paul had probably dozed off on the couch already. He must be on some kind of medication, she thought. How else could he sleep ten and twelve hours a night? She should have sent him to a motel the day he came.

But they'd been married. Didn't that still count? It counted for Anna—even if their child was dead and they were divorced and they didn't own anything in common and they lived two thousand miles apart. Even if Paul was strange and they didn't do anything except argue, somehow the marriage still counted.

They had never argued at the start. He had courted her with persistence, but he was also easygoing and sociable. He took to her friends with enthusiasm, clapped them across the back when they met and made plans with them as readily as with his own friends. Whatever jealousy he felt, he kept in check. Anna had three or four male friends who had once been her lovers. When introduced to them, Paul greeted them with a handshake and a direct look.

Later she discovered that alcohol had a lot to do with how relaxed he came across. On their way to a dinner or party he would drink three or four beers in as many minutes, power-jacking the cans like a fraternity drinking champion. Then he would laugh and talk and carry on. After they were married he sometimes drank to get out of the house, and he once drank his way out of a good job in electronics—though he quit drinking afterward for six months, to prove he could do it.

Anna's mother once wrote her from England, "Whatever first attracts you to a man is usually what you hate about him later."

Paul was an only child and often complained of the fact. Before Anna married him they had talked openly about children. Paul didn't want to have only one. "Let's have two or three," he said.

"Two at the most," Anna said. "I don't want to get in over our heads."

After Kevin's birth, Anna gave herself over to motherhood. She stopped working for a year and a half, spent all her time with her son and moved through time in a fog, perfectly content. At eighteen months she finally weaned Kevin and moved his crib to another room—and opened her eyes to find the rest of the world still moving at full tilt, hardly aware of infants and small children. She arranged day care for Kevin and went back to work, first twenty hours a week and then full time.

When Paul started mentioning another child, Anna looked at him coolly. She had taken care of Kevin as an infant and she went on taking care of him as a young boy. Paul returned from work, played with Kevin for a few minutes, then found something else to do. He had no patience for tears or dirty work, or for the endless routine demanded by a four-year-old.

Still, he didn't want Kevin to be an only child. "It wasn't easy for me," he said, "I was lonely all the time. Don't you think Kevin should have a brother?"

"A brother?"

"Or a sister, either way."

"I've got my hands full," Anna said. They sat at the kitchen table after dinner, the dishes cleared but not yet washed.

"We always said we'd have more than one."

"Then you have the next one."

"Just what does that mean?"

"I'll bear it," Anna said, "and you can take care of it."

"Oh sure. How am I going to take care of some baby?" Paul stood up, pulled a beer out of the refrigerator and popped the cap.

With the backs of her fingers, Anna pushed the can toward the edge of the table. "Do me a favor and put that beer in the icebox until we talk this out. You don't need it."

Paul stared at her across the table. "You put it back."

"All right, I will." She opened the door and slid the can onto the refrigerator shelf. "It gets on my nerves," she said, "that you hardly ever help out with Kevin."

"What do you mean? I take him out almost every Saturday."

"I've been thinking about it. I don't see why you shouldn't look after him as much as I do. Half the time."

"Come on, Anna . . ."

"Half the time. Take him to day care half the time, pick him up half the time, fix his dinner every other night and wash his clothes. Wash *your* clothes. Shit, I'd be happy if you did a quarter of the work around here. I'm working a forty-hour job the same as you are, and now you're talking about having another child and sticking me with all the work? You better think it over."

"Hey, who earns more money? You work over at that stupid greenhouse, and they barely pay you more than minimum wage. I bring home twice what you do."

Anna stood up from the table and looked into the living room, where Kevin was playing on the rug. She closed the door and lowered her voice.

"You know, Paul, I've taken a lot of crap in this marriage. I've been telling you that, but you don't listen. I know you love Kevin, but you don't spend enough time with him, and you dump all the work on me. And until you stop doing that, I don't even want to hear you mention another child."

"Get off your fucking high horse, Anna. Who was it who read him a story last night? And who took him to Portland to see the Trail Blazers' game? Anyway, it's not for me we should have another child, it's for Kevin."

"*Half.* You start doing half, and then I'll talk about it."

"I'm not going to do half of that stuff. When you had Kevin, the first couple of years you loved it."

"Mommy," Kevin yelled from the living room, "don't argue." He opened the door and looked in—and, at the sight of their faces, burst out crying.

Anna looked at her son, and then at Paul. She had always picked Kevin up, had always been the one to comfort him. She wanted to now, the same as ever, but she folded her arms and held back. "You do it," she told Paul.

"Oh Anna, just pick him up. Look how he's crying."

"I always do it. This time you pick him up." She fought, not against Kevin or Paul, but against herself, to stop from giving in.

Paul thrust a finger at her. *"Pick up that kid."*

Kevin dropped to the floor, wailing. "Don't *argue*," he cried.

Anna turned away from Paul's bulging eyes and started to walk out the back door. He grabbed her arm and wheeled her around. "Pick him up," he shouted.

"Let go of my arm."

He slapped her across the face, hard.

Filled with remorse, he immediately stooped and raised a wide-eyed, gasping Kevin to his arms. "Anna I'm sorry, I'm sorry, I didn't mean to do it." He apologized over and over.

He never hit her again, but she never forgot. She flushed with anger even now, lying in her sleeping bag on a black night in the middle of the woods, to think about Paul's slap. They'd stayed together for another year, but in retrospect it would have been simpler if she had left that night.

Anna stood up in the middle of the woods, as far from sleep as ever. She had no idea how long she'd been lying on the ground. Something had changed among the trees, but she couldn't figure out what it was until she took a few steps toward the pond. The clearing was lighter. She could make out individual trees across the water, and the opening of the path. The waning moon, only two days past full, had risen behind the clouds. Anna stepped back into the trees, suddenly aware that she was barefoot on the noisy floor of the woods, wearing only her underwear and a shirt.

The woods had grown perceptibly lighter. Anna made out the dark rectangle of her sleeping bag against the ground, walked to it and put on her pants and shoes. She carried the bag farther into the woods, but even there the night was no longer pitch black. From anywhere close by, the dark bulk of her sleeping bag showed up against the ground. She left it and tiptoed back to where she could see the pond. There she crouched among the rhododendron leaves and waited.

No one would come to the pond in the middle of the night, she thought. But then, it was probably still only twelve o'clock, or one at the latest. If men came, they'd build a fire and drink beer, and she'd have to crouch in the woods away from her sleeping bag until they left.

It was as humiliating as a slap in the face. Why did she have to lose her sleep because of men? Animals didn't scare her. She knew that snakes, which she sometimes feared during the day, would be safely curled up at night. But goddamned men. If you didn't know a man, he was dangerous. Sometimes even if you did know him. Anna had camped out on her own a few times before and never been afraid, but she couldn't stop trembling now. Looking out from the edge of the trees across the water, she saw something move, and went rigid. It was nothing. She focused a few yards to the side, for better night vision. No, nothing.

What if Paul tracked her here? Well, that was crazy, he didn't even know where she was. But other men might come with flashlights, and swim and get drunk. They might build a fire and stay all night, and Anna would be trapped in the woods. What if she sneezed? What if they found her lying inside her bag, unable to run? A single woman in the dark, they'd rape her.

She picked up a stone and flung it into the woods, where it thudded against a tree. She threw another, and another. There was probably enough light now to follow the path down to her car, but she didn't want to go back to her house, and Paul. She wanted to make it through the night. Lying down on her sleeping bag, she turned one way and then the other. At every sound she sat up and stared into the woods. She wasn't afraid, she was furious. She almost wished men would come so she could have it out with them. Scream and howl, or run terrified through the trees.

She must have slipped off, for the grey first light surprised her. She stood up, exhausted. No one had come, of course. She had wasted a night's sleep. Stuffing her bag into its sack, she walked carelessly through the woods to the edge of the pond, knelt beside the water and splashed her face. The first birds were already singing, whippoorwills and catbirds and jays. They made her think of Aldo Leopold, sitting comfortably with a pot of coffee in the Sand County predawn, listening to the birds and taking notes for his book. And of Thoreau, who also loved the first hour of light. Fuck Thoreau, and Leopold, too. Goddamned men, free to do what they wanted.

Anna stormed down the path, snapping dead branches out of her way and listening to the domestic sounds of the forest. There was nothing to be scared of. By the time she reached the open space of the road, the sky had turned lemon against an eastern line of poplars, and a pair of roosters crowed from a nearby farm. A rangy black dog with a swinging tail loped up the road and stopped to investigate her car. When it lifted its leg against the front tire, Anna blasted it in the gut with her shoe, lofting it into the air. The dog howled and raced back along the road, turning twice to make sure it was safe. Anna picked up a rock and threw it. *Get out of here you piece of shit.* Next time it's a kick in the balls. She jumped into her car, turned around on the narrow road and roared home, throwing dust over everything behind her.

TWO DAYS LATER she drove Paul to Fell River, cashed his check at her bank and let him treat her to lunch before dropping him off at his new house. Sitting at a window table at the Bradford Hotel, they talked about their days in San Francisco and Eugene, and about their first trips to Seal Rock. For almost a decade they had shared trips, holidays, arguments, the birth of their son, disappointments, sex and laughter. No one else, not even Anna's father, knew Kevin the way Paul did. No one else had the history.

All through lunch and a long cup of coffee, Paul was considerate and alert. He spoke about their past, Anna thought, as if they often carried on such conversations. But later, as she drove him to Hinman Street, he grew distant. "I've only rented a room," he said. "I share the kitchen and bath with everyone else."

He got out in front of the house, picked up his suitcase and a desk lamp Anna had loaned him, and led the way up the stairs of a large clapboard house with a broken screen door. Somewhere upstairs a Jimi Hendrix record played, obscuring the conversation of two young men sitting in armchairs on the open porch. They didn't look up until Paul stood next to them and asked, "Is Margo around?"

"Margo? No, I don't think so. I think she's at work."

Paul set his bag on the floor next to the armchairs. "I'm going to live here," he said. "Margo rented me a room."

"Good," the second man said. "Why don't you move in?"

Paul lifted his suitcase and set it down inside the door, then rested the lamp on top of it. "I guess I'll move in," he said to Anna, and gestured minutely with his hand. "Thanks for bringing me. I'll . . . I'll give you a call."

"Fine," Anna said. "Do that, or I'll come visit." Paul didn't move, even when she got into her car and waved good-bye. He looked awkward and shabby, standing in the doorway of a house full of people he didn't know. It made Anna sad.

CHAPTER 3

———— ❦ ————

ON A WARM SATURDAY NIGHT Alex walked down to Ling's Kitchen for an early dinner. He liked to eat when the restaurant was almost empty. Later in the evening the room would fill up with students, couples and noisy groups, but before six o'clock some of the Lings still sat around a large table after their own meal, telling jokes in Chinese. At least Alex imagined they were telling jokes. Their soft recurrent laughter fluttered up from across the room.

He ate duck, and rice as white as the tablecloths. He drank a Chinese beer, then a second. His fortune cookie read, "Your advancement has no limits." By the time two middle-aged couples came in for dinner, he was slightly drunk; he leaned back in his chair and blatantly appraised the two women.

Both overweight, they wore double-knit pants suits and low-heeled sandals. They angled for a fit at their table, rocking their wide buttocks as they adjusted to the restaurant's cane chairs. They might have been sisters from the identical way they fanned themselves with their menus and patted the backs of their cropped, overtreated hair.

Alex could not imagine caressing such hair or sliding into bed next to such buttocks. Freya had probably been older than these two matrons when she returned from England, but even at the age of fifty-five Freya had moved like a young woman. She wore her hair loose and hadn't been to a beauty parlor in twenty years except to get a haircut. Of course she was no young girl. She had plenty of serious wrinkles.

When other customers entered the restaurant, Alex paid his bill and stepped outside into the sunset. Dazed for a moment by the brilliant light, he wandered past the courthouse, walked down High Street and emerged at the river.

Alex still found weekends difficult. For his entire adult life he had gone out on weekend nights, either with Freya or some other woman, or with friends. He still went out, to movies, concerts and plays, or occasionally to a bar—though in a college town like Fell River the bars belonged to the students. At this hour some of them played Frisbee or lay on the banks of the Ohio and read. Alex watched the girls: their long legs and the lovely flesh of their underarms. The sky was the color of apricots. Near the path, two girls leaned back on their elbows on a blanket, talking, their shoes kicked off. One of them rolled onto her side to face the other. They lay close together, almost touching, one girl in jeans and the other in a skirt.

Alex sat down on the grass where he could watch them out of the corner of his eye. He felt like a lascivious old man. What if they were asking each other in whispers, "Who's that creep?" He couldn't imagine sitting down next to two coeds and striking up a conversation about classes and rock and roll concerts—if that was what they talked about.

Women close to his own age usually looked like the buttocky sisters in Ling's Kitchen. In the last year he had met a few younger women in their late forties or fifties, but they were all married. A month ago at a tennis club party, Elena Mars had followed Alex outside onto the lawn, slid her hand around the back of his neck and surprised the blue Christ out of him by swabbing out his mouth with her tongue. Later he heard that Elena's husband wore a famous set of horns.

After his last two years with Freya, Alex had no heart for light affairs. He might have slept with some woman he didn't know, but not with Elena, a bored mother of three grown children. He liked Elena—if only because she flirted with him so freely and then laughed at his surprise—but he didn't want her to tongue him without warning or invite him over for a drink when her husband left town on a geology expedition.

It was only three years ago that Alex had lain with Freya on a blanket beside Lake Harriet, one intimate couple among many. Freya read him pornography from Anaïs Nin and ran a covert hand down the front of his pants. "He likes to hear about smooth young girls," she said, laughing. "Without me he'd be a ferocious lecher."

Storm clouds built up over the Ohio, darkening the sky across the river. The two girls talked on, heedless of the weather, and of Alex. The one wearing a skirt rolled to one side until he could see the smooth skin of her thighs and the white recess of her underpants.

When Alex stood up, both girls turned to look at him. He passed them virtuously, eyes straight ahead, then left the bank of the river for Front Street. Down in the commercial end of town no one walked the pavement, and few cars groaned over the bricked purple streets. An air conditioner hummed above the metal door of Hank's Nightingale Bar, and a neon sign advertising Robin Hood Ale quivered against the flat western light. Through his pocket, Alex grazed a steady erection. He imagined laying his cheek against the cool underside of the girl's thighs, pushing up her skirt and licking around the white line of her panties.

The sky darkened and waves of heat lightning broke out behind him as he walked to the center of town, where he sat on a bench near the courthouse. Thunder shook the wooden slats of the bench, and the air, pungent with ozone, turned a deep blue. The flashes came no closer, but single drops of rain plunged onto the brick walkways and exploded like globs of silver and mercury. A few hit Alex's white cotton shirt and left watermarks the size of quarters. The wind gusted, died down, then blew hard again. Hidden until the last minute by the buildings and dark skies, the rain swept over the courthouse like surf. Alex bolted before it to the theater marquee across the street.

The teenage girl who sold movie tickets stepped outside her glass-and-metal booth in front of the theater to watch the rain.

Alex knew her a little. The theater had given him a senior citizen's card allowing him a dollar off on the price of tickets, and after the first couple of months the girl told him not to bother pulling it out, she remembered him.

He had never seen her outside the booth before. The management had dressed her in a tight, short blue skirt. Or was it her own choice? Alex had often noticed when buying a ticket how her bony knees stuck straight out from her stool, almost at a level with the cash register. She wore too much makeup.

"A regular toad strangler," she said, taking a step back to keep her feet dry. "People inside, they don't even know it's raining."

Alex glanced around at the posters. "What are you showing?" he asked.

"An old Cary Grant movie, *North By Northwest.* You can go in if you want, you don't need a ticket."

"I saw that movie, with Eva Marie Saint."

"Is it any good?"

"It's sexy."

The girl laughed and rewrapped her ponytail with an elastic band and a flick of her wrist. "It must be thirty years old," she said. "I didn't think they made any sexy movies back then."

"Not X-rated sexy, just . . . arousing. They're on a train."

"Yeah? Listen, you watch things here for a minute, I'll be right back. No one'll show up in this downpour." The girl locked the door to the booth and skipped into the theater.

Alex wondered how she could stand working in the tiny glass booth, since everyone who came along the sidewalk stared at her. The rain flung down on the metal top of the marquee, drumming wildly, and ran over the sidewalk in sheets. Five minutes later the girl returned, her thin arms folded over her chest.

"Was it sexy?" Alex asked her.

"Not to me. They were eating dinner in a restaurant on the train."

Alex smiled. "Sounds pretty old-fashioned. I guess these days that's pretty tame eating." He broke off and laughed. "Who knows what they show in those X-rated movies."

"You've never seen one?" The girl didn't laugh or look away.

"No. Have you?"

"Sure, they show 'em here at midnight sometimes. X, double X, triple X, you name it."

"And you've seen them?"

"Parts, after I close down the booth. They're all the same. I just look in sometimes. You've never been to one?"

"I guess not." Alex put his hands in his pockets. "What do they show?"

"Everything you could think of. You know. . . ."

"Well, I guess I know. Unless they've come up with something new."

They both laughed, and the girl said, "Come around for a midnight show sometime. It's only two bucks, and you get a dollar off with your card. It's cheap."

"And a thrill."

The girl smiled lightly. She was probably used to selling tickets to horny men, Alex thought. Or maybe she figured he was just a harmless old twink, turned on by Eva Marie Saint.

He stepped out on the sidewalk to look up and down the street. The rain had let up. He told the girl he'd try to come in some midnight if he ever stayed up that late, and then he set off for home in the light rain, avoiding the streams of water that ran past the limestone curbs and sloshed around the wheels of cars.

Thinking about the girl by the river, his erection came back. He was glad to be aroused, for after Freya's death his sexual drive had all but vanished. At home, he took off all his clothes, lay down on his bed and dripped hand cream over his penis. He imagined the girl by the river telling him to come on over and lie down beside her. Her friend disappeared; everyone on the riverbank was gone. Raising her skirt, she opened her legs toward him and let him slide his fingers beneath the elastic of her panties. She pulled her skirt above her waist, took his head in her hands and guided it between her legs. She pressed his eyes and cheeks and mouth to her cunt, and he ate.

THE FOLLOWING MONDAY MORNING, Alex left his hospital office and walked upstairs to the rehabilitation ward. His jogging shoes gave him a quiet step, and when he rounded Susan Rupert's doorway he found her staring at the wall in front of her. She turned to him sharply, her brown hair pushed up against the pillow and her dark eyes ringed with purple streaks. Except for the violet bruises, her face looked pale. Her legs stretched to the bottom of the bed, where her feet stuck up in two separate hummocks, covered by the sheet. Other than a folded wheelchair leaning against the far wall and a single book on the bedside table, the room looked unoccupied: no magazines, no flowers, no Kleenex, and the television turned off.

"I'm Alex Delaney," he said, extending his hand. "I'm the vocational counselor."

"Ah, Mr. Delaney, I've been expecting you. Every day I've wondered, When is my vocational counselor going to show up? And now here you are." She shook his hand lightly, turning their wrists at an angle. "You've got your folders with you, so I'm sure you know my history."

"I've glanced at it," Alex said. He stepped back from the bed and stood near the door. "I thought we might go over it together."

Susan's eyes flattened beneath her discolored brows. One arm flicked away from the side of the bed, as if throwing something to a dog. Her legs, outlined beneath the white sheet, didn't move.

"I've gone over it twenty times," she said. "Don't you have my history from Albuquerque?"

"I know you spent a week on the critical list and five months in the hospital," Alex said without looking at her folder. "And you're thirty-four years old, and you've had a few reconstructive operations."

"Three. I looked like a rhesus monkey when they started. My face was all scrunched up under my forehead. I should be grateful they got me back together as smoothly as they did. I am, really, I've just been in the hospital too long."

"You fell off a cliff?"

Susan put both hands at her sides and sat up straighter in bed, restraining herself visibly. "Tell me it's all in there. Tell me everything you need to know about me is already written down."

"I do remember one note in particular," Alex said, "from the administration. Perhaps you've seen their comment?"

"No, I haven't."

" 'Miss Rupert,' " he quoted to her after opening her folder, " 'has not always been a helpful patient.' "

"They said that? Let me see. Who wrote that?" She reached for the folder, but Alex closed it and tucked it under his arm.

"The signature's just a scribble," he said. He stood at a safe distance from the bed. She could not, after all, get up and walk across the floor to him.

"Let me see it," she demanded, her arm still out.

"I'm sorry, I shouldn't have read it to you." Alex looked around the room. "It hardly seems like you've moved in here. No TV, only one book, no clothes . . ."

"My clothes are in the closet. I'm not interested in making a home out of this room, I'll be out of here soon enough."

"Back to your parents?"

"I just spent a month with my parents, in Hobart. That was enough."

Alex crossed the room, moved a chair next to the bed and sat down. "When's the last time before that that you lived with your parents?"

"When I was eighteen." She touched her fingers to the smooth, discolored flesh above her cheeks, tracing the thin scars from plastic surgery. "As soon as my kidney infection clears up, I get out of here. And I've already been counseled and reha-bilitated within an inch of my life. I was in the hospital a long time in New Mexico—five months, just like it says there. About the only thing they couldn't manage was getting me to walk again. I tried that, but it didn't go."

"That's one of the questions I wanted—"

"Don't worry, Mr. Delaney, I'm not going to slash my wrists. And don't look so bleak, you're supposed to be helping me out." She held her wrists up to his view. "See, no scars. I'm not one of those. I never thought about it, not even on the worst days."

Alex leaned forward and inspected the smooth underside of her wrists. "I'm not in charge of your mental health," he said, "but I'm relieved, anyway. It makes for terrible statistics, which is hell on our funding."

"Ah, a sarcastic counselor." Susan smiled for the first time. "No one else has a sense of humor around here. I prefer it to commiseration."

"I once recommended we hire a stand-up comedian to perform in the rec room on Saturday nights," Alex said. "I really did, I wrote a letter to a board member. I doubt if it strengthened my tenure at the hospital. The board didn't think rehabilitation was the right place for a comedian."

"He'd probably make paraplegic jokes."

"He wouldn't, but the patients might."

"We ought to," Susan said. "There's a couple of us here who can still laugh. Listen, maybe you could help me out with something after all."

"Sure."

"Drive me around someday so I can look at apartments. I could go in my wheelchair, but it would take me forever. Most places are no good. They've got to be on the ground floor and have some kind of access."

"What about your parents?"

"What about them?"

"They think you should live with them a while longer."

"How do you know that?"

"They called me."

"Jesus Christ, it's war. No wonder I'm not a helpful patient." Susan jammed her index finger against the bed control until the head locked in its upright position. She glared at him. "Do you want to take a side right now? Their side, or mine?"

"Can you afford to live on your own?"

"I can afford whatever I want. For a while, anyway. I've got the world's best insurance plan."

"Apartments are cheap in Fell River. You might find a nice place."

"If I could get out and look."

Alex stepped to her wheelchair and unfolded it. "What did you run this through, the Southern 500?"

"Just about," she said with another faint smile. Her face had the round, flat look and unlikely colors of a kindergartner's crayon portrait. "I can go anywhere except the steepest hills. But I still need a place to move to the day they let me out of here. My parents have already got the Wells County social workers on their side, and they all think I should go home. But here in the hospital I'm the client, not them."

"True."

"So when this infection clears up, and my parents refuse to help, a man with your sense of humor just might drive me around town to look for an apartment. Don't you think?"

"Seems like I might," Alex said. "All I'd have to do is take the heat from your parents, the welfare department, the head of the rehabilitation unit and the hospital board of directors. No problem."

Susan leaned back against her pillow, holding back a smile. "I'm tired now, all of a sudden. I think it's time for my nap."

AT TEN AFTER SEVEN Alex parked his car illegally in the doctor's lot, ran to the rehabilitation entrance and took the stairs to the rec room two at a time. His arms were empty, his briefcase left at home. He grabbed the banister with one hand and swung around the stair landings. Under his jogging suit the smell of sweat rose from his chest.

Susan Rupert and May Dorling, who had been waiting in a far corner of the room, pivoted smoothly toward him in their wheelchairs, the chrome spokes of the wheels shining against the tile floor. Such graceful movements, Alex thought, belied the awkwardness of the catheters, urine bags and other hardware that allowed paraplegics what mobility they had. He looked at the women's motionless feet. Susan wore sneakers and white anklet socks with a fluffy yellow ball above the heel. May wore blue hospital slippers. Their ankles looked smooth and domestic—completely ordinary—as if there were nothing to stop the women from getting up and walking away from their wheelchairs.

Alex thought they'd hate him for his easy clothes and the smell of exercise. Instead, they stared at him greedily. Even before he found a seat, Susan turned her bruised eyes to him and asked, "What have you been doing?"

"Playing tennis with a friend. We got into a long second set." Alex was short of breath after running up the stairs. "I didn't realize the time until we finished."

"Did you win?"

"Yes, but it went to a tiebreaker."

"I used to play tennis," May said. She swung her arm away from the table as if hitting a forehand. Older than Anna, she had only been in her wheelchair for a month. She looked away as she raised and lowered her torso in the chair to help her circulation.

"Me too," Susan said. "I played on my college team."

"A couple of athletes," Alex said.

They both laughed. Susan flexed her arm, raising her biceps. "We're hard core from the waist up."

"What do you say we talk about jobs?" Alex offered.

They wavered, adopting serious looks for a moment. "Shit," Susan said, "let's talk about sports."

May looked at her. "That would be a change."

"Let's talk dirty," Susan said. "Let's talk about walking and running."

The two women rolled their chairs an inch forward. When a nurse entered the room, Susan waited for her to pass through the far door before saying, "I played on a grass court one time, in North Carolina. It was gorgeous. When I go to heaven I want to play tennis every day on a grass court."

"And walk through the waves on the beach," May said.

"And run the high hurdles. I wanted to run them in high school and never did. I always loved the name: *the high hurdles.*"

They might go too far, Alex thought. His worried expression held them back, or at least no one spoke until Susan shifted in her chair and looked across at him, her eyes faintly enshrouded under the fluorescent lights.

"And what would you do in heaven, Mr. Delaney? After all, you can already do everything we want to do."

"Alex. Everyone here calls me Alex."

If he went to heaven, he thought, he'd see Freya. Well, that was stupid. He didn't believe in heaven, and he knew Freya didn't live in the clouds. But Susan meant, what did he want in life that he didn't have? What would he rectify, if he had the chance?

"So?" she asked.

"I don't know. Maybe eat all day and never put on weight."

"No, really."

A moment passed. "I'd like to lie down with my wife."

No one said a word until he added, "She died two years ago." He looked from May to Susan and finally smiled. "Hey, don't go somber on me. I didn't get all bent out of shape when you said you wanted to run the high hurdles, did I?"

He hadn't meant to talk about his wife. The thought had simply come to him as he looked at Susan.

Alex had found that his clients in the hospital inevitably sought out whatever was not disabled or handicapped. In the rehabilitation program they learned to get in and out of wheelchairs, onto toilets, into bathtubs, into cars. They paid attention when Alex talked about buildings without elevators and problems with employers. What quickened them, however, was the nondisabled world.

They were careful with each other. They shared the heartbreak. But socially and sexually, the patients were drawn to the nondisabled. The men watched the long-legged nurses. The women, though more surreptitious, watched the men who could walk, whose whole bodies functioned.

"Did anyone see Lendl play Connors?" Alex asked.

He led the two women to a discussion of spectator sports, stadiums, public buildings and barrier-free design. Shortly after eight, he let them go. May rolled silently out of the room, but Susan hung back. Twisting her upper body, she reached behind her and pulled a copy of the *Fell River Express* out of a bag strapped to the back of her wheelchair. Among the classifieds she had circled almost a dozen ads in red.

"You've done some homework," Alex said.

"The doctor told me I can leave in five days if I'm an obedient patient. How about you? Have you talked to my family, and Wells County Welfare?"

"I haven't, actually."

"Too busy playing tennis?"

"I only work half time," Alex said.

"And can you drive me around?"

"Yes, I can do that."

"Good." Susan smiled broadly. "I need to win a few battles. Besides, I can love my parents at a distance. They're not so bad. They've adjusted so far to how I live my life."

"Even to this?" Alex opened his hand toward her knees.

Susan laid her hands on her thighs. "I think at first it was harder on my mother that I fell off a cliff roped to a married man, than that I couldn't walk anymore. Of course, before the first couple of operations she wasn't too happy about my face, either."

"What happened to him?"

"Who?"

"The married man."

"He died."

Susan kept her eyes on his but said nothing else. They set up a time for the following day to drive around Fell River in Alex's car and look at apartments.

ONCE PAST the hospital's front door, Susan looked back at Alex's hands, first at one and then the other, until he dropped them from the wheelchair handles. "I'll take it from here," she said. "This is what I practice for. Where's your car?" She rolled ahead of him down the slight incline of the parking lot, wheeled to a stop next to his Buick and turned her face to the sun.

Using the steering wheel to pull herself in, Susan got into the car from the driver's side, slid across the front seat and arranged her legs. She wore her white tennis shoes and ankle socks, a pair of blue slacks and a white blouse. On a small pad of paper she had listed the addresses of a half-dozen apartments.

"All of these are on the ground floor. My idea is to drive around first and see which ones look best. Could we do that?"

"Whatever you like. I'm yours until two o'clock."

"And then?"

"Then I have a meeting with a young man who dove into the Ohio River last week and fractured his fifth cervical vertebra."

"A quad."

"He may be able to move his left shoulder a little."

"Those are the ones who break your heart," Susan said. "They live and die on human spirit, that's all they've got. Me, I'm just a happy-go-lucky para. Do the twist and it goes like this. And today's the big day for me, I want to see if I can live in the world after seven straight months in hospitals and at my parents' house. I'm real glad to be out here."

Alex was glad, too. Glad the sun was shining, glad Susan wasn't a quadraplegic, glad she could do the twist on the front seat of his car. Glad that her eyelashes were long and that she was smiling.

They followed a zigzag course through Fell River, tracking down the houses and apartment buildings on Susan's list. At the first three places, she got out of the car and into her wheelchair to have a look. But it was a time-consuming process, and in the end she asked Alex to investigate and report back to her while she sat in his car and listened to the wind rustle the leaves of maples and sweet gums. Alex returned with details from the backs of the buildings. As they drove from one place to the next, he asked about her history.

"If you didn't want to live with your family, why did you come back to Ohio?"

"Personal reasons."

"They always are."

Susan looked at him across the width of the Buick's front seat. "I came back because I couldn't stay with the man I lived with before the accident."

"Why not?"

"Because I couldn't walk."

"Some couples stay together."

"It was more complicated than that. I think we were breaking up anyway. I had kind of moved out of Scott's house and then I started sleeping with Mel."

"The one who died."

"Yes, the climber. I only knew him for a couple of months. But I was the one who broke things off with Scott, you see? So how could I go back after the accident when I couldn't even walk? My mother practically said it served me right. She's kind of born again, a big churchgoer. Her heart's good underneath, but the Baptists have twisted her up. Anyway, when Scott came to see me in the hospital we could hardly look at each other. There was sex to think about, too. After a couple of visits I told him I didn't want him to come anymore, but I'd go see him when I could walk again. That didn't pan out. Did they put down in my history how hard I tried to walk?"

"They did."

"All the same, I still might go back to New Mexico. Scott's living with another woman, but I spent years in Santa Fe and I have a lot of friends there."

"How about friends in Ohio?"

"I grew up in Columbus but I went away to school at UC in Cincinnati. My parents moved to Hobart ten years ago, so I don't know anybody there. How about you? Do you come from around here?"

"I was born thirty miles up the river," Alex said, "but my family moved to Minneapolis when I was in grade school."

"I can't believe you're sixty-three."

"How do you know how old I am?"

"I asked a nurse."

"How'd she know?"

"Don't ask me. But you don't look your age."

"I always win the guess-your-age game. Or else everyone's being polite."

"I'm never polite," Susan said, thumping her hands on her legs. "You think I'm the polite type?"

Alex laughed. "Not at all. If you didn't like someone, I think you'd chew him up and throw him in the weeds like an old wad of Red Man."

"I like to think I would," she said. A tiny piece of her gums showed at the top of her two front teeth whenever she smiled.

After finishing their tour, Susan thought the best apartment was the bottom half of a duplex with a clear view of the Ohio. She asked Alex to drive her there a second time. The owner lived upstairs.

Alex held the wheelchair, Susan slid into it from the car, and they rang the doorbell at the side entrance of the house. A small man in grey pants and a white undershirt came down the carpeted stairs and stepped outside, holding the screen door open with the nicotine-stained fingers of his right hand.

"I think we talked on the phone," Susan said. "I wonder if

I could have a look at the apartment you have for rent?"

"Are you . . . you two together?"

"Yes," said Alex.

"No," said Susan.

"I'm helping her find a place," he explained.

"I need an apartment on the ground floor I can get in and out of easily. You've got a nice view here."

"Real nice. But . . . there's this couple looked at the place already I think they're gonna take it. Anyway, the kitchen needs painted. No, it's . . . it's taken, the place is taken."

Fucking redneck, Alex thought.

Susan stared at the man for ten seconds, then lifted her front wheels off the ground and spun her chair, almost clipping his shins. "Let's go," she said, and rolled down the concrete path without looking back.

The man leaned toward Alex. "You understand, mister. How's she gonna take care of the place? This other couple, they come around earlier this morning."

Alex turned and walked to his car. Susan had already climbed in and was pulling the folded wheelchair across her lap, banging it and pushing it into the back seat. "The prick bastard," she said.

"You wouldn't want to live downstairs from a guy like that anyway."

"Little nerd in his sleeveless undershirt."

"You were polite," Alex said after a few blocks. "You surprised me."

"I was polite? Fuck that. Take me back, I want to tell that turkey off."

He looked at her cautiously. She laughed. "Hey, don't go all somber on me. You didn't get bent out of shape when I said I wanted to run the high hurdles, did you?"

"No."

"Well, when I start swearin' at some dingbat who don't know jack shit 'bout nothin', you can laugh if you feel like it." He

did, for she had the redneck accent down to a cruelty. "Polite-
ness is a disease," she said. "They ought to give us a cure at the
hospital."

Alex pulled the car over under some shade and parked. He
let Susan cool down for a moment before suggesting, "Maybe I
should talk to the next landlord."

"What do you mean?"

"I could say I was looking for a place for my . . . sister or
something. No one would know until you signed the lease."

"Is that what you tell your clients to do at the hospital?"

"No."

"What do you tell them?"

"I tell them to stand up for their rights."

"Then let me stand up."

But the next interview, with a smooth, balding storeowner,
was no better. He had already told Susan over the phone the
apartment he had for rent was downstairs, but now he looked
surprised at that idea.

"No, no, the one downstairs is already rented. The one I
have available is upstairs, and I'm afraid it would be quite un-
suitable. A building that small doesn't have an elevator, of
course."

Susan stared him down but said nothing. Back in Alex's car,
she slumped against the door. "Yeah, don't tell me about it.
That guy was one unctuous mother. What do I have to do, take
these guys to court?"

"You could."

"But I get out of the hospital in four days, and if we go on
like this, I might lose all the good places. Maybe you should try
the next one for me."

Alex picked up the next key without any trouble, from a
middle-aged woman who owned a small house on Mayfold. The
house wasn't close to the river, but it wasn't a duplex, either, so
no one else lived under the same roof. All the floors were hard-
wood, the small back patio faced a wooded bank below the houses

on the road above, and there was a driveway. Susan would have to enter through the kitchen door because of the front steps, but a bricked path led around the side of the house.

"Maybe I could talk to the landlady," Susan said. "Maybe she'd be glad to have me live there."

"You want to risk it?"

"No, it's too good, and the rent's fair. Go ahead, Alex, if you can get the lease, I'll sign it."

He chatted up the landlady, telling her his niece had landed a job at the university and was moving to Fell River the next week. The owner was delighted to rent to an educated, single woman and made Alex stay for a cup of tea before she accepted a hundred-dollar deposit and handed over the lease. He felt like a shark on the way back to his car but was glad it had all worked out.

"Now," he told Susan, "you can do battle with your parents."

"They'll give in. At first they'll complain, but they'll wind up helping me out. I get along with my dad real well. I just can't let him decide where I'm going to live."

Susan read over the form lease and gave Alex a check for a hundred dollars. Then they drove across town and ate lunch in McDonald's sunny parking lot. With the end of her tongue Susan cleaned the milkshake frost from her upper lip and licked clean the tartar sauce that had dropped into the webs of her fingers.

Her gracefulness surprised and pleased him, and her good humor. Her loose tongue, too. He couldn't imagine his daughter saying "fuck that" or "he don't know jack shit." Maybe Anna talked that way—probably she did sometimes—but not to him.

All the same, Susan was a paraplegic. She couldn't walk through the woods or play tennis, or feel anything below the waist. And as she had said herself, there was sex to think about.

"You still miss your wife," she asked him, "don't you?"

"Sure."

"Every day?"

"I think about her every day. It's different now. I don't get as sad, but I still want to ask her things."

"Like what?"

"Like what her life was like when we were divorced. She went to live in England and didn't come back for ten years. And when she did, I was so glad I hardly asked her anything about it. I felt like a kid, I didn't care what she'd done all those years. But when she died I wanted to know all her secrets. I had some letters—I still have them—but I didn't ask her enough when she was alive."

"Did you fight?"

"Only the year we split up, before she left. But terribly then, like dogs. How about you and . . . what was his name? Scott?"

"Scott's an American male."

Alex laughed. "What a sneer. So am I, and half the population. What do you mean?"

"I mean he wouldn't talk. Scott would never have admitted to someone he didn't know that he missed a woman and wanted to sleep with her. Not in a million years. Even when we lived together I had to wheedle and pry to get him to talk about what he felt."

Alex himself wasn't going to say what he felt at that moment—that he found Susan an interesting and attractive woman and would like to see her again. He told her instead that if he could help her out with anything else, he'd be glad to.

"There is one other thing. I'm looking for a car. A nice fat American car I can pull the wheelchair into without killing myself. A Ford or a Chevy, nothing too expensive. Needless to say, my parents don't want me to have one."

THE DAY Susan's parents helped her move to her new apartment, Alex made himself scarce, in case they wanted to corner him in his office and complain about his helping her find a place. Part of the day he toured the local car agencies, and the following afternoon he pulled into Susan's driveway in a yellow four-door Malibu with only twenty-four thousand miles on it. Susan opened the front door of her house and let herself down the two brick steps, her chair tilted back on its rear wheels.

"It's perfect," she said. "It's gorgeous. What do they want for it?"

"Thirty-two hundred," Alex said. "They're giving away these gas hogs. But the Chevy dealer doesn't install hand controls. I'd have to take it to Columbus or Cincinnati."

"Would you? We could go together. I feel like I'm sixteen and almost have my license." She grasped Alex's shirt at the collar, pulled his head down and kissed him on the cheek. She reminded him of the young girl in Minneapolis who had taken Freya's clothes.

The following week he helped her with another project, a ramp over the two front steps. He consulted a book on carpentry, had the lumberyard deliver pressure-treated two-by-sixes, one-inch boards and galvanized nails, and managed to build a serviceable entrance ramp between the holly and lilac bushes that bracketed the door.

"When the landlady comes around, stonewall her. Act like nothing could be more natural than a ramp to the front door."

"You are the sweetest of devious men, Alex. It'll never pay you back, but I'll fix you a dinner for every hour you've worked here."

"No, this is strictly apprentice work."

"I'll fix you apprentice dinners."

The next afternoon he took her to the hard-surface tennis courts behind the high school and set up a ball caddy across the net. Susan had a good swing, even from her chair, but it took all Alex's skill to hit the ball to where she could reach it. They achieved a few volleys. He spent a lot of time gathering up his stock of tennis balls.

The wind blew back Susan's hair, exposing her temples. When she wheeled off the court at the end of an hour, she was still excited. "I hardly care where the balls go," she said. "I just want to thwack at them and see them fly off the racquet."

Fair enough, he thought—but the only way she could play tennis was if he hit to her precisely and was willing to chase the balls all over the court. She would never be able to warm up on her own against the backboard.

"For God's sake, Alex, don't give me that responsible look. I'd rather pay some teenager to throw balls for me and run after them. I can buy the help, you know. I'd rather have you as a friend."

He glanced away. At the edge of the court, the whitened underleaves of young maples flared up in the wind. Two thrushes chased each other into the air, then fluttered back onto the grass. He said, "I'm almost thirty years older than you are."

"I never think about that."

Her words discharged softly in his mind, buoying his forehead into the gusty air. He had thought about their ages a lot.

"I've had other things to worry about recently," she said. "Like my legs. I used to be proud of my legs, and they've wilted down to these sticks." She thumped her knees lightly with the strings of the tennis racquet, and her voice broke. "I'm a fake, Alex. I only show you my good side."

"I know."

"Do you?" She turned her head into the wind and dried her eyes. Her glossy hair was the last shade of brown before black.

"I want to," he said.

A bell went off inside the high school, even though the building was closed for summer vacation. Susan raised and lowered herself in her chair.

"When I came out of the coma, I knew I'd have to fight to live. And that was all I cared about—just to live. I got through the worst of the pain on that desire." She stretched her neck to one side. "I didn't want to say all this to you so soon."

Alex, who had been standing beside her chair, sat down on the grass. "Go ahead."

"At some point I knew I was going to make it. Eventually they unwired my jaw, and my ribs got better, and I didn't hurt

as much. But at the same time, I lost that sure feeling. Other
desires took over, beyond just living. I wanted to walk, and feel
my legs. I thought about sex and sports. Everything has changed
for me."

"I'm sure it has."

"That night when you came to the meeting late and we talked
about tennis—I hardly slept at all that night. I lay in bed and
thought about running and tennis and every sport I'd ever
played. I thought the blood would break out of my heart."

"I was afraid of that. I worried about it all the next day."

"Don't worry for me, Alex. Don't ever worry. Anyway, I
need to think about sports, they're part of my past. Hell, running is how I survived adolescence."

"I can't imagine you had much trouble with adolescence."

"I was shy."

"You weren't," Alex said. "There's not a shy bone in your
body."

"I was. I was as shy as an otter. Sophomore year in high
school I was six feet tall. Six feet even, the same as today. My
social life was zilch. I pretended boys didn't interest me, but
every night before bed I massaged both my lips and my breasts
for ten minutes. My lips filled out, but no dice on the breasts,
they never got any bigger than lemons. I was the shyest kid in
the class except for Martin Dinko."

"Who must have been in love with you."

"No, I don't think so. Martin was five six, he weighed about
a hundred and twenty pounds. His pulse rate was so low he
sometimes passed out in the cafeteria before lunch. We both
ran cross-country in the fall. I was on the boy's varsity because
no one except Martin could outrun me."

"You never beat him?"

"I'd lead him for the first two and a quarter miles, every
race, and then he'd pull up beside me as we went onto the
cinders. We always ran ahead of everyone else. We finished
one, two in the districts. The course ended with two laps on the
track so everyone could watch, and around we'd go, side by

side, gasping for air, two beanpoles in our only moment of glory."
Susan stopped to laugh. "For a couple of minutes it must have
looked like a parody of screwing between the two shyest kids
in school. Then, no more than fifty yards from the finish line,
Martin would kick out a couple of yards on me and take first
place. Every goddamn time. I don't know how he came up
with it."

"You never got to be friends?"

"God no, I just wanted to beat him. And then Jeb Downy,
who ran back around fifth place, told me that Martin only stayed
behind me for most of the race so he could watch my ass as he
ran. That helped him win, Jeb said. I smacked Jeb across the
mouth in front of the whole team. Drew blood, too. I almost
knocked him off his feet." Susan laughed outright. "I'd like to
bust Jeb Downy one more time. If anything was sacred to me
then, it was competition."

"You can still compete," Alex said. "There are plenty of
wheelchair sports."

"You're right, I could. I probably will. Anyway, I better stop
worrying about these legs and how skinny they're getting. You
never look at them."

"I look at them," Alex said. "Sometimes."

"Less today." Susan had worn shorts for the first time. Her
thighs, lying white and indolent on the vinyl chair, were as long
as channel catfish. "With legs like these," she said, "I could have
had a hell of a social life in high school. I could have been the
hit of the drive-in and never felt a thing. Go ahead, Alex, touch
me. It won't hurt you."

He rested his left hand on her leg, just above the knee.
He half expected the muscles to tense, but of course they
never moved.

ON SUNDAY MORNING Alex and his daughter warmed up on a
clay court at the tennis club, marking the newly brushed surface with long footslides and the landing streak of balls. After

two hard sets in the evaporative morning light, they retired to a bench facing the courts.

"Paul's lost a tooth," Anna said, "here." She curled back her upper lip to show her father, placing a finger on one of her own white incisors. "It completely changes his face. He looks ten years older."

"I know, I ran into him at the grocery store."

"You did?" Anna sat up straight on the bench. "When was that?"

"A couple of days ago."

"What did he say?"

"He acted as if we were old acquaintances—which I guess we are. He was polite. We talked at the checkout counter, but just for a couple of minutes. What does he do all day?"

"I don't know, I haven't seen him since he moved into that house on Hinman. He sends me postcards. Yesterday he sent one with my horoscope taped on the back. Here." Anna pulled a small clipping out of her wallet. *Look for travel and new adventures. Let yourself go.*

"How come he doesn't get that tooth fixed?" Alex asked.

"I think he likes it. It gives him a sinister look."

Alex adjusted the strings on his racquet and watched the long, vigorous strokes of the couple on the near court. "Don't you worry about him living around here?"

"You mean because they had him locked up in California."

"Partly. And because he's strange. He could hardly look at me when we were talking."

Anna lifted her hair off the back of her neck, still cooling down from tennis. "Paul's a completely different man from the one I married. I don't know what our history means anymore, but somehow I'm still tied to him."

"What does any history mean?"

"Garbage, probably."

"Oh no, Anna."

They sat on the bench in silence, listening to the repetitive thudding of tennis balls and to the cries and comments from a half-dozen games in progress. Alex had the same problem with history his daughter had. He couldn't make the past apply. What he had learned from Freya didn't help him now with a woman thirty years his junior, recently paralyzed from the waist down.

"I've met someone interesting," he told Anna. "A woman from the hospital."

Anna drew up one foot to the bench and tucked it under the white shorts of her other leg. "Someone you like?" she asked.

"I don't know, I like lots of people."

"You know what I mean."

"Well, I guess I do, but I'm not sure how I like her. She's much younger than I am."

"So am I," Anna said, laughing, "and look what good friends we've become."

"And she's a paraplegic."

"Oh. . . ."

"That makes a difference, doesn't it?"

"For some things. What's her name? How old is she?"

"Susan Rupert. She's younger than you are."

Anna looked at him askance. "She might not have guessed your age right. Most people wouldn't."

"She knows. I told her."

"Ah, this is serious. And she likes you?"

"I guess."

"Then don't panic, papá." Anna leaned forward, smiling, and kissed him on the cheek. "Let it go and see what happens."

Alex wondered if, as he got older, women were going to start kissing his cheeks. Susan had, a few days ago, and now Anna.

AT SIX O'CLOCK, as the bells of St. John's Church sounded over the town of Fell River, Susan disappeared to her room for the third time in twenty minutes to dress for dinner. Alex, who had already set the dining room table, stepped to the back door to listen to the thirty irregular peals from the church tower. Preparations for the meal of Cornish game hen and ratatouille had begun at four, under Susan's tutelage.

Thick summer weather had engulfed the town. The temperature outdoors was eighty-five, and the kitchen hotter still. Susan rolled into the room wearing an expensive-looking green blouse at odds with the rest of her clothing. A film of perspiration rose on her forehead.

"We've fixed quite a dinner," Alex said. "I don't eat this way at home."

"Me neither, usually. How about Anna?"

"Soyburgers and steamed broccoli, the last time I ate at her house. She's no gourmet."

"So why have we done this?" Susan laughed.

"To prove that I'm domestically proficient, I suppose. And that you can do anything."

Susan opened the oven, basted the pair of game hens one last time and turned off the gas. "Have we proved it?"

"Sure. But I wonder if you're as nervous as you look."

Wheeling up beside his chair, Susan leaned over and kissed him on the mouth. She held her lips against his own for a surprising pair of seconds. "I'm nervous," she admitted, "but I'll get over it. And you?"

"Cool as a cucumber," Alex said. In fact, Susan's lips had been the cool ones against his own.

Anna rang the doorbell. Susan let her in, and Alex introduced the two women. They sat in a triangle in the living room, eating cashews and talking about the heat wave of the last few days.

"Are those bruises?" Anna asked abruptly. She stared at the soft lilac marks around Susan's eyes. "I'm sorry, my father didn't tell me how you wound up in a wheelchair. I don't know anything about you."

"Hardly anyone does in Fell River. Except your father, a little. I broke my back by falling off a cliff in the Bandelier National Monument. The bruises are recent, from plastic surgery. They've just started to clear up."

"You broke your back," Anna said. "You could have died."

"The man I was climbing with did. We were on the same rope."

Anna stared at her.

"He was the climber, I was just a novice. But he's the one who fell and dragged me off. The first thing I knew Mel was in the air scrambling to hold on, and then he shot past me in midair. He died when he hit."

"At least it wasn't you who fell and dragged him off."

"And killed him, you mean. That's true. But maybe if I'd fallen, it wouldn't have happened that way. My ideas about fate have changed in the last year."

"How do you mean?"

"I don't believe in it."

Anna nodded but didn't speak.

"Why should this be my fate?" Susan asked, gripping the arms of her wheelchair. "Everything they say about karma and fortune and destiny—it's all bullshit. I'm sorry, I get a little heated up on the topic."

She sat up straight in her chair, her shoulders tight and her mouth turned down. "You tell me," she asked Anna, "do you think everything that happens to us is determined beforehand?"

"No, I don't believe that either."

"Why should we swallow that? It's like saying we did something to deserve it. That's the message that floats around in people's eyes, though, have you noticed?"

Anna glanced at her father.

"Oh no, not from Alex."

"Dad's had enough history himself."

"For which," Alex said, making light of the subject, "women come and kiss me on the cheek."

"*You* kiss *me* on the cheek," Susan said. "I'm more outgoing."

After dinner and dessert they stacked the unwashed dishes in the sink. "I'll do them in the morning," Susan explained.

"Besides, we have to leave early if I'm going to make it to the movie at my own speed. When someone pushes me I start feeling like an invalid."

They made their way toward the university through the late sunshine, past other pedestrians and a few joggers. Squirrels flipped from tree to tree, and a black Labrador bounded out to the sidewalk from the backyard of an older brick house. Susan stopped to rest her arms and pet the animal.

"Some dogs love me," she said, "and others can't get used to the chair. This one seems friendly."

The young Lab ducked its head and broad shoulders, squiggling back and forth. Susan turned to Anna to explain that she wanted to buy a lighter, faster wheelchair for such fair-weather trips through town.

"*Hey*," Alex yelled, and jammed his foot hard under the dog's backside; the Labrador had lifted its leg against the side of the wheelchair. It howled and ran.

"I'll be damned," Susan said, raising her hand above the endangered wheel. "The goddamned dog took me for a parked car."

A man appeared at the side of the house with the Labrador circling his legs. "What's going on?" he asked.

"I just stopped your dog from pissing on our wheelchair," Alex yelled, louder than necessary.

A few steps down the sidewalk, Anna asked, "Was that my father the dog lover who blasted that poor puppy in the groin?"

"Stupid mutt. He was aiming for Susan's guide wheel, he might as well have peed on her hand."

"You can never tell when someone's personality is going to change," Anna said, teasing. "There was a time when my father belonged to an antivivisection society."

"Oh, I just got some mail from them. Go ahead, laugh. Next time I'll ask the dog first if he really needs to go. I wouldn't want to mistreat an animal for no reason."

"No, no," Susan said. "Better to stomp on 'em before they get me."

At exactly eight they walked into the university's film department. A young student had set up a card table in the hall outside the screening room to sell tickets for the movie. He wore a shirt without sleeves and an irregular hair style—a buzz-cut over the top with longer hair hanging down the back of his neck. He looked at Susan briefly, then turned to Alex. "I'm afraid you'll have to sit in the back. Wheelchairs aren't allowed in the aisles."

"Are you talking to me?" Susan asked.

"Yes, it's . . ." He looked at her for an instant, then jerked back to Alex and finished the sentence to him. "It's fire regulations."

"Sure thing," Alex said, grabbing the handles on the back of Susan's chair and pushing it through the door. He went down the aisle of the small auditorium and stopped near the front. "If this is good," he told Susan, "you can put your brakes on and we'll watch the movie from here."

Behind them came the young boy, holding the cash box in his hands.

"It isn't allowed by the state," he said without speaking directly to anyone. He glanced over his shoulder to see how much of a display he was causing in front of the sparse crowd.

Alex raised his index finger to the boy's chest and pushed. "You call the fire marshal if you're so hot about it." Then he dropped his voice and added, "You should think less about the rules and more about other people." The boy hesitated, then walked back up the aisle, holding the cash box to his chest where Alex's finger had pressed against him. Alex said quietly, "He's just young. He got confused."

"You can't even get the bastards to look at you when they're telling you not to do something," Susan said. "If I'd come alone, he probably wouldn't have had the courage to follow me in here. They'd rather pretend they didn't see you."

Everyone else in the theater acted as if nothing had happened. Alex sat down on the aisle with Anna on his right. The flurry of ruffled feelings subsided, and he lost himself in the movie. For a while he rested his hand over Susan's, on the arm of her wheelchair.

After the movie they trailed the crowd outside, then started home along the darkened streets. The small front wheels of Susan's chair clanked rhythmically on the scored concrete of the sidewalk. A few blocks from home, Susan told Anna her arms were tired and asked her if she'd push the chair.

Anna stopped at Susan's front door, at the foot of the ramp. "I won't come in," she said. "I have farming in the morning."

"You could have a drink with us if you like," Alex said, "or just sit for a while."

"No, Mondays are always busy. Time for me to go."

She said good night and walked to her car, leaving them in front of the small house. The night had cooled. Susan snapped a pair of lilac sprigs from the dark foliage, stuck them above her ears and opened the front door.

Alex followed her inside. She parked her chair under the floor lamp in the living room and watched him as he paced back and forth, examining her books and magazines. "Have you read all these?" he asked.

"Most of them." She laid the lilac twigs in her lap.

Alex had never visited her house at eleven at night with only one light on, with no dinner to be made or books to be discussed—or with Susan sitting like an animal in her chair, staring at him. I ought to leave, he thought. Instead, he kept moving around the room.

"Come and sit down."

Alex glanced at her, then lowered himself carefully into the armchair beside her.

"It's perfectly safe," she said, smiling. "After all, I can't feel anything below the waist. We could even go to the drive-in."

"Oh yeah?"

"That's a joke, Alex, you could laugh."

He tittered a little and squeezed his knees to stop them from shaking.

"Even the psychologists are afraid to talk to us about sex,"

Susan said. "Don't you ever ask your patients what they're going to do about it?"

"I have, a couple of times."

"But you didn't ask me."

"No."

Gently, she passed the two switches of lilac over his eyes, then dropped them into the opening of her blouse. Their new leaves were a lighter green than the cloth. Alex reached the end of one twig with his fingers and softly pulled it away from her chest. He laid it across her mouth and kissed her through the small, waxy leaves.

The other twig had disappeared, fallen down. Susan undid two buttons and leaned forward so he could see her breasts. He looked at her face.

"Go ahead," she told him. "I want you to look."

With the tips of his fingers, he opened her blouse enough to see her nipples resting against the cloth. He asked her, "How far down can you feel?"

"To here." She placed a leveled hand below her breasts, at her navel.

"So here you feel everything?" he said, grazing her chest with his hand.

Susan unbuttoned her blouse completely and closed her eyes as Alex passed his fingertips over the soft skin of her breasts. He felt her sternum and the smooth ladder of her ribs. Her skin was beautiful to him. Her healed ribs were beautiful, and the small plane of flesh over her collarbone.

"One day the skin around my eyes will be as clear as this," she said, placing a hand between her breasts.

"Your eyes are lovely."

"But these won't change." She laid her hands palm down, one on either leg.

"I don't care," Alex said. He drew her toward him.

"You might care later."

"I might, I don't know about later."

"We shouldn't go too fast," she said.

"No, we won't."

"But if you like, you can spend the night here."

He almost went to sleep before she finished in the bathroom. She wore a nightgown with long sleeves and faced away from him in bed. He pulled her toward him so the thinning globes of her bottom rested against his lap.

"Shy as an otter," he said.

"If you want me now, Alex, you have to court me. I've taken all the first steps." A few minutes later she slept in his arms.

CHAPTER 4

J ACK ELLISON gave his first Fourth of July party for his children forty years ago. Now he gave them for his grandchildren. The Ellison house overlooked the Ohio from a lap of flat land two hundred feet above the river; flower gardens, an expansive lawn and a dozen large oak trees surrounded the house.

Anna sought out the host and introduced herself. Ellison, one of her father's tennis partners, pumped her arm and followed her gaze across the lawn.

"Yes, there's Alex," he said. "He's taken on old Batty Bates, the croquet wizard. Go ahead then, see what they're up to."

Alex, soberly dressed in flannel pants and a white shirt, stood next to Susan's wheelchair. The two of them had teamed up against an elderly man and woman, both dressed entirely in white. The man was explaining the tactics of the English-style game with its central stake and six narrow wickets.

Susan's wheelchair tires had fluted the grassy surface of the court. "I'm going to be an athlete yet!" she told Anna. She leaned precariously over one side of the chair and hammered her ball neatly toward a wicket, golf style. The ball struck but did not go through, and the turn passed to the other woman—who also missed a shot.

"It's an exacting game," the man in white said in a clipped eastern accent. "The wickets are only an eighth of an inch wider than the balls."

"But the balls really fly off these mallets," Susan said, laughing. "I can knock one from one end of the court to the other, easy."

The man tightened his lips and pointed a finger at the wicket her ball had failed to pass. "Bravado won't get you through. You need strategy, and more work on your stroke. But you could play well, young lady."

The croquet court, planted to creeping bentgrass and rolled as smooth as a putting green, looked as if it belonged to an English estate. Closer to the large Ellison house, two serving men passed among a scattered crowd of a hundred people, bearing appetizers and glasses of champagne. It was not a scene Anna had expected to find in the Ohio Valley. Few guests, however, other than Bates the croquet expert and his wife, were formally dressed. Jack Ellison himself wore jogging shoes and a pair of blue shorts. He disengaged himself from a noisy group and strolled to the edge of the court. Standing close to Anna, he considered the match. "Bates is the master," he said. "Watch this."

Bates tapped the black ball toward a far corner, almost out of bounds.

"He's enticing your father. If Alex is smart, he won't bite."

Ellison inclined his head close to Anna's, in sympathy with her father's stroke. Tufts of white hair sprouted from his protuberant ears like miniature clumps of broom sedge, and his pale blue eyes locked on the game. He'd had two cardiac arrests in the last five years, Alex had told Anna, but he still put up a fight on the tennis court.

"From now on," Ellison said, "I'm just going to play games. When I'm too old for tennis I'll drop back to golf and croquet. I played the commodities market for forty years and now all I want to do is play games, like my grandchildren."

He pointed toward a dozen children playing dodgeball on the grass. In the middle of a limed circle a boy and girl, both about ten, sidestepped the rubber balls thrown at them from all sides.

Anna froze, for the boy looked like Kevin. He had the same high cheekbones and curly hair, and the same wild look. He laughed as the balls flew past. One narrowly missed his ear. He grinned, then a second ball caught him on the arm. Another child took his place, but from outside the circle he kept up the same banter and good spirits.

Anna turned away from the croquet court without a word and walked across the grass to watch the children play. The girls screamed and the boys showed off. A few of the younger kids hung back from the circle, but when a ball came to them they picked it up and threw it. No adult regulated the game.

Close to the edge of the lawn, but at a safe distance from the children, Anna sat down to watch. Two hundred feet below her the brown swath of the Ohio curved west and disappeared among low hills. Her ears rang and her legs stretched away from her. Her head, disembodied, seemed to float into the middle of the game, where the balls winged past her as in a dream. She watched the curly-haired young boy in secret. In fact, he bore only a faint resemblance to Kevin—but the first moment had been a shock.

Ever since Kevin died, the beauty of young children had embarrassed Anna. Her stares, even for the youngest children, bordered on the gluttonous and sexual. Now, watching the game of dodgeball, she only wanted to see the unconscious bodies of the young pass graciously through the summer air. But even that seemed reprehensible. Kevin's death had shut her out of the great circle of parents and children.

The game broke up, the kids scattered, and Anna walked back toward the house across the soft manicured turf. Her father and Susan were sitting with a group of others on the front porch, the lavender doughnuts of flesh around Susan's eyes noticeable from a distance. No one would take the two of them as father and daughter, for Alex was fair and Susan dark. Nor did they seem too far apart in years to be a couple.

Alex welcomed his daughter with a nod and continued a story about growing up on the Ohio River. Relieved that he didn't stop to introduce her to everyone, Anna stayed just outside the group, trying to remember what people talked about. to other people they hardly knew. It surprised her, how adept her father was.

The two of them went through the dinner line carrying an extra plate for Susan. They loaded up with barbecued ribs, potato salad and snap peas and made a second trip for plastic glasses of red wine. They all balanced their overloaded paper plates on their knees as they ate.

"Were those all Jack Ellison's grandchildren playing dodgeball?" Anna asked.

"Some of them. Others probably came as friends, as we did." Alex placed a minuscule emphasis on the word *we*. "You can imagine how much it takes to put this show on," he said, turning to Susan. "I've heard Ellison spends a couple of thousand on fireworks alone, not to mention all this food."

"One year we played dodgeball at Lisa's birthday party," Anna said, "at Lake Harriet. Both you and Mom were there."

"My daughter is the family chronicler. She remembers things about Minneapolis that are a complete blank to me. I forget we ever did them, but Anna can remember the year and month, and sometimes even the day."

"August fifteenth, of course, that's Lisa's birthday. I'd say around 1955."

"See what I mean?" Alex said. He turned back to Anna. "We missed our lunch together last week. How about this Tuesday, for sure?"

His brusque tone and the reminder of their lunch at the Bradford were warnings that he didn't want to talk about the past in front of Susan. Mainly, Anna knew, he didn't want to talk about Freya or Freya's death. Probably not about Kevin, either.

After dinner Anna forced herself to wander across the lawn and talk to other people. She hadn't been to a party in over a year and felt shy about approaching groups of people she didn't know. Yet when she did, no one put her on the spot or asked whom she knew at the party. The first group of women she joined talked about children, the work habits of driven husbands and the race for county commissioner. Another pair of women talked about Edith Wharton and Lily Bart, then went on to gossip openly about some man named Fred. Larger groups, dominated by men, talked about university politics, sports and the stock market. An older man asked Anna what she did. He showed only mild surprise when she answered, "I farm."

Anna discovered that dozens of people led lives she had never imagined in Fell River. She had not met there, as her father had through the tennis club and his job, contractors, university professors, wives with plenty of money, and young men in their thirties wearing Cincinnati Reds baseball caps and polyester shorts. After almost two years, Anna still thought of Fell River as a half-hidden town on the edge of Appalachia with a state university, a couple of moribund industries and a narrow strip of first-rate tomato and melon soil along the river. It still seemed an anomaly to her to live in that part of the world—yet in one conversation after another she discovered an undercurrent of loyalty to the town.

With the approach of dusk a few guests strolled to the southern brink of the lawn in anticipation of the fireworks. Anna stepped inside to use the bathroom—and surprised a woman in a full-length mirror. *Oh,* it was herself. Did she appear that somber to others?

Her figure hadn't changed. Paul Dunham used to call her the Big Woman. He'd lay his own big hands on her thighs and tell her she was "made for midnight." When was the last time he'd said that? At six three, Paul towered over her, so when he called her the Big Woman, she liked it. A long time ago, that seemed. Anna didn't want to wind up strange and sad, like Paul. At least she still had her waist, she thought, smoothing out her dress in front of the mirror. And work, and her sanity.

Stepping outside through a pair of French doors onto the side porch, Anna turned at the sound of a girl's laughter. Ice cubes lay splattered over the slate floor, and an empty glass dangled from the girl's hand. In front of her, bent with exaggeration at the waist, a man pulled the wet cloth of his pants away from his lap.

"Oh Dad," the girl said, glancing at Anna and laughing. "Don't you have any control?"

The man was less amused. "She did it," he said, pointing at the girl with his elbow. "And I'm not so sure it was an accident."

"It was. It was an accident!" The girl laughed until Anna joined in. The man held out his wet pants with clenched thumbs and forefingers. "Sometimes my dad can't hold it!" the girl said.

"You want me to tell stories about you, Daria?"

"That was when I was *little*." She laughed. "You're an *adult*!"

The girl was older than the children who'd played dodgeball. She took her father's arm and told him she was sorry—but in the middle of apologizing she glanced down at his soaked pants and broke out laughing again.

"See what happens when your daughter grows up?" the man said, turning toward Anna. "You give your whole life to her and you can't get any respect. She just loves it when some stranger comes along and thinks you've peed in your pants." The girl shrieked.

"I'm a grown man. Do you think I go around peeing in my pants? Have you ever seen anyone my age pee in his pants? Only little kids do that. This is just soda pop or something. . . ."

"Lemonade," the girl managed to get out. "A whole glass of lemonade! But it was an accident, Dad, I swear."

"A likely story. You might have planned the whole thing just to embarrass me." He wiggled like a dog after a swim and straightened up. "But I know how we might even the score, Daria. How about walking around the party right now, arm in arm? Or else maybe I should visit you in school sometime. I could drop in to see you, with my pants looking just like this."

"You wouldn't dare."

"I might. I bet I could get a big laugh in your homeroom."

"*Dad,* that's not funny."

"Ah, so there's a limit to this after all?"

The girl pouted momentarily but laughed again when her father plucked at the front of his pants and minced across the patio as if he'd crapped in his pants.

"Here I am in the middle of a party," he said. "I'm as wet as a seal, and my daughter's laughing at me in front of strangers."

"Oh Dad." The girl put her arm through his. "It was my fault. And you can wear anything you want to my school, I don't care who sees you."

"There is a sweet streak to her," the man said. He looked at Anna. "And who are you? Now that you've caught me with my pants down, so to speak."

"If you don't have anything to change into," Anna said, "there's a dryer inside." She glanced behind her.

"Yes, but who are you? What do I wear in the meantime, a towel?"

"There were some in the bathroom, I don't know. . . ."

"Do you live here?" he asked.

"Me? I hardly know anyone here. Aren't you . . . an Ellison or something?"

"We're friends of friends. I thought maybe you were an Ellison. How do you know about the dryer?"

"I went by the washroom on the way to the bathroom."

Anna's unpremeditated rhyme hung in the air. The seam between the man's lips widened fractionally, the embryo of a smile. His angular tanned face was capped by an uneven haircut. Done at home? Anna wondered.

Having stared at the man's wet lap, she now forced herself to endure his candid look. Finally she stepped off the patio onto the grass but after a few paces glanced back at the man and his daughter. They stood silently upright, watching her go. The man waved.

At the far end of the lawn, overlooking the river, clusters of people swatted mosquitoes, talked and waited for the fireworks. "Come on, Jack," someone yelled, "set 'em off." But Ellison held back the display until the final blue light of dusk had faded from the sky.

Anna stood next to her father, behind Susan's chair. Far below, in a small field by the edge of the river, two men scuttled back and forth. Finally, when not even their white shirts could be seen in the dark, Ellison signaled to them with a flashlight. The first rocket whistled up from below and exploded in front of the crowd in an orange burst, followed by another and another. A concussive explosion punctuated each flush of color. In the white antimony light of the finale, Anna glanced to one side and saw the man from the patio standing next to his daughter, his arm around the girl's shoulder. He was watching Anna, not the fireworks.

FOR A DAY AND A HALF at the end of the week, Anna, Shelley, Deal and six teenage helpers picked the farm's first tomatoes. They'd missed the Fourth of July market but still had some of the earliest tomatoes in the state, and prices in Cleveland and Toledo were twice what they'd be a month later. At four o'clock Saturday afternoon Anna delivered the last load to the produce docks in Fell River. She spoke briefly with the farm's crop broker, then parked the big flatbed in an empty market lot and walked downtown to the public library.

Heat floated above the steaming sidewalks. In front of the post office a pair of oscillating sprinklers overshot the grass and wet her ankles—twice, for she paused to let the sprinklers go around a second time. Skipping up the stairs to the library, she checked on farm prices in the *Dispatch*, browsed through the anthropology section and sat down in the reading room.

An hour later, two books in hand, Anna stepped outside into the town's baked blue air—and stopped just outside the door. On the sidewalk below, the man from the party was talking to his daughter. Anna went down the stairs, her eyes on the smooth hollows worn into the limestone steps by the tread of generations. At the last minute the girl said, "Dad, there's that woman. . . ."

Anna stopped. The man said, "Say, hello there." He took a

step toward her and stuck out his hand. Anna's own hands and forearms, even after a full scrub, still showed the green-and-golden tint of tomato dust.

"You're the one who saw my disgrace," he said. "The one who caught me after I had that accident."

"*Dad.*" The girl pulled at the sleeve of his shirt and looked away. Her hair was in braids, she wore shorts and a yellow T-shirt. She looked younger: eleven or twelve.

"Okay, so I didn't actually pee. . . ."

"*Dad,* I'm going to the library."

He ignored her embarrassment. "You're Anna Delaney, aren't you?"

Anna took a half step back. "How do you know that?"

"It's a small town."

"But I never saw you before that party."

"Me neither." He smiled, almost.

"So how do you know who I am?"

"I asked Jack Ellison."

"Well, he doesn't know me at all. What did he tell you?"

"He knows your father, and your name, and where you work. He didn't have your telephone number, but I found it in the book."

"And what were you going to do with it?"

"Call you up and invite you to have a cup of coffee this afternoon at the Elephant Cafe."

His daughter took a step back and folded her arms, looking away pointedly. The girl's bashfulness diffused Anna's own.

"I'm Jay Corman," he said. "This is Daria, who's on her way to the library to pick out some books."

"With you," the girl said in a pout.

"I said I'd go with you, Daria, but I didn't know this would come up." He looked at Anna, then back at his daughter. "How about if we meet here at six when the library closes?" Daria frowned, scuffed her sandals on the first step and agreed. She went up the stairs without looking back.

"You will come for coffee won't you?" Jay asked.

They started down High Street, Anna lagging slightly behind. Jay wore a pair of loose green corduroys and running
shoes the same color.

"You embarrassed your daughter," Anna said.

"It happens all the time. No one can mortify a girl like her
father."

"How old is she?"

"Twelve. Sometimes she's oblivious to everything and everybody, and other times she thinks the Big Eye is on her. I'm
usually not proper enough for her. Do you have any children?"

"No."

Anna's curt response silenced him for a block. Car tires
burred over the brick streets, and the dilated whistle of a freight
train sounded from the eastern edge of town.

In the Elephant Cafe, seated face to face, they ordered coffee and reopened a neutral conversation. They talked about
the pollution of oceans and the rate of inflation.

Anna felt light-headed over the unaccustomed late-afternoon
coffee. Or perhaps it was Jay's motionless, imperturbable look.
He sat without twitching or looking away or playing with the
silverware. Almost without blinking, Anna noticed. His obvious
composure highlighted her own restlessness as she turned her
empty cup in its saucer, curled a lock of hair around one finger
and shifted in her seat.

"Do you have any other children?" she asked.

"No. I've got my hands full with Daria."

"She's a spirited girl."

"You mean all that sulking at the library?"

"That, and how she laughed at the party. She was having a
good time there."

"At my expense," Jay said, laughing. "Imagine if I'd spilled
lemonade over *her*. Fireworks or no, she'd have had me drive
home so she could change clothes."

"And you would have?"

"Probably. The things you do for your child—you know,
they never end."

She knew. Had Jack Ellison told him about Kevin?

Turning in his seat, Jay lifted his cup and signaled the waitress. "You want another?" he asked Anna.

"No thanks. Too much coffee makes me nervous." In fact, her foot had begun to jiggle up and down. She stopped it, but it started again. "So at your house," she said, "there are only three of you?"

"Only two."

"And her mother?"

"She lives in Boston."

"But Daria stays with you?"

"Martine had her for five years, now we're on the second five-year plan. Martine's a busy woman these days, she's on the executive track."

"What does she do?"

"Buys for Filene's."

Fi-lene's, he said it, looking across the room and tightening his lips. There was a history behind Jay's tone of voice, Anna thought—some trouble, like everyone else. It made him seem less threatening.

"Apparently you already know what I do for a living," she said. "What about you?"

He pulled a white card out of his wallet. *The River Dance Studio,* it read, along with an address and his name.

"The river," Anna said. "You mean the Ohio?"

"That, and the bedfellow of Time."

A man as attractive as Jay must go through a lot of women, she thought. The bedfellow. "You mean *Of Time and the River*?"

"I guess that's where it came from."

"I don't dance," Anna said. "What kind of dance is it?"

"Modern and ballet. I taught for the university before they closed down the department. In fact, I rent their old studio. I'd like to do just modern, but more people come for ballet. Kids, a lot of them."

"Do you . . . what is it, choreograph your dances?"

"I choreograph some, sure. I don't get to perform as often as I used to."

"What do you dance about?"

Jay's elbows rested on the table. "Things I see in the street," he said. "Or the way people move."

"Such as?"

"Such as . . . the way you walk with your left shoulder a little higher than your right."

"Oh." Anna leaned back.

"No, really, that's part of a dance. Dancing's made up of things like that."

"I thought dancing was steps and flying through the air."

"There's that, too, but it has to come from something. How often do you walk down the street and see someone flying through the air? It's more like telling a story, or getting a feeling across. For me, most dances start out with a position or a gesture."

"Like what?"

Jay's shoulders, though broad, sloped steeply away from his neck. He nudged his empty cup with the tip of one finger, in a slow circle. "Different gestures. Maybe it's something I hardly notice at the time but comes back to me later."

"Like what? Give me an example."

"I don't know, usually it's something personal."

"Like my name and address," Anna said, sitting up. "That's personal. Or a glass of lemonade spilled all over your lap. Give me an example. Tell me about one of your dances."

"All right, let me try. I've been working on a dance for the last couple of weeks, and it comes from a particular motion, like I said. It's a departure. It looks like this."

He stood up and moved away from the table, inclining his torso to one side and looking back over his shoulder.

"The legs are almost straight. Most of the movement is in the upper body, since departures take place in the heart. I'll do this same movement over and over—the way separations are

repeated. The first dancer goes offstage and then returns, perhaps many times. The rest—I'm not sure what they'll be doing,
or even if there'll be any. I'm still working on the piece, but
this is the seminal motion, the one that sets off everything else.
Of course, when the choreography is done it looks abstract,
and ten different people would have ten different reactions to
it. It doesn't have to mean anything specific."

"But the original movement is specific," Anna said. "It comes
from something."

"Yes, it's this." Again Jay arched himself away from the table, his eyes turning back to her, his emotional carriage out of
place in the small cafe. After a moment he came back and stood
with his hands on the edge of the table. His fingers were tanned
and ringless, the backs of his hands lined with strong veins.

"It does come from something," he admitted. "I probably
shouldn't tell you what it is because you'll get fixed with an
image that isn't really part of the dance. It happened one afternoon last spring when Daria rode off on her bicycle, leaving
me in a little park by the Fell. She looked back to tell me she
was going for a ride—I think first she started to go and then
she remembered to tell me. She stood up on one pedal, about
thirty yards away, one leg stretched down and the other raised,
leaning to one side the way I was just doing. She's grown four
inches in the last year. The bicycle was banked on the asphalt.
She turned to wave—and suddenly it looked like the way all
children leave their parents. Her hair was in the sunlight, and
her body outlined against the trees. All around her the air turned
glassy and thick. Maybe cars were passing or doors slamming,
probably other children were walking nearby. But none of that
meant anything. I was only aware of her coasting away and
looking back as children sometimes do when they leave you.
Maybe I only saw it because she looked back, and they don't
always."

"No," Anna said, "they don't." She was silent a minute before asking, "Why would she leave you?"

"Just part of growing up. I've been thinking about it for the last few days because she's leaving for the summer. I never thought I'd miss her this way."

Jay sat down, his cavalier demeanor gone, his hair lying close to his scalp. "You must have a child," he said.

Anna pushed her cup across the table with the back of her hand. "So Ellison told you that, too."

"No, he didn't tell me that. It was what you said."

"I did have a child once, but he died in an accident." She said it quickly and turned to look out the window.

"Is that how you got your scar?"

The small scar on her forehead, barely an inch long, followed the curve of her eyebrows. Anna traced the smooth, raised tissue with her finger. "I went part way through a windshield."

"I noticed it at the party."

Anna stood up and pushed away her chair. "I'm sure you did. You probably made a note about it so you could put it in a dance." She threw a dollar bill on the table as Jay stood up. She didn't want to get angry. After all, he had opened up to her and shown her his dance. But having talked about Daria, wouldn't he expect her to tell him something about Kevin? She wasn't going to do that.

They walked back up High Street a rigid four feet apart, as if locked on the separate tracks of a railroad line. Anna still held his dance studio card in her right hand. At the library steps she apologized.

"I'm sorry I got upset, I know I didn't have any call to. Maybe we can talk again some other time."

"I'd like to," Jay said, looking directly at her.

Back at her truck, Anna twisted the rearview mirror down to look at her forehead. How many times had her scar led a conversation where she didn't want to go? She breathed deeply and tried to unwind. Loss had so determined her last year that she hardly knew what anyone else lived for.

CREAKING WOODEN STEPS led up to Jay's studio on the second floor of a handsome but poorly maintained brick building on Merton Street. Anna put a hand on either banister and ascended, tread by tread, as far as the small landing. She laid her ear against the door, heard nothing and tried the doorknob. It was safely locked. A sign, printed in the same script as Jay's card, read, *The River Dance Studio.* Dance company posters were pinned to a bulletin board along with announcements of seminars, master classes and local performances. There were four framed photographs of dancers as well. Anna recognized the first as Isadora Duncan but didn't know the second. The third photo was a grainy enlargement showing, in the foreground, a woman on pointe, her arms and throat and chin all raised. Stepping closer to the picture, Anna discovered Jay on the periphery of the dance, looking wistful and young.

The last photo was a cover from *Dance World.* The caption read, "Jay Corman of José Limón," above which Jay was caught in midleap, one leg straight before him and the other bent behind. He looked like an animal, magnificent, with curly hair to his shoulders and light, feral eyes. He looked possessed, literally separated from the earth. His eyes haven't changed, Anna thought.

She went down to the lobby, cased the sidewalk and stepped outside onto the street, walking past the railroad tracks and farm market as far as the river. She hadn't been attracted to a man since Kevin's death.

The stately Ohio flowed before her, it had no debate. Yet sometimes the river seemed like a whore to Anna, carrying whatever leapt between its legs: human sewage and chemical waste, overpowered V8 playcraft and chrome houseboats that mooned about the eddies like floating Winnebagos. And soil. Whole fields of topsoil stripped from Pennsylvania and Ohio and Kentucky farms. Sixty tons of topsoil a minute passing by Fell River in a giant colloidal wedge.

If only the rules for people were as clear as those for water. Follow gravity, boil at 212, freeze at 32. No morality to it. But human choices were never as rudimentary or inevitable. Some people mated and others didn't. Some bred and others didn't.

Anna did not want to control everything about her life. She wanted it to happen to her, and for everything to work out well. As her friend Michelle used to say in Eugene, "You want to be loose, but you don't want to get fucked." That was the trouble, they'd agreed; sleeping with a man usually meant you got fucked by something larger. Anna wanted to lie up sometimes in the palm of the world, but for the last few years she'd been too careful to let it happen.

Sitting on a bench beside the river, she wrote a note on the back of an envelope. She carried it to the studio and left it in Jay's mailbox.

Dear Jay,
  I stopped by and found you in photographs, but not in person. I've thought a lot about your dance—and your showing it to me. Thanks for that.

Anna

Three days later an envelope arrived at her house, addressed in a spidery hand to Anna Delaney, Indian Trouble Farm, Fell River, Ohio.

Dear Anna,
  I was surprised and delighted to get your note—read it just before class and ran amok with my warm-ups. May I have the pleasure of this dance? How about the Hayes Cafeteria for dinner, or else the Carriage House for cocktails? You pick. Sometime this weekend?

Jay

He mocked her for cowardice—she had written a thank-you note instead of admitting she wanted to see him again—then deftly returned the initiative to her hands. The Hayes Cafeteria was a self-service restaurant with bright lights and metal chairs; the Carriage House an intimate, expensive warren of booths and tables for two.

On Saturday night she found Jay leaning against the fender

of his car in the Carriage House parking lot. He sported brown-and-white shoes, a pair of cream slacks and a blazer. Anna looked formal herself, in a dress and low heels.

"I wasn't sure what to wear," she said. "I thought you might come in sneakers." The ventilated uppers of Jay's shoes looked like the rattan seats of an old railway car.

"I wish I had. The soles on these Italian jobs are paper thin. They were my father's, years ago, but I think they're coming back in style."

"So you chose style over comfort?"

"If we'd met at the Hayes Cafeteria," he said, smiling, "I would've worn my running shoes."

The two of them swayed infinitesimally on the balls of their feet, side to side. Conversation was only a pretense that let them stand a yard apart and watch each other's chests rise and fall.

After the bright, almost empty parking lot, the restaurant seemed artificially dark and close. A man played soft piano, waiters hovered, and the major-domo seated the two of them at a small table, perilously face to face. Anna felt like a young girl. Her heart muscled against her ribs and her knees went loose under the table.

Jay ordered and ate handily a great platter of food. Anna asked for a small salad and a baked potato but couldn't finish either. They skipped coffee and dessert and returned to the parking lot before dark.

"The atmosphere in there was a little tight," Jay said, "wasn't it?"

"Thanks for coming out so soon. I felt like I was in a cloche."

The only place to stand outside the restaurant, however, was on the asphalt lot. All around Anna the metal shards of a mysterious culture were parked in orderly rows: cars and pickup trucks, their metallic paint reflecting the light of early dusk. Anna would have liked to take a walk, but the parking lot gave onto a busy street with no sidewalks.

Jay leaned against her Datsun. "Sometimes I think about putting a car on stage and choreographing a dance around it."

"You can have this one if it keeps breaking down," Anna said, raising her foot to tap the car's fender. "Damn junker."

Jay laughed. "Aren't you fond of your car?"

"I suppose I should be. But I'm annoyed at it because the clutch is going and I've only had it for a year. What about your Dodge?"

"The generic automobile?" Jay considered his car with the hooded eye of a New York art critic at a Midwest opening. "I'm kind of attached to it, though it does have certain irrefutable flaws. For one thing, it's too dirty to play with. And if I were going to put a car on the stage, I'd want something a bit more exalted. An automobile with grandeur."

Jay strolled down the line of cars and paused in front of a polished, light green Chrysler LeBaron. His shoulders rolled forward and his hands hung palms out, away from his legs. He looked like a little boy who needed to urinate.

"I like a car that's been kept up," he said, "don't you? Look how clean this LeBaron is. Don't you think you could love and respect a car like this?"

Anna considered the car doubtfully as Jay approached with delicate, ingratiating steps. He rested the pads of his fingertips on the chrome streak running along one side, touched the mirror and the door handle, and passed his open hand over the textured roof.

"Such a beautiful car," he said. "So perfect in every line. Sleeker than any human, more trustworthy than any lover." He brought his shoulders forward and rubbed them against the low roof. "*LeBaron.* May I call you LeBaron? I've watched you passing on the streets. I've wanted you for years."

Anna stiffened, but Jay went on caressing the car with his chest, ignoring her. He sidled and twisted his way around to the hood and squirmed out of his blazer without ever losing touch with the metal. The coat dropped to the ground. Anna knelt and picked it up, but Jay paid no attention. He moaned softly, his chest lying on the hood as he raised his knees and caressed the grille with his thighs. He slithered up onto the car and rolled over on his back, his eyes closed and his jaw clenched. His entire body undulated as he gasped, "Le Baron, you have carried . . . *America.*"

Slowly his throat and shoulders relaxed. He slid off the hood and stood up, looking at Anna without expression. She handed him his jacket.

"That was kind of disgusting," she said.

"Sure, but so are these cars. Big cars like this have been planking America for years. It's hard to believe they still make them."

His tone was conversational. It spooked Anna to see him change so fast. "You were pretty convincing," she said.

"I probably have a little desire for luxury, the same as whoever owns this thing. You, too, I bet. I doubt if either one of us would buy a car like this, but—be honest—wouldn't you like to go for a drive in a big gas hog like this with plenty of power and electric everything? It's part of our culture. Wouldn't you like to get behind the wheel of this baby?"

Anna nudged one of the LeBaron's tires with her toe. "I don't think I know the kind of people who'd spend this much money for a car. What do you think they'd say if they came out of the Carriage House and found you draped over their hood?"

"I imagine they would be displeased."

"But then again," she admitted, "when I was growing up, my mother had a fifty-eight Buick with a gigantic leather back seat. We used to take it to the drive-in."

"I'll bet you did," Jay said, grinning.

"No, no, we just . . ." Then she laughed, thinking of how often she'd made out in the back seat of that car. Jay stood in front of her, smiling and handsome. How much easier it would be, she thought, if they were teenagers.

Leaning forward, she kissed him softly on the lips, then told him she was going home. He tried to maintain his smile, but she could see he was disappointed. "It's not even nine o'clock," he said.

"This is all new ground for me. I have to take one step and

then another step, and not get lost. But I'd like to go out again."

He nodded. Anna walked to her car and pulled out into the Saturday-night traffic, leaving Jay standing in the lot next to his Dodge. She drove back to her farm in the warm early night with the last of the June bugs slapping against the windshield, and softer insects melting against the glass in yellow splats.

OVER THE NEXT FEW DAYS Anna took a politic view of Jay Corman. He was a couple of years older than she was; he had a daughter, almost a teenager, whom he looked after full time; and he ran a business, of sorts. Maybe his life was full enough so he wouldn't have to take over hers. He'd given her a sad face at the end of the night—but he'd let her go without complaining.

Three days later he called and told her he had a surprise, something he had to show her in person. She resisted his smiling voice over the telephone. What surprise was that?

Only in person, he insisted. Avoiding both her house and his, she agreed to meet him after work the next day beside the courthouse in Fell River. But when she parked her car in the empty municipal lot, Jay was nowhere in sight. She sat down on one of the wooden benches—and immediately heard a whistle. She stood up, but no Jay. Then another whistle, from one of the cars parked along the street. Walking toward the sound, she discovered Jay slouched behind the wheel of an enormous Chrysler Imperial, a grey fedora pulled low on his forehead.

"Ace Dude here," he said. "Wanna take a ride in this deluxe set of wheels?"

"You're kidding. You didn't buy this thing?"

"It's a friend's, but he let me have it for the night."

"And just what did you have in mind to do with it?"

"I don't know, we could have dinner at Tony's and take a moonlight drive."

"I see you've got it all planned out."

Jay sat up straight and laid his hat on the seat. "I thought of some things, but it kind of depends on you."

"That's nice to hear."

Maybe she ought to lay everything on the line, tell him, Look, my child died fifteen months ago, and now my ex-husband has moved to Fell River, all of which makes me nervous. And I hardly know you. So would you take things easy, please?

Jay looked chastened, however, without her explaining anything. "Let's go to Tony's," she offered. "I've never eaten there."

"Never eaten at Tony's in the summertime?" He was immediately brighter. "Daria would say you're neglected and underprivileged."

Tony's was a drive-in pizza and hamburger stand with a blue neon sign as large as the restaurant itself. A circle of parked cars jutted out like spokes from the round kitchen, and outdoor waitresses in short red skirts and checked aprons went from car to car. Sitting on their hoods, skinny boys drank quarts of Pepsi-Cola, and young girls in satin shorts darted over the pavement to whisper in their friends' ears.

"I come here all the time with Daria," Jay said. "She insists she likes it because of the food."

Anna relaxed in the Chrysler's massive front seat. The teenagers at the restaurant looked blind and innocent, driven toward a sexual world they knew nothing about. Their grace of movement, she thought, obscured the fact that before they were twenty, half of them would have screwed up their lives with early marriages and unwanted children. But Anna remembered the sexual obsession that had come over her the last year in high school.

"I used to go to restaurants like this in Minneapolis," she said. "I acted just like these girls, all I could think about was boys. But I was older than Daria."

"She just likes the scene. She's not interested in boys yet."

"No? She might not be possessed, but I'll bet she's interested. She's going into the seventh grade, isn't she?"

"When I was in the seventh grade," Jay said, "all I wanted to do was play soccer and baseball."

"You were a boy."

"Okay, she's interested, I see her looking around sometimes. But I figure I've a couple of years left before it gets wild."

"And then?"

He shrugged. "We'll get by."

"Where is she tonight, with a baby-sitter?"

"She's almost too old for a baby-sitter. She's at a friend's for
the night." Jay looked out at a teenage couple walking by arm
in arm, their hands stuck into each other's back pockets.
"Sometimes I think it would be easier for me if I had a boy
instead of a girl. I know what teenage boys are like, but adolescent girls are a mystery to me. I didn't know anything about
them when I was that age, and I still don't know."

"What about Daria's mother?"

"That's what I'm afraid of, that she'll get to be fourteen and
want to go back to her mother. Maybe I'm not the right model
for her. Maybe a man shouldn't bring up a teenage girl."

"Lots of women bring up boys and do a good job," Anna
said.

"But not so many men bring up girls. Sometimes I worry
about it."

After a pizza and a milkshake Jay took the river road downstream as far as the bridge at Deeter, where they crossed over
to Kentucky.

"Wouldn't you like to slide over next to me while I drive?"
he said, smiling. "It seems like the right thing, after Tony's."

"Sure." Anna laughed. "The girl is supposed to stick close
to her guy, right? Like a little puppy dog."

"Or you could drive and I'd sit next to you."

"You would?"

"If we were steadies and you wore my anklet, I would for
sure." His laughter was completely free of affectation.

"So where are we headed?"

"There's a park beside the river a few miles down."

"And that's where you usually go?"

"Anna, I haven't been parking since I was in college."

"So what are we going to do there?"

"I thought maybe we could . . . kiss and all that."

"All that?"

Jay lifted both hands from the steering wheel. "Hey, we can sit and talk about ballet and eggplants if you like. Or we could go somewhere else. I'm not trying to sneak anything over on you."

They sat facing the river in the small Kentucky park, at either end of the Chrysler's wide front seat.

"I'll be out there in a week," Jay said, gesturing into the darkness.

"Out where?"

"Working on the river, on a towboat. I do it every summer when Daria goes to Boston to see her mother. Thirty days on the river. Sometimes we go as far as New Orleans."

"Thirty straight days?"

"Twelve hours a day, seven days a week, at fourteen thirty-two an hour. Everything over forty hours is time and a half, and weekends are double time. I make a lot more money working in the engine room of one of those towboats than I ever will at dancing. Anyway, I kind of like it. I get a month of no phone calls, no visitors and no parents complaining about their kids' ballet classes. Just the river in front of me and the boat moaning through the water, day and night. Most of the guys work month on and month off all year round, but a few of us get on for just thirty days in the summer when the traffic is heaviest."

"You don't look like an engine-room type," Anna said.

"I was in the merchant marine every summer through college. I still have my card."

She meant he didn't look big enough. He was only an inch taller than she was. "A grease monkey. Isn't that what they call guys who work in the engine room?"

"I get hired on as a deckhand," he said. "Not a grease monkey."

She could always get to him. She didn't really mean to but somehow couldn't stop herself. Having put up a barrier between them, she slid part way across the seat to knock it down.

"I'm a little slow at parking," she said. "I'm out of practice."

He hunched over and put his arm around her. "Surely it's like riding a bicycle," he said. "You never forget how."

Jay lowered all four windows at once, and the muddy smell of the river engulfed them. Anna listened to the flap of tiny waves against the shore and the whine of an errant mosquito. She turned to Jay and touched his face, then kissed him. He was slow, she had to initiate every step. Maybe she'd resisted him too much, because now, when she wanted him to lead, he wouldn't. He followed her, but she was the first to put her hands on his chest, the first to pass her tongue along the inside of his lips.

Stretched diagonally across the front seat of the car, Anna removed both their shirts. Of course she remembered how the moves went. What she had forgotten was that she could feel so excited. She wanted Jay's hands on her body and passed her fingertips over his thighs so he would do the same. She stretched and spread her legs toward him. The pads of his fingers grazed her neck and breasts, so lightly she lost track of where he was touching her. He moved closer, tracing small circles on her flesh. Anna wanted him to touch her—but not to take off her underwear or his pants. She didn't want to sleep with Jay or touch his penis. She just wanted to go on lying against his shoulder while he caressed her over and over with his fingers, as if they were still in high school.

He put his mouth to hers and drew the breath out of her lungs, passing his hands over her thighs and spreading her legs even wider. Her pelvis jerked up and down, moving on its own. She wanted Jay, but she didn't want him to lose control, or to lose control herself.

Jay wanted to fuck, of course. Sex was nothing to men unless they came. Some would stop when you asked, and some wouldn't. But Anna hadn't planned on sleeping with Jay or anyone else, and her womb was unprotected. Above all else, to thy womb be true.

Now that she didn't want him to, he led. Anna lay flat on the car seat, gone limp. Wouldn't he notice? She felt his erection against her leg as he pressed his chest against her own. He kissed and kissed her—then slowly let up. And as he did, the wheedle of mosquitoes filled the car. They must have been there the whole time without her hearing, but now Jay twisted one arm behind him to fend them off. She could have kept his back clear by passing her hands up and down, but she didn't. She didn't want to move, only to lie there.

"*Damn*," Jay said, "these things are voracious."

Just be glad they're not on your balls, she thought. That made her giggle, and the next moment she was laughing under his weight.

"Sex and mosquitoes don't go together," he said, annoyed.

"Jay, can we wait?"

"Of course we can wait."

"I just want you to hold me, I'm not ready for sex. My body is, but I'm not. I need a little time."

Jay pulled his shirt on against the mosquitoes and covered both their heads with Anna's pullover. Lying together in the darkness, his breath smelled like an infant's.

"You don't have to be ready, Anna, today or any other day. If I forget myself, just tap me on the shoulder and tell me. I'll come around fast enough."

"It's not even that I want you to come around," she said. "But I'm not ready. I don't feel like an adult anymore, I feel like those kids we saw at Tony's—as if I'd never done this before. I have, but I can't remember it. Not *this*. Can you remember this from high school? Were you sleeping with girls then?"

"No, I was halfway through college before I went to bed with a woman."

"But you went parking in high school."

"A couple of times. I was a shy kid."

Anna kissed his mouth and eyes. She liked lying next to Jay in the absolute dark, half-naked, covered by his chest. When she spoke, her mouth was so close to him she felt her voice vibrate off his lips.

"I remember this feeling," she said, "except I was so young. My senior year in high school I went out with a boy named Carlos. He wanted to sleep with me and I wouldn't let him. We'd go out on Saturday night and come home before midnight and park in my driveway. My dad always waited up for me, but once I got home he'd go to bed. Usually he'd come to the door first and wave, and I'd wave back. Then he'd leave Carlos and me sitting out there in the driveway by ourselves, close to the house but half-hidden by some junipers. It was like my parents gave me their permission to sit in the car as long as I didn't stay out too late or get in trouble somewhere else. They must have known what was going on. On chilly nights we steamed up the car windows so bad you couldn't see in or out— but there was always the chance someone might walk by or rap on the window, so everything had to look good. We couldn't take our clothes off, and we weren't going to screw. Carlos wanted to, but I'd ruled it out, I just wanted him to go on touching me. I wore skirts and front-release bras to make it easier. We'd make out for two or three hours in a row, way into the middle of the night. It was the greatest sex ever. And we never screwed, even though we made out in that car almost every Saturday night for six months. I never came, of course, I didn't know what it was. Carlos came all the time in his pants, but we never talked about it. And he never complained, either. Maybe he thought nice girls shouldn't sleep with anyone. Sometimes I felt like I was using him so I could have all that sex without . . . fucking. Fucking was definitely out. I didn't want to get pregnant, and I didn't want to see Carlos's prick. I just wanted him to touch me, and since we were always right outside my house and had most of our clothes on, I trusted him and didn't have to hold back."

Jay drew her toward him, his hands on the small of her back. "And it's a little hard to trust me?"

"No, I didn't mean that."

"But it might be true. You don't know me that well."

"I don't know myself that well. It's been a long time since I've done this. Not since Kevin died."

Jay was silent for a moment. "I can be trusted," he said, "but you'll probably have to learn that for yourself over a period of time."

Would they have a period of time? Did Jay assume they'd go out again and do something like this? Anna could hardly remember what it was like to go out with a man. She felt that everything she'd ever learned had been unlearned by having a child, and having him die.

AT HOME during lunch or dinner, Anna read. She read obsessively, as she had done as a young girl—only now it was Rudolf Steiner on agriculture, William Albrecht on soils, or extension service reports on bell pepper trials. She read *American Vegetable Grower*, the Nasco farm catalog and the *Fell River Express*. In the fall she turned from agronomy to novels, and in the winter to Eskimo folktales. Often she had two or three books going at a time. She read twice as much as when Kevin was alive.

She was in the middle of a magazine article when the telephone rang. A man said without preamble, "I need your help with something."

At first she thought it was Deal from the farmhouse, then she didn't know who it was.

"It's me," Paul said, "who do you think? How many people call you up, anyway?"

It was the first time she'd heard from him since dropping him off in Fell River two weeks before. "Your voice sounds funny," she said.

"Funny peculiar or funny ha-ha?"

"Peculiar. I didn't know who you were."

"I need to talk to you," he said.

Anna had gone an entire year without talking to Paul, until the day he showed up unannounced at the local bus stop. After squatting in her house for six days and draping himself all over her life, he moved to Fell River and had never called her until today. Yet Anna was curious. She wanted to know what had happened to him.

After work she showered and changed her clothes, choosing a print blouse and a pair of flannel slacks she hadn't worn in months. She and Paul could go out for a drink or a cup of coffee, she thought, like any other divorced couple who have kept in touch. Some couples with children met on a regular basis, picking up and dropping off their kids. She and Paul still had plenty to talk about.

He stepped down from his porch wearing chino pants, a wrinkled white shirt and a large pair of polished black shoes. All his clothes looked borrowed. His pale brow glistened in the heat of the late afternoon, and the dark gap of his missing incisor made the rest of his teeth luminous.

Taking her arm, he walked her down the sidewalk under the profusion of silver maples. Although two men—two different men from the last time—sat on the porch, they didn't look over at Paul, nor he at them. He clamped Anna to his side and asked her, loudly enough for them to hear, how her week had gone.

Why should he want to impress a couple of deadbeats on an unpainted porch? Maybe he'd told them a woman was coming to visit him—someone he went out with. Feeling sorry for him, she allowed Paul to guide her along the sidewalk, and she answered his bland questions about her health and the weather. Once out of sight of the house, however, she loosened his grip on her arm. Paul was so large, and moved so clumsily in his new shoes, that she imagined he could slip and fall on her. Disengaged, walking half a pace ahead of him, she asked if there was some emergency.

He just wanted to talk to her. It had been two whole weeks.

"You mean there's nothing? I thought you said you needed help."

"I want to talk. After all, we live in the same town now."

"You're going to stay here?"

"Maybe for a while. It's a free country."

Paul kept his eyes on the irregular bricks of the sidewalk, swollen from below by the growth of tree roots.

"What was that money you got," she asked him. "That check?"

"How come you're always on my case? Do I ask about your money? It's from the welfare department."

"What for?"

"They know you can't hold down a steady job after Napa State, so they pay you something to live on."

"They send it out here?"

"I've got a friend in San Francisco who forwards it."

"But don't you work?" she asked. "Don't you want to work?"

Paul shrugged his shoulders. "Sure."

He'd offered to help at the farm, but the last thing Anna wanted was to have him involved with her work. She wasn't sure if she wanted Paul to leave town or not and picked at the question the way a child picks at a scab. At a street corner she stopped and asked him where they were going.

"It's dinnertime," he said, touching his hand to the small of her back. "Let's go out to eat."

"And what if I don't want to have dinner? Where have you got in mind?"

"Relax, Anna. You go out to lunch with your father all the time, why can't you eat one dinner with me?"

"How do you know that?"

"You told me yourself. You eat at the Bradford Hotel every other Tuesday."

But Anna hadn't told him that. She was certain she had never mentioned it to him. "Have you been talking to my father?"

"I don't even know where he lives."

Could Paul have been spying on her? She let him lead the

way to a bar and restaurant she had never been in, where they took a table near the back. Paul sat down next to her, rather than across. When he ordered a couple of beers, Anna smelled the sharp dry odor of his breath. His tongue came out to wet his lips—and she could not remember ever touching that tongue with her own. Of course she had, hundreds of times, but she couldn't remember it. And the papery, acrid odor of his breath was nothing she had ever smelled before.

Anna sat back in her chair, maintaining a distance between them. She didn't want Paul's knee to brush up against her own or his hand to reach out suddenly and take hold of hers. Still, she wanted to hear him talk.

Because Paul was Kevin's father, Anna thought she had something to learn from him—yet she couldn't manage to steer the conversation to their past, or to anything Paul didn't want to talk about. At one point she asked him what he was doing the day Kevin died. He started to answer but went off on a tangent about the Golden Gate Bridge, San Francisco and Mexican immigrants to the city. When Anna asked him about his plans for the coming months, he answered with a diatribe about the fate of harp seals in the Atlantic. He was perfectly clever, he had the crazy man's perspicacity in ignoring what he didn't want to talk about and in directing the conversation to his own topics.

"So," he asked her, "have you been going out with anyone lately?"

Anna waved her hand over the table, dismissing the question.

"No, really. How's your sex life been since you came here?"

Paul asked the question as if her time in Fell River were all of a piece, ignoring Kevin's death and the months that followed. Anna was unwilling to explain what he should have known already and stared with satisfaction at the gap in his teeth. He didn't look much different from a bum off the street.

"Is that what you wanted to ask? Is that why you called me up?"

"No," he said mildly, "I just wondered about it. Is it so bad to ask?"

"I haven't slept with anyone since Kevin died."

She didn't tell him how close she had come only three nights before, parked with Jay across the river in Kentucky. If her sexual dormancy was breaking at last, it was nothing she wanted to show Paul.

"Maybe it's just the summertime," he said, "but I've been feeling pretty horny myself these days."

Men were so loose with their language, Anna thought. "Horny" was not a word she would have used about herself—yet wasn't that what she felt? Only the night before she had woken out of a dream in which she and Jay had walked into the woods naked and lain down together on a bed of leaves.

Paul ordered an appetizer and a sirloin steak. His expression softened as he ate, his mouth closing around large pieces of meat. His brow was smooth and white. For five silent minutes it seemed as if he'd forgotten Anna's presence.

"Why was it," she asked, "that you came back to Fell River?"

"I just came. I was thinking about Kevin, so I came."

"What were you thinking?"

"I missed him. I thought if he were alive, he'd be playing baseball. Little League or something. He could've played shortstop, where all the action is. I would have taken him to the games and worked out with him in practice, hit him some grounders."

Anna wanted to believe him. She wanted to believe Paul had come to Fell River because of Kevin, and that when he sat on the front porch of the house on Hinman Street he thought about his son, and when he wore the lost expression he sometimes had, it was because Kevin had died. She wanted him to be miserable for an honest reason.

"He's been dead for over a year now," she said.

"I had the feeling, so I got on a bus. Don't you ever do anything illogical, something in spite of yourself? Or do you always keep cool? You look so cool and reserved."

Anna thought of how she had cried herself to sleep on her bedroom floor for a month running, unable to touch the mattress she had sometimes shared with Kevin. Or of how she felt the day she tore his room apart, sweating and wild. But maybe other people thought she never lost her composure. What did anyone know of another's grief?

It didn't seem to her that Paul suffered—but maybe he hid it the same way she did. Maybe when he saw other fathers playing catch with their sons he broke out crying and turned away. Of course when Kevin was alive Paul hadn't played much ball with him. He was always working or busy with some project. Maybe in his present lazy incarnation, he and Kevin would have become better friends.

As if she had spoken out loud, Paul said, "I guess I should've spent more time with him when I had the chance."

"That's what I think every day," she said. Her stiffness toward Paul melted. "I should've spent more time with him and given him more attention. I shouldn't have left him alone so much. If I'd ever known . . ."

Paul leaned forward and took her hand. "You couldn't have known."

"No, I couldn't. But I go on missing him."

She started to cry—but at once Paul's assailant breath made her look up. He was practically on top of her, leaning over the corner of the table with his eyes on her face. He looked rapacious, nowhere close to tears. She pulled back and yanked away her hand.

"No, no," he said. "You should cry. It's good for you."

"Good for *you*, you mean. When have you ever cried? When have you ever missed him?" She stood up with a jerk, smashing her knees on the bottom of the table.

"Don't leave, Anna. Don't get angry. We could go to a movie or something."

"I don't want to do anything with you. Every time I see you I feel like I've been had. And you can pay for your end of this dinner, too."

Paul opened his wallet slowly. "All I've got is a fiver," he said, bringing his face closer to hers.

Anna pulled back and threw a ten-dollar bill on the table. She wanted to say, "Fuck it," or call him an asshole, but those were men's words. "You pay it," was all she said. She spun past the tables and pushed her way out the door. Before turning the first corner she looked back to make sure Paul wasn't following her, then broke into a jog down High Street to get back to her car before he did.

FELL RIVER remained a dangerous place to Anna. There Paul lived an unknown life among strangers, there boys the same age as Kevin played tag on front lawns or swung from the branches of trees. And there Jay was alone in his house. He called Anna after taking Daria to the airport and mentioned again that he only had a few days left before his month on the river began.

It felt dangerous, as well, for Anna to invite him to her house. She felt like a young girl around Jay, driven by something greater than hormonal desire, yet bound by a flat, adolescent perspective. She desired Jay but resisted his life. It was only because he was leaving for an entire month that she relaxed enough to ask him out for dinner and exposed to him the flimsy arrangements of her homelife.

She arranged her schedule so that when Jay came he'd find her doing a powerful, oversized job: not down on her knees in the dirt pruning an interminable row of late tomato plants, nor rogueing the fields already in production, but at the wheel of the expensive new John Deere.

One of the farm's current projects was the rejuvenation of a forty-acre field on the eastern edge of the property. Shelley's family had rented the piece to a neighboring farmer, and he had corned the land close to death. After twenty years of repeated ensilage harvests and wet-weather use of heavy machinery, the compacted soil was thick and cloddy, almost devoid of organic matter. The drainage was now the worst of any ground on the farm, and pools of water stood in the low sections after every rain. Deal had seeded the field to winter rye in the fall and planned to till it under in April, but the new tractor failed to arrive in time and the rye shot beyond the succulent stage into stalk. The old twenty-horsepower 9-N Ford bogged down before it, and the rye was fully headed before the new John Deere finally arrived at the local agency. Deal drove the tractor out from the edge of town, and he and Anna attached it to the farm's two-ton Miller disk.

The disk made a glory of tilling the rye. In two passes, the angled blades chopped and distributed the stalks throughout the top profile of the soil. It was an illusion, Anna knew, to think that heavy machinery made one's work more signifi-cant—yet she wanted to be on board the tractor when Jay came, rather than down on her knees.

Rounding a far corner of the field, she saw Jay walking toward her over the uneven, freshly turned ground. She cut through the rye to meet him and swung out of the cab like a truck driver, the engine still running. Jay smiled and was glad to see her—but soon turned his attention to the tractor. He touched the massive weighted tires and the new coulters of the disk. "This outdoes a LeBaron by plenty."

Anna offered to show him how the tractor worked, and with Jay perched against one of the fenders, they bumped out over the rough ground. She lowered the disk with a clank, the en-gine burrowed to a deeper vibration, and the tractor waded through the rye. Soil moisture was perfect for the job. Churned between the polished blades of the disk, the earth poured out between the blades, carrying strips of green leaves and stalk. For an instant, the soil behaved like a liquid.

"How many people would it take to do this by hand?" Jay asked over the pitch of the engine.

"Dozens," Anna yelled. "Hell, hundreds, you couldn't do this job by hand. They used to do it with animals, but they could never have chopped up a stand this well."

"Any chance of driving this rig myself?" Jay's expression was as hopeful as a fourteen-year-old boy's on a back road, trying to get behind the wheel of his dad's car.

Anna showed him the hydraulics and hovered over the controls. He drove like a beginner, careful of the slightest bump or veer, trying not to waver an inch off the line between tilled and untilled ground. With the wind behind them, dust rose and swirled around their heads. Jay, completely absorbed, blinked his eyes as he looked back to check on the disk.

After a couple of passes Anna began to resent his exaggerated concentration. With his innocent manner he had somehow taken possession of both her tractor and her job, and now drove around and around the field, having to all appearances forgotten her.

When Deal came across the road and stood at the edge of the field, ready for his shift, Anna traded places with Jay and drove the last round herself. She shut off the tractor this time, jumped down to the ground and introduced the two men.

They shook hands, then stood facing each other with their arms folded—Deal wearing his blue work pants from Montgomery Ward, Jay in a pair of beige corduroys—and talked farm machinery and cars. The farm's old 9-N Ford was a flathead, and Jay had owned a flathead pickup in high school. "Treat a flathead right and it never quits," Deal said. Jay agreed, nodding his head, his arms still held against his chest.

It was the Old Boys club all over again. When Anna met a woman she didn't know, they were usually slow to talk. They had to scout each other's reactions first and discover what camp they were in regarding men. How much easier it was, she thought, for two men to meet and start a conversation. They got onto cars or pro football and acted as if they had known each other for years. It hardly made any difference if they were both decent men like Deal and Jay or if one of them was a redneck lout who thought all women were whores. Any two men could stand around with their arms folded, rocking on their heels and talking about automobiles. One of them would have owned a '48 Merc as a kid, and the other would have been intimate with a Chevy Impala. One followed the Packers and the other the Dolphins, and none of it had anything to do with women.

After ten minutes, Deal mounted the tractor and drove off to finish the field. As they walked back to Anna's house, Jay asked her if it had been wrong for him to be driving.

"I don't think so, but I'm not sure. We loan out the trucks sometimes, but the tractor's brand new."

"If Deal were unhappy about it, would he have said something?"

"Probably not until later. But if he'd been upset, I would have noticed, and I didn't."

"All these years in farm country," Jay said, touching her arm, "and I never drove a tractor. I'm glad I got the chance."

His gentle tone, after his talk with Deal about trucks and machinery, surprised her. As they walked the path to her house, Jay snapped off a milkweed and placed the end of the green stalk on the back of his hand, where it bled a white circle. He slid out his tongue and nudged the surface tension of the ring.

"Don't," said Anna, "it's poisonous. And it's bitter."

"If it's so poisonous," Jay said laughing, "how do you know it's bitter?"

"I tried it. Just once."

"You would do that, wouldn't you?" he said, and laughed.

"Are you always so easy to get along with, Jay Corman? Don't you have days with low spirits?"

"Of course. You want me to invite you over the next time it happens?"

"Yes, I do."

"It wouldn't work, I'd pull out of it if you came over."

"What if you get blue next month when you're out on the river?"

"I'll write you a nasty letter and send it from the next lock. You shouldn't doubt I can be a grumpy son of a bitch sometimes, just like everyone else."

They went up the brick walkway to Anna's house. Her lawn was unmowed and the living room cluttered. Books and magazines lay on top of her desk. A couple of shirts, a tennis racquet and a can of balls had been thrown on the couch, and her bicycle rested upside down in the middle of the floor with both wheels off and the chain in a pan of kerosene.

"Not much time for housecleaning," Anna said. She cleared the couch so Jay could sit down, climbed the ladder to her room to change her clothes and set to work on dinner. There was still Boston lettuce from the fields, as well as broccoli, tomatoes and onions. Anna slid a package into the oven as Jay glanced through her library of garden books. The salad made, she set the table—then noticed Jay looking at her. She went back to the sink. She'd been humming some song unconsciously. It took her a couple of minutes to remember what it was, from Neil Young.

> Try to be sure right from the start,
> For only love can break your heart.

Had Jay recognized the song? Like dreams, music was moored to the subconscious, and somehow that word "love" had crept in. Anna spent extra time cleaning up the counter, deliberately humming another song. Finally she announced dinner. She set the salad on the table and brought out the package of fettucine Alfredo from the oven.

Jay laughed as he sat down, pointing a long finger at the Italian dish in its crimped aluminum pan. "This here don't look much like country woman's fixin's," he said.

Anna jumped in his face. "I worked from eight to six today with twenty minutes off for lunch, so I didn't have much time to cook the fancy meal. And as for being a country woman, I farmed my first five years inside the city limits of Eugene, Oregon. You can eat straight salad if you want."

Jay raised both hands and turned his head aside in mock humility. Perhaps she'd overreacted, but his ironic tone had gone straight up her spine. Sometimes Jay's easygoing manner grated on her. It was ridiculous, she knew; all her desires were contradictory. They ate slowly and politely until the conversation thawed.

Anna let him help clean up. They washed and dried at the sink, their arms touching repeatedly, then sat down on the sofa for coffee. The chirp of crickets and the high croak of tree frogs came through the open door.

Jay said, "You've never told me anything about Kevin."

Involuntarily, she looked aside at the empty space that had been Kevin's room. The light-colored marks of the wall partitions still stood out on the oak floor. Could a stranger feel Kevin's presence here? But Jay wasn't a stranger. He was a man she had thought about going to bed with.

"Tell me about him. What did he look like?"

"His hair was too long," she said, throwing herself at a detail. "He never wanted his hair cut, he said he was going to be an Indian. He told everyone at day care, 'When I grow up I'm going to be an Indian.' "

She looked at Jay. Maybe that was enough, maybe she didn't have to say any more. But he looked back at her, waiting.

"He got kicked out of day care. I know that sounds ridiculous. Probably they were kicking me and Paul out. They said Kevin couldn't stay out of the trees and he couldn't stay quiet and he wouldn't keep his shoes on. Can you believe that? They were lucky he kept his *clothes* on. My son was a wildman, an original. One Sunday morning he woke me up by putting canned peach slices on my eyes—and then he ate them for breakfast. Sometimes he'd get the giggle fits with his friend Greg and they'd laugh for an hour. I hated to stop them even in a restaurant, because they had such a great time. Kevin always wanted to fly in an airplane, and he never did. He loved big words. When he learned a new word he'd use it every hour for a couple of days. 'That's very *aggravating*,' he'd say, or, 'Let's go to the *cinema*.' He was a little afraid of dogs. He slept like a stone at night, you could tromp around in his bedroom and his breathing wouldn't even change—but if you mentioned his name, he woke up immediately. He used to answer the telephone by saying, 'Is that you?' It fooled everyone."

This was like falling out of the sky. She'd have a wonderful fall, she'd tell Jay all about Kevin, and then she'd hit the ground.

"What did he look like?"

Anna glanced up at the slight change in Jay's voice. Although the colors inside the house had faded, and then the light itself, she could see his eyes were moist. His face was soft. He wanted to know about her and Kevin—so she told him, with no idea of what she was supposed to get in return. In the end she cried, as she hadn't done since the fire.

Somehow it was safe to tell him. She felt he would keep the information without ever using it against her. She cried against his chest, breathing at twice his speed, inhaling the pungent odor of his body. Perhaps it would be all right to love Jay—to love someone other than Kevin.

"I'm so afraid of you," she whispered.

"Why afraid?"

"Because I should have been stronger before we met."

"I'm not going to stop you from growing stronger."

She didn't know if that was true or just another thing men said. But Jay could not have faked his tears, nor the catch in his voice. She asked him to come upstairs.

She hadn't exactly planned to go to bed with him—but she'd thought about it. She had bought a new tube of contraceptive jelly but hadn't allowed herself to get out her diaphragm, unused for almost two years. Now, as Jay stood beside the window staring out into the night, she looked through a pair of old suitcases to find it, rummaging among winter clothes and half-forgotten journals.

He was gentle at making love, almost somber. Anna felt only half as excited as she'd been the week before when they parked by the river, but she liked the way they moved together, neither one nor the other leading.

Afterward they drifted toward sleep. Jay was stretched out beneath her, the small pad of flesh next to his shoulder cushioning her head. Already his breathing was slow and steady. Through the south window, Anna heard a fox's high yelp— reminding her of some other animal. After a drowsy moment she recognized it. The cry sounded like the bark of a seal. When Kevin was only a year old Anna had carried him down to a beach in San Francisco close to the Golden Gate, and they'd found a pair of seals in the water. Kevin whirled in his carrier, never taking his eyes off them until they swam out to sea.

In the last reach before sleep, Anna realized that the vivid picture of seals with baleful eyes and long lashes was more than what she remembered, it was a dream. How beautiful were the images of dreams. She tried to steer the dream to Kevin so she could watch him as he stood up boldly in his carrier—then tried to hold on to the vision of the two seals swimming through the translucent waves. But having realized it was a dream, she could not go back. Beside her, Jay twitched and his breathing grew even slower. In the morning, she thought, she would wake before him. She'd lie still and watch him sleep in the first light, as the sparrows and towhees sang along the fence rows.

TWO WEEKS LATER she received a letter from Pittsburgh, written by Jay on two different sheets of paper, one in pen and one in pencil.

Dear Anna,

I'm on the *Bessie Jackson* getting used to the river again. I went home that morning, packed and closed up my house, and took off for Cairo. Six hours later I was tightening up barge cables with my thirty-pound ratchet, and by late afternoon we were on the river.

It's not very romantic out here—no Huck Finn and his raft. We run nonstop and try to cover 200 miles a day every day. That's all we do, just ride these big engines up and down the river. The Ohio never stops flowing, and the engines never stop running. Unless something goes wrong they'll run nonstop, upstream and down for ten thousand hours before their next overhaul. I do like the *BJ*, though. It's an older boat with a beaming grace, not one of those new river-specific tows, all square and low and efficient.

I read a lot, and watch the river. Even though we ooze oil and pollute the air with diesel exhaust and all the crap boats turn loose— at least we lead the river life. Everything else fades away. I forget about dancing and Daria and the rest of the world. Even the night we spent together seems distant.

I was up in the wheelhouse with the pilot, Bill Zank, when we passed your farm. But it was one A.M. and I didn't see any lights on. Bill knew your house, the way he knows everything else on the river.

We drop off coal, cement and scrap iron in Pittsburgh in two days (I'm talkin' river talk now) and pick up sheet steel, oil and chemicals for the trip downstream. If it looks like we'll pass by Fell River during daylight hours, I'll give you a call from the Gallipolis lock upstream, and maybe we can wave. I'll be headed back to Cairo, and from there on to New Orleans.

I'm glad we had that night at your house.

"Love, Jay," it was signed.

A few nights later, Anna returned from delivering a truck-load of eggplants to the farm's broker in Fell River, and found a message from Shelley on the kitchen table. In fourteen hours, if his boat kept to schedule, Jay would pass by Indian Trouble Point and would be on the lookout for her.

Early the next morning, Anna woke to one of the heaviest fogs of the summer. The fields directly beyond her house faded into the mist, and the farmhouse and barn were invisible. After breakfast she worked for an hour among the beets—a crop that didn't suffer for being touched when wet—then leaned her hoe against a fence post and set out for the point.

Save for the temperature, it might have been a winter day. The fog silenced the birds and muffled all other sounds. At the edge of the fields, butterfly weed, Queen Anne's lace and early asters stood erect and colorless, dripping with moisture.

Catalpas and willows lined the bank, below which tiny waves lapped against the shore and raised the smell of saturated mud. Near the end of the point, Anna catwalked down the trunk of a fallen sycamore and crouched on it just above waterline. Ten yards out the river disappeared.

Nine o'clock came and went with no sign of Jay's or any other boat. Hunkered down on the isolated tree trunk, Anna gave herself to the creamy, secretive fog, allowing her thoughts to travel free of harvests and farmwork. Nine-thirty. Completely lulled, she looked up at some change in the atmosphere, an infinitesimal grooming of the air. She felt, rather than heard it: a minuscule bolus of pressure: a sound. It came from nowhere, neither upstream nor down. A hum, a disruption no louder than the belly of a toad flopping on damp ground, it disappeared and then returned.

It was a boat. Lifting itself out of the distance, the sound divided into the separate beats of a throb, coming from everywhere, like the fog. It's furry diesel pulse grew louder and closer, until Anna feared the boat might crush her against the bank. *It's on me,* she thought, and scrambled up the tree trunk. She stepped back, poised for escape, and yelled Jay's name into the throat of the noise.

Unheeding, the boat came on. Anna stood on the balls of her feet, staring into the white wall. Somewhere overhead the sun was shining, for the fog had turned a milky color. Then she heard Jay shout.

"*Hey Anna,* I think we're going by Slate's Point. I can't hear you if you're there because of the engines. I've been thinking about you. I like you a lot. I thought we could wave but . . . it's so foggy. Send me a letter to Cairo. And a raspberry pie. We're turning the point right now."

Even as he spoke the engines changed pitch. How had he known when to yell? Anna stood on the sodden, muffled grass of the bank, peering into the opaque mist—then jumped back at a new sound. A two-foot wall of water whistled through the bushes and scrub at the edge of the river, slapping the muddy banks. The wake of the lead barges came out of the fog in a streak, headed for the end of the point and disappeared into open water.

A half hour later the swirling fog yielded to sunlight. The Kentucky bank of the river appeared and disappeared, and in twenty minutes more the last tatters of mist vanished under the expanded blue sky of full summer.

Dear Jay,

I heard you when you passed by—I was standing on the shore. I loved how your words came out of nowhere, and then you were gone.

So I made you a pie. That's what you said, wasn't it? Afterward I could hardly remember, it seemed so strange. But I took an hour off in the middle of tomato harvest and picked raspberries. Deal looked at me like I'd lost my wits, and told me I'd get covered with chigger bites. I did, but here's the pie.

Jay, what if I like you best in the fog? Maybe you could come to my house after dark, the way Cupid came to Psyche. We could speak and make love in whispers, and you could leave before dawn.

I'm a restless woman. Maybe we could see each other every once in a while. Maybe we could meet next time at the roller rink. Or on the Ferris wheel at the county fair. Is there a motel in Cairo? Let's go out on the river in two boats and talk back and forth in the fog. I'm still a little scared.

But I've been thinking about you, too.

She signed it "Love, Anna."

CHAPTER 5

— ❧ —

THE DAY AFTER JAY CAME HOME Anna took the afternoon off and drove to Fell River. They had agreed to meet at his house, but she had to knock three times before Jay heard her and opened the door.

He wore a headband, a damp T-shirt and a pair of gym shorts, and breathed as hard as if he'd been running around a track. The living room furniture behind him was pushed back from the varnished wood floor, and Chuck Berry's "School Days" played at high volume on the stereo.

"Come on in. Have a seat, how've you been?"

"I've interrupted you."

"No, no, I'm out of breath . . . I've been at this long enough." Jay leaned back against the wall holding one hand against his chest. "It's so great, though . . . to have space and a good floor. And Chuck Berry! Do you know this song? You must."

Anna nodded.

"I heard him play once in a bar in New York," Jay said. "It was a great show, all sex and rock and roll. He had wild yellow eyes. Just listen to this."

Jay stepped barefooted across the floor, lifted the needle and set it down again at the start of the song. "This is mad music," he said. "It's disruptive and wild. I'm surprised kids didn't run out of school when they heard it."

As Berry's raucous guitar flooded the living room, Jay stepped onto the floor and danced, his head tilted back and his feet as skittery as a colt's.

What was the way of men that was always strange to Anna? At her farm, Jay had taken over the job of disking in a matter of minutes—but here in his house, she couldn't even take over his attention. Having just stepped inside the door, she didn't feel like dancing to a song that was all sex and rock and roll.

Jay turned off the stereo, dried his face with a towel and steered her into the kitchen for a late lunch. He did all the talking: about dance, and Daria, and his month on the river. Twice he touched her forearm. What did he expect of her on a sunny Tuesday afternoon? She would rather have met him at the Ferris wheel.

He invited her upstairs to see the rest of his house—Daria's room and his own. Standing in front of the windows overlooking the Fell from his bedroom, he circled his arm around her waist. Anna glanced down furtively at his arm, then across at his profile, trying to place Jay in the history of her affections. She couldn't do it. She could hardly remember him at all.

The white walls of the room were empty save for a single photograph of Daria. The afternoon sunlight, strained through elm and maple leaves, tinted the walls a light green, and the smell of newly mown grass filled the room. Jay embraced her from behind, held his hands against her chest and grazed the back of her neck with his lips. He pulled off his shirt, walked her to his bed and began to undress her. He was full of kisses.

Anna wished she had come after dark. The room was too bright, and Jay too fast. He removed her dress, ran his fingers over her thighs, kissed the webbed skin between her toes—and put his mouth between her legs.

"Don't," she said, "I have my period."

"I don't care, I'm a horny dog. I've been at sea for twenty years. I love your blood."

"You'll ruin your sheets."

"I'll get new ones."

She pressed her hands gently against his temples and drew his head toward her own. She didn't want him to see. But he kissed her eyes closed and his hands kept moving: across her chest and down inside her hips. When he stripped off her underwear and came into her, she felt the pressure of his body on her own, but her mind stayed as clear white as the walls of the room. Jay thrust forward, moaning, his diligent fingers still at work.

Afterward, when Jay stirred and opened his eyes, Anna pulled a sheet over their heads, covering them up the way he'd done when they parked by the river. The sheet only muted the light.

"I don't know how old you are," Anna said. "You could be a stranger."

"I'm forty-one."

"Are you divorced?"

"I got divorced five years ago."

Anna pulled herself up on one elbow and grasped the sheet with her other hand. "I want to know if you go out with other women."

"I have some friends around town."

"What does that mean?"

"It means . . . there are a couple of women I sleep with sometimes."

With the back of her hand, Anna wiped away the beaded perspiration from her forehead. "I'm no good as a light-weight," she said. "I don't know if I'm good for any of this."

"I don't want it to be lightweight. I won't sleep with anyone else."

"I want to know if you'll lie to me."

"Anna, be merciful. You say that like you're driving nails."

"I want to know if you're honest."

Jay looked at her face to face, their eyes no more than a foot apart. "Usually, but not always."

"You tell lies."

"Not exactly, but sometimes without actually telling lies I'm not quite honest."

"Will you lie to me?"

Jay looked at her but didn't answer.

"Will you?" she insisted.

"I don't know."

"You will, you'll lie to me."

Her voice was calm. It wasn't the voice of one lover turning against another, but that of someone who stumbles across the truth and doesn't know what to do with it.

"When we're like this," she said, "you ought to believe you'll never lie to me. It might not be true, but you ought to believe it now."

"I'm so hot for you I could promise you anything. But haven't you said things at times like this, and found you couldn't live up to them later on?"

"I'm sure I have." She unfolded the sheet over their heads and blinked against the light. A network of wrinkles stood out around Jay's eyes and mouth. Without the softening influence of the sheet, Anna knew her own face must look as bright and stark as his. "I wasn't ready," she said.

Jay rested his hands on her waist. "You looked a little awkward over lunch, but I thought we might cure it like this."

"You're going to *cure* me, Jay Corman?"

Under her drill-press look he lowered his eyes. "I could use a little curing myself. It's not just one or the other of us."

"Then how come I always feel shy around you?" She stood up, pulled the sheet off the bed and walked across the room. "How come it always seems like you've got everything you need already?"

"I don't."

"No?" Anna looked at Daria's photograph hanging on the wall and cocked her head.

"She's growing up, and one of these days she's going to leave. Every time she visits her mother I think she won't come back."

Jay's voice was plaintive, but his posture belied him. He lay stretched out on the bed, completely naked, his penis folded calmly over one thigh. Was it Jay in particular, or was sex always easier for men?

"And you have those friends of yours," Anna said. "You don't need me."

"Those are easy arrangements where no one gets hurt. This is something else."

Anna stepped toward the bed holding the sheet against her shoulders, her hair curling in the damp air. "Aren't you going too fast?"

"I was attracted to you the minute I saw you at that party. Weren't you? Tell the truth."

"Maybe. But it's easier for a man." She stood above him next to the bed. "What'll you say later?"

Jay laughed. "You mean after I've stolen your virtue? I don't know anything about later. You want to beat on me for that?"

She did. She wanted to beat on him for looking so relaxed and happy and naked. But in the end, through pure good spirits, he broke down her resistance. She lay down on the bed beside him and relaxed, her chest against his, while they talked into the late afternoon.

At eight o'clock that night they sat on stools in the Plantation Bar, eating nachos with cheese and drinking shots of tequila. Anna rested her arm on Jay's shoulder. "This is getting easier," she said. "But I better stop drinking before you have to carry me out of here."

In the last light they walked down to the river end of town, a little drunk, swerving around the young ginkgoes and sweet gums planted at the edge of the sidewalk. Stride and stride, Jay's hand kept contact with her thigh, palming it softly, like a retriever mouthing a duck.

"You working on something down there?" she asked.

"One beautiful womanly leg," he said, "with good strong muscles."

There was no one else on the streets. Anna slowed, turned toward Jay and cupped the front of his pants with her hand. "And this muscle that keeps appearing?"

"Oh dear. That's the Repulsive Bulge. It just gets a man into trouble."

"You in trouble right now?"

"I think I am." Jay laughed. "You know how it goes when a horny dog comes back from his travels."

"I don't think I do. How does it go?"

"The Bulge gets insistent. It keeps rising up, over and over."

"Maybe this horny dog Bulge just needs to be petted." Glancing up and down the empty sidewalk, Anna slid her hand inside Jay's pants. His eyes went hazy. "Not all that repulsive," she whispered.

At the railroad tracks near the end of High Street they heard the first diesel whistle of a train, from a grade crossing at the eastern edge of town. They turned, walked out along the edge of the university's empty playing fields and sat down on the grass only thirty feet from the tracks. The train whistled its way past the water plant, the baseball fields, the feed store and the first university buildings.

Jay wormed his hand inside Anna's yard-sale cotton dress— and snapped one of its shoulder straps. "Oh dear," he said.

Had he meant to break it? Anna couldn't tell from his tone of voice. As the train whistle sounded from the Fort Street crossing, he reached behind her and fumbled with the straps of her bra.

"No you don't." She rolled onto her back and pinned his hand behind her.

"Yes I do." She heard him smiling in the dark.

He kissed her and smoothed her breasts with his free hand. The diesel engines grew louder and louder, until the train leapt into sight around the corner of a building, its elliptic headlight sluing across the empty field. Anna struggled to sit up—they were too close to the tracks. But Jay leaned across her and with a small laugh popped the second strap of her dress. *"Damn it,"* she said, *"no."* The first locomotive thundered by as she hooked a leg around Jay, rolled out from beneath him and pinned his arms. She pressed her chest against his face and squeezed him with her legs. The front of her dress fell down and the hem rode up over her waist. It wasn't a fight, Jay was much too willing.

The freight cars boomed and rumbled past, one car after another, the iron wheels shrieking against the curved rails. The air smelled of hot metal. Anna, still on top of Jay, pushed his

head to the ground with one hand and stripped off her underpants and pad with the other.

"You want blood?" she screamed. "You want your mouth
covered with blood? Then *here*." From her seat on his chest she
slid forward and kneaded her cunt into his face and yelled down
at him, "Are you a horny dog?"

Jay screamed back between her legs, "I am, I am!"

The train rolled on, twenty cars and twenty more and twenty
more, the shriek of the wheels unending. Truck trailers swayed
by on top of flatcars as Anna leaned back, unfastened Jay's pants
and lowered them to his knees. His skin was white, his prick as
dark as an eggplant. She mounted it, everything flowing, and
they mated like feverish hyenas, howling at each other in the
dark.

Jay came, the caboose passed with a *whoosh*, and Anna lay
forward in the expanding silence, her buttocks exposed to the
air. She looked out over the field and across the tracks, but
there was no sign of anyone. Beneath her, Jay's chest began to
shake.

"What are you laughing at?"

"You're wilder than Chuck Berry!" he said. "You're dangerous!"

"Hey, you ripped my dress apart. You're the pigdog who
started all this." But looking down at him, she laughed. "Before
your next engagement," she said, "you might want to scrub up
a little, starting with your face."

"How about my shirt, it's covered with blood."

"Yes, try explaining that to the police," Anna said, laughing.

"No problem, officer, it's nothing at all, really. I was just
watching the train go by with my woman here, and she pushed
me down and rubbed her pussy all over my face until I could
hardly breathe. After a few drinks she loosens up like that."

"Shut up, Jay. I feel a little shy now."

"Shy!" he said. "I don't think so."

"It was just the train that made me crazy."

"It made you beautiful."

"And I shouldn't drink tequila."

Anna pulled her underwear on and reached for the straps of her dress, both of which had ripped off flush. With a small stick she poked two holes below the seam in front, and managed to tie the straps back on.

Jay turned his shirt inside out. In a water fountain at the far end of the soccer field he splashed and scrubbed. Anna washed as well and drank, and then they walked back up High Street toward the center of town, listening to the whir of nighthawks in the black sky. Twice Jay broke out laughing; he had the most uncalculated laugh of anyone she knew.

Directly in front of them on Main Street, a man stumbled out of the ice-cream shop into their path, holding up a precarious cone in one hand and yelling back inside, "You bet your ass I will." In the shop, a pair of customers stared intently at the tubs of ice cream. Jay made to go around the man—but it was Paul. Anna dropped her arm from Jay's and took a half step away from him.

Paul straightened up, looking pleased with himself, and turned. "Look who's here," he said. "It's Anna, née Delaney. And some guy with her. Christ, when it rains it pours. You should have come by five minutes ago, the guy in here gives me free ice-cream cones. See this one? No limit."

Anna said nothing. After a moment Jay asked, "How come?"

"I do him certain favors. If you want to know. Hey, Anna, aren't you going to introduce us?"

Jay's eyebrows arched when she told him that Paul was Kevin's father. She had mentioned Paul's name before but never said he was in Fell River. In fact, after not hearing from Paul in over a month, she had started to think he'd left town. But here he was, bobbing up and down in front of her, a bear on the sidewalk, his ice-cream cone dripping a raspberry streak across his knuckles. He extended his left hand to shake with Jay—who started with his right, then switched to his left, creating a hesitation in which the two men shook hands longer than normal, with the wrong hands.

Paul's cone was melting fast in the heat. He licked twice around the outside and made a face. "Terrible. I don't know why they gave me this flavor. You want this cone, Anna? You?"

They didn't. He tilted the cone upside down at the curb, twirled it fastidiously into the pavement and wiped his hands on his pants. "Where are you folks headed?"

Again, Anna didn't answer. Jay said, "Somewhere, though we haven't talked about where. We might go for something to eat. Do you think, Anna?"

She looked into the distance, less animated than a stone, but Paul jumped in and said, "Let's go to the Eat Here Now. That's cozy, and it's close."

They took a table in the restaurant's open patio and ordered deep-fried potato skins and a couple of beers. Anna sat upright; she didn't want a beer. The waitress brought them three by mistake, but Paul waved them onto the table. "No problem," he said, "we'll drink 'em." The waitress looked like a college girl. She wore a short plaid skirt and a bright streak of makeup on either cheek. Paul claimed she was making it with a friend of his—but in fact, he said, she was a lez. "They're all gay in here. The bartender's queer as bait. This isn't much of a restaurant, they're just laundering drug money."

He ate the potato skins with his fingers and scarfed up his share before Anna and Jay were half-done. Stretching his feet out under the table, he gave Anna a steady look.

"So what have you two been up to?"

"We went for a walk," Anna said.

"Funny how your dress got ripped. You look like you've been rolling around on the ground." With his thumb and forefinger he picked a blade of grass out of Anna's hair.

Jay said, "I just got back into town, so we celebrated with a few shots of tequila."

Anna should have warned him about Paul. She'd been icy since they met him on the street. Couldn't Jay get the message?

"Been out of town, eh? You've got some blood on your shirt, bud."

"Oh, here. . . ."

"Yeah, and it looks like you cut your lip, too. How 'bout that?"

Anna saw for the first time a tiny smear of blood beneath Jay's left nostril. She touched her face at the same spot, trying to show him without having Paul see. Jay laughed and wiped his lip with some beer.

He was going to play the fool, while Paul's gaze came around and settled on her breasts.

"Never thought I'd see you this loose, Anna—your dress ripped, and pieces of grass in your hair. Hell, I guess it's summertime, isn't it?" He nudged Jay's arm playfully with his fist.

"And the livin' is easy," Jay said.

Paul broke into a smile. "So tell me, what's eight inches long and fits in the palm of Nancy's hand?"

"Look, Paul . . ."

"Ronnie's ray gun. It may be old, but it's bold."

Anna looked away. There were only five or six other customers on the patio.

"Did you hear the one about the guy who went out with his girlfriend for a whole year and still couldn't get laid? One night he gets so frustrated he whips out his dick and lays it on the kitchen counter. He's got a rod about a mile long and he says, 'Look, honey, you know what this is?'

" 'Oh my goodness,' she says, 'that looks like my mom's meat loaf. She must have left it out of the fridge by mistake.'

"Jesus Christ, the guy thinks, this girl is a moron.

"So a couple of days later he comes over to visit. There's no answer at the door, so he goes upstairs and looks through the keyhole into the girl's room, and she's in there with one of her girlfriends, suckin' and fuckin' like crazy. He springs another rod a mile long and bursts through the door. 'Now,' he says, 'you girls know what this is?'

" 'It sure does look like one of those Italian sausages my mom buys down at the deli,' the girl says. 'She loves to eat those.'

" 'Oh shit,' the guy says. 'Where is this mother of yours?'

" 'Probably downstairs watchin' TV.'

"So the guy runs downstairs, and there's a foxy-looking woman down there watching an X-rated movie on the cable. He walks up and sticks his dick right in her face. 'Look,' he says, 'you must know what this thing is.' She takes it in one hand and feels it up and down as she squirms around in her seat.

" 'Yeah,' she says, 'I know what this is. This here's a real nice-lookin' cock. But you might have better luck with it if it stuck out between your legs like everyone else, instead of out of one ear like that.' "

A laugh escaped from Jay. Paul brought his hand down on the table with a bang, making the bottles and glasses jump, and laughed hard and loud until the manager came out from inside.

"You guys better settle down out here," he said.

Anna waited for Jay to speak, to say something, to take charge. Instead, Paul looked up and said, "Say, Jack, what's the difference between a bowling ball and a nigger's pussy?"

"Time to go," the manager said. He grabbed Paul's chair and pulled it away from the table. Paul jumped up fast and wheeled to face him—but then thought better of it.

"I guess you're right, bud, we probably got a little out of line here telling some jokes and all. You know how it is when you're drinking beer. We're ready to go, anyway."

"You've paid the bill?"

"Hey, you know me." Paul laughed, turning to Anna. "I never have any money."

"I'll get it," Jay said. He paid, and the three of them filed out to the street, where they stood in a triangle, each at a distance.

"So now what?" Paul asked, smiling.

Anna put the end of her finger against his chest and pushed. "You go back to your house, or wherever you live. Jay and I go the other way. I've had enough of this."

"Loosen up, Anna, for Christ's sake. . . ."

She took Jay's arm and turned her back on Paul. When they looked back from the first street corner, he had disappeared.

Anna disengaged herself from Jay and walked with her arms folded across her chest. Her real complaint wasn't with Paul, it was with Jay. She'd wanted him to guess—without her having to say so—that Paul upset her. She didn't want Jay laughing at Paul's stupid jokes or going along with his insinuations. "I don't know why you had to invite him along," she said. "Couldn't you see what he was like?"

"How was I to know? I thought he was a character. You're the one who married him. He was just a guy on the street to me."

They walked to Jay's house in silence, as giant river moths beat their wings against the streetlights overhead and the summer's last cicadas ground down for the night.

"I'm angry because I should have taken care of it myself," Anna said, "and I didn't."

TICKING THEM OFF on her fingers, Anna thought: I'm surrounded by males. Paul, Jay, her father, Deal—and Kevin, never far from her thoughts. She sat on her front steps after a late dinner, the house dark behind her and the sky cloudless. She missed her women friends in Eugene. Except for Shelley, and perhaps Susan, she had no women to talk to in Fell River.

Something swept over the lawn, rose vertically and disappeared into the line of trees to the east. An owl, from the soundlessness of its flight. A dozen fireflies, the sparse remains of an early summer's multitude, glowed at random against a backdrop of sweet corn. A few discrete sounds poked out of the darkness: leaves rustling beside the drainage ditch, a clicking from a distant fencerow and the prehistoric conversation of a pair of tree frogs. Across the river in Kentucky, a string of dogs circulated an esoteric, canine message.

Anna stepped barefoot across her lawn onto the warm soil of the nearest field. The waning moon, half-full, allowed her to distinguish individual plants, but since nothing showed any color, she had to find the buoyant lobed peppers and dense tomatoes by feel alone. When she bit into the smooth skins of Moreton Hybrid and Red Pak tomatoes, warm juice ran down her arm; warmer than the night. From among the last of the beets a pair of rabbits burst into erratic flight, reminding Anna to approach the corn silently and listen for raccoons. Deal tried to scatter leather dust around the patch after each rain, but both coons and groundhogs had their way with the ears as they came ripe.

It wasn't true you could hear corn growing on a hot night— maybe field corn, but not the compact sweet corn they grew for fresh market. At the start of the first row, Anna dropped her shorts and urinated on the ground, marking her territory. She had read that wolves staked out their turf that way, and Deal said he did the same—though the cornfield was far too large for one man to autograph.

The process would be harder still for Anna, who would have to expose herself every few yards, squirting a little here, a little there, wetting her curly hairs in the process. It was another rueful case where the male organ was obviously the more ser- viceable. If Deal had to pee during the day, he turned his back, whipped out and stood there—*stood* there—with a certain ar- rogant languor, directing the stream of urine comfortably away from his feet. Then he squeezed and shook himself dry with little masturbatory movements, tucked everything away and zipped up his fly as he turned back to work. A marvelously practical operation. Anna, on the other hand, had to lower her naked backside to the ground, carefully judge the inclination of the terrain—or hop out of the way of a spreading yellow rivulet—and do her best not to spatter her ankles.

On the other hand, she thought, she wouldn't care to have a set of floppy organs protruding out of her body into the air, ever in danger of being knocked about or grabbed. Let men live with that.

Often when she walked in the fields at night, the pleasures

of horticulture returned to Anna, as strong as in a dream. Seven years before, she had taken a greenhouse job because of her gladness for everything that grew—but in the midst of commercial fieldwork, she often lost that feeling. During the day her thoughts ran to marketing plans and the timing of plant populations in the thousands and tens of thousands. With her mind on crops, she barely noticed individual plants. At night it was different. There was nothing to do in the fields except mark off a whimsical terrain, and explore, and tip up her nostrils to the odor of mud and willows carried inland from the river by a gentle wind.

She walked as far as the western edge of the farm, then turned and headed back to her house. There, she called Susan and made plans to go swimming with her at Sam Turner's pond.

ROLLING down the ramp in front of her house in Fell River, Susan looked rested and healthy. Her thighs, extending from a pair of khaki shorts, were as slender and brown as loaves of bread, and her strong forearms controlled a new lightweight chair with canted wheels and no armrests. Nevertheless, all Anna could think of for the first few minutes was Susan's *paraplegicness,* the fact that she couldn't walk.

Susan opened the door of her car and stationed her wheelchair next to the driver's seat. She lifted her upper body behind the steering wheel, pulled her legs in behind with her hands, folded the chair and stuck it in the back seat. "Jump in," she said.

They picked up a couple of oversized tubes from a tire store downtown, squeezed them fully inflated into the trunk of the Malibu and drove upriver to Turner's Run. The path leading up to Sam's pond curved into the woods, smooth and level for the first hundred yards. Susan wheeled ahead under the tree canopy, her hard rubber tires snicking on dead leaves and the dry ground. Farther on she had to wait for Anna to help her over the steep pitches.

August's blue air had settled into the valley after three days of hot, still weather. In the middle of the woods a breathless haze kept the surface of the pond as flat as linoleum and made the late afternoon feel like dusk.

Susan left her shorts on but pulled off her shirt. She didn't wear a bra; her breasts were no larger than a young girl's. After testing the water she spun her chair, lowered its front wheels into the pond and looked back over her shoulder. "How about tipping me in?"

"Just . . . dump you?"

"Gently. As long as I slide into the water and the chair doesn't follow me in."

Anna held on to the webbed backrest of Susan's chair. "Now?" As she lifted, Susan leaned forward and half dove into the pond. She emerged five feet out, her hair smoothed back and her eyelashes dripping wet.

The two women floated in the middle of the pond, legs draped over the tubes, shorts in the water, hands outstretched. There was no wake, no wind, no drift. The air and water were almost the same temperature.

"Your father worries that I'm too young for him."

"Do you think he's too old?"

Susan twirled herself through a slow circle in the water. "No. And we've talked about it a couple of times. But the truth is that living in a wheelchair has changed everything for me. If I could walk, maybe I'd think he was too old—probably I would. But everything looks different now. Not just your father, everything."

"I try to imagine what it feels like," Anna said. She stirred up a small whirlpool with each hand, disrupting the glassy surface of the pond.

"What I'm trying to say is that I didn't start going out with your father because I was desperate. I just liked him."

"I never think of you as desperate."

"I am, sometimes. Not when I'm doing something difficult—like getting out to a pond like this, or buying groceries. I like those challenges. But every once in a while something reminds me that I have to live this way forever—something most people wouldn't even see, or wouldn't think about."

Anna worried that she'd said something wrong. "What kind of thing?"

"Yesterday I saw a little boy at the supermarket trying to open the door of his mom's pickup. The handle was above his head, and it looked like the button was stiff. His mother wanted to get in the truck and go, but the boy stuck his little buns out at her and kept her away. He could push the button in, but he couldn't push it in and pull the door open at the same time. I really loved him for trying so hard to open that door. Even when he let his mother do it, he told her, 'I'm going to get bigger so I can open it by myself.'

"But that's what made me feel helpless. That little boy knew he was going to grow up and learn to do everything an adult can do—whereas for me, there's a limit. What difference does it make to try and play tennis or go up a path in my wheelchair, if I'm never going to walk again?"

"I try not to look at those little boys."

"Oh Anna, I'm sorry. I wasn't thinking."

"I just meant it's the same with me. Most days I get along fine, and then some incident like that slaps me across the face."

Susan looked off into the dense underbrush, as green as Guatemala. "The same thing happens to your father," she said, "though he hides it better. I've been trying to work up the courage to tell him something."

Anna rolled over on her tube. She didn't want Susan to say she was leaving her father.

"My whole past life in New Mexico is up in the air, and one of these days I have to go back and settle it. I should have told Alex right at the start—but I didn't know when the start was."

Anna nodded. Susan rolled over onto her stomach as well, and the two women floated face to face on the flat surface of the pond. The violet discolorations around Susan"s eyes had faded to smoky echoes. "It's not that I'm leaving him," she said.

"But you might not come back. You have friends in Santa Fe and you could get your job back."

"I doubt it. Anyway, Scott's there."

"Scott?"

"The man I lived with for three years. We might have been breaking up, I don't know. I starting dating another man— Mel, the one who died in the accident. I've told your father about it, but the story's too complicated. Anyway, when Scott came to see me in the hospital my face was a mess and my legs felt like cork. What was I going to tell him—that I wanted to go back to him now that I couldn't feel anything below the waist? After his third visit I told the hospital not to let him in, and I sent Scott a letter telling him I'd come to see him when I could walk again. I never have."

"He didn't write you back?"

"Scott's not much of a writer. And I hear another woman moved into his house. Still, I think I should see him."

The texture of the woods had turned amorphous with the approach of dusk, though the pond's lucent eye still reflected the light from above. Anna floated, her legs scissoring gently through the clear water. "What have you told my father?"

"That I lived with Scott and haven't seen him since right after the accident. But I haven't told him I want to go back. I guess some things don't get said, no matter how much you talk. I'm going to explain it, though. You won't tell him first, Anna, will you?"

"No, of course not."

"It won't be like leaving him."

CHAPTER 6

O N LABOR DAY MORNING Anna lay completely still on Jay's bed, the sheets tossed off onto the floor. Jay whistled as he packed a lunch downstairs, glad because Daria was coming home. Anna, however, didn't want to go to the airport and wasn't glad of anything. Her limbs felt encased. When a fly settled on her forehead she couldn't move her hand to slap it. She twitched her eyebrows and it buzzed off, but a moment later it returned to land on her knee, where it tortured her minutely by walking up and down her leg. Of course she could have moved her hands if she put her will to it—yet the fly continued to scurry along her thigh. She braced herself and sat up, placed the soles of her feet on the warm wooden floor and moved her eyes by slow degrees from one object to the next, as she did when hung over.

Sitting at the kitchen table with Jay, Anna dissembled, hoping her uneasiness would fade. It grew instead, as she struggled to finish a piece of toast and a glass of orange juice. She had no idea where the feeling had come from. Sometimes a bad dream carried over, but she couldn't remember any dreams from the night before. A bad biorhythm? A conjunctive planet out of whack? A hidden attack of the flu? If Jay hadn't been so eager to have her go with him to the airport at Louisville, she would have gone back to bed.

Cars clogged the highway in both directions. The other drivers looked grey and sedated—whole families looked the same. Only Jay drove with his window down. Where were so many people going, and why did anyone live in this pointless landscape? Why would anyone choose to live *here*? And why did every house face the bloodless highway, honoring those who never stopped, who lived elsewhere, who passed by at top speed in hermetic, air-conditioned capsules? Beyond the houses the land was tired, the rivers mud-bottomed and polluted. How far was it to a clean river? How far to the ocean? Impossibly far to the Pacific, Anna thought. She slumped in the front seat of Jay's car, the door handle elbowing her ribs.

Then it came to her, perfectly obvious. Every year for almost a decade she had spent Labor Day weekend at the ocean. She and Paul and another couple with children had rented a house at Seal Rock on the Oregon coast. Even after the divorce Paul drove up from San Francisco and they all stayed in the same green-and-white, wooden-frame cottage. It had a living room, a tiny kitchen and three small rooms with bunk beds. As cramped as it was, they returned to it every year and spoke as if they always would.

At this very moment the blue-black waves of the Pacific were curling and sliding onto the beach at Seal Rock, covering the sand with foam. September was a bright and fogless time at the ocean. Kevin built sand castles with the Farrell boys, chased the waves in and out, and allowed the water to bury his feet in the sand. Both families played and read and ate at the beach, never returning to the small house across the road until dinnertime.

Even inside the house Anna felt the unending power and elegance of the waves as they tumbled onto the beach. She listened to the ocean as she lay in bed at night, and all through her sleep, and upon the instant of waking. In the evening as they played cards—it was the only time Anna consented to play cards with adults—she sat at the small oilclothed table with only a tenth of her mind on the game, allowing the sweep and sack of the waves to take over her thoughts.

She had come to live far from the Pacific. Too far. In her entire life she might never spend another Labor Day at Seal Rock, eating provolone sandwiches with Bermuda onions, drinking spring water and Italian red wine. It never rained, it was cool at night, and every year they went to stand on a bluff and listen to the seals. Kevin barked down at them, intent and serious, and then walked back to the house holding his father's hand. The last time they went to Seal Rock, Kevin told Anna that Labor Day was more fun than his birthday.

The following year the two of them spent the entire holiday weekend driving from Oregon to Ohio, so Kevin could start school on time in Fell River. And the next year he was dead.

Jay hung his left hand out the window. He no longer whistled or offered bits of conversation, but Anna knew he was sunny underneath, thinking of Daria's return. His whistling had annoyed her, and now his failure to whistle annoyed her. Recognizing a dangerous mood, she told Jay she was sleepy and climbed into the back seat of the car to keep out of the way. Without meaning to, she slept. .

She walked on a tropical black-sand beach and waded through the glassy water with a dark-skinned man. He kissed her neck. Anna kissed him back, he wrapped his legs around her, and the creamy water held them up. From each crested wave they watched the palm trees and the long dark beach— and then the man was gone. The waves broke, and broke, and broke again, each one lifting her skyward before it passed beneath her and slid toward the shore.

She woke up in the airport parking lot, groggy and sweating in the hot back seat of Jay's Dodge. A note on the dashboard read, "TWA flight 426." Anna pulled herself out of Jay's car onto the asphalt and made for the terminal. Why had she floated arm in arm with some other man, in a foreign sea?

Inside the airport the floor shook under her feet in continuous tremor. The recessed lighting made white shirts and teeth look blue, and prolonged Anna's estrangement from the waking world. It took her ten minutes to reach the gate, where she found Jay hugging his daughter. She thought for a vicious instant: Jay has everything, he gets whatever he wants. Then Daria turned to her, smiling, her straight hair grown to her shoulders. She wore a pair of drawstring pants, heeled sandals and a *Boston* T-shirt with the name written in black script. In the two months she'd been away her breasts had grown.

"My young girl has grown up," Jay said.

"Just a little, Dad. Hi, Anna."

As Anna embraced her, she felt the girl withhold her chest. Such moments would have come with Kevin as well. Anna tried to imagine him as a young man, someone she hesitated to embrace.

On the way home Jay told stories of Daria as a child: of how she often laughed in her sleep; of how she loved to travel; of how she had once, on this same road at sixty miles an hour, slipped the keys out of the ignition and held them brightly in the air.

Only Anna was vile, only she had doubts and regrets and a metallic grip on affliction. The same highway she had despaired of earlier in the day was in fact only a neutral ribbon of concrete. She held to the burden of her past and, at the same time, worried that her future was closing in on her. She worried about turning forty in three years. She worried about the day menopause would slap her across the face and catapult her into middle age.

Riding in the car with Jay and Daria, she made an attempt to relax and join in the conversation. Daria let her arm rest against Anna's leg, yet no matter how comfortable they all appeared, it seemed to Anna the three of them were wrapped in two separate packages: Jay and his daughter in one, and she in another.

At the dining room table after dinner, Jay announced that he'd been asked to go to Salt Lake City for a week to give a series of master classes and perform one of his dances.

"But Dad, I just got home."

"It wouldn't be until the end of the month. We'll have plenty of time together before then."

"But who'd take care of me?"

"I haven't asked her, but I thought maybe Anna could." He looked across the table at Anna, his two eyebrows arched in identical Minoan curves. "You're almost old enough to look after yourself," he told his daughter. "You could help Anna with dinner the same way you help me, and she could stay here at night. Anna?"

Anna thought the idea was a little abrupt, but she said, "If Daria feels comfortable about it, I'd be glad to. She might want to think it over."

Jay did the dishes by himself, leaving Anna and Daria in the living room. "You two could read," he suggested.

Anna closed the door to the kitchen to keep out the noise and read to Daria from a book on Isadora Duncan. The girl read silently as Anna read out loud, and several times she corrected Anna after a mistake. Anna felt her breathing, all through the chapter. When they finished she asked the girl, "Does your father still read to you?"

"Sometimes. Sometimes we just read our own books."

"How about your mom?"

"No, she doesn't like to. We go to the movies."

"I used to read to Kevin every night. Did your dad tell you I had a son?"

"Yes. He was nine, wasn't he?"

"How'd you remember that?"

"Because I had a friend who died, and she was nine, too. She had leukemia and never told us, and then she went to the hospital and died."

Anna saw that Daria's eyes were moist. "Did your father tell you what happened to Kevin?"

"He said you had an accident."

"What did he say about it?"

"He said that when a child died, nothing was worse."

Anna's breath went out of her, as if she'd been punched in the chest.

"But I think it would be just as bad to have your parents die, because then you'd be an orphan."

The word "orphan" triggered a string of images in Anna's mind, one picture of Kevin after another. She wanted to tell Daria—or Jay, or someone—how beautiful Kevin had been as a baby. How he had freed her of all doubts and ambition, and how he had clung to her nipples with his entire, flawless body.

She couldn't say that to a young girl. She couldn't even cry in front of Daria. At home she could get drunk and throw hammers through the window and burn up part of her house, but in front of Daria she had to be responsible. Jay knew that. He'd asked her to stay at his house because of it, Anna thought.

SEPTEMBER passed quickly. The tomato harvest ended, and with it, Anna's frenetic work schedule of the past four months. She slept over a couple of times at Jay's and got to know the routine of the house. After he flew out to Salt Lake City, she drove in from the farm every day after work to fix supper and look after Daria.

Along with a half-dozen other kids, Daria lived a reckless neighborhood life in the streets and hardly spent any time at home except to eat dinner and do her homework. But at the end of the week it rained for two days. Anna and the girl played Scrabble, did a five-hundred-piece puzzle and went out for dinner one night at Tony's.

On Sunday afternoon Jay returned and found Anna reading on a lawn chair overlooking the Fell. He hopped out of his car and walked toward her in little steps like a rabbit, his eyes wide and his hair grown long. Wearing sandals and a checked shirt, he didn't look like a man with responsibilities. His suitcase was hardly any larger than a day pack.

"Hello, Anna Delancy. The Fell is still flowing? And Daria still breathing?"

"She's at Angela's, she's fine. How did it go?"

He kissed her, led her to the porch and kissed her again. "I can still manage in the real world." His lips brushed against Anna's as he spoke. "I taught well, and the faculty liked my dance."

"You're in your prime," Anna said, speaking against his mouth.

"I'm not. But hey, no one asked my age the whole week. Either I fooled them or scared them."

"Fooled them. You're not so scary."

"Sometimes I scare you a little."

"That's different. I'm not scared, I'm just . . . slower."

"You heat up my electrons. Once they get moving I can't hold back."

Anna laughed. "Those aren't your electrons, they're your gonads."

In the clear light of his bedroom Jay moved slowly, holding and kissing her, over and over. When she stopped to put in her diaphragm he gave her plenty of time, massaging her shoulders as she covered the ringed, elastic membrane with gel, raised one knee, inserted the diaphragm and checked its fit. They went on kissing after that; perhaps he worried about going too fast, after her comment. But once inside her he came in a hurry. His back arched, his breathing turned sharp and his eyes went out of focus. At the last moment he cried out, *"Oh Anna, I love you."*

She lay under his words as under water. Even though all his weight pressed down on her, she felt his words, not his body. He seemed to weigh no more than a child. His breaths came slower and deeper. His arms twitched as he glided toward sleep.

But before dropping off he roused himself. He rolled over and faced her, supporting his head with his right hand, and began to talk. He told her what had happened in Utah: a woman had invited him home (he wasn't interested); there was a student who could have danced with any company in New York; he had borrowed a car and driven into the dry mountains near Salt Lake. Finally he got up, padded down the hall to the bathroom and returned to bed to ask Anna about Daria and farming.

They both acted as if he'd never said anything while making love—as if they'd both been unconscious. Did it annul his words, that he'd said them in the midst of an orgasm?

Jay didn't want to get up, he said he'd drive over to Angela's when it got dark. He was full of stories and plans:

"This fall," he said, "we could go to West Virginia."

"When we meet Frank you'll see what I mean."

"Sometime we'll visit the River Museum in Cincinnati."

He didn't seem to notice her silence.

Anna wanted to tell him she wasn't ready, that he shouldn't assume anything. She couldn't tell him she loved him, she didn't even know what that meant anymore.

And as Jay talked, her thoughts wandered. How arbitrary life was with a man, and how simple with a child. An affair or a marriage might end at any moment, but not life with a child.

She woke up from such thoughts to hear Jay ask, "If a woman has a child at thirty-five or forty, is it a problem for her?"

"You mean from this afternoon?"

"No, I mean in general."

She wanted to smack his face. She didn't want him to even think about her being pregnant—and at the same time, she hated him for pointing out that she was "thirty-five or forty" and childless. She didn't want to have a child out of desperation and didn't see how she was ever going to be ready.

Jay always moved too fast for her. It was not enough for him that they should lie down together in the afternoon, make the cries of small animals and stretch out afterward with their legs entangled. But it was enough for her.

THREE WEEKS LATER Anna drove to town through a light rain. She climbed the steps to the landing outside Jay's studio, paused at the door and took off her damp jacket. Inside, someone played the piano. As quietly as she could, Anna opened the door and sat down on a bench along the back wall.

Jay hesitated, and with him, the accompanist, so that everyone in the room turned toward Anna. Jay took a step toward her, but she waved him off with one hand, retracting her shoulders and squaring them against the wall. He gave her a puzzled look, then faced the class, nodded at the pianist and went on.

The students were all women or girls. Anna didn't know any of them, and even Jay, who was dressed in tights and leg warmers, looked like a stranger to her. The class moved from one exercise to another in a warm-up as studied and beautiful as a performance. The women dropped to the floor, stretched left and right, arched backward and rose like crabs. On leg kicks and rolls, their pastel leotards spun through the air in unison. Jay called out the changes. No one missed a beat.

Anna had come during a class on purpose, so she could feel Jay's presence, but not his bias. She had a decision to make, and if she asked Jay about it first, she would never be sure of her own choice. Recently, nothing had seemed more important than knowing her own will.

She left the class before it ended. Outside, the rain had stopped, though the young trees along Merton Street dripped onto her shoulders as she passed beneath them, her head down and her jacket under one arm. According to the hospital clinic, she was pregnant.

She had gone for a test after missing her period. For three months after Kevin's death she hadn't menstruated at all, but once started again she'd locked onto the moon's exact cycle, to the point of beginning all her periods either Monday night or Tuesday morning. Yet somehow she'd been tricked. She'd used her diaphragm as regularly as the Pope gave benedictions, but it didn't do any good. The goddamn Pope. He was so hot on pregnancy, *he* should swell up with child and waddle around the Vatican.

The clinic secretary read her the results of the test over the phone. For a day Anna raged against the news. Feeling as awkward as an adolescent, she finally drove to the clinic and asked if they would please, even though they had already told her over the phone, on the faint possibility they'd read her the wrong results, would they check one more time to make sure she was actually pregnant? She was.

After visiting Jay's class, Anna walked through the streets of town for an hour. She wound up at the Hayes Cafeteria, where she managed to eat dinner without ever looking at the face of another diner. By the time she drove home the sky had cleared and the temperature fallen. She unplugged the telephone, wrapped herself in a sleeping bag and sat alone on her front steps until well after midnight.

The following afternoon she told Jay that she was pregnant but wouldn't have the child. She had already made an appointment for an abortion at the Cincinnati Women's Center.

Jay slumped in his chair at the small table in the Elephant Cafe where they'd first talked. He rarely misplaced his posture that way. He coughed and stuck one hand into his shirt to scratch himself. A button popped off and fell to the floor with a click. Unable to find it after a short search, he sat up again, wearing the sad look of a spaniel.

"We've only known each other for two or three months," Anna said. "That's not enough time."

"No, I guess not."

"And I still feel delicate about it. I don't know if I'll ever have another child."

"I'm not pushing you, Anna."

"But you don't like it."

He examined the restaurant's new red tablecloth and picked at the embroidery. "I'm afraid of it."

She saw how easily she could hurt him. She didn't want to, but it was remarkable to think she could, since Jay had always been the invulnerable, cheerful partner. It's true he'd been the one to say he loved her. But that was easy for him, the way everything was easy. And what did such a passionate moment come to, after all, held up against childbearing, child care and love of a child? One was fucking, the other a responsibility that never ended.

"Afraid of what?" she asked.

"Of what happens with abortions. How they drive couples apart."

The waitress brought two cups of coffee from the fuming espresso machine on the back counter. The coffee was too hot to drink. "I have to choose to have another child," Anna said. "I can't just let it happen."

"That's a choice, too, letting it happen."

"Jay, how can you want another child? You have a wonderful twelve-year-old girl. Isn't that enough?"

"I always wanted a family."

"But you have a family, with Daria. And you had one with her mother."

"We were too young, it didn't work out."

"Do you really want to start over again?"

Jay sat up and blew on his coffee, folded his hands and stared at Anna. "I'm forty-one years old, and I have everything else. I have friends, I have dancing, I have a daughter. I've had lovers. So of course I want the one thing I've never had, a family that works."

"What if we didn't work?"

"I think we would."

"Jay, I've made up my mind."

"I know. It's all right."

"It doesn't mean I'm leaving you."

"No."

His insecurity thrilled her. There was no other word for it; an electric current ran up and down her back, and her skull grew light. But she fought the sensation because she didn't want to take pleasure in disappointing him. "Sometimes I feel a little distant," she said.

He smiled briefly. "I know, and sometimes I get angry about it and don't want anything to do with you or a family."

The waitress fussed with the next table, and other customers came and went. Outside, the wind waved the trees back and forth in the sunlight.

"Don't you think we need more time?"

"If you'd asked me that yesterday," Jay said, "I probably would have agreed. But today you're pregnant. That changes things."

"Who'd look after a child, if we ever had one? It's always the woman who winds up under a baby, like a toad under a stone. And I don't want to stop farming."

"I'd help out. I've had Daria since she was seven."

"That's different, seven-year-olds are easy. They've already lost half their crushing power."

Jay's sad expression had eased, and there was no argument to his tone of voice. "I just don't want you to leave," he said.

"I won't. I promise."

"You know, Anna, even if I never saw you again, I'd be glad we came this far."

JAY OFFERED to drive her to the clinic, but she turned him down. She didn't want to fight his silent will, and her own indecision, all the way to Cincinnati.

On the morning of her appointment the alarm clock next to his bed went off at five-thirty. Anna clapped her hand on it but immediately dropped back onto a sea-green lawn bordered by shiny rhododendrons. In the middle of the lawn, as Anna and Jay walked arm in arm around the perimeter, a little girl turned somersaults on the mown grass.

"Don't drift off," Jay said. He nudged her feet with his own and circled one arm over her belly. But when she rose and dressed, he floated back into sleep.

Anna set out on the empty river road, driving fast. The chill dawn light, turning from grey to mauve, revealed the first frost of the year, a faint white sheathing of ice on field corn and leaf-stripped soybeans. Halfway through the trip, Anna stopped for tea and toast in one of the small river towns; the clinic had told her not to eat anything, but the morning was too long to go without a semblance of breakfast. Back on the road, the sun rose over the hills behind her, lighting up the yellow sugar maples like beacons.

The outskirts of Cincinnati quickly dismantled her peace of mind as she left the farmland along the river and plunged into a chaos of shopping malls and commuter traffic. The city looked insufferable, all graceless commerce and claptrap on billboards. Long before reaching the crowded center of town, Anna knew she had allowed herself to be fooled: by the dawn, by the peaceful roll of hills, by the unblemished tartan designs of agriculture. This operation—this procedure, as they called it— could not go well, no matter how they treated her. Over the phone, the woman who had answered her questions had sounded gentle and reassuring, but that was a peripheral kindness that had nothing to do with the act itself.

The clinic, isolated on the second floor of a ten-story steel office building, was not what Anna had imagined, or hoped for. The receptionist checked her name off a list and gave her a form on a clipboard to fill out in the waiting room. Anna took the clipboard, barely listening to what the woman said.

She was thinking of an appointment she had kept at another abortion clinic, in San Francisco, shortly before she met Paul. On that morning fog lay across the bay, white gulls swept over the quiet streets, and a couple of pedestrians smiled at her on the way to the tram. In front of the clinic, in the cool August sunlight, blue hydrangeas flowered in a square redwood frame. She was twenty-six years old.

She had been a little foolish, and a little careless, and let herself get pregnant by a drifter she hardly knew. She met him in a bookstore. He bumped into her bedroom, bumped again and was gone from sight before she realized what had happened. Mildly ashamed, she went camping by herself at Point Reyes after the abortion and told no one about it, glad to have escaped from such a mistake so easily. Yet here she was, eleven years older, pregnant again, at an abortion mill in downtown Cincinnati.

Have you ever had an abortion?

She was a second offender. And it was an offense, no question about that. No matter how bad the alternative, the impeccable moral position on abortions was not to have one.

If so, were there any complications?

Not really. Certainly nothing physical. On occasion in recent years, Anna had spoken adamantly about the right of all women to abortion on demand—and her opinion remained firm on that right. That was politics. But as she sat in a plush chair in a color-coordinated, windowless waiting room, she wasn't absolutely certain she wanted an eight-week fetus to be sucked out of her womb by some doctor with a machine.

Only a week before—was this purely by chance?—Deal had told her a story about his travels in Nepal. One morning, not far from Katmandu on one of the country's few roads, Deal had come upon a group of men in loose pants and brightly knit hats, clearing the road of a mud slide. He saw one of the workers stoop over his mattock, pick up an earthworm and place it in his palm. The man carried it matter-of-factly away from the work site and laid it on the ground, then returned to digging. Deal, fascinated, sat down within view of the road and saw the same incident repeated over and over: one of the men would pause, bend down to extricate some worm or beetle and carry it out of harm's way. The foreman gave no mind to the interruption.

A middle-aged woman entered the waiting room and called out five names, then led the way down a corridor, the metal cleats of her high heels clicking on the linoleum floor. She wore a tight knit dress and dark stockings. Her legs were stylishly thin below the knee, but had gone fat higher up. From one end of an oblong table in a miniature conference room, she counseled the five clients, explaining the procedure clearly and efficiently. From her tone, she might have been talking about a self-cleaning oven rather than a uterus. Anna understood she was giving them a chance to back out.

They were all fully decided. One girl looked no more than fifteen, her pale blond hair tied in braids. She had come with her mother. A second girl wore boots and designer jeans, and a third carried a bookbag, as if she might get in some studying. The last woman looked fifty years old—looked even older than that—and said quickly when asked about her motive: "It's because of the money. It's a financial question."

Since when, thought Anna, was an abortion only a financial question? She wanted to know what the older woman actually thought about abortions—and what the young blond girl thought, and what the student thought. But the session remained doggedly impersonal, and Anna learned nothing about the other women. Had this counselor, who led them so crisply toward their abortions, ever had one herself? Had she had *two* abortions?

In a tiny, private dressing room Anna changed into a hospital gown. She placed her clothes, her watch and two rings in a beige plastic container, the kind she soaked laundry in at home. Though the room was warm—even the tiled floor was warm against her bare feet—Anna felt exposed in the surgical gown. It was a flimsy scrap of blue cloth that only came down to the middle of her thighs and that lifted almost to her buttocks when she leaned forward.

A nurse opened the door without a knock, holding a syringe in her right hand and a piece of cotton in her left. "This is a tranquilizer," she explained as she maneuvered behind Anna. "It'll help you feel more relaxed." She twitched Anna's gown to one side and planted the needle.

Three minutes later, feeling identically unrelaxed, Anna was taken to a third room, directed onto a table and told to raise her feet to the metal stirrups. The rush was premature; the doctor did not appear. When the nurse went out Anna lowered her legs. She would have preferred the dignity of being naked to wearing the clinic's gown. After a few minutes the nurse stuck her head in the doorway and announced, "We're running behind on the first group, so the doctor will be delayed a few moments."

The doctor might be a woman. After all, everyone else in the clinic was a woman. Anna had refrained until now from imagining the doctor as either male or female—but from the way the nurse said "the doctor," she knew he was a man. If he had been a woman, the nurse would have said "Doctor So-and-so."

As the tranquilizer took effect Anna felt calmer and more detached. She heard a woman's cry, cut off suddenly, and tried to remember if her first abortion had been painful. It must have been, she thought, but in fact she could not remember. Strangely, though she remembered the sunken blue color of the hydrangeas growing outside the clinic, and the lit, rectangular doorbell that made the entrance look like part of someone's home, she couldn't remember if the operation was painful or not, or if women called out from other rooms. The doctor was a man.

The nurse returned, followed by Dr. Salis. He introduced himself and touched his hand briefly to Anna's forearm—a calculated, civilized touch, she thought, to be given before he started groping around inside her cunt. He was young, slightly bald, and had a small patch of rough skin on one cheek. He seemed to move slowly, and he looked down on her from far above. He opened a manila folder with Anna's form in it, laid it on a table by the sink and glanced at it as he washed his hands.

"There were no complications the first time?"

"No," Anna said. The word came out of her mouth like a cube. She shouldn't have let them give her a tranquilizer; she'd rather be honestly nervous.

"Feet up," he said, "and let's have a look."

He went directly to the mark, easing a lubricated, gloved hand into her vagina. Anna worried that she would lose control of her sphincter. With half his hand buried inside her, the doctor turned his face aside as if his sense of touch would be more faithful if he looked at something across the room.

"Let's have twenty cc's of lidocaine," he told the nurse.

Anna asked him what that was for.

"It's a local anesthetic. It helps when we introduce the cervical dilators."

His tone was neutral, neither chatty nor solemn. He had entered the room with authority, but now, standing beside the table with nothing to occupy his hands, he looked a little gawky. His long neck bent forward slightly. He was younger than Anna by some years.

"How many of these do you do a day?" She wanted to hear him talk.

He looked away, waiting for the syringe, and for a moment she thought he wasn't going to answer. "About twenty," he said, "if there are no snags."

"All day long?"

"Oh no, I finish here before noon. After lunch I'm at the hospital."

The nurse passed him the syringe. He placed the needle against his middle finger and slid it up to Anna's cervix. She felt a brief stab of pain.

"Doesn't it get to you," she asked, "aborting fetuses every day, one after another?"

He threw the syringe into a wastebasket lined with plastic and turned back to Anna, still supine on the table. "I think about it," he said. His right hand started toward the rough patch of skin on his face, but at the last minute the tips of his fingers veered off. "It does happen sometimes that we save a woman's life. Usually we only save her from a child she doesn't want. It's not the most pleasant practice in medicine, but . . ."

Anna waited.

"But it's certainly not the most difficult. Before this I spent a year in the cancer wing at Cincinnati General. Mostly uterine and cervical cancer. We helped some people there, too, but I lost patient after patient."

Anna felt the nurse stiffen against her side. Dr. Salis, as well, must have heard the woman's starched uniform rustle against the table, but he went on.

"I don't mind you asking." He stripped off his gloves, laid them next to the sink and told Anna it would be a few minutes before the local took effect. He paused at the door before leaving. "I think about it every day. It's not something you get used to."

After he disappeared down the hall, the nurse rolled a machine to the side of the table. One hose projected from its top and another led to a large bottle on casters. Anna raised herself to look at the wide-mouthed glass receptacle. She had once made wine in such a bottle.

The doctor reappeared in ten minutes, washed his hands again and began to slide the dilators into Anna's uterus, each tube slightly larger than the one before. They hurt. No longer detached or calm, she tightened her jaw to keep from crying out. Once the final dilator was in place, the nurse turned on the machine. The doctor guided the first hose inside her as the metal canister—a vacuum cleaner by any name—hummed and breathed. Then an uneven sputtering. Moving through the opaque, lower tube, Anna saw a line of dark, uneven lumps. She twisted her head to look. *"Don't,"* the doctor said, but she had already seen the coagulates dropping soundlessly toward the bottom of the jar, where they were hidden by the metal stand.

Dr. Salis swabbed out the inside of her uterus. Although not as painful as the dilators, the act infringed on a deep, barely imagined part of her body. Anna held herself tense until everything was withdrawn. As her breath came back the doctor put his hand on her knee. "That's done," he said.

And that was all for him, since there had been no snags. Dr. Salis helped the nurse for a moment, shook Anna's hand wordlessly and offered her a thin smile before leaving the room. With hardly a complaint, her body had released its store, its secret second life.

Now she was free and without obligation—yet in two weeks her uterus would once again do its best to get her pregnant. Almost every month for thirty-five years she was fated to slough and bleed. Unless, of course, some male slithered in, came blithely and disrupted the pattern. To interrupt the disruption it took another male: a doctor who put his hand inside her, then a machine inside her, and freed her to begin the cycle once again.

Anna didn't want Dr. Salis to have any part in her life. She was glad he had been correct and neutral. At the same time, a resentment surprised her at how quickly he could disappear to his rounds somewhere else and have done with her.

After a rest and a lunch of insipid ham sandwiches, the same five women were subjected to another session with the same counselor. Anna felt irascible but understood that composure was the key to the highway. All the women were composed, and all were grateful. No one had any suggestions or complaints about how the clinic was run. They would all be more careful next time. They all want to get the hell out of here, Anna thought.

It was after two when she finally reached her car. The clinic had given her a month's supply of the pill, mounted on a strip of paper beneath plastic bubbles. Anna threw them into the back seat. How could they still give women the pill? Reaching into the bottom of her purse, she felt for the oval case of her diaphragm. Not for the first time, she was surprised by the flimsiness of the case and its cheap snap closure. Stamped on the back were the words "Made in Korea." Without question, her diaphragm was her single most important possession, yet it knocked around inside a ten-cent case of blue plastic. One way or the other, it hadn't done her much good. She was exhausted. She would never do this again.

IN THE DAYS THAT FOLLOWED, Anna stayed close to farmwork. The tomato and pepper harvests dwindled to a close, and the high school kids stopped coming by to work a couple of hours after school. Anna and Shelley cleaned the fields of stakes, twine and black plastic, while Deal greased and overhauled the farm machinery. A few harvests continued: turnips, spinach and brussels sprouts.

Early-morning frosts yielded to the matchless, clarified skies of mid-October. Dusk came early. Each afternoon at four Anna stopped for a bite to eat, then worked until dark. She cooked dinner and ate at her round oak table, listening to the news on the radio. At nine she lay down on the couch with a book. Twice Jay called after putting Daria to bed. Sometimes Anna read late into the night but she was always up the next morning by six.

On a quiet evening a week after the abortion, as the last blue light faded from the sky, Anna uncoiled her garden hose and watered the herbs planted in front of her house. The evening was windless and the air redolent with the odors of parsley, basil and cumin. Three crows flapped past, barely visible against the sky, and not ten feet away from her a ghostly possum scuttled into the crawl space of the house. She was going to be late with dinner.

Late for what? she wondered, raising her head. Then she understood. Late for Kevin's dinner, late for reading him a story, late for his bedtime. In the year and a half since Kevin's death she hadn't changed her schedule by ten minutes. She still got up on time to get him to the bus, she still interrupted work when the same bus passed by on the river road after school, and she read to herself every night at the same hour she had always read to Kevin. Even when she stayed at Jay's house her schedule was the same, because of Daria.

Since the abortion she hadn't cried, hadn't dreamed and hadn't spent the night at Jay's. She kept as busy as possible, stayed away from the farmhouse and begged off her Tuesday lunch at the Bradford with her father. But as she coiled the wet hose and listened to the possum scuffling around under her house, she had to fight back her tears.

Her experience at the clinic had kept her under a cold anesthesia all week. It wasn't that she believed she had killed a child. *Kevin* was a child; a fetus was something else. Yet something had changed for her. She threw the last coils of the hose onto the ground and set off at a hard walk toward the Ohio.

Under the trees near the end of Slate's Point, in almost complete darkness, she found the toppled trunk of the syca-more jutting down from the bank into the river. Feet first, her hands gripping the smooth, barkless surface of the tree, she crabwalked down the trunk as far as the water. The river's dark surface showed no sign of movement, but the slow heavy slurp coming from the underside of the trunk, and from half-submerged branches, signaled the current's relentless work. Sliding forward on her haunches, Anna dipped her hands into the river. The water was warmer than the night air. She cupped it to her face and cried, weeping for all the children born unwanted and for all the mothers thrown into pregnancy against their will. She wept, too, for Kevin, who had sprung mys-teriously out of her body, grown up in a perfect match of desires and been taken from her in the unspeakable beauty of his tenth year.

She wanted once, in this her only life, to conceive a child out of love and to live as a family until the child grew up and left. Crouched beside the Ohio, in retreat from her house and dinner and all her habits, she was convinced that the rounds of birth and death were not over for her.

JAY CALLED on the phone and said, "Paul's here."

"At your house?"

"Exactly."

"What the hell is he doing there?"

"I'd like to know that myself." Jay's voice was clipped. "He's sitting here on the couch. He says he needs to spend the night because he's been locked out of his place."

Anna swore coldly. "I'll be there in fifteen minutes."

Paul made a claim on her and she jumped. How long would it go on like that? She drove straight to Jay's, where she found Paul already stretched out in his sleeping bag on the couch, his spiky hair bunched up at the back of his head. He raised his hands between them, placating her the minute she came in the door.

"Now don't get all upset, Anna, I told Jay you didn't have to come in. I'm not making any trouble here. I just got locked out of my house because I'm a little late on the rent. I only need a place to stay for tonight, and I know Jay doesn't mind."

Jay minded, which was obvious from the drawn lines of his mouth and his stiff, folded arms.

"Jay doesn't want you here and neither do I."

"For chrissakes, Anna, relax. It's an emergency. It's just for one night. My check is due in any day." Paul looked at her without blinking. He was easily the calmest person in the room.

The kitchen door swung open and Daria walked in with a schoolbook in one hand. She said hello to Anna but was more curious about what Paul was doing—or still doing—on the couch.

Jay stepped in front of his daughter with professional speed. "Brush your teeth," he said, "and go to bed."

"Go to bed? I haven't finished my homework, and it's only—"

"You can finish your homework in bed. I want you to go upstairs now."

Anna had occasionally seen Daria wheedle her father, but not this time. She gave a sour face, stepped to one side to take a last look at Paul and went up the stairs. Her sock feet slipped a little on the polished wooden treads, and the muffled sound of her steps faded along the upstairs hallway.

Paul hadn't moved, other than to settle farther into the cushions of Jay's couch. He didn't pay any attention to Daria, neither when she entered the room nor when she disappeared up the stairs.

Jay motioned for Anna to follow him through the door into the kitchen, where they talked in whispers. He didn't want Paul in his house but had already asked him to leave without result; Paul had been polite but ignored him. Jay didn't want to turn him out by force, or try to, and Anna didn't want to call the police. After a long, hushed talk, they went back into the living room. Anna told Paul he could stay, but they wanted him out in the morning. Otherwise, Jay would call the police.

"Don't talk cops, Anna, they get everybody in trouble. Don't worry about it, I'll hit the road early."

Everyone in the house was in bed by nine, and all the lights off except for in the upstairs hall. Jay went twice to check on Daria, then lay down on his bed, still dressed, with the door to the hallway partly open.

"What's he up to?" Jay asked, barely above a whisper. "What does he want?"

"I hardly know him anymore, he could be a stranger."

"He's still in love with you, isn't he?"

"I don't know, maybe a little."

"Does he ever . . . come on to you? Is that what he wants?"

"He probably isn't very happy about me going out with someone else. He makes comments, you've heard him. And those dirty jokes."

Jay tiptoed to the door a third time and looked down the hall. "I hate to have him in the house with Daria here."

"He's not that dumb. Didn't you see how careful he was? When she came in from the kitchen he didn't even look at her."

"It still makes me nervous."

Anna nodded. "But he isn't after Daria, and I don't think he wants anything from you, either, even though he showed up over here. I'm the one he thinks about."

"What do you mean?"

"He's unhappy about Kevin and he wants me to do something about it."

"But what can you do?"

"Nobody can do anything." Anna undressed and changed into a nightgown she kept in Jay's closet. "It's so lonely when someone dies, you think you'll never get through it. Every day is bad. But you make it through a day, and then a month, and then a year—and by then you've learned something. It's still bad, but at least you know that sadness doesn't kill you. For a long time I thought I was going to die because of Kevin. But I don't think Paul ever went through anything like that."

"He looks like he went through something."

"He does. I don't know, maybe I'm wrong about him. I know they locked him up in a mental hospital, which must have been terrible. But it didn't do any good. He didn't mourn, he didn't cry, he just . . . took more drugs or something. Sometimes I don't think he even knows Kevin's gone and can't ever come back. Shit, I sound hysterical. But instead of suffering himself, Paul wants me to hand over what I've learned to him, so he doesn't have to go through it on his own. If I try to say something about it, he changes the subject."

"He just shows up whenever he feels like it?"

"I can't ignore him. We're tied by blood. He'll always be out there somewhere."

"He's so creepy. And what nerve, to come over here and settle down on my couch."

"I'm sorry we ever met him that night," Anna said. "And that I've got you wrapped up in this."

Early the next morning she found Paul in the kitchen, eating an omelet. He had helped himself to eggs, cheese and green peppers from the refrigerator and made a pot of coffee. Anna glanced in the living room and saw his rolled-up sleeping bag and army-surplus duffle lying neatly beside the front door. Although he'd stayed at Anna's house for weeks without ever touching a dirty dish, he washed his pan and plate at Jay's immediately after eating, sponged off the table and set out a cup of coffee for Anna.

When Jay and Daria came downstairs, Paul went into the living room and picked up his duffle bag. Jay and Anna followed him to the door, where he thanked them for putting him up. They'd been good to him, he said, and he'd repay the favor someday. He sounded like a polite, effusive cousin. He was out the door and gone before eight o'clock. Jay drove Daria to school rather than let her walk, but there was no sign of Paul along the way.

Two weeks passed, during which Anna heard nothing from Kevin's father. Finally he telephoned to say he was leaving town in a couple of days but wanted to take her and Jay out to dinner first, since they'd been a help to him. He was coherent and well spoken over the phone. With some misgivings, Anna accepted the invitation.

At Ling's Kitchen, Paul spoke urbanely about Chinese food and translated into English the names of all the dishes on the menu. Anna had never known him to study Chinese. He told none of his former stories about living in stolen vans and getting into arguments with hotel managers and the police. But for the entire meal, he didn't look Jay in the eyes. With some ostentation, he took the check and paid for it with a fifty-dollar bill. When Anna asked where he'd been living, he said he was going to pack that night and leave tomorrow for the East Coast.

First, though, he wanted to buy them a gift. "No, no," he said, "this is something I want to do." At a carryout close to the restaurant he chose a magnum of the most expensive champagne and placed it on the rubber mat next to the register. He murmured something about getting a bottle of beer as well and, after browsing for some minutes in front of the cooler, pulled out a full case of Pabst and set it next to the champagne.

Anna could not suppress a comment. "You're leaving town tomorrow morning and buying a case of beer tonight?"

"Yeah," Paul said. "You think I don't have the cash?"

"I guess you have the money, but I don't see how you could drink that much in one night."

"You know, Anna, you can make a scene out of anything. Who says all that beer's for me? In the whole time I've been here have you seen me drunk once? Not even close. You must think you're the only friends I have."

Anna apologized. It was true that, as far as she could tell, Paul had become a moderate drinker. She shifted her weight onto her left foot, leaning back slightly until she felt Jay's shoulder against her own. Paul stared at the two of them, his expression thickening. Under the store's fluorescent light his skin looked pale and slack.

Muttering under his breath, he looked over the rack of candy bars to one side of the register. At dinner, Anna had noticed how delicately he'd handled his silverware—but now his hands looked clumsy and oversized, their backs covered with thick black hair. He picked up an Almond Joy, squeezed it a couple of times and tossed it back in the carton, then chose a peanut-butter cup. The clerk looked at his thumb, still planted in the middle of the cup, and said, "Unless you're going to buy those, I'd appreciate it if you wouldn't finger them."

"If I wouldn't *finger* them, eh? Don't get yourself in a dither, buddy." Paul looped the candy back into its carton, but it bounced out and fell on the floor. He looked away.

"Hey, pick that up."

"Pick it up yourself. You money men are all slimeheads."

The man behind the counter was bigger than Paul, heavyset and over six feet. He picked up the case of beer with one hand and the bottle of champagne with the other and set them on the floor behind the register. "You can forget about these, I don't need business from guys like you."

"Hey fuckknuckle, gimme that beer."

"I'm not selling you any beer."

"You goddamn well are selling me some beer. I got rights in here like anybody else."

The man turned to Jay. "You better take your friend outside."

"What are you talking to him for?" Paul said. "You give me that case of beer or I'm coming around to get it."

The man turned the key in the register, slipped it into his pocket and picked up a telephone receiver off the wall. He pushed seven quick buttons on it from memory. "You can talk this over with the police."

"Police, *fuck*." Paul leaned over the counter with one hand and snagged the cord, flinging the telephone into the air. With a single yank he ripped it away from the box on the wall. "You're going to call the police on me?" He spat on the floor. "I hate the goddamned police. You can't handle this on your own, so you call the cops. Here's what you can do with the police, shithead."

With one hand he tipped the sales rack forward, spilling hundreds of candy bars, beef jerkies and peanuts onto the floor. Instantly the man started over the counter—but he never made it. Paul hit him like a football player, then put his fist in the man's chest.

Jay grabbed the back of Paul's coat and was flung off like a child. Paul never even looked at him. He stepped into the nearest aisle, grabbed a pair of bottles and threw them on the tile floor, sending glass and red wine over Anna's ankles. He smashed a third bottle and held it by the neck, jabbing the broken glass toward the clerk. "You get the fuck out of my face, Jack. And you," he said, looking at Anna. "You make me sick."

He held the broken bottle in front of him and backed as far as the door. "And you, fag dancer, you better go home and take care of your prissy little daughter." He turned into the darkness, and by the time Anna got to the door he had disappeared.

They went to Jay's immediately. Daria was watching television and reading a magazine; no one had been there. Both Jay and the man at the carryout talked to the police, but Paul was not to be found. The police guessed he had left town but promised to keep an eye on Jay's neighborhood. There was never any sign that they did. Paul never wrote or called.

ANNA HAD NEVER KNOWN a man as peaceful as Jay Corman. There was no fret to him, no need to stay eternally busy. He lay around her house like a dog allowed on the furniture, one arm trailing over the edge of the sofa, his running shoes kicked into the middle of the floor. As he fixed lunch or washed the dishes after supper, he hummed tunes and shifted back and forth on the balls of his feet. He never asked for directions but put the pans and dishes away wherever they seemed to fit.

He liked to make love to Anna on Sunday afternoons in his bedroom overlooking the Fell. He pulled her on top of him, raised her up with his thighs and came into her with his eyes open, his mouth softened and dark. He watched her through the entire act. Afterward, in the lambent yellow air of October afternoons, he didn't want to get up, or eat, or do any work; he liked to stay in the moist sheen of her flesh. If she started to get out of bed, he pulled her back and said, "Don't go. Let's lie around for a while."

Yet five days a week he went to his studio and was inaccessible to everyone, including Anna. There was no question of lying around with him on Monday or Tuesday afternoon. Although he taught classes for only part of the day, he was busy choreographing dances for a spring concert.

In town one day on business, Anna dropped by his studio. She could hear music inside, but the door was locked and she had to rap hard on the varnished wooden panel to let Jay know she was there. Finally he opened the door—but only twelve inches. He stood with his bare feet apart, one hand on the knob, wearing a pair of sweat pants and the top of a leotard.

"Not again?" he said with some humor. The last time she'd come to the studio, she'd been pregnant.

"No, I was just in town with the truck and thought I'd drop by."

"Ah," Jay said. He didn't move to let her in.

"I guess it's a bad time to visit."

"I'm in the middle of something, yes. How about meeting after my classes are over?"

Anna nodded. In fact, she would have liked to stay. She would have liked to sit by the window and watch the thin dark slice of the Ohio, flowing beyond the trees. She would have liked to watch Jay in the midst of choreography as he went over and over the same piece of music, his chest rising and falling, the waistband on his grey sweat pants wet with perspiration.

She had come to the studio because she wanted to see him absorbed in his own world, with his attention locked on something other than her.

Inevitably, she was most attracted to Jay when something else had caught his interest or imagination. When he wasn't thinking about her. It was easier for her when she didn't feel threatened by his desire. She didn't like repeating the limp words "I'm not ready."

The following Saturday she spent the afternoon and evening at his house. Daria was at a friend's. After an elaborate dinner prepared by Jay, Anna wanted to go out for a walk, or to a movie. She wanted to go dancing. She wanted to change into a dress and talk to people and look into windows and see what the rest of Fell River did on Saturday night. She didn't want to make love so early, leaving him too much time afterward to trail his fingers over her face, to put his mouth to her navel and hum, and to ask her questions.

Jay didn't want to go out. He took off his clothes and said he was too naked to go anywhere. Sitting in a chair in front of her, he rested his feet on her lap, kneading her thighs with his toes. Anna was self-conscious about her thighs, she thought they were too heavy. Jay, on the other hand, was perfectly relaxed about his body. There was no debate in him, no discontent.

"We've never talked about other men and women," she said.

"No, we haven't."

Jay's tranquillity and attention nettled her; she wanted to slow his relentless progression toward intimacy. "What do you think about it?" she asked. She was aware of a perverse desire to make Jay hop.

He sat up cross-legged on his chair and straightened his back. His penis lay on one thigh like a soft microphone, intimate party to this and a long line of previous conversations. It made Anna feel that Jay was not quite alone, while she was.

"I think," he said slowly, "that if you have something to tell me, you should do so, instead of asking me questions about it."

It was almost impossible to make Jay squirm. It wasn't in

him. He never tapped his feet on the floor or ground his teeth or drummed his fingers. He hardly ever yawned or scratched himself, and at moments like this, his composure made Anna feel scattered and unprepared.

"All right," she said. "We've never talked it over, but sometimes I think about it. I want to be free to go out with other men if it comes up."

"Have you got someone in mind?" Jay shifted his weight. His penis rolled down between his legs, less visible.

"No, I don't have anyone in mind, but I thought we should talk about it. I don't even know if you've been seeing other women in the last four months."

"You mean sleeping with other women?"

"Yes."

"I haven't."

"Have you wanted to?"

Jay breathed as slowly as ever, his breaths coming only half as often as Anna's. "I've been attracted to women, but I haven't slept with anyone. What about you?"

"I haven't seen anyone since we started to go out. But I want to."

That wasn't exactly true. She'd barely thought about other men. She only said it now to see if she could interrupt Jay's steady, naked breathing. When she found that she could, she relented. "It's not that I want to," she said, "but I want to be free to. I'm not ready to be exclusive."

"You've been ready for the last four months."

"Yes, but we never talked about it. I didn't know what you were doing with other women."

"Even if we never talked about it, you knew I wasn't doing anything."

Anna remembered how Jay had said, "I love you," the words uncoiling in the midst of sex as if from some uncontrolled storeroom in his chest. It was true, she knew he hadn't been with other women.

"I don't want to feel boxed in," she said.

Jay stood up smoothly, abruptly, and went to stand by the window. At forty-one he still had a boy's body, thin-waisted and hollowed at the top of the buttocks. He stooped and put on the pair of corduroys he'd dropped on the floor earlier. Then he turned and spoke.

"You're too old to give me this 'I need freedom' line, and I'm too old to listen to it. You don't want to get boxed in. Then do whatever you goddamn well feel like doing."

"Don't be angry at me, Jay. I want to come and see you, but I don't want it to be so inevitable. Couldn't we loosen it up a little?"

"Listen, you do what you want. If you don't want to come around, don't come around. I know how these things go. I'm in love with you and now that it's obvious, the soles of your feet are burning up."

"Jay . . ."

He pointed a finger at her. "Have I ever held you down and breathed on you so you couldn't get enough air? Just do what you have to and don't let me hear about it, because I've been through this before."

He picked up his shoes and walked out of the room. Anna sat on her chair, close to tears, listening to him as he banged around in the kitchen. This wasn't what she wanted. But nothing was what she wanted. She wanted to know if she could live with a man again and not have to retreat to her bedroom, and to Sam Turner's pond, and to these obscure rituals. She wanted to know what to do about Kevin, and her father, and Paul.

She wanted to know if she should ever have another child.

In the kitchen she found Jay scrubbing the refrigerator, his naked back still tanned and smooth and . . . *honorable*, Anna thought. He smelled of curry powder and chlorine. Fighting not to give in to him, she tied her thick blond hair back from her neck, stuck her hands in her pockets and waited for him to turn around. There was nothing meek about his look when he did; he wasn't humbled by the sponge and Ajax cleanser he held in either hand. But his eyes curled.

There was no way for him to know how attractive she found him at that moment. In the end, all she could do was say she was sorry and walk outside. Without Jay, there was nothing she wanted to do in Fell River, so she got into her car and drove back to her farm, the last insects of the fall slapping and dying against the windshield.

ANNA WENT OUT with the first man to attract her, a friend of Deal's. Deal had given up rock and roll touring years before and sold his pedal steel guitar, but now and again he filled in with a group from town called Peach Eater, playing slide with them on his old Stratocaster. The band did Talking Heads, Stevie Wonder, Stones and Third World tunes, as well as a few originals. Ross was their bass player.

Deal invited her to come down to the Club House on Friday night. Hesitant about going out to a bar alone, she showed up late, in the middle of the second set. Deal waved at her and jumped around the stage as he played, uncharacteristically ebullient. A New Deal, she thought, laughing back at him. Ross stood calmly to one side, wearing a yellow shirt and go-aheads, laying down a bass line that kept everyone dancing. In the smoky, ninety-degree club, he was the only one who looked composed.

But what attracted Anna to him was his high, sweet voice as he sang the lead on two of the band's originals. At the end of the set Deal stepped clear of the monitors and jumped down to the dance floor beside Anna—and Ross followed him. She was surprised at how short he was and how unlike a rock and roller he seemed without his guitar.

Ross turned out to be twenty-nine. Eight years younger than Anna, but certainly an adult. She let him do the courting. He bought her a margarita, he asked her questions, he touched her waist with his hand. He had straight white teeth.

She left before the last set was over, but the following day Ross called and asked if she'd like to go to Cincinnati with him, to make a club date for the band. Without knowing if it was an overnight invitation, she said yes. They met for breakfast at ten A.M. ("My earliest hour," Ross said), then drove to the city. He made a booking at one club, left a demo at another, and they were free for the rest of the afternoon.

"Have you ever been to the art museum at Mt. Adams?"

"A museum?" he asked skeptically.

She persuaded him. At Mt. Adams they found two touring exhibits, one a collection of ceramics, the other a display of erotic art from Persia. Ross scrutinized the Persian painting as if memorizing each detail. He put his nose close to the glass and tilted his forehead back, exposing a receding hairline. He didn't look like a musician—nor like a lover, Anna thought. Yet outside the museum, when she asked him what he thought of the paintings, he said flatly, "Sex is my life."

Anna almost laughed, he sounded so matter-of-fact. For herself, she'd never been able to separate the act of sex from the relationship as a whole. "I don't think it's my life," she said. "In fact, I'm not sure it exists on its own."

Ross looked dismayed.

"Don't get me wrong." She laughed. "I'm fond of it myself."

In the unseasonably warm afternoon, they found a grassy, secluded spot some distance from the museum. There, with the passion of initiates, they lay down on the grass and traded kisses. Ross unzipped his pants and slid his hands under Anna's dress. As families with children passed by on a distant sidewalk, they lay side by side, their lips touching, their hands on each other's genitals.

They went out to dinner, necked through the second half of a movie and found a motel room near the river, where Ross insisted on paying the entire bill. They made love twice. Anna surprised herself at feeling so relaxed with a man she hardly knew and perhaps did not approve of. It helped to be in an anonymous motel, and to feel she'd been taken there. But as the near-stranger beside her drifted off to sleep, she came fully awake and lay on her side of the bed, thinking how arbitrary it was to be in this particular place, with this particular person.

She had been right: sex was not divisible from the man, nor was a trip to Cincinnati divisible from her life with Jay, nor was Jay divisible from her history with Kevin. With some sadness, lying beneath the diffused neon light coming through the curtains of a Best Western motel room on the outskirts of Cincinnati, she knew that Ross was irrelevant to her. She had nothing to learn from him. Surely she had known that from the start, but somehow it took remembering. She thought for a moment of calling Jay up and telling him on the spot, but she held herself back.

A WEEK LATER, Anna told Jay she had gone out with another man.

"It was only one time. I don't think we'll do it again. Do you want me to tell you about it?"

Jay hesitated, his lips drawn together. "No, I don't. But I guess if you do go out again, I want to hear about it. Or even if you just feel like it."

"You got angry the last time I told you that."

"That's right, but I still want to know."

Jay was constrained with her for a few days, which, in the natural balance of couples, led Anna to be more affectionate. By Thanksgiving they had smoothed things out. Jay admitted to a jealousy he had never been able to control, and Anna tried to explain why she had needed to wander.

Thanksgiving marked the start of Anna's holiday: no work on the farm until next February, when the first seeds for the new season would be started in the greenhouse. Deal and Shelley took part-time Christmas jobs in Fell River, but Anna was free.

She invited Jay and Daria, her father and Susan, to Thanksgiving dinner at her house. Alex cooked the turkey and brought it out to the farm in a steaming pan, straight from his oven. Susan brought creamed onions, Jay a broccoli plate, everyone helped out.

198 · JOHN THORNDIKE

Daria, however, caught sight of the white, spongy lumps in Anna's mashed-potato gravy. "Yuck, what did you put in there, tofu?"

"Oh Daria, I'm sorry, I completely forgot. Maybe you could separate them out."

"No way. I don't want any of that stuff."

She wasn't any happier when the creamed onions were passed around, or her father's broccoli. "You know I hate sauce on broccoli," she told him. She was polite to Susan and Alex but passed over everything on the table except turkey and mashed potatoes and silently made it clear that those were the only foods she could possibly force down. As everyone else heaped their plates, Daria sat, begrudging the wait, with a flattened pile of mashed potatoes—no butter—and two slices of white turkey breast. A white dinner on a white plate.

"It wasn't the food," Jay said afterward as they all took a walk around the farm, with Daria some distance ahead of the rest of them. "She's angry that I'm going to the Outer Banks without her." He and Anna had planned a trip to the North Carolina beach for the three days after Thanksgiving.

"We could take her along," Anna said. "I wouldn't mind."

"I'd like her to come, in a way. But we've never gone anywhere alone."

Susan interrupted them. "I'd be glad to look after her if you need some help. Or take her to the movies or something."

"Thanks," Jay said. "But to be honest, she'd rather stay with Angela. She'd be shy with someone she didn't know well. Maybe a movie, though. She won't stay angry, she'll hardly think about me once I go."

The ground was hard and dry, so they followed the path all the way to the Ohio, walking in single file: Daria out ahead, beating the dried heads of ironweed and goldenrod with a stick, then Susan in her chair, then Alex, Anna and Jay. The trees along the river had all dropped their leaves.

"If I'd told Kevin I was going to the beach without him," Anna said, "he'd have had a seizure."

"For the greater glory of parents," Jay said, "children sometimes have to be denied."

Anna turned and looked at him, but there was no sign of mockery on his face. "They really do," he said. "It's only fair."

Recently, Anna had discovered she could bring Kevin's name up in front of Jay without putting a chill on the conversation; he took references to her son with equanimity, sometimes even with humor. Her heart still jumped up in her chest when she mentioned Kevin's name in front of others, but it was a help that Jay found the topic neither sacred nor scary.

Early the next morning Anna and Jay set out from Fell River through the frosted brown-and-grey landscape of late November. They crossed the aging Smokies, descended to the red claylands of North Carolina and drove out of the last of the pine woods onto Pamlico Sound just before dark. It was twenty degrees warmer than in Fell River. They turned south at Whalebone Junction onto a trafficless spit of land on which there was no more red clay, no earth at all, only sand, salt vegetation and the smell of the sea.

At Cape Hatteras, in the aural tumult of the national park campsite, Anna helped Jay pitch his new dome tent. They chose a secluded spot behind low pines, but even there the wind whistled at them over the dunes, pushing the sound of breaking waves through the scrub. The campground was almost empty. After anchoring the tent with oversized pegs, Jay took Anna's arm and led her toward the beach, their feet mushing out beneath them in the sand.

As they rose over the last low dune into the gusty wind, the sound of the ocean doubled. Except for white streaks of breaking surf forty yards out, and the roil of foam that slapped up onto the beach, the water was almost invisible. Anna's face opened. She smelled the wrack and tar thrown up by the last high tide and sucked in the salt air over her tongue. She watched one wave after the next crash onto the shore, each one spinning a billion sand particles against a billion others, busily rearranging the eternal convergence of water and earth. *All this time,* she thought. Every hour of every day, ignoring all human arrangements, the ocean continued to thunder onto the shore. Nostalgia meant less to it than a cork. Beyond the horizon, the next land was Morocco.

The following morning they walked along the beach, fed the black-headed laughing gulls and took the ferry to Ocracoke. The wind died down in the warm afternoon. After dark they explored the village and found a restaurant in the front room of someone's house. The menu offered only scallops, bluefish and baked potatoes.

Across the table, Jay looked windblown and tanned. Anna asked him if life with him would always be as easy as it was on this trip.

"I like to think so."

"Sometimes I worry that I'm too somber for you. I'm afraid I'll hold you back."

"I've adapted so far," he said, smiling.

"But I don't want you to adapt. I don't want to hold you down."

"I have my own worries, Anna. I can keep clear of yours."

"It doesn't work that way. You know it doesn't."

The waitress interrupted them with a pan of shucked scallops in butter and a large plate of bluefish. She looked like a grey-haired college professor. "This is what I've been eating for two weeks straight," she said, "Thanksgiving included."

They ate in silence, until Anna said, "Things are easier for me now."

"I've noticed that."

"But it still comes and goes. If I start thinking about Kevin, everything looks bad to me and I get depressed. Then I don't care about my father, or Susan, or the farm, or anything. Or you. Sometimes I think about you and I don't even know who you are. That still happens. Then it passes."

"What do you want me to do, Anna, give you up? Look how good it is now."

"I'd like to be swept away like a young girl, but I'm not. I don't know if I'm too old, or too careful, or what it is. We don't use the word 'love.' "

"No," Jay said, "we don't. Not usually."

"Sometimes I think I'm too hard-headed. And sometimes I worry about Daria."

"She was a tyrant at Thanksgiving, wasn't she?"

Anna put down her fork and lowered both hands to her lap. "She made this trip a test case. I'm not saying you should have brought her. I'm glad we came by ourselves. But at home . . ." She paused, thinking out what she wanted to say. "I hope you give Daria all the attention she needs at home. If she ever got the idea you were leaving her for me, she'd fight me every chance she got."

"That won't happen, Anna. I might come to the ocean with you instead of her, but I'd never leave Daria for you or anyone else. She comes first, she has to."

"It could get more complex," Anna said, looking down at her plate.

"How?"

"If you ever had another child."

"I've thought about that," he said. "I've even talked to Daria about it."

Anna added quickly, "It's just one of those questions that comes to mind."

After dinner the wind died away completely and the temperature rose under the cover of low clouds. The Ocracoke campground was as empty as the one at Hatteras. Jay assembled the tent, then suggested they move it to the beach; four aluminum wands maintained its form, and it only weighed a few pounds. He set it down just above high-tide level, Anna threw in the sleeping bags, and they crawled inside.

In the windless night, the beach still hummed and shook under large waves, the residue of yesterday's storm. The sound of the ocean filled the tent and overwhelmed Anna's thoughts.

She unzipped the two sleeping bags and climbed between them, but when Jay started to take off her clothes and she made a move to help him, he stopped her. Placing her hands at her side, palms to the ground, he told her to stay with the ocean.

Engulfed by everything marine, buoyed by the soprano curl of the waves and the tremulous chatter of stones at the break, Anna stretched her hands and feet to the four corners of the tent. In the pitch black, Jay passed his mouth over her lips, over her neck and breasts, giving her no chance to kiss him back. When she raised her head, he placed his palm on her forehead and pressed gently until she lowered her head back onto the sleeping bag. He turned her over, and over again, laying his palm on her mouth, his penis on her chest, his lips on her navel. He wouldn't let her rise or touch him.

I'm not responsible for this night, she thought.

She lay on the clement earth, under the black sky, beside the intrusive, unstoppable ocean. Jay, or some part of Jay, passed from her navel to her anus to the base of her spine, all the way up her back to her skull. Anna floated. She knew early on that she was going to come. Jay entered her, left her and drove into her again wildly, pushing her into a corner of the tent. She let him. She led him. She lifted him off the ground with her strong, smooth hips and grabbed his buttocks with her hands. In her breathless, expanded moment, the cries of sea animals and birds filled the black air of the tent and lifted her off the ground.

She didn't know if Jay came. She didn't know anything. He lay on top of her, slumped and still, loading her hips into the sand. He might have been dead save that his chest rose and fell. When she finally touched him on the shoulder, he raised his head slowly.

"I'm wide awake," she said. "Let's talk."

"Haven't we said everything?"

"Let's tell stories."

"I'm fresh out of stories."

Anna wrapped her legs around his thighs and squeezed. *Tell* me," she said. "Tell me about coming."

"Ah, that. I think you go to a different world. I'm a bear, I've got nothing to tell a seal."

"But you like me to go there."

"I do. I like you to go there, and come back, and go again."

CHAPTER 7

S ITTING in the bucket seat of Alex's small car on the way to the Columbus airport, Susan was acutely aware of leaving her Chevrolet behind.

"I thought about taking it," she said, "but it's an ungodly long trip to Santa Fe. I'm not up to a thousand miles of Route Forty."

"You wouldn't want to have a breakdown in the middle of Oklahoma."

Alex's profuse, greying hair hung over his collar. As she had done more often in recent weeks, Susan thought about him being sixty-three years old. It didn't make sense for her to go out with someone that old, because by the time she got to be fifty, he'd be eighty. *Dios guarde.* But dressed in Eddie Bauer hiking pants, a plaid shirt and a pair of running shoes, Alex looked, as always, much younger than his age.

"I have to go back, Alex. I never decided to leave in the first place, they just took me from one hospital to the next. First to St. Vincent's, then to Albuquerque Presbyterian and then back to rehab in Fell River. My old life went out the window, it vanished. I have to say good-bye to it, at least."

By choosing to go back to Santa Fe she had turned up Alex's soft side. He talked sparingly and listened to every word she said. Glancing across at him as he drove, she noticed how his eyebrows had grown bushy and rebellious.

"I don't even know if your ticket is one-way or round trip."

"I'll come back after I settle things in New Mexico. It's one-way, but I'll come back."

He drove, looking straight ahead. "I hated it when Freya left, but she had to go and there was no stopping her."

"But she left for ten years. I only want a couple of months."

Alex gave her a thin smile. "Can I have a sworn affidavit on that?"

"We could have gone to the mayor. 'I, Susan Rupert, hereby promise not to stay in New Mexico for more than three months.' "

"Don't make a vow you can't be sure of. Besides, it's better for everybody if you just do what you have to. Or what you want to."

"You're so wise, Alex. I wish I could be that wise."

"The older I get, the less I care about being wise. I'd rather be happy."

The quivering blue light and textured decor of Columbus's new terminal, identical to a hundred other airports, made Susan feel like she'd already left the Midwest. They checked her bags and sat in a corner of the gate area, avoiding cigarette smoke and other people's conversations. Alex was cold; he crossed his arms over his chest and tapped his feet on the carpeted floor.

The man at the counter announced Susan's flight, with a first boarding call for anyone requiring assistance. Alex kissed her on the mouth and stood up.

"I'm lousy at good-byes," she said. "They never mean anything to me. But later on I'll miss you."

Susan turned toward the gate, but before she reached the door two elderly women rolled by in a pair of airport wheelchairs, pushed by their husbands. The chairs flew small metal pennants mounted on aluminum poles but had no hand rims. Susan held Alex's arm for a moment, then turned and let her chair roll free down the carpeted incline as far as the first turn, where she skidded to a stop like a kid hotdogging a bicycle. Alex stood at the door. She waved a last time, rolled around the corner and caught up to the two women as they entered the accordion chamber joining airport to airplane.

The two husbands, looking portly and golfish in checked double-knit pants, held the wheelchairs steady—and the two women stood up, gathered their purses and sweaters, and walked into the airplane past the solicitous faces of the attendants.

There was nothing wrong with them! Susan wheeled onto the plane, handed her boarding pass to a stewardess and watched the two women walk down the aisle. They had *chosen* to sit in wheelchairs as if they were invalids. Christ Almighty, they took such treatment as an honor.

Susan found her own aisle seat and lifted herself into it. She couldn't get the image of the two women out of her mind: their pastel blouses and blue hair. Screw old women, she thought. Maybe they had liver troubles or something. But they had walked down the aisle easily enough, chatting away. She wanted to ram her chair into their shins.

Where did this rage come from? Two minutes after leaving Alex she wanted to knock down a couple of old women and rip out their puckered lips.

As soon as the plane took off she fell asleep and didn't fully wake until the pilot announced their approach to Albuquerque. The plane furrowed directly into the sunlight, dipped repeatedly through the yellow evening air and landed with a thump.

Susan, the last one off, found Scott's wide blond face above the dwindling crowd of families and travelers. He held his index finger up in the air, angled toward her, an old greeting. He'd finally cut his long hair.

"It's great to see you again," he said. "You look good, you really do." He took her hand and bent down to kiss her on the cheek. His chipper formality shrank Susan's heart, and when he stepped behind her to push her chair up the long corridor, she cut him off.

"I can manage. It's the only way I keep in shape."

They talked desultorily while waiting for her bags, then passed through a pair of electric doors into the sunlight. Susan inhaled the dry air. December tenth and seventy degrees.

"We're having a heat wave," Scott said. "Hey!" An airport cop in a white shirt stood beside his Buick, writing a ticket. The car was parked in a handicapped space. "Here we come," Scott said, waving and pointing at Susan.

The cop tore the yellow ticket in half. "No problem. No problem."

"Well, that's something." Scott was pleased. He had always loved a good deal.

In the day's last light they drove north past rabbit brush, piñon trees and Rocky Mountain junipers. Susan sat beside her door with the window open and the wind whipping her hair. Magpies drifted across the highway and jack rabbits snipped into the grey-green chamisa lining the pavement.

"So how's your new woman?"

"Beth? She's fine."

Scott gave her the gossip from Santa Fe, almost all of it about dissolving marriages and couples who had drifted apart. Susan waited for him to ask about her life in Ohio, but he didn't. How wonderfully Scott could talk on and on, she thought, without letting her know how he felt about anything. She had written him about Alex and her struggles in Fell River, but he didn't seem to be curious about any of that. He gave her a complicated history of recent water problems in Santa Fe and told her about his last camping trip into the desert. Although he had clearly gone with Beth, he kept saying, "I climbed this . . . I found that . . ."

"Do you fuck a lot? You and this woman you live with?"

Scott sat up. He moistened his dry lips with his tongue and prepared a speech. "I tried to make this clear over the phone, Susan. You're welcome to stay at my house, and there's no reason we can't be friends. But I live with Beth. You were the one who told me not to visit you anymore at the hospital. The last time I went they wouldn't let me upstairs."

"Yes, and on top of that I can't walk anymore, and I said I wouldn't come to see you until I could. But I've come anyway."

"I'm glad you have."

"But you're going to act as if we accidentally passed out of each other's lives. As if we didn't sleep together for three years and talk about having children and promise to meet every Halloween for the rest of our lives. You're not going to ask me how I feel, or let me start telling you how dreadful this is and how much I hate it." She banged her hand on the dash. Scott looked over, his lips tight. "Just because I can't walk," she said quietly, "doesn't mean I'm not a woman anymore. I am. I have a man in Ohio and I'm not going to throw myself at you. So you don't have to treat me like a piece of stoneware."

Before they reached Santa Fe the night had cooled; a few pockets of snow even showed up beside the road. Susan asked him to pull over so she could breathe the dry air and smell the desert. Scott stopped at an abandoned rest stop, where they sat side by side in the dark as the rush of truck tires and diesel engines approached them from behind, passed, and droned off into the night. She wanted him to unbutton both their shirts and hold her against his chest.

She couldn't have explained that to him, at least not the way she felt it. She had been sleeping with Alex—successfully, as the books said—and that wasn't what she wanted with Scott. She wanted to be acknowledged. She wanted to touch his skin and lie next to him, and not feel that sex was all genitalia. She wanted to feel Scott's hands on her breasts and to smell the odor of his body, the hint of potter's clay that was always with him.

She couldn't ask for that, so she leaned against him inside the protected car, silent, taking what she could get. She knew he wouldn't sit there long, and he didn't.

Beth turned out to be pretty, ten years younger than Susan, with long chestnut hair. She was also twenty pounds over-weight—almost fat, Susan thought—though she had good posture and an easy gait. She asked, without embarrassment, if Susan needed any help around the house or any special ar-rangements in the bathroom. Susan liked her immediately. Beth didn't seem threatened, nor did she treat Susan as if she were an able-bodied woman who just happened to be spending her time in a wheelchair.

"I'm a masseuse," Beth said, "but I've never worked with the disabled."

Scott relaxed in the living room—Susan saw him visibly unwind as Beth assumed the responsibility for her visit. She showed Susan to the guest bedroom, in the corner of which were stacked ten identical cardboard boxes, each one labeled "Susan" in black Magic Marker. The handwriting wasn't Scott's.

"Those are my things?"

"I packed them away, I hope that was all right. Scott still has some pictures of you in his room. I know this is awkward. Do you want to see them?"

"No. I'll get this stuff out of here eventually."

"It was hard on him." Beth lifted Susan's suitcase to a small table. "He still misses you, though he doesn't like to show it."

"But he has you."

"I only moved in a few months ago. We didn't go out together when you lived here. I knew him, but we were just friends."

"He was free," Susan said. "I'd half moved into my own house, and I was fucking Mel."

Beth's eyes opened wide, but she didn't say anything. Susan hardly knew where such language came from. She wanted to shake up Beth as she had shaken up Scott. It was all too smooth: the quiet roll of her wheels on the tile floors and the orderly bedroom with its stack of uniform cardboard boxes.

"Do you think you'll move back to Santa Fe?"

"I guess I could. I have a lot of history here, I came to Santa Fe thirteen years ago."

"I was only eleven years old then."

During the next few days Susan called her friends on the phone, many of whom came to visit her. Scott kept to his studio, and Beth went to work every day. Susan lost the urge to shock her, and the two women relaxed. Beth didn't have the least hesitation at leaving her and Scott together. She's not the jealous type, Susan thought.

But one night Beth answered the phone and passed it abruptly to Scott. He started a conversation standing up, then pulled the cord behind him and went to sit outside the front door. Beth and Susan went on talking, but when Scott came back, Beth stopped in midsentence and asked him who had called.

"Adele."

"And you have to talk to her outside in the cold?"

She was jealous. She was jealous of some woman who had called on the phone, yet she wasn't jealous of Susan, who had lived with Scott in that same house, who had come back from Ohio to see him, and who still wanted to lie down beside him and touch his chest.

In that moment, Beth erased Susan as a woman. Because Susan couldn't feel anything below the waist, she was no threat. Beth threw her out of the sexual leagues without a thought, and Susan hated her for it. But she couldn't say anything about it. She couldn't convince her to be jealous.

So she drank. She had Scott reach her the bottle of mescal, a large clear bottle with a white worm resting on the bottom. *Con Gusano*, the label assured her; each bottle with a worm. Scott drank a little, Beth a little, and Susan drank the rest of the bottle.

In pure forgetfulness she got as drunk as an Indian—as the true Indians of Mexico and Guatemala, who still live Indian lives. She took the last of the bottle, left the house without a word and wheeled up Canyon Road, then off onto side streets to get away from the lights. She tried to count the stars but only got to forty before losing track. The brighter ones shone through the glass of the empty mescal bottle, tipped overhead. She spat out the worm.

In the eyes of the world she was no longer sexual. She knocked on her thighs, raised her knees one by one and let them drop. She thought about Alex and how she had been seductive with him, needing some affirmation that she hadn't withered sexually. Maybe he didn't notice that, in his own need. But she was clever and led him on, too fast for either of them.

Drunker and drunker, wheeling around the back streets of Santa Fe, she felt she didn't have to have Alex, or Scott, or anyone else. Of course she was a woman, and wanted intimacy. Sex was still part of her being. When she took a man between her legs, even if she didn't feel him, she took the force that women have taken forever and gave the same force back. If a man came to her, fine. She didn't want to seduce him in order to define herself as a sexual being. She was a sexual being.

Scott found her an hour later, her coat unbuttoned in the cold night, the empty bottle wedged between her legs. A neighbor who had seen her outside Scott's house called to tell him the woman in the wheelchair was whirling around in the alley, singing songs and "howling." Susan didn't remember that the next day, but it was probably so. She sang Sonoran tributes to mescal. She forgave Beth. She thought, No matter what, I'll always have the night.

The next morning she woke up like an Indian, with no hangover—but so blue the world seemed to have come unraveled. Scott's kitchen disintegrated when she rolled into it, the toaster and blender flying around in her vision until she stared at the floor tiles and backed out into the living room. She ran a bath to clean up, but the water coming out of the faucet looked like an animal, and the toothbrushes over the sink jumped up and down. She knew that wasn't so and stared at them to make them stop, but the more she stared, the more they skittered around. She had to bathe with her eyes shut.

She waited half the day for her vision to settle down. She thought, Maybe this is what Indians have instead of hangovers. By the time Beth came home from work Susan was able to talk, and the three of them went out to a movie. But Susan knew she could no longer be comfortable in Scott's house, and the next day she went to stay near Tesuque at her friend Laura's.

TWICE Susan began a letter to Alex, but got no further than writing, "You might not know me anymore, for the bitterness that's come over me in the last month."

In Fell River she had always been calm. At Laura's house she wept and screamed, facing the fact she could no longer explore silent rivers at night, or walk up dry arroyos past coyote spoor, or run after sagebrush in the rolling wind. Never to kick a ball, never to feel her calves ache with work, never to feel a man moving inside her. It was beyond words.

Each day the sun rose with the same mocking clarity of perfect weather. Gloom was out of place in the desert. In the entire ecology only Susan was morbid, writing in her notebook and wheeling herself about on the polished floors of Laura's house. She felt it was wrong to be embittered, outlandish to be disabled.

She began another letter to Alex. "I'll never be as disabled as I am here, in this savage land. A foot off the road and I'm mired down. I had to come back to the desert to find my worst rage."

Every morning Laura got up at five and painted for three hours before going to work. Her diligence threw Susan's lack of will into relief. She lived without a man. She had owned her house for five years, mudding it herself and varnishing the pine vigas. She was a collector of skulls. Perched around her living room sat the bleached white braincases of foxes, hares, prairie dogs and raccoons. With exactitude, Laura had mounted the miniature skulls of birds on vertical wires, so delicate that the skulls quivered when the front door of the house opened or closed. Susan thought she knew the desert well herself but had never found the skull of a bird there.

Two weeks after moving in she sat on the patio in back of Laura's house, warming herself in the winter sun and listening to the sound of *rancheras norteñas* from a radio somewhere out in the desert. Desert, she thought, was not the right word. That was only the word people used for this stark, dry, almost tree-less land. The air of the desert—the lack of air, the absence of anything whatsoever in the sky—was the invention of a purist.

Chattering on the washboard road and trailing a plume of dust, a vehicle approached from the village of Tesuque. A sag-ging blue fifties pickup slowed and stopped. Susan heard its metal door groan open and close with a bang. There was a knock. Opening the front door, she found a woman dressed in blue jeans and a white TVLKING HEVDS sweat shirt. A few years older than Susan, the woman had short black uneven hair and black eyes. She was Spanish, Susan thought, rather than Indian. Or maybe both. She held her arms slightly away from her body and carried her weight on the balls of her feet.

"I'm Elena Resgado."

Susan rolled her chair back six inches. Elena stood motion-less in the doorway. She said, "You knew my husband, Mel."

"Yes."

"You can't walk at all?"

"No."

Elena didn't move a whisper. Not her hands, not her feet, not her eyes. Susan kept the footrest of her chair between them.

"Are you unhappy?" Elena asked.

Susan stared at her. "Sometimes I am," she admitted.

"You didn't think that could happen, did you? That some-thing that bad could happen. I should never have let Mel go climbing with you. There were bad signs all over it."

"I tried to write you, but the letters came back. I knew Mel was married, but he told me you had . . . an open marriage."

"He told women anything he felt like. What is this 'open marriage'?"

Susan looked away. "I don't know."

"Of course you don't know. You were never married. Mel and I got married in a church in Barcelona, did you know that? Did you know we had two children?"

"No, I didn't. I'm sorry, Mel never told me anything about you."

214 · JOHN THORNDIKE

"And you didn't ask. But I know plenty about you."

"You do?"

"I know you were tired of your job. I know you're a foot taller than I am, and you like to screw on top. I know plenty."

"What do you want?" Susan asked. "How did you find out I was here?"

"Mel used to tell me those little details. And when I got jealous enough, we'd go to bed and make love until the house shook. You think you were the only one?"

Susan rolled her chair an inch forward and said coldly, "I don't screw on top anymore."

"Maybe not." Elena relaxed her posture and slid her hands into the back pockets of her jeans. "I guess not."

The two women remained in the doorway without saying anything. Finally Susan asked, "Do you want to come in and sit down?"

Elena nodded. "Yes, I want to."

They sat upright on two straight-backed chairs, drinking coffee. Elena said, "I left town after Mel died. Everything was dangerous here, so I went to live with my grandmother in Oaxaca. I hadn't been there since I was a child. I thought I could get through all this on my own, but I still have questions."

Susan thought her questions would be jealous ones about sex with Mel, or how they had met, or what he had told her about his marriage. But there was none of that. Elena only asked about the day Mel died. What the weather was like, what Susan had worn, what animals and birds they saw on the way out to the Bandelier, whether or not the waning moon was visible before sunrise.

Because her memory of the accident had only come back to her in pieces, and there were still gaps, Susan couldn't tell Elena everything she wanted to know. But the dark-haired woman simply leaned forward in her chair and asked another question. She asked about every detail of the climb, down to the striations in the rock in which Mel had driven pitons. She wanted to know what position he had been in when he died. Of course Susan didn't know that. Elena never got angry, she just asked another question.

"Did you talk to the Debarrs?" Susan asked. "They probably remember that day much better than I do."

Elena flicked her hand. "Gone. Left town."

That she wanted to know everything about the day of her husband's death—Susan could understand that. But some questions made no sense. When Mel coiled the rope at the start of the climb, had he taken it up in free coils, or had he wrapped it between his thumb and his elbow? Did he whistle or hum or make any noises when he climbed?

Elena paused, looking out across the patio at the pincushion cactus and sagebrush of the overgrazed field beyond, and asked if Susan had worn Mel's climbing helmet. She had. Of course, if Mel had been wearing the helmet instead of Susan, or if they had both had helmets . . .

Or if they had gone some other day, or if they had picked another route up the rock face, or if they had said something different or laughed at a different time, if they had done anything at all to change the exact moment at which Mel lost his grip, they might never have fallen.

So many of Elena's questions were about climbing that Susan finally asked her if she had climbed with her husband— though it was one of the few things she had heard about Elena, that she didn't climb.

"You don't ask me anything," Elena said. "I ask you."

Then she started in on even smaller particulars. Had Mel ever stuttered, did he look closely at his hands, was there wind from the south? In the end, Susan's answers disappointed her. She sighed and looked out through the window.

Susan told her she was sorry.

"Sorrow is unimportant, it's baggage. You've suffered more than I have, and more than Mel." Abruptly, she knelt on one knee next to the wheelchair. Raising her hands to Susan's face, she asked, "May I?" Susan thought she wanted to touch her.

But Elena cupped her hands and stared at her left eye. "Your back is strained," she said finally, "and your liver is swollen. You should stop drinking."

"How do you know I've been drinking?"

"The eye speaks for the body. I'm an iridologist. You survived the fall that killed another person. Now what are you going to do with your life?"

That was it. Susan had spent a month in New Mexico and decided nothing. She didn't know what she was going to do about the desert, or work, or men, or even where she ought to live. Elena's sharp look brought her to the edge of tears.

"I'm going to take you to the Fuentes de Lima," Elena said, "and you can bathe in the waters. That will help your back, and if you stop drinking, your liver will return to normal. Then you can make some decisions. If I come back in two days, can you leave then?"

"It's so sudden. And why would you do this for me?"

"*Porque su muerte nos amarra.* His death binds us. And I have more questions. Perhaps I'll always have more."

NEITHER SUSAN NOR LAURA had ever heard of the Fuentes de Lima, nor were the hot springs listed in Laura's guidebook to New Mexico.

"This Elena Resgado," Laura said. "I asked a couple of friends about her. She has an eccentric reputation."

"Like what?"

"One woman said she saw her go into a trance at a party. She smokes dope and drinks."

"That doesn't seem too eccentric, considering her husband died less than a year ago."

"You know, Susan, you don't owe this woman anything. It wasn't your fault he fell off the cliff and died. Does she blame you?"

"I don't think she came to see me out of revenge."

"Then why?"

"She wanted to hear about Mel's death."

"Do you have to go with her to these springs?"

"I don't have to, but I want to. I'll be careful."

"How careful can you be?" Laura asked. "Headed off to some unknown place at the other end of the state."

"And in a wheelchair."

"Exactly."

"I take a lot on faith," Susan said. "Every day."

Two days later Elena returned, honked the horn and started throwing things out of the pickup cab into the bed: jumper cables, a tow chain, a couple of cans of oil, a rucksack and a bag of food. Susan threw in her coat and borrowed sleeping bag, and managed to haul herself up onto the soft, dusty front seat of the truck. With hardly a word exchanged, the two women headed south on Route 285, passed Santa Fe and drove on into open country.

Behind the wheel of her truck, Elena looked hardly bigger than a child. She drove for thirty minutes without saying a word, then broke the silence with an abrupt, isolated comment: "Mel had a son by another woman, years ago."

A half hour later, as if they'd been carrying on a steady conversation, she said, "The desert is always most alive during the third quarter of the moon."

"That's where the moon is now, isn't it?"

"You should learn to pay attention to your body so you can tell when your kidneys or liver are under strain. I shouldn't have to look in your eyes to find that out." Then she retired into silence again behind the unmuffled roar of the truck engine. The Rocky Mountain junipers and piñon pines of the high plains gave way to four-wing saltbush, Mormon tea and creosote bush, the true plants of the desert. As the altitude dropped, the temperature grew warmer.

After dark they stopped for a bowl of chili at Los Corderos. Four men playing pool in the back of the restaurant paused to look them over, then went back to their game. Though Susan had heard grotesque stories to the contrary, she found that generally her wheelchair soothed men. They didn't feel the need to hustle and strut about and make comments.

Elena ordered her chili in a flat, unstressed tone of voice. Her southwest accent came and went. She hardly paid Susan any more attention than she had in the truck.

Beyond Los Corderos the serrated profile of black mountains jutted into the western sky. The road looked half-abandoned, its crumbling asphalt devoid of markings. After a turn west and another turn south, Elena slowed and stared into the dark, looking for something at the sandy edge of the pavement. Three identical roads appeared, none of them marked. After slowing almost to a stop at each one, Elena accelerated and drove on. She passed the fourth road completely before backing up, staring, and turning onto it, leaving the pavement behind.

"How did you know which one to take?"

"There were stones."

"Where? I didn't see anything."

"No one lives on this ranch anymore. The owner died mysteriously, so the people here think the springs are evil. They're all superstitious *pendejos*. I've bathed here many times. Mel brought a friend here once and cured him of lupus after two days in the pools."

Susan folded her hands over her kneecaps. "You don't think to cure me of this, do you?"

"Not exactly, no."

After a ten-mile run into the foothills, the road ended abruptly in the courtyard of an abandoned ranch. Three or four buildings, still luminous with whitewash, stood out behind a line of dead trees. Lime trees, Elena said. Once the marvel of the ranch, but now as dead as the owner. Parked in front of the roofless main house, the two women waited for their eyes to adjust to the darkness. A path led around one side of the building.

After an easy first hundred yards the trail turned sharply

uphill. Elena pushed the wheelchair from behind until they topped the rise onto a small horseshoe of land. The bottom pool, cut into the rock and fed by water dripping down from two pools above, had raised the temperature of the night air by ten degrees.

Elena took her clothes off and stood beside the pool with nothing on. A small, thin woman, she had practically no rear end.

Eventually, Susan's desire to get into the water overcame her embarrassment. She disconnected her catheter tube, removed her clothes and let herself down onto the cold stone like a lizard. The night air was warmer than in Santa Fe, but not tropical.

Elena hunkered down on the stone ledge beside her, lowered one foot into the water, then the other, and slid off the rock into the pool. "Go in slowly," she said. "You won't get burned. Put your legs in an inch at a time and tell me what you feel."

At first Susan felt nothing; neither the hot water, nor the cold rock against her bottom. The water gave off an acrid dry smell as it trickled from pool to pool and drained toward the mesa. Only a few points of light, distant mercury-vapor lamps, broke the darkness to the east. Susan's vision began to flicker, the way it did after drinking mescal. Although her feet were only immersed to the knees, she felt the pressure of the water on them. That couldn't be so, for her legs were completely insensate—yet there was something she felt.

"Slowly," Elena whispered. "What do you feel here?" She lifted herself out of the water and laid her palm against her own stomach.

Susan didn't answer, but a bittersweet tingling filled her body.

"That thrill that spreads up into your chest—that comes from your kidneys. Slide into the pool, but go slow."

The closer the water came to her navel, the less Susan understood her own sensations. Perched on a stone step at the edge of the pool, she dropped into the water an eighth of an inch at a time. Other than the trickling spill of water and the distant call of a crow, the night was silent. As the water rose to her navel, waves of feeling rushed over her. Her breasts felt gorgeous. On the eastern horizon a milky silver glow spread into the sky: the third-quarter moon, preparing to rise.

After drying her hands on her shirt, Elena removed a single small joint from a plastic film case. "Pure indicus bud," she said.

Susan didn't care to smoke. But when Elena held the lighted joint to her mouth, she inhaled, keeping her own wet hands off the paper. Within seconds she felt high. Perhaps it was the marijuana, or perhaps Elena's talk had made her light-headed, or perhaps it was the strange fact of bathing in the middle of the night, miles from nowhere. Whatever, Susan grew even more confused about what she could feel and what she couldn't. She ran her fingers lightly up and down her legs.

Elena floated with no apparent effort on the opposite side of the small pool, her head a disembodied globe on the dark water. "The heart and the genitals," she said, "are the two strongest seats of feeling. Any heart attack victim can tell you how much the heart feels. You should keep track of it, always. And you should know your genitals as well—both what they look like and what they feel like. Some women know nothing of their own bodies. Touch your breasts, pretend a man is touching them."

As Susan circled her nipples, an underwater thread ran down her chest to her genitals—and for the first time since the accident, she felt her clitoris. Sweet Jesus, she felt it. Maybe it's only the dope, she thought, or the water. But when she explored her vagina, and then her anus, she felt the touch of her fingers. It was faint but sure, she had feeling. It went on and on, it was no illusion. She laughed and almost cried. "I can feel my hand!" she said.

"You're a lucky woman."

Susan had never once seen Elena smile, but even in the dark she could tell she was smiling now.

THE NEXT MORNING, after only a few hours' sleep, Susan watched the eastern sky change from grey to rose to yellow. The sun waded into sight, quivered as it broke contact with the horizon, and sprang into the sky in little charged hops, as if irregularly wired. Vapor from the hot springs rose straight up into the windless sky.

Elena, tucked into a down sleeping bag, slept as late as a teenager. Susan watched the progress of the sun, opened her own bag to its direct rays and finally drifted back to sleep. It was noon before the two women got up, ate a breakfast of yogurt and apples, and maneuvered Susan's chair up to the next pool.

The water in the middle pool was too hot for Susan to stay in for more than a few minutes at a time; her heart wouldn't slow down. Elena jumped in and out, drying off her small brown body in the sunshine and giving Susan long, strange looks.

Susan wondered why this woman, whose husband she had taken to bed, was doing so much for her. In return she had answered a few questions—but what was that? As the afternoon went on, Elena smoked a lot of dope, stayed silent for long periods and delivered the same kind of isolated flat comments as she had on the drive down.

"Mel could stay in the top pool for an hour, he was impervious to heat."

"All the trees here have died. No one looked after them."

"You still don't know what you're going to do with your life."

After each remark Elena turned aside and surveyed the horizon, as if to avoid any further conversation. The guarded neutral expression on her face disappeared, and she wore the exaggerated look of someone deep in thought, or pain.

Susan asked her how long she and Mel had been married. Elena didn't hear, or didn't answer. "Mel told me you had an arrangement. The way I understood it, everything was out in the open."

222 • JOHN THORNDIKE

"How could he resist a young woman like you?"

"I didn't chase him, Elena. He asked me out three times before I even said I'd have a beer with him."

"Mel was five years younger than me."

"He was?"

That meant Elena was almost fifty. "Was he really?" Susan asked again.

"Did I tell you once, or not?"

Susan had taken Elena to be a woman of elfin grace, forty at most.

Ten minutes later, floating on the far side of the pool, Elena said in her flat tone: "You killed my husband."

"I didn't kill Mel, he almost killed me."

"You didn't even love him."

"How could I, I didn't know him that well."

"Then why?"

With a single smooth motion, Elena lifted herself out of the water and walked to her clothes. Without once looking back she started down the path to the ranch house, holding her pants and shirt in one hand and her sneakers in the other. Her wet flanks steamed as she felt her way down barefooted.

"Where are you going?" Susan yelled after her.

Halfway down the path and half out of sight, Elena turned around. *"Cago en tu madre,"* she screamed. "I'm going to Mexico. I've had enough of your *pendejadas."*

Ten more steps and she disappeared. Susan yelled again, but no answer. Two minutes later the truck started, backed once, and shot straight out the road, in third gear by the time it emerged into sight.

It was no trick. She had gone, leaving Susan with nothing but her clothes, the sleeping bags and a couple of apples. Had the whole trip been a setup to punish her for sleeping with Mel—for killing him, as Elena said?

It was ten miles at least from the springs to the paved road. Susan had often walked that far across the desert with Scott, but she'd never done more than three or four miles at a stretch in her wheelchair, even on a paved surface.

Either she had to walk it or wait for Elena to come back—which might be worse. She got dressed and managed to pull herself up into the wheelchair, thinking someone else might come. But there was no evidence that anyone ever visited the springs—not even beer cans, the desert sign of human passage.

After the sun set behind the beige-and-black mountains to the west, the temperature began to drop. Susan draped her coat over her shoulders and stationed her chair close to the edge of the pool. She drank, slowly, for ten minutes, lowering her hand over and over into the water, taking in as much liquid as she could. The astringent spring water smelled faintly of soda, but she had drunk some the night before with no ill effect. Unless she could dig for it, there would be no water between the ranch and Los Corderos.

The closer it grew to dusk, the calmer she felt. Sitting on one sleeping bag and folding the other one on her lap, she started down the path. Twice she almost fell out of her chair as it skidded over the rock outcroppings, but she made it to the lowest pool, and from there down the path to the abandoned ranch house.

For the first five hundred yards the road ran downhill in an easy coast. When the ground flattened she settled into a working rhythm. She had thought her arms were strong, but they soon ached. Twice she stopped to rest and to calculate how far she had come. Three and four jack rabbits at a time crept across the road ahead.

Just before dark, after more than a decade in New Mexico, she saw her first desert fox. It crossed the road at a run fifty yards ahead and never noticed her. Smaller and greyer than a coyote, its tail floated straight out behind it.

After three or four miles she stopped to eat an apple. Even if she had to sleep in her chair along the way, she knew she could make it to the highway. The thought of the fox excited her: its silky few steps across the light-colored road. She knew the coyotes would howl at night but never come close. Instead of being afraid, she felt wonderfully powerful and alone, embarked on a journey she had never planned.

She had covered another couple of miles when a metallic clattering disengaged itself from the desert's near-silence. The road, which Susan remembered as being perfectly straight, actually had a few dips and bends, and around one of these a pair of drunken headlights appeared, one beam askew and the other pointing into the sky. Elena's truck. Like a rabbit hit by a beam of light, Susan hesitated, then jerked to the side of the road. But where there was cover for hares, there was nothing large enough to hide a grown woman in a wheelchair. The chair's rubber wheels sank immediately into the sand, and she couldn't bring herself to dive out of her seat onto the ground. In any case, Elena was already slowing down. She let the pickup out of gear and rolled the last fifty yards to where Susan was mired down behind a couple of sparse creosote bushes.

"Good girl," Elena said pleasantly. She turned off the motor and lights, opened the creaking driver's door and jumped to the ground. "I knew you'd make out 'til I got back. So you took a little trip at night, no problem." A strong southwestern accent had come into her voice. She pulled Susan back onto the road, leaned into the cab of the truck and held out a burrito wrapped in wax paper.

"Loaded with beans and *salsa verde. Y por la sed,* a six-pack of Coors. Less the two I finished on the way out from town. Even a little *borracha,* I have thought of your hunger and thirst."

Elena was convincingly drunk: talkative, friendly and sloppy. She told Susan she was a brave girl to have come so far on her own.

Halfway through the torrid burrito, Susan opened a Coors. "How come you give me beer, after telling me I shouldn't drink?"

"Once in a while won't hurt. *Pues,* the truth is you should stay away from alcohol."

"You didn't mean to come back, did you? When you left."

Elena took three steps into the dark and turned around. "I hated you and I hated Mel," she said. Her English was completely clear. "I left so I could keep the feeling. Sometimes I need to hate. If I had stayed, I might have hurt you, or else we would have talked. When you talk you lose your feelings."

"Why did you bring me here?"

Elena looked offended. "Some things you do because it's right. You learned something, didn't you?"

The drive back to Santa Fe lasted until almost four in the morning. Elena drank coffee and sobered up while Susan sat upright on the truck's wide, crumbling front seat. Neither woman spoke, but Susan stayed alert the whole way back, thinking about the hot springs, the abandoned ranch and the miles she'd covered on her own.

CHAPTER 8

— ❦ —

AFTER a mild early winter, a bitter cold front swept into the Ohio Valley in late January, turning the ground at Anna's farm to metal. For two straight weeks the temperature at night dropped to twenty below or worse. The unprotected earth froze three feet down, and on poorly drained stretches of the river road the frost raised six-inch chunks of pavement like flakes. The immaculate frozen air purified human breath but stopped all construction and farm-work. Everything exposed to the weather turned brittle: machinery, hand tools and the vinyl seats of automobiles. The branches of Anna's lilacs snapped, when she brushed against them, like the bones of small birds.

The Ohio River froze twelve inches deep, which stopped even the massive coal and salt barges from plowing through the ice. Anna walked the quarter of a mile to the Kentucky shore and clambered over the tumultuous slabs of bulk ice driven against the bank. She stared back at Ohio like a foreigner. In the late afternoon, padding homeward in her felt-lined boots, she might have been approaching the ice-rimmed shingle of the Bering Sea. The scene was abstracted and unearthly in the frozen purple light of dusk, every object in nature wrapped and shrunk by the cold.

Yet twelve inches down, the river still flowed. Men had been fishing on the ice as they hadn't done for ten years, using power augers to drill down to the water. A half inch of ice had already formed at the top of a recent bore; when Anna smashed it with her foot the water slurped up to the surface, alive and dark.

Through the coldest weather, when her wood stove could

barely keep up, she often abandoned her house and sought shelter at the university. Early in the morning she claimed one of the large oak desks in the high-ceilinged reading room of the anthropology library. The room's iron radiators, enclosed by wooden cabinets, clanked reassuringly as a white, heatless sun lit up the room through windows of beveled glass. Steam from the university's central heating plant fed the building, and by afternoon it was sometimes so warm inside, the librarian had to crack a window.

Stimulated by the frigid weather, Anna read all of Stefansson's and Freuchen's books about the Arctic. The Eskimos, she learned, disliked warm climates and felt uncomfortable out-doors when the temperature rose to over fifty degrees. They thought of their land as the most beautiful in the world; in-deed, they felt sorry for those who lived farther south. Along with frozen seal and narwhal meat, they ate fermented fish and birds of horrendous description. And they did, in fact, occa-sionally loan their husbands and wives—though never in secret. Their tales of starvation and survival made Anna sit straight up in her chair.

Some days she read a novel instead, or a biography. The library was warm and dry, the phone was never for her, and she came so often the woman who ran the place no longer paid her any attention. Anna brought a lunch in her briefcase and ate it in the lobby beside a bust of Margaret Mead. Sometimes if Jay had a free hour in the late afternoon, they played a game of racquetball at the Y.

With her house stone cold and her water supply frozen, Anna accepted Jay's offer to move into his house for a few days—and wound up staying for three weeks. Daria acted as if it were nothing out of the ordinary. Jay was nervous at first; he didn't want Anna's come-cries or their midnight laughter to drift down the hall toward Daria's room.

"It won't hurt her to know we laugh a lot and lie around together," Anna said.

"Maybe not, but I don't want to upset her."

"You don't want her to freak out and go live with her mother, you mean."

"All right. I think about that sometimes."

"Jay, relax. This isn't like you. Or is it?"

"Hey, I told you I could worry and be a cranky son of a gun as much as the next guy."

Winter broke before the end of February. The ice on the Ohio boomed, cracked and drove itself into shelves along the riverbank. In early March the temperature rose into the sixties for a full week, which allowed the first towboats to pass upstream, loaded with coal for the steel mills in Pittsburgh. On the farm, creeks ran and the surface of the fields unfroze—but when Anna took the small tractor out on St. Patrick's Day to seed potatoes, she ran the furrowing plow into frost, ten inches down.

Anna invited Jay and Daria to spend a weekend at the farm. When asked on a Wednesday, Daria said sure, she'd like to go— but by Saturday morning she was not so eager. "For the whole weekend?" she said. None of her friends would be there, and Anna didn't have a television set. In the end Jay told her, "You agreed to come, so you're coming."

She pouted elaborately on the way out to the farm, pulling back the corners of her mouth and staring out of the car across the fields. No one spoke. When Jay turned into the gates, Anna directed him to the greenhouse with her finger.

"I didn't know we were coming out here to *work,*" Daria said, eyeing the benches and plastic trays with animosity.

Anna held out a package of seeds. "You don't have to work if you don't want to. But if you do, the farm will pay you two fifty an hour."

"What do I have to do?"

"Seed tomatoes. But only if you want to."

Anna set up the job for her. First she filled a dozen grower trays with a seeding mix of peat moss, soil and perlite, then tapped a pile of Sweet 100 tomato seeds onto a stiff piece of gasket paper. She used a sharp pencil to push two seeds into each cell of the tray. Daria paid little attention to the demonstration, gazing around the greenhouse with a show of boredom. "Got it?" Anna asked flatly.

Fifteen minutes later she passed behind the girl to see how the job was going. Daria turned slightly as Anna passed, presenting her back to the inspection. But Anna could see she was moving at a snail's pace, picking up each small, fuzzy tomato seed with two fingers and poking it into the peat mixture in the cells. It was fifty-cents-an-hour work, Anna thought.

Even so, she left the girl alone for an hour—and held Jay back when he started down the aisle toward her. The number of seeded flats beside Daria eventually grew, and at one point she announced to the greenhouse at large, "Forty trays." Passing by at a distance, Anna saw that Daria had developed her own technique. She spread the seeds out evenly along the edge of the gasket paper, taking extra time to lay them out precisely so the seeding went as fast as possible.

It had frosted during the night, but under clear skies the air in the greenhouse soon reached the temperature and humidity of coastal Ecuador. Daria took off her sweater and rolled up her sleeves, then pulled her shirttails out and tied them around her waist. Her smooth complexion shone with moisture. Her hair was almost the same color as Susan's, Anna thought. a chocolate, almost purple brown.

Just before one o'clock Daria announced, "A hundred trays!" It was a good time to quit, and Anna paid her on the spot with a ten-dollar bill.

After lunch, Anna suggested they might be able to take the farm's old rowboat out onto the river. Shelley's father had used it for duck hunting, and Anna had come across it the previous fall, chained to a young sycamore beside the Ohio. Half-covered with leaves, blackberry canes and wild-grape vines, it hadn't been in the water for years. But Anna found a single life jacket hanging in the barn next to a pair of oars, and the meticulous Shelley came up with the key to the padlock.

"A rowboat on the Ohio?" Daria said. She told Anna her friends had motorboats and houseboats, not rowboats. Still, she led Anna and Jay across the spongy fields to the river, knocking down dried seedpods of milkweed and burdock with a stick, and when the river came in sight she ran ahead yelling, "Icebergs! Giant icebergs!"

Along with the usual spring runoff of branches, boards and refuse, slabs of ice pocked the river, some of them as large as cars. On the south-facing Ohio shore almost all the ice had already melted, but on the shaded Kentucky side of the river grey-and-white slabs still lined the banks, and the sheltered mouths of creeks were still capped with ice.

Daria, oblivious to the mud, scrambled down to have a closer look at the river. Then she jumped back up on the bank to help Anna pull the rowboat out from under the vines and brambles, and the three of them slid it down the bank to the water. It floated without a leak. Even the oarlocks, the need for which Anna had forgotten, hung in place at the end of rusted chains. Daria jumped into the boat and called for the oars.

"Hold on," Jay said, "hold on. First put on this life jacket. And I don't know if this boat is big enough for all of us. I don't know if it's safe."

Anna stepped gingerly into the boat and took the middle seat. "It looks all right to me," she said. "I think it has Styrofoam under the seats."

Daria fussed with the life jacket but didn't tie it to Jay's satisfaction. He made her sit down in the back of the boat while he fastened the corroded buckles.

"You don't have to wear one of these stupid things," she said, "so how come I do?"

"Because you're a girl and we're adults, and I don't want you to drown."

"I'm not going to drown. I bet I can swim better than you can."

"Just wear it."

The skiff was reasonably buoyant, even with all three of them aboard. Anna took the oars and edged away from the shore into the current, rowing steadily to keep abreast of the current. Daria, in the bow, kept on the lookout for slabs of ice, which rose only an inch or two above the brown surface of the water and were difficult to see more than a few yards upstream.

"We're in the middle of the North Atlantic," Daria said, half rising from her seat. "We might get hit by an iceberg any minute now and go down like the *Titanic*."

"We might turn over," her father said, "if you don't sit down up there."

Large or small, there was no other boat on the river. Close to shore, a pair of muskrats made easier progress against the current than Anna could, while overhead, two dozen Canada geese beat their way up the flyway in an unbalanced V.

"Let's ram an iceberg, Anna. Let's smack into one."

"All right, but you have to sit down."

Daria strained forward, hovering an inch off the seat as the rowboat angled farther into the river. She made out a smooth patch on the water ahead and urged Anna forward. "Full steam," she cried, "full ahead." Anna leaned into the oars, propelling the skiff upriver until it crunched against a block of ice. The boat stopped dead in the water, Jay pitched forward into Anna's lap, and Daria laughed from her seat in the bow. "Bammo!" she said. "Down goes the *Andrea Doria*."

"Any leaks?" Anna asked, looking under the seats. "I'm not sure how much this old boat can take."

"Don't worry," Daria said. "It's all metal."

"So were the *Titanic* and the *Andrea Doria*. Where'd you learn about those ships?"

"In a book. Here comes another one."

They attacked a dozen blocks of ice on the raw surface of the river, jarring their ocean liner against the icebergs. Sometimes the skiff jammed itself up onto a slab and had to be wedged off, with Daria half in and half out of the boat.

After twenty minutes Jay crawled into the middle seat and relieved Anna at the oars. He didn't row as well as she did—

Anna had grown up on Minnesota lakes—and all his movements were hesitant. Although he had passed up and down the Ohio many times on towboats, it was a different matter to wobble along in a small rowboat with only ten inches of freeboard.

The skiff traveled erratically as Jay missed strokes with one or both oars. In addition, he had trouble steering to Daria's imperious commands. "Go left," she said. "No, *my* left. Now straight ahead. *Hard.* We're going to miss this one, too."

She stood up to look for more ice and rocked the boat. "Sit down," Jay said. "Sit down so I don't tip this thing over."

"But we'll never hit one if I don't see them far enough away. You can't row fast enough."

"Daria, sit down."

"Just because you can't row you want me to sit down."

Jay turned, grabbed his daughter by the life jacket and jerked her down onto the seat. "Now *stay* down," he said.

Anna had never seen him manhandle Daria before except in play. The girl turned away in the bow, shaking her head. After thirty seconds she turned back and said, just loud enough to be heard, "I don't care if you are my father, you're a bastard and you can go to hell."

Jay went on rowing in silence, headed for Kentucky. No one said anything and no one looked at anyone else. When they reached the shore Daria jumped out and scrambled up the icy bank, holding the rope taut as the two adults got out of the boat. She looked conspicuously away from her father.

Downstream on the Ohio side of the river they could see docks, farmhouses and the town of Fell River, but the Kentucky shore where they had landed was heavily wooded, without roads or houses. One small meadow opened into the trees but looked as if it hadn't been hayed in years. Black alder, hawthorn and poplar saplings had taken over much of the field. On a roadbed above the bank, a single pair of railroad tracks followed the curve of the river, the rails shiny and smooth.

They walked downstream along the tracks, Daria in the lead,

no one talking. Ash and hickory trees arched overhead, while ancient beech trees, as grey as battleships, climbed the steep bank to their left. In the protection of rock outcrops lay curved wings of old snow, the granular white surface half-covered with the detritus of understory growth: twigs, bits of dry grass and pieces of bark and moss.

Anna and Jay left the track to investigate some lichens rising in a ladder up one side of a fallen trunk. The growths were as green as Caribbean waters, but soft and dry. Daria walked ahead, balancing on a single rail. She was a hundred yards beyond them when they heard the sound of a train, its diesel pulse echoing along the tunneled roadbed. Daria walked on unheeding as the train grew louder. "Daria," Jay yelled. "*Daria.*" The girl finally looked around. He gestured along the tracks. "*A train,*" he yelled.

Daria waved back with an insouciant hand. Feeling her way along the rail with her feet, she turned her head toward the river.

"What the hell is she doing?" Jay said, speeding up his walk. The noise of the train pushed toward them under the arching trees. Jay started to run toward his daughter, but Anna grabbed his arm.

"She's twelve years old. She knows what she's doing."

A giant blue locomotive appeared around the bend, making the air and ground quiver. The engineer let out a savage blast of the horn. Daria turned her head slowly toward the train and at the last minute skipped off the track toward the edge of the roadbed. She waved to the engineer as nonchalantly as she had to Jay, then was hidden by the four locomotives.

The train came past in a roar, the engineer sour-faced at his open window. The shriek of iron wheels reminded Anna of the mad time she and Jay had screwed in Fell River on the soccer field next to the tracks. But Jay didn't look at her now. He studied the long line of tankers, flatbeds and boxcars. When the caboose finally sucked by, drawing with it the reverberations of the final cars, Daria hopped back on the same rail and walked toward them in idle balance, her eyes still turned to the river.

"She's too clever for me," Jay said. "God knows what she'll do in the next few years."

"I'm going to take notes," Anna said. "And lessons."

Daria announced as they met, "A hundred and fourteen cars." She pirouetted on her rail, making a full circle without stepping off. "Do you want to go back to the boat?"

Daria and her father tightroped back along either rail, throwing out an occasional arm to keep their balance. On the trip over, the current had carried them a hundred yards downstream, so they decided to pull the skiff up along the Kentucky shoreline before starting back. The lower bank, however, was muddy and covered with chunks of ice. Daria had to ride in the boat and fend it off from shore as Anna and Jay pulled from the top of the bank. When the rope caught in a jumble of ice slabs, Jay scrambled down to free it, slipped, and landed flat on his back in the mud. "Shit," he said.

Daria laughed. She pulled even with her father, who stood up holding both muddy hands in the air. "I don't know if I can allow you on board like that," she said. "I've been trying to keep the ship clean. Is this an emergency?"

"It'll be an emergency if you don't let me in there."

Anna rowed them back across the river. Daria kept a steady lookout without standing up, and they charged into a half-dozen icebergs. "Frigate lost in the Arctic Ocean," Daria said. "All hands drowned except the captain and two mates. You're the captain," she told Anna. "Dad and I are the mates."

That night after Daria went to sleep on the couch, Anna took Jay out for a walk. On the way back they stopped to check the temperature in the greenhouse. Sixty-seven. The air was heavy with the wet smell of soil, peat moss and fish emulsion. Anna stood in front of Jay, placing her fingers on his chest as if putting the shot.

"How come when we argue," she said, "it takes us so long to get over it?"

"We don't argue that often."

"No, but sometimes. Do you always get over it that fast with Daria?"

"I guess so." Jay thought for a moment and then laughed. "Imagine calling your own father a bastard. And she's only twelve. Sometimes I think I'm too loose with her."

"I don't think so. At least your troubles don't last."

"She's too clever for me. How's an adult going to keep up?"

"Maybe you don't have to," Anna said, "since kids don't hold grudges that long."

"I think it's something else." Jay leaned back against a bench, brushing his fingers over a tray of young tomato seedlings. "I think it's knowing you're never going to split up, because when you're sure of that, you can argue like crazy and get over it. If you and I got into a bad argument, one of us might say to hell with it, I'm not going to put up with this shit. But Daria and I can blow off steam without being afraid, because we know we're never going to leave each other."

"But that's not true," Anna said, her fingers still touching Jay's chest. "You're not going to stay together forever. It won't be that long before Daria grows up and leaves home. I know you worry about that."

"Yes, but that's different from the way an adult would leave."

"Then what about adults?"

"It's not the same. It's harder." Jay took Anna's hand and led her back to her house under the light of the waxing half-moon. Daria didn't wake up on the couch or stir. They climbed the ladder to Anna's bedroom and closed the trap door.

"So how does it work with two adults?" Anna asked again.

Jay took off her shirt. He undid the first button, then rested the tips of his fingers on her throat and chest before going on to the next. Releasing her cuffs, he pushed her shirt off and let it drop to the floor.

"It would be easier for them if they knew they were going to stay together," he said.

"But how can anyone know that? Nobody stays together anymore."

"It's just a feeling people get."

They knelt on Anna's bed, their voices at a whisper. "So Jay, let's say you wanted to get that feeling, how would you go about it?"

"Probably it has to come to you."

"You don't have any special tricks up your sleeve?"

"If you were desperate, you could try taking care of me and looking after all my needs." Anna could hear him smiling. "That's an old trick that used to work for women. Scrub a man's floors and clean the stove, that kind of thing."

"Forget that kind of thing," Anna said. "Sometimes I do get the feeling—but I don't say anything about it because I'm afraid it won't last."

"When do you get it?"

"Sometimes . . . when we make love."

Jay brought his mouth close to her, kissing her neck and shoulders, blowing softly on her chest. She had the feeling, so she told him.

The next morning, nuthatches called from the nearest trees and sunlight bathed the room. Anna was light-hearted. She spread her hands out and drummed softly on Jay's chest. "I'm fond of you this morning."

"Are you now?" he asked in an English accent. "Are you fond of me?"

"Last night I had the feeling, and this morning I'm still fond of you. At the very least, fond of you."

Daria came up the ladder from below, knocked, opened the trap door and latched it against the wall. Standing at the end of the bed, she stared at the four feet poking out from under the blanket.

"What have you two been doing?" she asked disdainfully. "Making love?" She touched a big toe with her thumb. "This is

Anna's foot, I can tell. Dad's feet are all calloused."

"Your dad and I might lie around in bed all day and never get up," Anna said. "I'm terribly fond of him this morning."

"All day? It's already ten o'clock, I've been reading for an hour."

They agreed to get up if Daria would make them her famous breakfast of eggs, home fries and biscuits. The girl went through a dozen pots and pans, washed nothing as she cooked, and proudly surveyed the full sink and littered countertops after the meal. "You guys clean up," she said. "That's the way it works." Then she surprised them both by asking if she could go back to the greenhouse and seed more tomatoes, and get paid. As she walked off, Jay stared after her with exaggerated bug eyes.

"That was my daughter?"

"Money," Anna said. "Money drives the young. Besides, she likes having a project."

"How about this project?" Jay asked. He laughed and looked at the sink. "Is this what I get?"

"No, I'll do it. You plant the trees."

As a late gift for Anna's birthday, Jay had bought her a pair of Chinese chestnuts from a local nursery. The native chestnuts on the farm had all died of blight, long ago.

"You know the blossoms smell like come," Jay told her.

"Like what?"

"Like come, like semen. If I plant them too close to the house, you'll think you're swimming in come, every June."

"A dubious pleasure," Anna said, laughing. "But go ahead, I'll risk it."

She explained where she wanted the trees, at either end of the blackened oval behind her house. Jay went to the greenhouse for a load of peat moss and a shovel, and Anna started in on the dishes. When he came back, she watched him through the kitchen window.

He used a shovel with a strip of rolled steel at the top and pushed the handle away from him so the blade pointed straight down. He jumped a dozen times on the shovel, scribing a full circle and then slicing it into quadrants. Kneeling down, he pulled out the clumps of turf and stacked them to one side of the hole. They looked like heavy scalps. Jay bent over the excavation, completely absorbed by the job.

After removing the first layer of soil, he dug into the fibrous loam below. He was a meticulous gardener, much more so than Anna. He dug round and round the hole, keeping the walls perpendicular. After finishing the first hole he jumped down into it for a moment and stood without moving. Anna watched his chest rise and fall. He lined the bottom of the hole with peat moss and set in one of the trees, gently packing the roots with crumbled soil and layers of peat until the hole was filled almost to the level of the grass.

Anna remembered spying on Kevin the same way. One day she had watched him playing behind their house in Eugene, where he had constructed an elaborate playroad of hills and banked curves, using a toy dump truck and a bulldozer. Unaware of her presence, he plied his small machinery, hummed like a diesel engine and growled through elaborate gear changes. Anna wanted to pick him up and hold him in her arms—he was only six—but, instead, stepped back quietly and left him to his work.

Her first reaction to Jay was the same. She wanted to run outside and hold him, put her hands on him and feel the heat coming off his chest. Instead, she remained by the window and watched as he finished tamping in the last of the peat. He made a small circular depression around the trunk, poured in two buckets of water and tested the tree for firmness. He let the water seep into the ground, and still Anna kept to one side of the window. She watched as the wind blew his hair back from his eyes, and as he stared off toward the river. She wanted to see, over and over, how his body moved through space. What else could love be?

EVEN BY THE END OF MARCH the farm had only peas, spinach and lettuce in the ground. The greenhouse bulged with transplants ready for field setting, but the weather remained too cold and wet to move them out.

Anna, Shelley and Deal spent a full day erecting an emergency greenhouse of galvanized pipe and twenty-mil sheet plastic, to cover the plants that should already have been set out. Late in the day after the others left, Anna stayed on the job to gather up the ratchets, pipe wrenches and other tools. She didn't mind staying until the end. In fact, she was glad of an excuse to remain outside through the approach of dusk, watching the knobby stalks of sumac and ailanthus turn grey with night. By the river, somber colors or none at all. At the edge of the high meadows across the road, tulip poplars rose like poles next to shagbark hickories and red oaks.

Her father was due for dinner, but she'd told him to come late. He drove through the farm gates just as she finished cleaning up, climbed out of his car and gave her a hug through his bulky sweater. At her house, he brought back the fire in her wood stove while she started dinner.

"Are you getting by out here?" he asked. "It looks like you're stretching your wardrobe." He looked down at the white skin of her ankles. Both socks on both feet had holes in the back.

"These are just work socks."

"But how about it? Do you make enough money at this business?"

"About as much as I made in Eugene. But enough, I guess. No rent, and plenty of food. You know farming, it's always a squeeze."

"But you like it? You're going to stay with the farm?"

Anna turned to face him. "I love the work here. I have my own house, I'm a full partner in the business, I learn something every day." She stood upright with a spoon in her hand, her hand on her hip, her hip against the counter. "What are you after, Dad? You know all this."

"I'm thinking about giving up my apartment."

"To move in with Susan?"

"Since she came back she's already asked me twice. I think maybe I should. But then, what if she wanted to move or something?"

"You could move with her."

Alex fed the wood stove and stood in front of it, his shoulders hunched. "Yeah, I could."

"But what?"

"I don't know. I like Susan, a lot. Of course I'm so much older, and she can't walk, but even so we spend half our time laughing. We hold hands and kiss . . . do everything."

"Good," Anna said.

Alex smiled. "It is, it's good. But . . ."

Against the plaid collar of his shirt, her father's hair was greyer than Anna remembered. He stood upright, still the patriarch, but a little awkward. Anna put her arm around his neck.

"Spill it, Dad."

"I just thought that if I moved in with Susan, I'd have to get rid of some things."

"Like what?"

"A lot of junk around my place." Wandering into the kitchen, he looked out the window onto the dark lawn in back of Anna's house. The spring grass had barely established a tonsure-hold around the edges of the black patch of earth where Anna had burned everything from Kevin's room.

"What kind of junk do you mean?"

"Yesterday I was reading a Willa Cather book about the Southwest."

"*Death Comes for the Archbishop?*" Anna said.

"Yes, that one. It was one of your mother's. Susan's been telling me so much about that part of the country I thought I'd read something about it. This fell out."

He unfolded a slip of paper, softened by the years, with four lines on it in fading red ink. Anna recognized her mother's minute, legible handwriting.

Clean typewriter
Call B. Lundgren
Black beans
Alex's birthday

"Mom must have been reading the book," Anna said. "How old is the note?"

"I can't tell. It must have been early November, because my birthday's on the fourteenth. But what year, I don't know."

"Who was B. Lundgren?"

"Never heard of him. Or her."

"And the black beans?"

"They were for a Mexican dinner your mother gave. Maybe she got the idea from the book, I don't know. I've completely forgotten the dinner—who came or even which house we were living in at the time. I only remember the beans because Freya burned them in the pressure cooker. 'Plenty black,' I told her. She was not amused."

Alex's face settled below the cheekbones, his muscles gone slack. "I don't know why, but her handwriting still gets to me. I've put away everything she wrote, but her words keep showing up—on the tag of a set of keys or on the back of some photograph or on a tax form."

Anna knew that Alex kept all her mother's papers, all her correspondence and files, in a set of waxed cardboard cartons beneath his bed.

"I've got all her journals in my apartment," he said, reading Anna's mind with ease. "And photographs and poems and clippings out of the newspaper. I taped all the boxes shut before I left Minneapolis."

"But you sleep over them every night."

"That sounds bad, doesn't it? One night I dreamed I was riding the boxes around a miniature track, like freight cars. The whole time I was terrified they'd spill open."

"So now you want to burn them."

"How could I take your mother's things to Susan's? Of course

I could store everything, but that's not the question. It's having Freya with me all the time, around my neck. Here I am thinking about living with another woman—maybe even marrying her someday—and then I find four lines written on a piece of paper by Freya, and I can't think about anything else for days. I still miss her, and I don't want to."

A rainy wind drove against the west windows of the house. Anna slid a casserole into the oven and sat down with her father at the kitchen table over a couple of beers.

"I don't know if it would help or not," she said, "but maybe you should get rid of some of that stuff you brought from Minneapolis. Everything that was Mom's. Her papers, her books, her furniture—you could let all that junk go. I could borrow the farm's stake bed and we could take it all to the dump."

"What if I ever wanted it back? What if you wanted it?"

"No return of goods. I know, maybe you'd regret it someday. Maybe you and Susan won't work out after all. But I'll tell you, Dad, I'd rather see you free of all that stuff. What do you think Mom would tell you to do if she knew what was going on?"

Alex laughed. "She'd tell me to get on the stick. She'd wonder why in hell I was still sleeping on our old mattress and thinking about her when I had Susan."

"Let's face it, Dad, she's probably lying around on the cloud cushions with some guy, maybe some Italian poet who hit a truck on his Lambretta. Anyway, she wouldn't want you to mope around. If you ask me, you should have a party and get rid of that stuff."

Two days later Anna showed up at her father's apartment with the farm's one-ton truck. Alex looked gloomy, standing in the middle of his living room surrounded by boxes and gear.

"I don't know what should go."

"Everything that makes you think of Freya." Anna shook out her long hair from under a wool cap. "Just pile it up."

It all went into the truck in a heap: the mattress and box

springs, Freya's old couch, a couple of chairs, some of Alex's clothes dating back to the forties and fifties.

"It must be wrong to throw these clothes away," he said. "We should give them to someone, or sell them."

"With styles like these, you've got about thirty bucks' worth of clothing here."

Alex drew up to his full height. "You're implying that my wardrobe is out of date?"

"So few people dress like Perry Como anymore, Dad, you'd be surprised. The style might come back, but not in your life-time. Hang on to your tennis and running clothes."

They paid four dollars at the county dump for the privilege of unloading Alex's belongings. Jolting over the littered moon-scape, they skirted ruts, mudholes and the porcelain mounds of old refrigerators. Scraps of cloth and bent pieces of alumi-num stuck out of the soil, exposing how much of the landfill had already been laced with garbage. The dirt road led to a trench, ten feet deep, which city sanitation trucks and private pickups had lined with construction detritus, brush cuttings and household garbage.

Anna backed up to the trench and parked. She and her father climbed up into the stake bed and cleared a space on the sofa, throwing out an old lamp and a chair to make room for themselves. Though it was a chill day for a picnic, Anna had brought one of the farm's peck baskets filled with sandwiches, hard-boiled eggs and a bottle of Italian red. They propped their feet on cardboard boxes, unwrapped the sandwiches and poured the wine into plastic cups. The wind blew in puffs, lifting curls of paper into the air and volleying them over the chaos of the dump. In the distance, a bulldozer worried a mountain of old tires.

"A gourmet lunch," Anna said, "in a noble surround. The taste of aged cheese, the bouquet of a fine wine . . ."

"Many lovely bouquets." Alex laughed. "Isn't that Amana sixty-two I smell? And a hint of La-Z-Boy, seventy-four?"

"I think you're right. Along with the fabled aroma of Lemon Pledge and New Blue Cheer. There's a certain *je ne sais quoi* about coming to the dump, don't you think?"

"Yes, it's like the ocean. We have this sea of leavings."

A Chevy half ton backed up close by, carrying a pile of black plastic garbage bags and a couch. The couch looked like Alex's, though it was maroon instead of green.

Alex stood up to see what kind of shape it was in. "Look at that, Anna. Maybe I could pull a trade with this guy."

A skinny drink of water jumped out of the pickup, his sandy hair flopping in his face and his pants stuck in jackboots. He looked over once in greeting, then set to pitching his garbage bags into the trench. Still holding a plastic cup of wine, Alex leaned over the wooden slats of Anna's truck and spoke loudly into the wind. "Say, that looks like a decent sort of couch you have there."

The man paused between garbage bags and said agreeably, "Yeah, but the fuckin' dog diarrheaed the thing. Think you could give me a hand with it?"

"You give him a hand," Anna said, laughing. "I'll keep your place warm."

Jumping to the ground, Alex helped pull the couch off the pickup, and the two men rocked it over the lip of the trench. Alex invited the fellow around to the back of Anna's truck and asked him if he wouldn't like this other couch, it was quite clean.

"No, we're gettin' a new one. I ain't takin' anything back from this place." The man climbed back into his cab and took off in a V8 rumble.

Anna was still laughing. "Dad thought he'd do a little dealing," she said. "Thought he could kind of let go of his old green couch and kind of not."

Alex straightened his shoulders. "The dump is a great teacher."

Mildly drunk from the wine, they began to discharge Alex's past into the bottom of the trench. Alex recalled the origins of a few items, and they assigned a vintage to everything that went over the back of the truck.

"Grand Rapids, fifty-six," Alex said as he heaved a bedside lamp.

"Nashville, sixty-eight." Anna underhanded a dented Thermos.

"Boston, thirty-one."

"Of mysterious inception."

They threw over Freya's papers, all six boxes of them, without a comment. Then the mattress and the couch. Alex swept out the truck with the sober air of an English valet. Half of what he owned when he lived with Freya now lay in a clay pit, jumbled up with orange-juice bottles, lawn chairs and chicken wire. And removing all doubts they had committed an irrevocable act, the dump bulldozer clanked past them on the way to the trench. The giant D9 pivoted, waded down to the level of the garbage and ground past below them, pushing a mound of refuse before it to the far end of the pit. The driver sat stolidly behind the controls, his jaw thick and his eyes bagged. Repeatedly, he leaned out from his seat to void a shot of tobacco juice onto the treads of the Caterpillar.

"No respect for history," Alex said.

"That's just as well. We came out here to shake it."

CHAPTER 9

——— ❦ ———

COASTING in long sweeps, Jay and Daria turned bicycle figure eights across the football stadium parking lot. Anna unpacked a picnic lunch on the grass nearby, wearing her dark glasses against the brightness of the newly finished asphalt. The unpainted surface of the lot looked as smooth and black as the pebbled cover of a Bible.

Just at noon Alex and Susan rode into sight, Alex on a three-speed Raleigh he'd held back from the dump and Susan on a new racing wheelchair. Susan threaded her way past the wooden sawhorses at the lot's east gate and took off toward Jay and Daria, her smile visible from sixty yards off.

Pulling up in front of Anna, she said, "Your father has given me the world's greatest gift! This thing is *fast*. All Campagnolo equipment. Reynolds tubing—it's a pro's bike. It must have cost a fortune."

The chair had twelve gears, hand pedals, a long front fork and a vinyl seat slung between two skinny rear tires.

Alex rode up and dismounted, fluttering his hand. "It is fast. She took off coming over here and outran me easy." He parked his old Raleigh against the asphalt perimeter of the lot. "I'm ready for lunch, how about everyone else?"

"I'm too excited to eat," Susan said. "But the rest of you go ahead, don't wait for me."

Only Daria and Susan stayed out on the lot, speeding past each other on the smooth new pavement. Susan shouted back, something lost in the wind, and a moment later both she and Daria disappeared around the back side of the stadium. A couple of pigeons flapped over the leafless dogwoods near the picnic site, and a puff of wind turned into a dust devil that swirled toward the parked cars on Hilary Street.

The riders reappeared side by side, pedaling hard. Jay pulled a towel out of the wicker basket, stepped onto the lot and waved it like a checkered flag as they approached. *"Once around the stadium,"* he yelled. *"And you're off."*

Daria stood up in her toe straps, shifted down and missed a gear. Her chain rattled over the sprocket. Susan glanced over at the sound and immediately took the lead. She pedaled furiously with her hands, setting a course around the perimeter of the lot. Immediately behind, with her front wheel almost touching the seat of the chair, Daria rode in a tuck. The two cyclists disappeared behind the stadium only inches apart.

Alex, Anna and Jay waited, standing on the small tumulus of asphalt at the edge of the lot. There was no sound: no lawnmowers spitting grass, no dogs barking, not even the whine of cars passing over the nearby brick streets. Three more pigeons dropped into midair from their roosts on the stadium and flew off toward the white softball clouds above the river.

The riders sprinted into view, clinging to the eastern edge of the lot and heading for the final corner. They came straight on, Daria's forehead visible behind Susan's grinning, tanned face. Susan looked like a sure winner—until Daria rose up in her traps, pedaled hard and passed Susan's chair with only twenty yards to go. At the finish she was pulling away. Jay waved the towel, the spectators cheered, and the two racers veered off into the lot like gulls peeling away from the stern of a ship.

Susan returned first, breathing hard, her face wide open. "Alex . . . I'm going to . . . ride every day. . . . It's so beautiful . . . to be out of breath."

"Some people think it's painful," he said, laughing.

"No, it's wonderful . . . my heart is thundering . . . it's great. You don't know how long it's been. I could never get this far out of breath in a wheelchair . . . no matter how hard I worked at it. My arms get tired too fast. But this is like running . . . the pain is beautiful."

Daria rolled up and dismounted, loosening her toe straps with a professional flick.

"Good girl," her father said. "You pulled that one out at the last minute."

"Oh Dad."

"I thought she had you for sure."

"Come on, you know I cheated."

"You what?"

Daria looked at him as if he were simple. "I drafted her the whole way. The chair's so wide it was easy. I practically coasted until the sprint."

"Ha!" Susan said. "So that's what you were doing so close behind me."

Daria could not restrain a smile. "It's kind of like cheating, but the racers do it all the time. Anyway, Dad's the one who showed me how. Don't you remember, Dad?"

"I've raised a monster," Jay said, laughing. "Adults are clay in her hands."

"Kids are taking over, face it."

Bicycles down, they settled around the wicker basket for sandwiches, hard-boiled eggs and provolone cheese. Jay did without wine. He had to leave in an hour for Cincinnati, for the second of two performances at the Music Hall. The previous Saturday night they had all gone to see him dance his solo, "Daria Leaving," at the first of two dance festival weekends. Today he was making the trip alone.

Daria ate quickly and picked up her bike. She was headed for Angela's.

"How can you go *bowling* on a day like this?" Jay asked her.

"You should try it, Dad, it's great. Besides, you're going to spend your whole day in that theater, aren't you? *Dancing*? That's indoors, too—if you get my drift."

"Okay, I got it. Anna will cook you dinner and look after you tonight. I'll be back late."

"We're going to a movie," Daria said. "Me and Angela and Anna. She already promised."

The girl bent forward, fastening her toe clips as her bike rolled slowly out onto the lot. She stood up straight on one leg, looking back over her shoulder, and held the position for ten seconds. Her pose came straight out of Jay's dance. It was the same gesture Jay had described to Anna at the Elephant Cafe when they first met.

"I'm leaving," Daria said.

"You're not. You're too young."

"Oh Dad. Get a clue in life. Wake me up when you get back, I don't care how late it is."

AFTER Daria rode off, Jay and Alex took their own bikes and idled around the back side of the stadium, leaving Anna and Susan with the remains of lunch. Anna repacked the basket with glasses, plates and uneaten sandwiches.

"For a while I thought you weren't going to come back from New Mexico," she told Susan.

"Because I was gone so long?"

"I guess. And because I thought you'd want to live out there. The weather's good, isn't it?"

"The winter in Santa Fe is longer and colder than it is here. What's today, the eighth? They could have snow for another month, right into May."

"I know Dad thought about it."

"If Alex gets enough time off, we might drive out for a vacation next summer. But we're going to live here."

Anna folded up the tablecloth. "Because?"

"We both grew up here, for one thing. Alex has a job, and I've got a lead on work myself. I might do some stringing for the *Cincinnati Inquirer*. Just part time to get started. Or I could free-lance."

"You could find work in New Mexico just as easily."

"Alex thinks a lot about family. He'd miss you if he left Fell River. And he kind of thinks you and Jay might get together."

"We are together."

"Yes, but . . . more together."

"You mean have a child."

"That's not unreasonable, is it? I think about it myself."

"You and Alex?"

"Sure, why not?"

Anna stood up, frowning. "I guess stranger things have happened."

"Screw that, what's so strange about me having a child?"

"Oh no, it's not you. I meant my father, that he's so much older. If Alex had a child next year, he'd be sixty-five. Susan, I'm sorry, I didn't mean *you* shouldn't do it."

Susan settled back in her seat. "It's true we're a little unbalanced in age. But Alex'll probably live to be a hundred, he's in such good shape."

"Or he could go out tomorrow. Anyone could."

"Me too. I can't expect to live as long in a wheelchair as otherwise. But I'm not going to shut down my life because of that."

"No, you shouldn't."

"People think everything changes for you when you're paralyzed—especially things like sex. But sex isn't that different for me. I know that sounds crazy, since I can't feel anything below the waist. Or hardly anything. But sex isn't just nerve endings. It's in your nature, it's part of your whole life. And the same with birth. I didn't stop wanting to have a child just because I fell off a cliff."

"Would you have to have a Caesarean?"

"Not necessarily, I could probably have a normal birth. It's just an idea, anyway, it's not something I've decided on. Alex and I haven't been together that long, less than a year."

"The same with me and Jay."

"Do you think about having another child?"

"Sure. Every month I think about it, and every month I put off thinking about it until later. I still get confused because of Kevin. You know I had an abortion last fall."

Susan laid her hands on her thighs. "Alex told me."

"I won't do that again."

Anna turned her face to the wind. She put off thinking about children because the topic always made her cry. She almost cried now. "What does my father think?" she asked.

"You know Alex, how considerate he is. But it's my idea, pretty much. Here he comes, we could ask him."

"You ask him," Anna said.

"Ask me what?" Alex got off his bike, looking from Susan to Anna and back again.

"We've been talking about children. And fathers."

"At my age? I'm getting up there, you know, I'll soon be doddering about."

"Bull. You jog all over town and play tennis like a pro. Besides"—Susan laughed—"you're a whiz around the house."

"What do you think about it, Dad?"

"I'm too old, I'd look ridiculous."

"No you wouldn't."

Alex stood upright, his hands in the pockets of his khaki pants. "It's not what I'd planned for my next twenty years, I'll say that. Though I admit, there's something seductive about a young woman who thinks your seed's still good for something. It might keep me young."

"I have to go," Jay said.

Alex laughed. "Before you get the grill?"

"Yeah, I guess so. Anna knows where I stand. But I am late, I've got some lighting changes to work on at the Music Hall."

Anna walked him across the grass to his car. "I still wish you'd let me come see the second show."

"You saw all three rehearsals and the opening performance. I'd think you'd be bored by now. Besides, I'll be more relaxed without you in the audience. I was terrified last week."

"You were? You never said."

"I'm always scared before I go on. Twenty years on stage and I still can't relax."

"You're the most relaxed man I've ever known."

"Not waiting to go on. I'm a wreck. And with friends watching it's worse."

"I'll watch you tonight, when you come home. Wake *me* up, too."

THREE MINUTES LATER Anna turned at the sound of a car entering the parking lot. It plowed sedately through the construction sawhorses at the east gate and veered toward Anna, swaying over the asphalt on bad shocks. One of the sawhorses hung from the front bumper, dragging along the ground.

The back and side windows of the twenty-year-old Ford had all been tinted blue, making it impossible to see the driver. But the timing was so close Anna knew it was Paul. Smiling widely, he opened a rusted door and stepped out into the sunlight, waving at Anna as if he'd showed up a little late for an appointment.

Paul rested his hands on his hips and surveyed the car. "Doesn't look like much, does it? But it runs fine out on the road. How you doing, Anna girl?"

He hadn't called her that in years. He strolled back to the car and lifted the sawhorse off the bumper with the toe of his boot. "I got it for a couple of yards and a lid of Mexican breeze. It came with a title, but I figure it's hot anyway." He kept smiling. "Howdy," he said, tipping a nonexistent hat toward Alex and Susan.

"You picked your moment," Anna said. "Did you have to wait long for Jay to leave?"

"Not too long. Got anything in that basket? I haven't eaten since Richmond."

The car had Virginia plates. Also STP and Mopar decals, a "Sit On a Happy Face" bumper sticker and a small sign in the vent window: "If You Value Your Life As Much As I Do This Ford—Don't Fuck With It."

"Is that where you've been," Anna asked, "in Virginia?"

"Newport News, mainly. It broke their hearts to see me go. I don't suppose you've been worrying about me, have you?"

"Not really. The police called a couple of times to ask if I knew where you were."

"And if they find you in town," Alex said, "they'll want to sit down with you for a while. Maybe a long while."

"Hi, Alex, it's nice to see you again. I hope you've been well. The big bad Fell River police, right? Where are they now, with all these sawhorses busted up and me a sitting duck in here? Maybe they don't work weekends. How about it, Anna, would you have turned me in?"

"I was angry enough, it's just as well you got out of town fast. I thought by now you'd have gone back to San Francisco. I see you got your tooth fixed."

"You noticed." He drew back his upper lip and tapped with his fingernail. "And to think you might have had to look at that crooked smile of mine for the rest of your life."

For the rest of her life? What an idea. Sometimes she wasn't sure she would know him a year from now.

He leaned back against the car, elbows on the hood. "How about it, you got any sandwiches in there? I drove all night on coffee and country music. I'm off the sauce, you believe that?"

"I think we have egg salad," Susan said, leaning over and pulling the picnic basket toward her.

"And hello, Susan. We've never met, but I've heard some nice things about you."

Paul's civility ran counter to a shadowy set of clothes and a three-day growth. He wore black jeans, a black T-shirt and a black satin jacket sporting a pair of dragons on the front and a map of Vietnam on the back, with the names Saigon, Hanoi, Da Nang and Camranh Bay stitched across the map in green and scarlet thread. Paul had never been to Vietnam. In spite of needing a shave and dressing all in black, Anna thought he looked better than he had when he left Fell River. His new tooth was a good job, she couldn't tell it from the others.

He ate with abandon, polishing off three sandwiches and

an apple, but he refused the last of the wine. "Honest," he said, "I'm off that stuff."

His eyebrows lifted, giving him a benign, youthful expression. He asked Anna if he could speak to her, and the two of them walked off along the curb. Alex looked after them, more than once.

"What is it?"

"I'd like to talk to you without all these people around."

"Okay."

"No, I mean alone. Couldn't we go to your house?"

"What for?"

"Because I want to ask you some things. And I brought a couple of pictures of Kevin, for his book."

"Pictures I haven't seen?" Anna couldn't keep her voice from rising.

"I don't think you have. A friend of mine took them on the Golden Gate one of those times Kevin came down."

Anna folded her arms over her chest. "How long are you going to be here?"

"For chrissakes, Anna, relax, I'm just passing through. I'm headed straight to San Francisco. What do you think, I'd go through Ohio without stopping to see you?"

"Last time you camped out in my house for three weeks."

"I thought we could work on a truce."

She wondered if he had come back for Kevin's album. "We could use a truce," she said. "Let me talk to my father."

She took Alex aside and asked him if he'd look after Daria. "Jay would die," she said, "if he knew Paul was floating around town and Daria wasn't covered. Maybe you and Susan could pick her and Angela up and take them to a movie. I promised them."

"That's not what Paul's up to, is it?"

"No, I just want to be careful."

"How about you? Will you be safe?"

"With Paul? Sure."

"What're you going to do?"

"Go to my house and talk. Or try to."

The back of Paul's car was filled with cardboard boxes and loose clothes. A tire pump lay across the dilapidated front seat, magazines and newspapers littered the floor, and half a dozen Styrofoam coffee cups lay crushed above the dash. Anna tossed the pump in back and got in. "You still keep house the same way, Paul."

"Believe it or not, everything has its place. Look at the boxes, they're all labeled. I did build up a little road trash here, but I thought I could throw it away at your house."

Anna glanced across at him as he threaded his way past the splattered remains of the sawhorses onto the street. His tone of voice surprised her: clear, gentle, devoid of sarcasm. Not everyone would have noticed the change, but she recognized immediately the evanescent voiceprint of a younger, more tranquil Paul—the man she had married.

He drove out of town in silence, his right hand curled over the top of the steering wheel. The heater, stuck half on, blew the odor of antifreeze and rubber hoses onto the empty seat between them. Anna let Paul find his own way onto the river road toward her farm.

After a cold early spring, the broccoli, cabbage and cauliflower fields along the Ohio were filling out. As usual, agriculture had outstripped nature. Patches of winter rye were still the greenest crop on earth, while the first redbuds had yet to bloom along the edges of the grey woods.

On the pasture beyond the curve where she'd had the accident, a few Holsteins grazed on early bromegrass and alsike clover. Anna asked Paul to stop the car.

"Here? Pull off here?"

"I want to show you something."

He had never asked where Kevin died. They'd driven past the double curve on the way to the funeral, and a half-dozen times since then, but Anna had never said anything.

The Fairlane slapped through a puddle of water before swaying to a stop on the soft ground. Anna stepped out and walked to the tree. Spring grass grew around the trunk, but as yet no weeds: no Queen Anne's lace, no goldenrod, no ironweed or chicory. The grass looked as clean as a lawn. April, Anna thought, was actually the gentlest month for walking. She laid her palm against a smooth, swollen patch on the face of the sycamore.

"I hit this tree. The car turned upside down and landed in the field. You can't see anything now except for the mark."

When she moved her hand, Paul touched the place she had touched. But only for a moment. Then he reached out for the fence that had been restrung along the edge of the field, curving his fingers around the top strand of barbed wire. The sun, past its meridian, threw shadows of the naked branches onto the grass around them.

"Right here?"

"The road was covered with ice. It still has a drainage problem, you can see. I should have been going slower."

"And you stop by here sometimes?"

"It's the only road to town."

Paul lifted his hand from the barbed wire but caught the forearm of his satin jacket on one of the barbs. With a brusque gesture he ripped it free. "You're crazy," he said, "you know that?"

Anna said nothing.

"I don't want to know anything about this tree, or this field, or any goddamned thing about this place. Why the hell do you live in Ohio, anyway?"

"Where do you think I should live?"

"You always lived on the coast before. Ohio's in the middle of nowhere."

"Then how come you keep coming back?"

"I don't know why the hell I do. But I'm getting out of here today, I can tell you that. As long as my car holds up."

He felt for the rip in his sleeve, took off his jacket and flung it into the back seat. Then he opened the hood of the car and pulled the dipstick out of the crankcase. The oil was dark and viscous, in need of a change. Paul stooped, wiped the rod on a tuft of grass and plunged it back into the case for a reading. "Down a quart, as usual. The rings are shot." He seated the dipstick in its narrow tube and slammed the hood.

Anna knew something had registered. Paul could cover up with talk about engine oil and bad rings, but later he'd have to think about this place. She wanted him to do that.

He drove them to the farm in silence. Before following Anna inside he rummaged among the cardboard boxes in the back seat of his car and came up with an envelope. He carried it in between his thumb and forefinger and laid it on the kitchen table. "Go ahead," he said, "open it."

The two photos were almost identical. Kevin was six, maybe seven, standing on the Golden Gate Bridge looking west toward the ocean. Paul held him firmly around the chest. The wind blew, and a background sun lit up the dark Marin coast.

Anna sat down at the table, holding the two photos in either hand. After a while she said, "Maybe I should have let him visit you more often."

Paul stood in the middle of the room. He looked defiant at first, as if he'd expected some other comment. Then he lowered his hands from his hips and spoke with the same clear tone of voice that had surprised Anna earlier.

"Sometimes Kevin got bored when he came, because he didn't have any friends in San Francisco. Sometimes we argued, too. I wasn't a very good father on my own."

Paul had never admitted such a thing. Anna studied his face. "Maybe if you'd had enough time," she said.

He worked his lower lip. "Maybe so."

Anna scarcely remembered this side of Paul. As if locked in a déjà vu, she recognized his softened posture and gentler tone of voice but had no idea what he'd say next.

With a fingernail, Paul traced the cracks in the kitchen table. "I thought you could add these pictures to his book. You still have it, don't you? I know you wouldn't burn that." His voice rose slightly.

The day after the fire, Anna had stored the book in a suit-case under her bed. She retrieved it now from her loft and set it on the table, along with a tube of glue.

"You don't keep this very close. Don't you ever look at it?"

"I haven't, recently."

"I bought it at Cowen's Stationery the day Kevin was born. You remember that? I took a tram all the way down Market to get it."

"I remember you bought it. You pasted in the front page of the *Chronicle*."

"That's right, I started this whole book." Ridges appeared and disappeared on Paul's forehead. He skimmed through the album page by page, his neck cords standing out like an old man's. "It ought to be my turn, I should keep this now."

"All right. I think you should."

"You do?"

"I had trouble with it anyway."

"What do you mean?"

"I almost burned it. Only my father stopped me. But you'll take care of it?"

"Of course I'll take care of it."

"You could keep it in one of those boxes until you got back to San Francisco."

"I kept these pictures safe, didn't I?" Paul stood up, held the book to his chest and shuffled to the couch. He looked back at her. "You're going to give this to me?"

He sat down with a thump and looked around the room as if he'd never been there before—as if, the previous summer, he hadn't slept on that same couch for three straight weeks. He leafed through the album, going slower and slower. "I remem-ber this picture," he said. "We all went to the zoo. And I took this one out on the avenues." He raised his feet and stretched out lengthwise on the couch. The album dipped, closed and settled on his chest. Finally his arms let go and the book slid to the floor. He opened his eyes for a moment when it hit, then closed them and went to sleep.

Anna retrieved the album and placed it on top of the refrigerator, just as her father had, twelve months before. On the porcelain finish she could still make out the faint black words "There's a hole in the bottom of my life, and when I get drunk I fall into it." That wasn't true anymore. Or she hoped it wasn't true. She hadn't been drunk all year.

Paul quivered into sleep. His breathing, interrupted by shallow sighs, slowed, and slowed again. His left hand lay on the pine floor, knuckles down on the dusty yellow wood. Anna didn't understand how anyone could sleep like that. She slept, herself, with both hands tucked between her legs or against her chest. When she was certain Paul had dropped off completely, she lifted his hand and tucked it beneath his left knee.

She sat at the kitchen table on a straight-backed chair, completely alert. She didn't want to eat, or read, or even stand up. She thought about Paul and how she had heard, just for a moment, his original tone of voice, his autonomous, native speech. The same Paul Dunham she first knew—handsome, easygoing, sometimes a joker—lay contained in the sleeping form on her couch. She had heard him. She got up and covered him with a blanket.

There was a time when she had loved Paul. Because it worked out badly didn't mean she had made a mistake or that they had never gotten along. They had.

Once when they first knew each other they drove all the way to Mexico on a three-day weekend. God, they were young. Paul showed up in a borrowed station wagon after work one Friday, and they drove turn and turnabout all night long, passing through L.A. before dawn and crossing the border at Mexicali. They continued a couple of hours past the Mexican checkpoint, then turned off the main road and slept in the back of the car.

Late in the afternoon they woke into the dry air and empty space of the desert, and drove on. They ate enchiladas at dusk in an open-sided restaurant as the last rays of the sun turned the kitchen's adobe walls pink. After dark they climbed back into the station wagon and took off on a new road.

"Let's turn here," Anna said, and they turned. "Now here." They doubled back at dead ends, followed sandier and smaller roads, and drove on until completely lost. Anna thought they were headed south, Paul west. The road ran through tumbled hills, and the skies had clouded over. Finally they parked the car on a flat shoulder, unzipped the two sleeping bags and made love.

The sun rose directly in front of the car. Paul got up to urinate and climbed back inside. "Who knows where this road goes," he said.

"Enough. We've come too far already. Let's climb a hill instead. Let's walk around and see where we are."

Paul laughed. "We're on a little bend on a dirt road much too small to show up on the map. Don't you want to keep going?"

"Where is there to go? It's all the same."

He put his arms around her, his skin still cold from standing naked outside in the chill air. "We could have our first argument," he said.

"Paul, let's not."

"You really don't want to go on?"

"This is crazy. All we have is the weekend."

"Ah, what a man gives up for a woman. The adventures, the open road . . ."

"I have to be at work at nine o'clock on Tuesday morning, and so do you." And, she thought of saying, she hardly knew him.

"You're probably right. I could drive us all the way to Veracruz, and then we'd really be in trouble. Let's get dressed and explore around here."

That was all she remembered from the trip: the long drive, sex in the car and almost an argument. But Paul had listened to her, he'd been fair.

Sitting at the kitchen table, Anna thought about their marriage. Paul, his position unchanged, looked as if he lay in state, dead on her couch.

What if Paul had been the one to die in an accident? she thought. Would that have been more fair? Or Anna, what if *she* had died?

She stood up. Spots of light flecked her vision, and her neck felt as if it were stretched out in a long elastic column. Kevin's death had been unfair to her, she thought—but not to Kevin. He'd lived for nine full years, almost ten. That was his term.

Forgetting Paul, she walked down the front steps of her house. A cool wind blew from across the Ohio, playing among the lilacs and peonies. The revelation ran through Anna like blood, that Kevin's life had been completely fair. He had lived all his years, and when he died nature boomed up over his tracks with no sign of mourning. Relentless soybeans and clover grew rank beyond the scarred sycamore, which had healed itself of an insignificant wound.

Anna wondered how Paul could go on sleeping anywhere near her; she felt herself as if she might never sleep again. Returning inside, she crouched on one knee beside the couch, her face only inches away from his. All her fear of him was gone, and all her anger.

PAUL WOKE at five o'clock, confused. He pulled his hand out from under his leg and rubbed the circulation back into it. "I had a dream about Kevin," he said, hitching himself up on his elbow. "But I can't remember it. He was tiny. I could have held him in my palm."

Anna went to him and put her arms around his chest. They hadn't embraced in years, yet at first, Paul hardly acknowledged her. She might have been hugging a sea turtle.

"Paul, do you want to cry?"

"I don't think I can."

Allowing her head to slope over his shoulder, Anna breathed the stale air of the couch upholstery and Paul's acidulous, dried perspiration. She held back from tears herself. Finally Paul embraced her, circling her back with his long arms. He put his hands on her shoulder blades and pressed her to him. She couldn't feel his breathing at all. His hand dipped to the small of her back, then to her waist. It inched downward.

"I'm not doing that," she said. She twisted away from him and scrambled up from the couch. "You'll never change, will you?"

"Doing what? What'd I do?"

"You bastard. You know what you were doing. In another minute you'd have had your hand between my legs. No wonder you don't have any goddamn friends."

Paul sat up, glaring. "I've got plenty of friends. You don't know anything about my life."

"I know plenty. I know you want to feel my ass instead of crying."

"Tell me about it, you cunt."

"I ought to slap you across the face."

"Go ahead, try it. Try it and see how far you get."

Anna walked to the sink, her hands shaking. She straightened up, keeping busy, then ran the hot water and washed a few dirty dishes. When she finally went back to the table and sat down, Paul stood up and paced the room, back and forth in front of her. He hugged his armpits, then let his arms fly into the air. Every time she saw him he had a new set of gestures.

"All right, I'm sorry. You don't know what it's like being on the road and practically living out of your car with a bunch of guys trying to rip you off all the time. But I'm sorry. I'll watch where I put my hands."

"I'd appreciate it." They looked at each other eye to eye, a rare moment. "You know, Paul, I hope you work out whatever you have to. I hope you can pick up your life in San Francisco and stay out of trouble with the law, and just . . . be happy. That's what I'm trying to do. But I don't think you can help me very much, or I can help you."

His eyes averted, Paul stood by the open door. Finally he

turned back to her and shivered. "You got an extra sweater? It's cold in here."

She went up to her room and brought down a couple of work sweaters, one for each of them. "That's where you're going, isn't it? Back to San Francisco?"

"Sure. I told you, I'm just passing through."

"What are you going to do when you get back?"

"I needed some sleep was all. I couldn't drive it straight through by myself. You don't want to go to California, do you, Anna? Hah, we'd probably argue the whole way, it'd be a rough trip. But if I leave now, I'll probably make St. Louis before I drop for the night."

"You're going to leave now?"

"Yeah, I might as well."

His decision caught her off guard. It saddened her to think of him getting back in his car and driving across the vast, empty country. What a lonely life.

"Look, Paul, you can spend the night if you want. I'll stay over at the farmhouse with Shelley and Deal. You only slept for about an hour, that's not enough."

"I'll be okay. But I need some gas money. I couldn't make it halfway on what I've got."

Anna opened her wallet: fifteen dollars.

"Shit," Paul said. "How about borrowing some from your father? Or getting it out of the machine at the bank? You've got one of those cards, don't you?" He tapped the inside of her wallet with his index finger.

"I could get a hundred out of it. There's a daily limit."

That was a lie. There was some limit, but Anna didn't know what it was.

They walked to his car and both got in before Anna remembered the album. Paul went back for it and returned carrying it under one arm, like a schoolboy. "You sure about this?"

"Take care of it, please. Do your best with it."

At the pocket teller outside the bank, Anna inserted her

264 · JOHN THORNDIKE

card, then entered her four-letter code, KEVN. She hit With-drawal; From Checking; one hundred dollars and zero cents. The machine clacked internally, rolled out four new twenties and two tens, and returned her card along with a receipt.

"Let me see that card," Paul said.

One side was a bank card for the automatic teller, the other was a Visa credit card. Anna didn't want that in Paul's hands.

"Hold on," she said, "maybe I can get another hundred out of this thing. She inserted the card and entered her code, KEVM. INCORRECT CODE, TRY AGAIN.

"I must have made a mistake." She entered the code again, KEVM. The machine clacked, paused—and swallowed the card.

THIS TRANSACTION TERMINATED. CARDS MAY BE RETRIEVED DURING BUSINESS HOURS. A glass plate dropped in front of the keys.

"Shit," Anna said, "this thing's always breaking down. But here, at least we got a hundred."

With cash in hand, Paul didn't complain. He wadded the fresh bills and stuck them into his front pocket.

"I'd like to take you one more place before you go," Anna said.

"Where's that?"

"Kevin's grave. I go up there sometimes."

The last shadows around the cemetery's shrubs and head-stones had already vanished into the trailing end of dusk, though the spruce and cedar trees were still outlined against the sky. Paul walked unsteadily over the tufts of spring grass toward Kevin's small granite stone, engraved only with his name, Kevin Durward Dunham, and the years of his birth and death.

"What do you do up here?"

"Just sit. Sometimes I come with my father and we talk."

She moved a few steps to the side, then walked off and leaned against the trunk of a cedar. There was no wind, no noise at all. Paul dropped to one knee, his back to her, his form visible only as an outline. Anna wasn't sure why she'd brought him to the cemetery, or what she wanted him to do.

He remained in one spot longer than she'd imagined he could keep still. In between what angered and frustrated her about Paul, a small unhappy part of him kept showing.

"All right," he said finally, "let's go."

The road climbed slightly to a lip, then curved down toward the lights of Fell River. Anna didn't want Paul to drive past Susan's house, or Jay's, either, so she asked him to drop her off on High Street. And then what? They shake hands in front of the courthouse, and Paul drives off into the night with a hundred dollars, Kevin's album and a collection of cardboard boxes?

He drove through town on Merton, not High. They were halfway to the river by the time Anna said, "We've passed the courthouse, you could drop me here."

"Sure," he said, but didn't slow down. He turned sharply onto the iron bridge over the Fell, ran the single red light on the other side of the river and stepped on the gas.

"What the hell are you doing, Paul?"

Hunched over the wheel, he passed three slow-moving cars in a swoop. The last of the city street lights dropped behind.

"Goddamn it, let me out of this car."

"I think you ought to come back for a visit. I've been to this dipwick state three times, and you never even mentioned coming out, not once. You used to love San Francisco."

"Look, Paul, I gave you a hundred dollars, and you've got Kevin's album. What else do you want?"

"I want to hear you talk. I'll fall asleep at the wheel if I'm all alone. You want to talk about Kevin, don't you?"

"Slow down, you're doing seventy miles an hour. When are you going to let me out?"

"Not out here in the middle of nowhere. You don't want to get out in the dark, do you?"

He dropped his speed to fifty-five—still unsafe, Anna

thought, in a car with flabby shocks. She didn't feel as if she were being kidnapped, exactly. At least this wasn't newspaper headline material. She just didn't want Paul to hit another car or run off the road.

"Every time I come back," he said, "you treat me like I'm buggo." The green instrument panel lit up his face from below, giving him a spectral look.

"You did act a little strange at the funeral."

"Me? How about you? You looked like a stone the whole time. No tears, no nothing."

"They came later. And you were speeding."

"So what? You think I'm weird because I did a little crystal? Don't give me that look. I loved my kid the same as you. The only difference is you had custody."

Anna softened. "I know you loved him, Paul."

He drove on in silence, the speedometer needle drifting down below fifty. "All right, I should have played more ball with him. Go ahead, you might as well say I told you so. If I'd had more time, I would have. I always thought it'd be easier when he got older and I could talk to him. The last time he came we went over to Golden Gate Park almost every day and threw a football around. A little rubber football I bought him, small enough to get his hands on. You think I never did anything with him, but I did."

The speed limit dropped to thirty-five miles an hour as they drove into a small river town. There was only one traffic light. Paul slowed, caught the light on green and drove through without stopping. He watched Anna nervously, as if she might jump out of the car. Back on the road he stepped it up to fifty again.

"We didn't have such a bad time that visit. The only reason he wanted to go back early was because he didn't have any friends."

Anna let Paul talk. What was she going to say—that when Kevin came home he told her his dad had left him alone in the apartment at night, twice, and he was too scared to go to sleep by himself? If Paul wanted to reconstruct that history, what harm could it do him? Or her?

"I know we fought too much," he said. "You and me, I mean. I'm not saying we shouldn't have gotten divorced. But I made a mistake going back to San Francisco. There are too many crazies there, you can't think straight with so many schizos running around. It's worse now than ever. Eugene's not a bad town, I don't know why you left. If I'd stayed there, I could have seen Kevin every week. We could have worked on his pitching arm and his batting, he was a natural at baseball. How about it, don't you ever think about going back to Oregon?"

"No."

"You've still got friends there, you could get work easy."

"I've got work here, and friends here."

"You've got some ballerina you go to bed with, too. You got him on a little chain?" Paul barked like a Pekingese.

"Stick to Kevin," Anna said. "We were talking about Kevin."

"I was talking about anything I felt like." Paul leaned across the front seat and barked again, then laughed. "You're in my car, you know. I'm just trying to get you into the mood for the trip. I thought you might want to go to Eugene instead of San Francisco. What do you think?"

"I think you missed your chance with Kevin when he was alive, and now you have to live with it. And I think you ought to know Kevin wasn't a natural at baseball, either. Even in peewee league he was afraid of the ball. He was better at soccer."

"Well, soccer then, I'd play soccer with him."

In silence, they rolled into another, larger river town. Paul drove through the tail end of one yellow light but got stuck at the next light behind a couple of pickup trucks. With the car stopped, Anna could have opened her door and stepped out onto the Saturday-night streets of Ripley, Ohio, free. But she didn't. She didn't even put her hand to the door latch. Paul grunted in acknowledgment as he gunned it out of town, and two minutes later he was doing sixty again.

"Slow down, will you? You don't have any seat belts, and the shocks in this car are terrible. You'll be lucky to make it across the country."

"Oh I will? You think I don't drive well enough?"

"You drive too fast for me, on a two-lane road like this."

"But who is it who has the accidents?"

"One accident," Anna said, her voice lowered. "In my whole life."

"Yeah, one was enough."

She could have killed Paul then. She could have beaten his head in with a two-by-four and mashed his skull to a pulp. "You piece of shit."

Paul drove on through the dark Ohio farmland, still huddled over the steering wheel in the green light.

"All right," he said, "I'm sorry. I shouldn't have said that. But you're always telling me what to do. I ought to slow down, I ought to get seat belts, I ought to clean up the back of my car. I ought to cry. You think because they locked me up in Napa State you've got everything figured out."

Anna waited a moment before speaking. "I think you're a little screwhouse sometimes. You fly off the handle too easy and you talk a lot of nonsense. Like this crazy idea about me driving out west with you."

"What's so crazy about that?"

"We're never going to get back together as a couple. You know that, don't you? If we can be friends, fine, but if you press me too hard, I'll lock you out."

"What're you talking about, look whose car you're in. We aren't going through any more little towns, either."

"Look, Paul, I know you're not crazy. But I also know you could go that way if you don't look out."

"Oh yeah? Tell me about it."

"Do you want to hear this?"

"Now you got something big on me, right?"

"I think you've done some strange things, yes. They locked you up for something, didn't they? I wasn't there, I don't know what it was—but I've seen you in Fell River. You didn't have to throw over that candy stand or drive through that barricade, and you didn't have to take off out of Fell River with me in your car. You just like feeling wild. Isn't that right?"

"Huh."

"Maybe you have to go a little crazy, maybe it helps. I lost my head about Kevin sometimes and did some stupid things— but I always knew I had a choice. And no one's got a lock on you, either. Every day you can choose to do the crazy thing or not."

"And you're the one who's going to tell me what's crazy."

"It would be crazy not to let me out of this car when I want to get out."

"Forget it, Anna, you're not getting out. I don't care how smooth you talk."

She settled back against the seat, having said her piece. If her words lodged in Paul's brain and rustled around in there, good. If not, fine, his mind was still a mystery to her. She believed it worked like her own, but she didn't know for sure.

The first street lights of the city shone on lawns, sidewalks and storefronts. Paul accelerated, let up on the gas, surged forward and let up again as Route 52 turned into the Columbia Parkway. At fifty miles an hour he made almost all the lights. He ran a single red one, keeping a lookout for cops.

On their left, a hundred feet below the parkway, the river reflected the lights of Newport, Kentucky. On the right, sky-scrapers rose above the graph of downtown streets. Taxis drove past with comforting yellow lights on the roof, and couples walked along the sidewalks. Cincinnati, which had often felt large and alien to Anna, now seemed a haven.

When the parkway merged with Interstate 71, Paul increased his speed. They passed Riverfront Stadium doing sixty.

"This is it, Paul. I want to get off at the next exit."

"No way. No more red lights and no more stops. Thirty miles and we cross into Indiana, you won't even think about Ohio anymore."

"I want you to stop the car now."

He clutched the wheel. "Nothing doing. Not a chance."

"Paul, *let me out.*"

He shook his head, his lips pursed.

"All right, then." She leaned across the seat, caught hold of the keys and pulled them out of the ignition. The engine died.

"*What the shit.* Give me those."

He grabbed her left arm. She held the keys in her other fist, close to the door.

"Give me those keys, goddamn it." He braked to thirty as a semi roared by in the next lane. Coasting, still in third gear, he swore again before pulling off onto the emergency lane and braking hard.

Anna opened her door and jumped out before the car stopped rolling. "Here," she said, and tossed the keys under the door. They jingled on the asphalt.

A chain-link fence lined the highway. Anna ran for it, jumped halfway up and scrambled to the top. When she looked back Paul was on his hands and knees, groping beneath the car in the darkness.

"You bitch," he yelled. "I can't find the keys."

"Good luck, you'll find them. Let me know how you're doing when you get to San Francisco."

"You're crazy, where're you going?"

Anna swung both legs over the top of the fence and jumped. She landed in a patch of tufted grass, then slid down an embankment to the sidewalk. Paul was out of sight, though she could still could hear the whine of tires from the highway. Blowing off adrenaline, she broke into a run down the middle of the city street.

After a few blocks she slowed to a walk. The shops were lit and the pedestrians well dressed. Anna wanted to tell someone how she'd escaped from Paul's car and jumped over the fence—how exciting it had been. But a stranger, she realized, would think she'd dropped a bolt, might even call the police.

Half skipping along the sidewalk in her cushioned running

shoes, she covered the distance to the Music Hall in ten minutes. Floodlights from the park across the street illuminated the hall's stone façade, and a couple of ushers in black suits lounged outside, smoking cigarettes.

Anna took the steps to the lobby two at a time and pulled her wallet out of her front pocket. Behind the bars of the ticket window a woman sat upright on a high stool, her thighs compressed by a white gown. Dressed like a countess, she was made up like a whore. Anna, smiling wildly, her heart still thumping from the brisk walk, asked to buy a ticket.

"The intermission is already over, they'll be finished soon. And all I have is the balcony."

"A friend is dancing, I don't want to miss him."

The woman leaned forward from the waist, inspecting Anna's torn sweater and corduroy pants. She touched her fingers to the cosmetic mask about her own eyes. What did she imagine? Anna wondered. That the two carmine stripes on her cheeks evoked the rosy color of apples? They looked more like smudges from an exhaust system. Anna laid a crumpled ten-dollar bill on the marble counter.

"Oh, you might as well go in. Just go up to the balcony, the ushers are probably inside watching." The countess laid a single forefinger, tipped by a half-inch magenta nail, on top of Anna's bill and nudged it back out from under the bars.

"Thanks," Anna said. She climbed to the top of the stairs, followed a soft runner of red carpeting to the door and let herself into the hall. A few heads turned. She took an empty seat by the aisle and sank into the darkness.

On the stage, two women in body suits jumped forward and back. Had Anna missed this dance the week before? She had no memory of either woman. In fact, from high in the upper balcony everything looked different: the tiers of plush red seats, the dark audience and the waxy yellow light of the stage.

Her heart rate slowed and her eyes adjusted. She remembered the next dance, though the choreography looked entirely different from high up. When the dance ended, another round

272 · JOHN THORNDIKE

of applause welled up from the orchestra seats below. Was the audience moved or merely polite? She couldn't tell.

The house lights dimmed and went out, and a moment later a spotlight flared onto the back right corner of the stage. Jay stood on the balls of his feet within its white ellipse, his back to the audience. He wore his green sneakers and drawstring pants, and spread his hands at the level of his waist. He didn't move— not a muscle—for fifteen seconds. Then his head turned and his shoulders rotated, one isolation on top of another.

Anna had seen him perform exactly the same dance only a week before, but the man on the stage looked nothing like Jay.

Of course it was Jay. Each restrained movement was clearly visible even from the upper balcony. Yet as he stood up on the pedals of an imaginary bicycle and turned to say good-bye, Anna barely recognized him. And what did this dance mean? It was supposed to be about Daria leaving—but only this morning Anna had seen Daria riding around on the same bicycle. The girl was still growing up, no one had left anyone.

Lit by the spotlight's beam, Jay moved across the stage in pony steps. There was no music, and save for the single spot, the entire hall was dark. Anna leaned forward in her chair as if to follow the dance more exactly, from ten inches closer to the stage. And leaning, she felt as if she'd floated up out of her seat into the dark plenum of the hall. She hovered next to the chandelier, drifting closer and closer to the stage through the compressed black air.

All Jay's motions were contained within the spotlight. He never reached outside it until halfway through the dance, when everything broke. The floor lights turned the stage a bright rose, the extruded wail of a saxophone erupted in midnote, and Jay leapt into the air. Then he spun and rolled across the floor, beating the wood with his palms. Five times Anna had seen him perform this same dance, yet the movement was all new to her. She rocked back and forth in her chair, holding her arms to her chest so as not to sing out or cry.

The audience broke into applause, and Anna came to.

Somehow she'd missed the end of the dance. Jay was bowing in the rose light at center stage, his arms hanging straight down from his shoulders. He looked like himself.

She hardly noticed the last dance on the program, thinking about Jay and the drive back to Fell River. She'd have to find him backstage and explain how Paul had tried to carry her off to San Francisco and how she'd escaped. Jay would ask about Daria. They could call Alex to make sure the girl was safe, then drive home together through the spring night, sitting side by side in Jay's car. They could stop at the same twenty-four-hour restaurant as the week before, order home fries, biscuits and black coffee, and then stand on the unkempt bank of the Ohio, smelling the dark mud and debris of the spring runoff. They could stay up all night, talking and making love, and in the first light drive out to Sam Turner's pond to see the redwing blackbirds. They could do anything they wanted.

PLUME

LITERARY ORIGINALS

☐ **THE CARNIVOROUS LAMB by Augustin Gomez-Arcos.** A shocking, irresistably erotic tale filled with black humor. Into a shuttered house, haunted by ghosts of past rebellions and Franco's regime, Ignatio is born. His mother despises him; his failed father ignores him; his older brother becomes his savior, his confidant . . . his lover. Their forbidden relationship becomes the center of this savagely funny, stunningly controversial novel. (258200—$6.95)

☐ **EQUAL DISTANCE by Brad Leithauser.** Danny Ott, a young Harvard law student on leave in a paradoxical Japan of Zen masters and McDonalds, plans to "grow up" and "accomplish" things in his year abroad. But when he meets another young American, Greg Blaising, who introduces him to the irresistable neon nightlife of Kyoto, Danny's plans are increasingly upset. Then along comes Carrie. . . . "Constantly surprising, tender and exact."—*Newsweek*
(258189—$6.95)

☐ **SELF-HELP: Stories by Lorrie Moore.** In these nine stories Lorrie Moore probes relationships we all recognize, giving poignant, but wickedly funny advice on "How to Be an Other Woman," "How to Talk to Your Mother (Notes)," "How to Become a Writer," and on surviving other modern crises of loss and love by finding the absurd humor at life's core. "Brisk, Ironic . . . Scalpel-sharp."
—*New York Times Book Review*   (258219—$6.95)

Prices slightly higher in Canada.

Buy them at your local bookstore or use this convenient
coupon for ordering.

NEW AMERICAN LIBRARY
P.O. Box 999, Bergenfield, New Jersey 07621

Please send me the PLUME BOOKS I have checked above. I am enclosing
$_____ (please add $1.50 to this order to cover postage and handling). Send
check or money order—no cash or C.O.D.'s. Prices and numbers are subject to
change without notice.

Name _____

Address _____

City _____ State _____ Zip Code _____

Allow 4-6 weeks for delivery.
This offer subject to withdrawal without notice.